ELLY Griffiths

The Chalk Pit

Quercus

First published in Great Britain in 2017 by Quercus
This paperback edition published in 2017 by

Quercus Editions Ltd
Carmelite House
50 Victoria Embankment
London EC4Y 0DZ

An Hachette UK company

A CIP catalogue record for this book is available
from the British Library

PB ISBN 978 1 78429 662 9
EBOOK ISBN 978 1 78429 661 2

10 9

Typeset by CC Book Production

Printed and bound in Great Britain by Clays Ltd, Elcograf S.p.A.

For Sarah K. Huber

Praise for the Dr Ruth Galloway series

'*The Chalk Pit* is the most intriguing case written by the
prolific Elly Griffiths to date. A five-star thriller'
Daily Express

'Griffiths' great strength lies in her creation of a cast of
returning characters that readers can and do care about'
Mail on Sunday

'Ruth Galloway is one of the most engaging characters
in modern crime fiction'
Kate Mosse

'Griffiths has become a dab hand at plotting and cranking
up the tension. The murders, and the muddled humanity of
the characters, keep us turning the pages'
Independent

'Crime that doesn't sacrifice good writing and clever
characterisation for the sake of the plot'
Red Magazine

'Elly Griffiths writes ever-more ingenious detective
stories with a powerful sense of place and a varied cast of
sympathetic and unusual characters. Her heroine is a winner'
The Times

'Griffiths weaves superstition and myth into her
crime novels, skilfully treading a line between credulity
and modern methods of detection'
Sunday Times

Elly Griffiths was born in London. The inspiration for her books about forensic archaeologist Ruth Galloway came from her husband who gave up a city job to train as an archaeologist. The Ruth Galloway series has now been on the *Sunday Times* bestseller list, and has won the CWA Dagger in the Library. Elly's Stephens and Mephisto series is set in 1950s Brighton. Elly herself lives in Brighton but often spends holidays on the wild Norfolk coast. She has two children and a cat.

PROLOGUE

3.20 a.m., 3 June 2015

He shouldn't really be driving; they all know that. But Solly has probably had the least to drink of all of them and, besides, he has a calm self-possession that makes him able to carry off all sorts of excesses and still remain the reliable, charming boy next door. 'Boy from the next-door mansion,' as Dennis once put it.

But there are no buses and no one has the money for a taxi so Solly takes the keys from Em and drives slowly and carefully round the one-way system. Dennis and Em don't help by going 'Whee' at the corners and shouting witticisms to the few pedestrians to be seen in Norwich at three o'clock on a Wednesday morning. One of them, a police officer pushing a bike, looks up and shakes his fist.

'Get off and milk it!' yells Dennis.

'Shut up, Dennis,' says Grace. 'People hate students enough as it is.'

Grace is sitting next to Solly and feels obliged to talk to

him, to keep him concentrating on the road. This is difficult enough when the road in question keeps swooping up in front of her and tying itself in knots. God, just how much had she drunk? Those tabs on top of it too.

Solly is doing well though, not speeding, looking from left to right at junctions. They are heading out of town now on the A147. Dennis and Em have fallen asleep but Grace tries to stay awake for Solly's sake. They take the turn into Denning Road. Solly goes slightly wide but there's nothing coming so no harm done.

'I like this road,' says Grace. 'I'd love to live in one of those big houses.'

'Then you'll have to marry a rich man, darling,' says Solly, slurring slightly.

'That's a bit . . .' She can't think of the word. 'Crap,' she settles for. 'I might get rich on my . . . on my own . . . in my . . . Christ! Solly!'

But he has seen it too. A man standing in the middle of the road with his arms outstretched. There's something biblical about him: long hair and beard, wearing robes or some kind of cloak. Grace yells and Solly jams on the brakes. The car skids to the other side of the road and Dennis and Em wake up.

'What the . . . ?'

'There was a man . . . a man in the road,' says Grace.

But when they get out of the car there is no one there, just the long road between the tall dark houses.

CHAPTER 1

'Today our acronym is COAST. Concentration, observation, anticipation, space and time.'

The speaker, a woman in her fifties, with short hair and keen-looking spectacles, beams around the room. DCI Harry Nelson, in the back row, stares back, stony faced. In his head he works on another acronym: crap, outrageous, abysmal . . .

'You might be saying to yourself,' says the woman, 'why am I wasting a morning at a speed awareness course? The answer is because it can save lives.'

She looks at them solemnly, glasses glinting. The man next to Nelson, who earlier introduced himself as a minicab driver called Steve, is apparently asleep. Nelson gave his name simply as Harry and didn't vouchsafe an occupation.

The woman writes her name – Bev Flinders – in insultingly large letters on the whiteboard. She says that she is a driving instructor. 'Definitely not a policewoman!' Some of the more unctuous class members laugh.

'So why do we have speed limits at all?'

Bev's voice drones on. The room, a prefab in the station

car park, is too warm and smells of instant coffee. Unlike Steve, now snoring gently, Nelson doesn't feel tempted to sleep. He's too busy brooding on his wrongs. He shouldn't be here at all. He should be out solving crimes, maybe speeding slightly in the process but you can't catch criminals keeping to the thirty-mile-an-hour speed limit, can you? But his boss has ordered him to attend this course along with Steve, two HGV drivers and a clutch of women who seem to view it as a pleasant morning out. Yes, not content with giving him a tangled love life and a stressful working life, God has now delivered the biggest blow of all. Nelson has a woman boss.

Ruth has no time for such introspection. She is currently delving deep, not into her own life but into the ground below Norwich. She is in a cellar below the Guildhall, a square, crenellated building that stands like a little castle in the heart of the city. The Guildhall is now council offices but it has, in its past, been a toll house, a court and a prison. The most dangerous prisoners were kept here, in underground cells. The undercroft, this lower region is called, and plans are afoot to develop it as an exhibition space and even a restaurant. This part is quite pleasant, the walls are stone and there are some rather attractive vaulted pillars, but Ruth knows that things are about to get worse. She is going to have to go lower still, into a tunnel that has previously been closed off. Ted, from the Field Archaeology team, has removed the planks covering the tunnel entrance and is looking at her expectantly. Ruth knows that, as the head of

Forensic Archaeology, she should go first but the problem is that she has never been that keen on small, enclosed spaces . . .

'After you.' Ted grins, showing piratical gold teeth.

'Perhaps it would be better if I followed you. You've got the torch.'

Ted looks as if he knows what she's thinking. But, to his credit, he doesn't just hand her the torch but ducks his head and enters the tunnel. Ruth follows, taking care to keep close to Ted's high-vis tabard. The tunnel leads downwards and the plastered walls give way to chalk, the floor moving quickly from brick to rubble that crunches underfoot. Ted's torch picks out a well-crafted roof, lined with brick and flint.

'Probably an old chalk mine,' he says, his voice echoing slightly. 'Lots of chalk mines in Norwich.'

Ruth puts her hand on the wall. It's unpleasantly moist to the touch, as if it's sweating.

'There's a tunnel from the castle to the Guildhall,' says Ruth. She doesn't want to speak much as she has the idea that she has only so much breath to spare. She is unpleasantly conscious of all that stone and earth above her. Her hard hat feels as if it is pressing down on her head.

'Someone once told me that you could walk all the way from UEA to the town centre under ground,' says Ted. 'Shall we just keep going?'

Since the University of East Anglia is situated about three miles out of the city, Ruth doubts this. There's something disconcerting about the idea of these underground thoroughfares, as if the city has a dark twin, another life going on beneath its surface.

'I've heard that there's a tunnel from the Guildhall to St John's,' she says, not answering Ted's question.

'The Catholic cathedral?' says Ted. 'Maybe our body is a bricked-up nun or some such.'

He sounds incredibly cheery about the prospect. The reason Ted and Ruth are in the tunnel is because of a grisly discovery made by a surveyor working for an architect called Quentin Swan, who is planning to build an underground restaurant below the Guildhall. The surveyor, Mark Copeland, was assessing the site for health and safety risks. In the course of his investigations he sampled the ground using something called a borehole drilling machine. According to Copeland's report, which Ruth read that morning, the hand-held machine pulls out a vertical plug of soil, and in this sample were what looked like human bones. Copeland informed the council, which owns the building. The council called the police and then Ruth, in that order. When Ruth arrived at the Guildhall she had half expected to see Nelson waiting for her but there had only been Irish Ted in his high-vis vest and hard hat.

'The bones were buried, not bricked up,' says Ruth. 'We're nearly there, I think. Copeland said about halfway along.'

'Yes.' Ted shines his torch. 'Here are the little beauties, if I'm not mistaken.'

On the tunnel floor is a neat pile of earth, obviously excavated by the borehole machine. In amongst the chalky rubble, Ruth can see something that gleams even whiter in the darkness. She bends down. They are human bones; she can see that immediately. She thinks she can see a tibial shaft, maybe a femur. She takes a photograph and starts sketching the location in her notebook. She has almost forgotten that they are underground.

'Is it a whole skeleton?' says Ted, behind her.

'I don't think so,' says Ruth. 'Unless the rest of the body is still buried. We might need to get a proper excavation done.'

Ruth opens her backpack and takes out gloves, a trowel and a small brush. Ted kneels down beside her. He's an experienced field archaeologist and knows the procedure well. Ruth lifts out the first bone. It is a tibial shaft but it is broken, smashed almost, in the middle. Ruth shines her torch on it and sees faint parallel lines scored into the bone. She runs her gloved fingers over the end of the bone; it is blunt, not quite rounded.

'What is it?' says Ted.

'I don't know,' says Ruth, 'maybe nothing.' She passes the bone to Ted who marks it with a tiny number and places it in an evidence bag. Ruth then marks it on her skeleton sheet. It doesn't take them long. There are four long bones: two tibias, part of a femur and an arm bone, probably a humerus. There are also some smaller bones that look like ribs. All the bones have a dull shine, almost as if they are made of glass.

'How old do you think they are?' asks Ted. 'They're completely defleshed.'

'Yes,' says Ruth. 'That could mean that they're old but

they look so clean. You'd normally expect some discolouration with old bones.'

'These tunnels must be pretty old,' says Ted.

'Some of the chalk tunnels are medieval,' says Ruth, 'but
this doesn't look like a mining tunnel to me. It could be
linked to one of the churches, like I said. We must be some
way from the Guildhall by now.'

'Perhaps we've found our nun after all.'

'Perhaps. It's going to be hard to determine the sex
without the pelvic bones or the skull. Unless we can get
some DNA. We'll know more when we send the bones for
carbon-14 testing.'

'Do you think they're all from the same body?' says Ted.

'I think so,' says Ruth. 'The leg bones look the same
length.'

'Long bones,' says Ted, 'probably a man. I wonder where
the head is?'

'And the rest of the skeleton.'

'It's a mystery, Ruth,' says Ted, 'and I know how much
you like a mystery.'

Ruth is silent. She enjoys an intellectual puzzle as much
as the next archaeologist but she's not sure how much mystery she wants from bones buried in a medieval tunnel. It
would be nice to have an answer, actually. A nice, safe academic answer that could be filed away in a report.

Ruth packs the bones into a box marked Pathology. Ted
shines the torch on her while she does this and then hands
it over with a flourish.

'You go first. I'll carry the box.'

Ruth doesn't mind going first on the way back. Her back aches and her mouth is dry. She's longing to be above ground again, drinking tea in the Guildhall cafe. She thinks again of the layers of soil and stone above her head. It's almost as if the weight is crushing her, making it impossible for her lungs to expand . . .

'Are you all right?' says Ted, behind her. 'You're panting.'

'I'm fine,' says Ruth, making an effort to breathe properly. She can see the entrance now, the dim light in the under-croft looking as bright as a beacon.

When she steps through the archway, though, she sees that the light is partly coming from a torch held by DS Judy Johnson.

'Judy! I didn't think it would be you.'

'The boys are all busy,' says Judy. 'And when I heard that you'd found another body . . .'

'It's not a body,' says Ruth. 'Just a few bones. And I didn't find them. The surveyor did.'

'You didn't fancy coming down for a look?' says Ted, emerging from the tunnel with the box.

'No, you're all right,' says Judy. 'So, were the bones human?'

'Yes,' says Ruth, 'but we won't be able to tell how old they are until we get the carbon-14 analysis.'

'We're guessing old, though,' says Ted. 'My bet is medi-eval. Want to have a flutter?'

'No thanks,' says Judy, a bookie's daughter. 'When will you have the results?'

'I'll send the samples off today,' says Ruth. 'It'll probably take a couple of weeks.'

'And no idea what the bones were doing in the tunnel?'

'No,' says Ruth. 'It looks like they were buried and the surveyor disrupted them digging for samples.'

'Could be a bricked-up nun,' says Ted. 'Don't forget the nun.'

'Where are you off to now?' says Ruth to Judy, as they climb the stairs to the upper levels. 'Have you got time for a cup of coffee? There's a good cafe here.'

'That would be great,' says Judy. 'I've got a bit of time. Clough and Tanya are on a call out Denning Road way. A massive great hole appeared in the road last night.'

'What about the boss man?' asks Ted.

'Speed awareness course,' says Judy.

Ted and Ruth burst out laughing and after a few seconds Judy joins in. They are still laughing when Quentin Swan hurries in through the main doors, anxious about the fate of his subterranean dining experience.

CHAPTER 2

Nelson drives back to the station in a foul temper. He feels no compulsion to stay in third gear in order to keep below the speed limit, nor does he check his speed limit regularly or ease off the accelerator, all of which are recommended in the workbook which formed part of his 'National Speed Awareness Course Pack'. Instead he takes pride in breaking almost all the traffic rules in the short journey from the Portakabin to the police station. He screeches into the car park, parks at an angle and slams in through the back door.

The desk sergeant, a doughty warhorse called Tom Henty, hears the door slam and calls, 'DCI Nelson?'

Nelson opens the connecting door to the reception area. 'What is it, Tom?'

'You've got a visitor. Two visitors.'

'Who is it?'

'One's Aftershave Eddie. I've put him in Interview Room One because people started to complain. The other's a young woman called Grace Miller.'

Nelson groans. Aftershave Eddie – so called because he

is known to drink any substance containing alcohol – is a homeless man who sometimes sleeps in the police station porch. If Nelson sees him, he usually gives him money to buy a meal even though he knows that the meal will be entirely liquid. He used to encourage Eddie to contact a charity for the homeless but the man always refused, with some dignity. DS Judy Johnson has tried even harder, contacting charities and even booking Eddie into a hostel. But Eddie always replies that he is a free man and beholden to nobody. Nelson respects this even though he lives in fear of coming across Eddie's lifeless body in the street one day.

So what is Eddie, who once told him that 'with my family you steer clear of the police', doing in Interview Room 1?

'He said he wanted to talk to you and only you,' says Henty. 'DS Clough told him he could wait.'

Thanks a million, Cloughie. 'Is DS Clough still over at Denning Road?'

'Yes, sir.'

'What's taking him so long? It's just a hole in the road.'

'Takes me back to 1988,' says Tom, 'when that hole appeared in the Earlham Road. A bus disappeared into it, you know.'

Nelson sighs. Tom is about the tenth person to have told him about Earlham Road this morning. It's partly because of this historical precedent that the Serious Crimes Unit were required to attend but Nelson can't quite see what's keeping Clough there. He has probably checked into a cafe for a second breakfast. Mind you, he's with Tanya who never eats a carb if she can help it.

'What about the other visitor?' he says. 'Grace whatshername?'

'She's a student. Seems like a nice girl. Says she wants to talk to you about something odd that happened last night. Doesn't know if it's important but thought she should report it anyway.'

This sounds intriguing. Deciding to take the least appealing option first he heads for Interview Room 1.

The first thing that strikes him is the smell. He has only ever encountered Eddie in the open air before. Here, in the windowless interview room, the smell of unwashed clothes and alcohol is almost overpowering. No wonder people in the reception area were starting to complain.

Nelson keeps his face as expressionless and professional as he can. After all, he's pretty sure that Eddie would rather not smell this way.

'Hallo, Eddie. What can I do for you?'

'Hallo, chief.' Eddie has a faint Irish accent which reminds Nelson of parish priests in his youth. It gives Eddie a strange gravitas, helped by his Gandalf-like hair and beard. Looking at the man's face for almost the first time, though, Nelson is shocked to see that they might be almost the same age.

'I want to talk to you about a missing person,' said Eddie. He sounds very dignified and formal, even though a can of Tennent's Super is visible in his coat pocket.

'Talk away,' says Nelson, wondering why Eddie couldn't have had this conversation with Tom Henty.

'It's a woman,' says Eddie. 'A woman called Barbara

Murray. I haven't seen her for over a week and I'm starting to worry.'

'Is she . . .' Nelson tries to think of a tactful way to frame the next question.

'She's a rough sleeper,' says Eddie, coming to his rescue. 'She's only a young woman really, not more than forty, but she's had a very tough life, children taken into care and all the rest of it. I try to keep up with her quite regularly. I usually see her in the Vancouver Centre on a Wednesday because that's when they do the soup run. She wasn't there yesterday or the week before and nobody seems to have seen her.'

'Is it possible that she could be in a hostel? Or has she got family somewhere?'

'Her family are all in Scotland, as far as I know. I don't think she would have gone to them. She always said there was a lot of bad blood between them. It's possible that she's gone to a hostel but it's odd that no one has seen or heard of her. We're quite a close community. We look out for each other.'

Nelson thinks that it's rather touching that Eddie should refer to the rough sleepers as a community. But then he supposes that a life on the streets makes you value human contact. For his part, he can't even remember his neighbours' names, although Michelle is always inviting them over for drinks.

'So nobody's said anything to make you think that Barbara might be in danger?'

Eddie is silent for a minute. He runs a hand over his long

hair. The dirt is ingrained in his fingernails but the hand itself is rather beautiful, with long tapering fingers like a pianist.

'Someone said something. Could be nothing.' He pauses again. 'My friend Charlie who sleeps up by the Customs House, Charlie said that he heard a man talking to her, something about her children. He said that Barbara had seemed upset.'

'Did Charlie recognise the man who was talking to her?'

'No. He said that he looked like a do-gooder. A charity worker,' Eddie amends.

'Maybe he put Barbara in contact with her children.'

'Maybe. But Barbara told me that two of them were adopted and two in care. I don't think she had any contact with them.'

'She has four children?'

'Yes. The oldest must be grown up by now. Barbara told me once that she fell pregnant when she was still a teenager.'

It's not an unusual story, thinks Nelson, but no less sad for that. It is fairly unusual, though, to find a woman sleeping rough. Women tend to have support networks or, failing that, hostels take them in. Not Barbara evidently.

'Give me a description,' he says, 'and I'll have an officer check at the hostels and with local charities. I'll ask on the street too. But, as I say, she's an adult woman with no fixed address. It's more than likely that she's just moved away.'

'Thank you, DCI Nelson,' says Eddie. 'I knew you were a good man. That's why I asked for you. The others, they look through me or they give me the odd pound. That police-woman, she's been kind but you've always treated me like a human being.'

Nelson is moved by this tribute, even though he knows that it is largely undeserved. He doesn't do much for charity, beyond a couple of standing orders, and he's been guilty of hurrying past rough sleepers in the street. But he does have a social conscience; it's part of the reason why he became a policeman.

He takes a pad of paper from the desk. 'Let's have a description of this Barbara then.'

His second interviewee couldn't present a greater contrast. Grace Miller is pretty and blonde, dressed in jeans and a minty green T-shirt. She reminds Nelson of his daughters' friends, those impossibly slim young women with their lux-uriant manes of swishy hair. What's happened to all the overweight spotty teenagers? He's sure that when he was growing up, the girls at the neighbouring grammar school were nowhere near this confident and attractive. Mind you, by the time he was twenty-three he was married to Michelle, the most glamorous of the lot.

'Sorry to keep you,' says Nelson, sitting beside Grace in the Suite, the room usually reserved for sensitive interviews. It actually has comfortable chairs and a pot plant. There's also a two-way mirror, although today no one is on the other side.

'That's OK,' says Grace, twisting a paper cup in her hands. 'I know you're very busy.'

Nelson waits. He knows that nice middle-class girls (in his eyes being a student makes her middle class) don't just walk into police stations for fun. Eventually Grace says, 'It's something that happened last night. I know it'll sound a bit mad . . .'

Nelson waits some more. After a few more moments of cup-shredding Grace says, 'The thing is, I don't want to get my friends into trouble. We were quite drunk at the time. And my friend was driving.'

Nelson sighs. 'It's no offence to have been drunk. We can only charge you if we catch you while you're actually over the limit. I hope your friend doesn't make a habit of drinking and driving though.'

'Oh no,' says Grace. 'He's very sensible. He's studying law.'

In Nelson's eyes that's not a guarantee of sensible behaviour. He's no great fan of lawyers. He waits for Grace to continue with her story.

'We went to a club in Norwich and it was late, about three a.m. There were no buses and we couldn't afford a cab so Solly, my friend, drove Em's car. Em wasn't going to drink but she did in the end because her boyfriend . . .' She stops. 'Sorry. That isn't relevant. Anyway, Solly was driving back when we suddenly saw this man in the middle of the road. It was so scary. He just popped up from nowhere. Solly swerved to avoid him. Anyway, we stopped, and when we looked back, the man had vanished.'

'Vanished?'

'Yes. Just vanished into thin air. The thing is, we were all quite high . . . drunk . . . and we thought we must have imagined it. Solly just carried on driving. But now I keep thinking, what if we hit him? What if he's lying by the road somewhere?'

She looks really distressed, the last remnant of paper cup crushed in her hand. Nelson says, 'Where was this?'

'Denning Road.'

Denning Road . . . the site of the mysterious hole. Nelson looks at Grace. How can she sit there looking so clear-eyed and smooth-skinned when she was up drinking until the early hours last night? The young truly are a different species. Nowadays one extra pint in the pub can make Nelson feel rough as a dog the next day.

He asks Grace if she saw the local news that morning. 'No,' she says, 'I got up late and came straight here. I never really listen to the news anyway.'

'A two-metre-wide hole has appeared in Denning Road.'

Grace's eyes grow wide. 'Do you think my man fell into it?'

'I don't know,' says Nelson. 'But I'll tell my officers to have a good look. You did the right thing coming to see me. Can you give me a description of the man?'

'It sounds crazy,' says Grace, 'but he looked a bit like Jesus. You know, long hair and a beard. And he seemed to be wearing some sort of cloak.'

The long hair and beard reminds Nelson of Aftershave Eddie. But the cloak reminds him of someone else entirely: Cathbad, part-time druid and partner of DS Judy Johnson. Cathbad makes a speciality of turning up in odd places. Could he have materialised on Denning Road last night?

'Could you say roughly how old he was?' he asks.

Grace's smooth brow furrows. 'He could have been any age. I think his hair was quite dark though. He looked like he could have been a tramp. That's one reason why I came, really. I thought that if the man was sleeping rough, perhaps no one would notice if he went missing.'

Coming after his conversation with Aftershave Eddie, this makes Nelson look curiously at Grace Miller. It seems an oddly pertinent comment for a young woman. How old is Grace? Eighteen? Nineteen? He asks what she is studying.

'Sociology,' is the answer. She's a second year at the University of North Norfolk, where Ruth works. He assures Grace that they will look for her mysterious Jesus man. He also allows himself a brief lecture on drink and drugs (he hadn't missed the word 'high'). Grace looks as awkward and discomfited as if she were one of his daughters.

'I don't do drugs. Not really. Just a few tabs sometimes.'

Jesus. Do his daughters say the same thing? 'Don't take tabs,' he says. 'You never know what's in them. And don't drink and drive.'

'I can't drive,' she says. 'I failed my test for speeding.'

'I know the feeling,' says Nelson. Grace looks confused, as well she might. Showing her out, Nelson asks why Grace came into King's Lynn police station rather than going into Norwich.

'It's nearer uni,' says Grace simply. 'And I wanted to talk to you.'

'Why me?'

'I met your daughter at a party once,' she says. 'She said that you looked tough but you were a pussycat really.'

'She did, did she? Which daughter?'

'Rebecca.'

That figures. Rebecca was always the rebellious one but she has a degree now and a respectable job in Brighton. He wonders when the two girls met at a party. Rebecca comes home quite rarely now: Christmas and Easter and whenever she needs her car MOTed. On the plus side, his older daughter Laura has just moved back in after leaving her job (and her boyfriend) in Ibiza. She's signed up to do a teacher-training course at UEA.

'Well, take care, Grace. Good luck with your studies.'

'Thanks, DCI Nelson.' She gives him a cheerful wave as she sets off down the steps, blonde hair bouncing. He gazes after her for a few minutes.

'Staring at young girls, Nelson? You'll have to watch that.'

Nelson turns to face his new boss, Superintendent Jo Archer (Super Jo to her groupies). He notes with a sinking heart that she has her 'let's chat' face on.

CHAPTER 3

From his name Ruth expected Quentin Swan to be camp and at least sixty. In fact, the man who comes bursting in through the Guildhall doors is youngish and dark with horn-rimmed glasses. He looks like a cross between Harry Potter and Dr Who (David Tennant era).

'Have you found the bones?' is his first question.

In answer, Ted proffers the pathology box.

'Are you from the police?' asks Swan.

'I'm Detective Sergeant Judy Johnson,' says Judy, 'and this is Dr Ruth Galloway and Ted Houllihan from the University of North Norfolk. They excavated the bones.'

'Are they old?' asks Swan. 'Mark said they looked old.'

'We won't be able to tell until we do carbon-14 testing,' says Ruth. She guesses that Swan wants the bodies to be old because that won't affect his building plans. Nevertheless, there's something unseemly about his eagerness.

'Carbon-14 testing isn't that accurate though, is it?' he says now.

'It's accurate to plus or minus about a hundred years,'

says Ruth, which seems quite reasonable to her. 'Results can be skewed by sun spots, solar flares, that sort of thing. But we should be able to tell if this is a recent burial or not. We might be able to do DNA or isotope testing as well.'

'The thing is,' says Quentin Swan, fixing Ruth with what he obviously hopes is a hypnotic stare, 'I'm really keen to do this development.'

'Because Norwich really needs another cafe,' offers Ted helpfully.

'It's not a cafe,' says Swan. 'It's an underground experience. Gourmet food in the depths of the earth.'

'Well, I hope you get the go-ahead,' says Ruth. 'We should get the results in a couple of weeks.'

'A couple of weeks?' echoes Swan. 'Why can't you get them in twenty-four hours?'

'Because this isn't *CSI Miami*,' says Ruth. 'I'll be in touch with DS Johnson.'

Quentin Swan looks as if he wants to say more but Ruth is looking forward to her tea and cake so she waves in what she hopes is a friendly but firm dismissal. Judy and Ruth head off towards the cafe but, to Ruth's irritation, Quentin tags along with them, followed by Ted, still carrying the box of bones.

'How are you, Harry?' says Jo. 'How are you *really*?'

Nelson feels his stomach churn. This is one of Jo's favourite tactics. The faux concern, the leaning forward, the eye contact. The trouble is, after a question like this, any answer you give sounds like you're in denial. 'I'm fine,' sounds like a cry for help. Of course, Nelson thinks darkly, what Super Jo really wants is for him to burst into tears and say that he can no longer cope with the job, can she help him apply for early retirement? Then, after an insultingly short notice period and a leaving do in the Lord Nelson (ha ha), she can parachute a bright young psychology graduate into his place.

'I'm fine,' he says.

It makes Nelson laugh bitterly to think that he'd actually looked forward to Jo Archer's arrival. He hadn't much liked her predecessor, Superintendent Gerry Whitcliffe, and had thought that any change had to be a positive one. How could he have been so stupid? Whitcliffe was a career policeman, smooth and personable, addicted to press conferences and appearing on TV. It was no surprise when he got promoted to the Met, with a long job title and an even longer salary. 'Perhaps now we'll get a real policeman,' Nelson had said, when he read the email headed 'Sad news'. 'Real police officer,' Judy had corrected him, but she knew what he meant.

The thing is, Nelson isn't really sexist. He comes from a family of strong, independent women. He has three daughters and, whilst admittedly an overprotective father, he has always supported their right to a fair share of whatever's going. In addition, his older daughters, especially Rebecca, can spot patriarchal tyranny at a hundred paces (though they are less good, he often thinks, at identifying undue matriarchal interference). At work too he has always encouraged and promoted the women on his team. He may have left the course about 'Redefining Gender Roles in the Police Force' at lunchtime but he can see that sometimes they do need redefining. So, when he heard that his new boss was a woman, he had been cautiously optimistic. 'Put it this way,' he said to his wife Michelle, 'she can't be worse than Whitcliffe.'

How wrong he was.

From the moment that Jo Archer swept into King's Lynn police station carrying her yoga mat and balance ball, Nelson knew that he had met his match. Jo is thirty-eight, a social sciences graduate, with a sparkling CV and a mission to improve her fellow creatures. She's unmarried but, as she confided early on to Judy, 'not short of offers'. Nelson often thinks that Jo is not nearly as attractive as she thinks she is but, as with all these things, her insane self-belief rubs off on others, and after a week King's Lynn police were treating her as if she were Helen of Troy. Her technique is divide and rule. At first she tried to make a friend of Judy ('I always get on with other strong women'), but Judy is fiercely private and doesn't much want another friend. She then progressed to Tanya ('I've got a lot of gay friends') and fared a little better because Tanya is ambitious and usually oblivious to under-currents. With football-playing, politically incorrect Dave Clough, Jo veers between extreme flirtatiousness and a zeal for re-education. When Clough's son, Spencer, was born in January, Jo presented him with a pink teddy bear. 'But he's a boy,' Clough protested. 'Exactly,' said Jo, squeezing his arm.

But it's Nelson who presents Jo with her biggest challenge. Her vision for King's Lynn CID, presented in a slide show entitled 'A fresh start' and illustrated with images of phoenixes and rainbows, clearly does not include a forty-eight-year-old northern DCI with old-fashioned views on policing and a penchant for driving too fast. Hence the speed awareness course. Hence this chat.

'How was this morning, Harry?' asks Jo.

'Fine,' says Nelson. 'Very educational.'

'It's hard to get into new habits,' says Jo, 'especially as we get older.'

'Lucky I'm still young then,' says Nelson.

They are in Jo's office, unrecognisable from Whitcliffe's day. It's not just the balance ball, on which Jo sits, undulating gently, to conduct interviews. It's the fresh flowers (bought every few days by Jo's PA), the inspirational posters, the Macbook Air in place of the police-issue desktop, the mission statement on the wall, the photo of Jo in a plunging evening dress receiving a 21st Century Policing Award.

'Are you coping, Harry?' she asks now, pushing a box of tissues towards him.

'Coping?' he says. 'Coping with what?'

'With all the changes here. With being one officer short.' One of Nelson's sergeants, Tim Heathfield, left last year and hasn't been replaced. There isn't the budget, according to Jo. Nelson protested, for form's sake, but he has reasons of his own to be glad of Tim's absence. Tim was Nelson's protégé, who had followed him down from Blackpool and had established himself as the rising star of King's Lynn CID. The problem was that Tim had also established himself as the would-be lover of Nelson's wife.

'We're managing,' says Nelson, 'but I need to get on now. There's something I want DS Clough to check at the Denning Road site.'

'Information received?' says Jo, managing to make this sound both whimsical and sinister. 'Something to do with your visitor this morning? I saw that Aftershave Eddie was in reception.'

'A woman has been reported missing,' says Nelson. 'I'm going to follow it up.'

'A rough sleeper?' says Jo.

'A woman,' says Nelson. 'Now, if you'll excuse me . . .'

Ruth is pleased to see that both Ted and Quentin order cake in the cafe. That means that she can have some too. You can never rely on Judy. She's quite likely to have black tea or just a glass of water. But today Judy reaches towards the blueberry muffins so Ruth feels justified in doing the same.

The Cafe Britannia at the Guildhall always reminds Ruth of a fifties cafeteria, or her idea of one, at any rate. It's a high room with a mezzanine floor supported by little gold-topped pillars. She always feels as if there should be white-aproned waitresses whisking between the tables rather than a self-service bar with a cappuccino machine. There are home-made cakes, though, and sometimes there is music too, played on an upright piano in the corner and adding to the sense of having slipped into a golden age detective story.

The cafe is surprisingly crowded for a Wednesday morning and they take their food to a table on the upper level. Ruth is still rather irritated with Quentin for inviting himself to what should have been a cosy chat with Judy and Ted but he's not an intrusive presence at all. He chats easily to Ruth and Ted about the difficulties of building his subterranean restaurant.

'The trouble is there's not enough space on the surface any more. Have you heard about the super-basements people are building in London? The mega-rich all live in places like Belgravia and Chelsea and space is at a premium. They can't build horizontally any more so they build vertically. Down and down. Floor after floor with no natural light. Cinemas and gyms. Even swimming pools.'

'I've heard about that,' says Ted. 'They leave the diggers down there, don't they? It's too much trouble to get them to the surface so they just bury them.'

'I think that might be an urban myth,' says Quentin, 'but a friend of mine was employed as an architect on one of those developments. This guy – I think he was a Saudi prince – he wanted an eighty-foot-deep basement where he could keep his Ferrari collection. My friend had to put in a motorised lift to bring the cars to the surface.'

'I'd hate to have a room that was several metres underground,' says Ruth, remembering the tunnel earlier, 'even if it did have a swimming pool.'

'They think it's safer,' says Quentin. 'Architects are always talking about billionaire bunkers, panic rooms deep underground where the super-rich think they can sit out the next nuclear war. All the Russian oligarchs have them.'

'There aren't that many Russian oligarchs in Norfolk,'

says Judy, cutting her muffin into very small pieces. Ruth has already eaten hers.

'No, but there are a lot of very rich people,' says Quentin. 'That's lucky for architects, of course. There's always somebody wanting an extension or a barn conversion. But what I really like is building public spaces like art galleries or restaurants. Places where people can meet and exchange ideas, like the forum in Rome. You know, in the forum, the laws used to be written out for everyone to see. A bit of a change from today when you need to employ a solicitor at several hundred pounds an hour just to translate the law into English.'

'The word forensic comes from the Latin word forum,' says Ruth. She thinks that, as a highly paid architect, Quentin is probably complaining too much about lawyers. In his admiration for the Romans, Quentin reminds Ruth of her ex-boyfriend, Max, and she finds the comparison rather unsettling. She notices that Quentin is wearing a wedding ring and wonders if he's gay or straight. He has a slightly androgynous air to him.

'And your restaurant is going to be open to everyone, is it?' says Ted. 'You're planning a cheap menu then. Chips with everything?'

Quentin laughs. 'No, I'm afraid it'll probably end up being quite exclusive. But if it pays its way we can include some spaces that everyone can access – cafes and community centres and libraries.'

'An underground library,' says Ted. 'Now there's a thought.'

'Libraries are the cathedrals of the modern age,' says

Quentin. 'All that knowledge, available for anyone to use. It's quite a subversive thought; maybe underground is the right place for a library.'

'There's an underground cathedral in South America, isn't there?' says Ruth. 'I was reading about it recently. Isn't it in an abandoned salt mine?'

'Yes, the Salt Cathedral of Zipaquirá,' says Quentin. 'It's in Colombia. I went there once. It's an amazing place. It started off just as a refuge for the miners, an alcove carved into the rock where they could say their prayers, then it turned into this massive church, big enough for eight thousand people. That church was closed for safety reasons but the Spanish government held a competition to find an architect to build a new one. It was won by Roswell Garavito Pearl and he built this wonderful cathedral, below the old one, with a dome and balconies and icons carved into the halite rock.'

Quentin sounds quite evangelical when he describes the cathedral. Now he sounds less like Max and more like Erik, Ruth's old archaeology lecturer, in one of his messianic moods.

'Well, I hope you get to build your restaurant,' she says, 'even if I can never afford to eat there.'

'What will happen if the bones turn out to be of real archaeological interest?' says Quentin. 'If they turn out to be Richard III or someone like that.'

'They're unlikely to belong to a king,' says Ruth, who often wishes that she had been part of the team who found Richard's bones in Leicester. 'Though they do say Henry I is buried under a car park in Reading. If the bones are archaeologically interesting, we could apply for funding for an English Heritage grant. That's unlikely to be forthcoming though. The best we can hope is that we do another excavation, dig up whatever's there, log it and present the findings in a paper somewhere. It shouldn't hold up your building work for too long.'

'Of course, it might turn out to be a murder victim,' says Ted. 'She has quite an affinity with murder victims, does Ruth.'

This is considered very amusing, although Judy and Ruth laugh the least.

Clough and Tanya are also in a cafe, although this one is lighter on cakes and heavier on quinoa and tofu. Clough is eating an all-day breakfast which, to his horror, features vegan sausage. Tanya is sipping peppermint tea.

'We should get back to the station soon,' she says.

'Plenty of time,' says Clough, mopping up brown sauce. Hs phone rings and he answers it indistinctly.

'Are you eating again?' says Nelson.

'Keeping my blood sugar up,' says Clough.

'Your blood sugar must be sky high, in that case. Did you investigate the hole in the road?'

'Yes. It was a traffic case really. They've closed the road. All the commuters up in arms. Maintenance team are on their way.'

'Did you look in the hole?'

'Look in it? What do you mean, boss?' At the change in tone, Tanya looks up, glasses glinting keenly.

'Last night a student called Grace Miller saw a man standing in the middle of the Denning Road. She says that he disappeared. So you've got a hole and a disappearing man. Join up the dots yourself.'

'A student? Had she been smoking wacky baccy by any chance?'

'Very probably. That doesn't mean that we should discount her evidence. I want you and Fuller to go back and look in that hole.'

Grumbling, Clough pays the bill and he and Tanya head out into the June sunshine. The hole is fenced off and a maintenance van has just drawn up alongside it.

'Hang on a minute.' Clough shows his warrant card. 'We need to take another look.'

Denning Road is an attractive residential area, with detached houses surrounded by hedges and trees. There's a church opposite, also half-hidden by trees, and a park on the other side of the road. It's quiet now but at rush hour, the road is a major thoroughfare into the city. The hole is about two metres wide, a yawning abyss in the middle of the tarmac. It was only because it was spotted by a nurse on her way to the dawn shift at the hospital that the traffic police were able to cordon it off in time to prevent the morning traffic from disappearing into its maw.

'Have you got a torch?' Clough asks one of the maintenance crew. Before the man can reply though, Tanya produces a Maglite from her handbag.

'Bloody hell. What else have you got in there?'

'I like to be prepared,' says Tanya.

Clough shines the torch into the hole. It's deep, more than six feet down, he thinks. He can see smooth walls which look man-made, something which led the original investigating officer to believe that this was an old chalk mining tunnel. No one has yet been down but Clough is always keen to try anything once.

'I'm going in,' he says to Tanya, affecting a John Wayne drawl.

'Are you sure? Shouldn't you be wearing a hard hat?'

'I'm a risk taker, me.'

He lowers himself over the side, watched impassively by the three highway maintenance men. It's deeper than he thought. Clough is over six foot but the road surface is now at least another two feet over his head. He lands on rubble but when he straightens up, he can see that he is standing in what was once a tunnel. If he stretches his arms, he can touch both sides.

'Are you all right?'

He can see Tanya peering down, white face, black-rimmed glasses. Behind her one of the maintenance men says something about gas leaks.

'Can you smell gas?' asks Tanya.

'No. I can't see a body either.'

The hole is not very wide but it's wide enough for Clough to see something else, another tunnel leading off at right angles.

'I think we need to call the boss,' says Clough.

CHAPTER 4

Ruth hears about the Denning Road hole as she drives home that evening. It's the lead item on the local news.

'Should we be worried?' asks the interviewer. 'Are mysterious holes going to open up all over Norwich? A lot of our listeners will remember the famous Earlham Road hole in 1988.'

'Well,' says the unnamed male expert, sounding amused, 'Norwich is built on chalk and chalk is fairly easy to dig and yet can stand unsupported. There are all sorts of chalk mining tunnels under the city. Chalk was needed for the lime used in construction and Norwich was once one of the richest cities in Britain with a lot of building work going on. That's a lot of lime.'

'Can you say where the next hole will appear then?' says the interviewer, clearly unwilling to abandon the doomsday scenario.

'Not really,' says the expert. 'Tunnels have been found in all areas of the city, wherever chalk is available on the valley sides. Some of the tunnels have been filled in but many have been left as they were when they were abandoned.'

'So these holes could be opening up all over the place?'

'Let's not get carried away,' says the expert, still sounding admirably relaxed. 'The problems occur when stability is disturbed by external features, such as construction work or water leakage. I suspect that may have been the issue in Denning Road.'

'That's all we've got time for, I'm afraid,' says the interviewer, obviously not wanting to get drawn into discussing drainage. 'Thanks to Dr Martin Kellerman from the University of North Norfolk.'

Ruth is interested. It's not often that UNN gets its experts on the news, even the local station. Phil, her head of department, will be very jealous. She's never heard of Martin Kellerman but then the archaeologists don't mix much with other departments. Is he a geologist? A scientist? She'll have to ask Cathbad, who used to work as a technician in the sciences department. Cathbad knows everyone.

When she gets to her childminder's house, she finds Kate and two other charges playing on the trampoline in Sandra's garden. Sandra is watching them – she's too experienced a childminder to leave children unattended – but there's still something wild and uninhibited about the way the children are bouncing up and down, their shouts echoing in the still air. Ruth watches Kate's dark hair flying as she competes to be the highest. Kate's grown this year, she's nearly the tallest in the class, and her school dress is almost too short. 'They have to be short,' Kate informed

Ruth at the beginning of the summer term, 'and you have to wear them with frilly socks.' Hard to believe that Kate is six, nearly at the end of Year One. Most of the time she's still Ruth's baby but sometimes, especially when Ruth sees her with other children, Kate looks disconcertingly like a mini teenager. Ruth imagines that she looks like Nelson's older daughters, Kate's half-sisters, whom she has never met.

'Look at me, Mum!'

'I am looking,' says Ruth. I'm always looking, she thinks. But one day she will look and Kate will be gone, away to start her life without Ruth.

'They grow up so quickly, don't they?' says Sandra, in the empathetic way she sometimes has.

'Yes,' says Ruth. 'When Kate was a baby I longed for her to grow up but now I feel like I want her to stay this age for ever.'

'You wait until she's a teenager,' says Sandra, who has three grown-up children, two with children of their own. 'Mind you, teenagers are good company too. I miss the laughs we used to have when I had my lot here, their friends in and out of the house all the time.'

But Ruth's house is on the edge of the marshes, miles from anywhere. Will Kate's mythical teenage friends face the trek out to the Saltmarsh (dark road, no buses, taxis often refusing to make the journey), or is this something else to worry about? Maybe she should move to a house like Sandra's, with easy access to Lynn and trains and nightlife. The trouble is that Ruth loves her cottage, with its view of the endless sea and sky; she doesn't want to swap it for a Victorian terrace with a trampoline in the garden. Well, time enough to worry about that.

'Come on, Kate,' she calls. 'Time to be going home.'

After the usual hassle of putting on shoes and socks and finding lost book bags, Ruth and Kate are driving through the outskirts of King's Lynn on their way to the Saltmarsh. At first Kate sings Ruth a selection of songs from her end-of-term concert, which is only a few weeks away. 'One more step along the world I go,' she sings, in her sweet, slightly off-key soprano. 'And it's from the old I travel to the new. Keep me travelling along with you.' Ruth, concentrating on keeping to the actual road, wonders how on earth she is going to manage to get through the concert without collapsing into tears. And she hasn't really got any friends amongst the other mothers, who mostly seem just children themselves, so no one will offer her a tissue or a sympathetic look. After a while though, as Ruth takes the turning for the marshes, Kate grows silent and seems almost hypnotised by the grey-green expanse, the birds wheeling in the twilight, the line of blue that marks the tide coming in.

'Do you know what happened in Norwich today?' says Ruth. 'A hole appeared in the road. A great big hole. Big enough for a car to fall in, they said on the radio.'

'A hole?' says Kate. 'Where does it go to?'

'I don't know,' says Ruth. 'I don't think it goes anywhere.'

'Maybe it goes to the Land of Bism,' says Kate. 'Like in *The Silver Chair*.'

Ruth read *The Silver Chair* to Kate. She loves C.S. Lewis though she deplores his Christian moralising. She can't remember the Land of Bism though. Sometimes she worries that Kate is actually cleverer than her.

Back at the cottage, Kate disappears to find Ruth's cat, Flint. A loud thump from upstairs, followed by running feline footsteps, shows that Flint has been located. Kate follows Flint into the garden, having mysteriously managed to dress herself as Pocahontas in the interval. Ruth sets about cooking supper, macaroni cheese, one of her small repertoire of tried-and-trusted recipes guaranteed not to make Kate slump in her chair or pretend to vomit.

The phone rings just as she's pouring on the cheese sauce. She puts the casserole dish into the oven and goes into the sitting room to answer it. Kate and Flint are sitting on the sofa watching a DVD of *The Lion, the Witch and the Wardrobe*, maybe inspired by the conversation in the car.

'Hi, Ruth. It's Cassandra.'

Now this is a surprise. Cassandra Blackstock is Clough's partner and the mother of his baby. They are planning to marry in August. Ruth has seen Cassandra at various social events but has never really spoken to her beyond pleasantries about children. Cassandra is aristocratic and beautiful and a part-time actress, three factors that, in Ruth's eyes, make them unlikely ever to be friends. The fact that Cassandra is engaged to Clough is, according to Nelson, proof that there's hope for anyone. In fact, the two of them seem blissfully happy. But why is Cassandra phoning Ruth at home?

Luckily Cassandra doesn't waste much time getting down to business. 'You know I belong to a local theatre workshop?' Ruth didn't. 'It's called Jacob's Ladder and we're very keen on involving local people in our shows.' A pause. Is Cassandra about to offer Ruth a leading part in the next production? If so, Ruth will not have to spend long considering her answer. 'We're putting on a production of *Alice's Adventures Under Ground* for the festival. You know that was the original title of *Alice's Adventures in Wonderland*?' Ruth didn't. 'I'm playing Alice. A grown-up version, of course. It's quite a dark adaptation. Anyway, we want a child to play me as a young girl and I thought about Kate.'

'Kate? My Kate?'

'Yes. She's the right age and she's such a bright little thing. I remember her doing that magic trick at Dave's birthday party. And . . .' Slightly self-conscious laugh. 'She looks a little like me.'

Does she? Cassandra is dark and dramatic-looking, a real heroine type. Does Kate, who has inherited Nelson's dark eyes and hair, resemble her? Ruth can't help feeling a little flattered on her daughter's behalf.

'It's only a small part. One scene. I think she'd love it.'

Ruth is about to refuse. She has never wanted to act and she has certainly never wanted to be one of those mothers who is always pushing their daughter onto the stage, mouthing their lines in the wings and fighting with the other mothers about who has the biggest pair of fairy wings. She has even, so far, resisted Kate's demands for ballet lessons. But then she looks up and sees Kate, in the role of

Lucy, declaiming to Flint (Aslan), 'But how can I defeat the White Witch? I'm only a child.'

The truth is that Kate would love it.

Nelson does not have much luck in tracing Grace's Jesus man. After Clough rang with the news that the hole had exposed what looked like the beginning of a tunnel, Nelson drove over to Norwich to see the site for himself. He even went into the hole but he could see that the tunnel was completely blocked by stones and rubble. He set Tanya to find a geology expert at one of the universities and she came up with a Dr Martin Kellerman from UNN. Kellerman, sounding admirably calm and businesslike, said that the tunnel sounded like part of the old chalk mining system. 'I've been asked to look into it for *Look East*,' he said. 'Everyone's hoping that it will be as exciting as the Earlham Road hole in 1988.'

'Please,' said Nelson, 'don't talk to me about that bloody hole.'

Nelson also spoke to the Norwich police and heard from a PCSO Hobbs, a special constable who had been riding home on his bicycle in the early hours of Wednesday morning. He remembered a car full of young people who had shouted 'ribald' things at him out of the window. No, he couldn't remember exactly what they said but he got the strong impression that drink had been taken. No, Hobbs had not seen a bearded man standing in the middle of the road. He sounded quite affronted at the idea.

Kellerman duly visited Denning Road and gave it as his

opinion that the earth had subsided due to building works nearby. The council set about filling in the hole and opening the road to traffic. Nelson thought that he might as well call it a day.

He arrives home to a wild baying. His one-year-old German Shepherd, Bruno, greets him as if he's been away for a year. This is why people have dogs. Nelson doesn't know anyone else who would be so pleased to see him at the end of the day. Michelle barely looks up from the TV these days and his daughters stopped noticing him some time in their teens. He starts a play fight with the dog who breaks off to stare hopefully at his lead. That's the downside, of course. You're always having to take them for bloody walks.

He becomes dimly aware that there are noises from the kitchen accompanied by a tantalising smell of food. Has Michelle come home early from the salon in order to cook him a special supper? In the old days, she actually used to do things like that. But, on second thoughts Michelle is working late tonight and the aromas are slightly too spicy and foreign for her cooking. Nelson is not surprised to enter the kitchen and find his daughter, Laura, enveloped in a cloud of steam and trying to follow a recipe on her iPad.

'That's the only problem with cooking from a tablet,' she says, wiping the screen with her sleeve.

'Smells grand, love,' says Nelson, eying a sliced chilli with foreboding. 'What is it?'

'Thai green curry. I thought I'd cook as Mum'll be home late. And it's something to do.'

It's been great having Laura home for the last month but Nelson knows that his eldest daughter is becoming restless. Her PGCE course doesn't start until September and most of her friends are working or have left Norfolk. She works two nights a week in a local pub but otherwise spends her days at the gym or lying on the sofa watching reruns of *Friends*. She seems to have no setting between violent exercise and inertia. So the cooking is a definite step forward, though it might be nice if she occasionally made a shepherd's pie. Still, at least she's cooking a proper meal. Rebecca only ever makes cupcakes, which don't do his waistline any good ('You don't have to eat them all, Dad').

'Have you taken Bruno out today?' he asks. That's part of the deal. That she walks the dog on the days that he doesn't go to something called Doggy Daycare. Nelson can't say the name without deep, atavistic embarrassment.

'Yes,' she says vaguely. 'To the park.'

That means he'll need a longer walk later. Bruno is sitting in the doorway, staring at Nelson intently. Nelson turns his back. He'll just have a cup of tea first. Maybe even a beer.

Laura is listening to music on her headphones but the little kitchen television is on with the sound turned down. Nelson can see Denning Road with the police tape and the 'road closed' sign. A graphic helpfully demonstrates the size of the hole by comparing it to a basketball player lying down. Then a man appears on the screen, speaking earnestly. 'Dr Martin Kellerman,' Nelson reads, 'Senior Lecturer in Geology at the University of North Norfolk.'

What had happened to Grace Miller's mysterious man?

Perhaps he was just another drunk wandering in the road. At any rate, no one has been reported missing.

'Do you know a girl called Grace Miller?' he asks Laura.

Laura takes out her earphones and he repeats the question.

'I don't think so. Who is she?'

'She's a student at UNN. She's twenty.'

'No. I'm not going to know any twenty-year-olds, am I?' Laura is twenty-four, a fact that never ceases to take Nelson by surprise. She graduated three years ago with a degree in marine biology and immediately went to work in Ibiza as a travel rep. Nelson thanks whichever gods directed her back to Norfolk and a proper job.

'She's met Rebecca.'

Laura shrugs as if this is only to be expected. 'What's this Grace done?' she asks. 'Murdered someone?'

Nelson's daughters persist in believing that every case is a murder case. 'No,' he says, 'just a potential witness.'

Laura turns back to her curry, leaving Nelson to watch the silent television, now showing tennis players preparing for Wimbledon. Bruno appears beside him, radiating sympathy and goodwill and an urgent desire to be outside.

'Oh, all right,' says Nelson.

CHAPTER 5

'I'm sure I've seen Aftershave Eddie with a woman,' says Clough. 'I joked to him that he'd scored at last.'

'I bet he loved that,' says Judy.

'Oh, he's got a sense of humour, has Eddie.' The words 'unlike some' hover in the air.

It's been a slightly bad-tempered briefing all round. Judy arrived late, unusually for her, and Tanya has commiserated too loudly about 'childcare problems'. 'No, I overslept,' growled Judy. Clough, who always looks as if he's overslept, seems unwilling to take the disappearance of Barbara Murray seriously.

'I mean, tramps disappear all the time, that's what they do.'

'*They* don't do anything,' says Judy. 'Rough sleepers are all different. They're individuals.'

'I know that,' says Clough. 'I often have some banter with one bloke I see out jogging. He tells me Chelsea are a crap team, I tell him Man U can't play football.'

'I bet those little chats are a real comfort to him,' says Judy. 'The highlight of his day, in fact.'

'All right you two,' says Nelson. 'Fuller, you ring round the hostels. See if a woman called Barbara Murray has checked in. Johnson, I want you to go and talk to the rough sleepers around the town. See if any of them have seen Barbara. There's a man called Charlie who apparently heard someone talking to her about her children. Charlie's patch is by the Customs House. And Eddie said something about a soup run.'

'Cathbad does the soup run,' says Judy, surprising nobody. 'It's organised by the SVP. St Vincent de Paul Society,' she explains to Clough and Tanya. 'But anyone can help. That Italian restaurant, Toppolino's, they provide the soup.'

Nelson vaguely recognises the SVP Society. He thinks it's something his mother belongs to, visiting old people, taking them communion, playing Scrabble, that sort of thing. It's a shock to think that his mother counts as an old person herself these days.

'It's not a religious organisation,' says Judy, 'though lots of churches have SVP groups. Cathbad's is run by a man called Paul Pritchard. He runs the drop-in centre at St Matthew's.'

'Maybe we should pay him a visit too,' says Nelson. 'And ask Cathbad about Barbara.'

'I will,' says Judy. 'What about the man who disappeared on Denning Road?'

'We haven't had anyone else reported missing,' says Nelson. 'I suppose it's possible that he could have fallen into the hole, hidden there for a while and just climbed out. My student wasn't the most reliable of witnesses.'

'A man could have hidden down there,' says Clough. 'And

there weren't any other witnesses. Fuller and I went door-to-door.'

'OK,' says Nelson. 'Let's leave that one for now. Highway Maintenance are repairing the road. Anything else?'

'Human bones found below the Guildhall,' says Judy. 'Ruth and Irish Ted excavated them yesterday.'

'Human bones,' says Nelson warily. 'How old?'

'Medieval, Ruth thought.'

'Well, I won't put that top of my priority list,' says Nelson. 'Clough, you follow up on that GBH in Downham Market. Fuller, you can back him up when you've done the hostels. I've got to work on that strategy document.'

He doesn't catch the eyes of his team. They all know that Superintendent Archer disapproves of Nelson's habit of conducting investigations himself. He should be in the office, busying himself with strategy. Indeed, when the team has left, he does open up a document entitled 'Strategic Investigations 2015'. But after typing the word 'bollocks' three times, he closes the document and reaches for his phone.

'Ruth? I hear you've found some bones.'

Judy doesn't have to go far to find her first rough sleepers. There are a couple of men sitting in a bus shelter near the entrance to the Vancouver Centre. Judy asks them if they know a woman called Barbara Murray. The men, both huddled in blankets despite the warmth of the day, shake their heads. They are probably in their forties, thinks Judy. One is a ginger-haired giant with a face like a Viking raider. The other is smaller and wizened-looking, with a cough that shakes his whole body.

'She's dark-haired,' says Judy, 'with a gap between her teeth and a slight Scottish accent.' They have not been able to run to an e-fit but Judy always finds these unsatisfactory anyway. They never look like real-life humans and they make witnesses concentrate on the external rather than internal features. People don't always remember eye and hair colour, but they often do remember a voice or a mannerism. At all events, something in what she has said causes the two men to look at each other.

'Could be Babs,' says the ginger man.

'Babs?' says Judy.

'I've seen her around with Eddie,' says the smaller man.

'That could be her,' says Judy. 'Have you seen Babs recently?'

'No,' says the Viking. 'Not for a few weeks.'

'Do you know anyone who knows her? Who may have seen her?'

'There's Bilbo,' says the Viking. 'He knows Babs.'

'Do you know where I can find Bilbo?' asks Judy. Please don't say Bag End, she pleads silently.

But the answer is prosaic. 'This time of day, he'll be at the station,' says the small man. 'You can't miss him. He always wears a jester's hat.'

Judy gives the men five pounds each. It's not unethical, she tells herself, when it's her own money. Then she cuts through the bus terminus towards the rail station. She passes the museum on her way and spares a thought for Cathbad, who loves visiting the museum and communing with the timbers from the wood henge found on the Norfolk coast some seventeen years ago. At the time Cathbad had protested when the wood was removed to be stored in controlled conditions in the museum. 'It was meant to rot and become part of the landscape,' he told Judy. 'Change and decay and life and death – that's what it's all about.' Judy doesn't think much about change and decay, she tries to live in the present. But she does sometimes worry whether life as a childcarer, spiritual counsellor and dispenser of soup is exciting enough for Cathbad, the druid rebel who once stood on the henge timbers and shouted his defiance to the sea. He says he's happy but then he would say that, wouldn't he? Judy first met Cathbad when she was engaged to Darren and their subsequent relationship was passionate, unplanned and often tormented. Judy had married Darren and then Michael was born. The trouble was that, from the first, the baby had looked exactly like Cathbad. Now all that is sorted out, in a messy twenty-first century way. Cathbad and Judy are together and they have had another baby, Miranda. Darren still sees Michael and has recently remarried. If Judy still worries then maybe that's just because worry is her default position.

Judy finds Bilbo on the station steps. He is wearing his jester's hat and dispiritedly offering to dance a jig for the passengers hurrying past him. Judy introduces herself and offers him a cup of coffee.

They go, not to the rather charming Countryline Cafe in the station, but to a depressed-looking place across the road where Judy thinks it will be easier to talk. Even so, the cafe owner looks as though he would like to stop Bilbo from entering but Judy shows her warrant card and asks if he'd prefer a visit from Health and Safety. She buys Bilbo a coffee and a cheese roll and asks about Babs.

'She's a nice lady,' says Bilbo, eating with difficulty because he doesn't have many teeth. 'She's from Scotland and I'm from Wales so we've got a bond, like. She's had a hard life, children taken into care and all that.'

'When did you last see her?'

'A couple of weeks ago, on the soup run.'

'Is she usually there for the soup run?'

'Yes, there's a group of us who meet regular, like.' He makes it sound as if it's a social gathering. Which perhaps it is.

'So were you surprised when she didn't turn up?'

'Surprised?' Bilbo looks as if the word is new to him.

'Have you any idea where she could have gone? Have you heard anything? Any rumours?'

Bilbo is silent for a long time, tearing bits off his roll. He's so intent on his food that Judy thinks that he might have forgotten the question.

'I heard she'd gone underground,' he says at last.

'Underground?'

'Missing,' he says. 'You know.'

Judy doesn't know. She decides to try a new line of questioning. 'Do you know Charlie, who lives . . .' she isn't sure of the most tactful verb, 'by the Customs House? He said that he heard someone talking to Babs about her children. She seemed upset by it.'

'I know Charlie. He's another Scot. A clever man. He was a teacher once. Now, me, I left school at sixteen.'

Judy looks at Bilbo, who has taken off his hat to reveal sparse grey hair. In a different context, he would just be an elderly man at the golf club or shopping centre. It's so thin, the line between respectability and chaos.

'Do you know anything about Babs's background? Anything that might help us find her?'

Bilbo thinks, dabbing his mouth with a paper napkin.

'Like I said, she's from Scotland. We talked about the bagpipes once. I love music. I think she was married but he turned out to be no good. That happens a lot.' He nods wisely. 'We men cause a lot of problems in the world. Of course I've never been married.' He says this rather sadly, though. Judy can't imagine Bilbo young but he must have been. He may once have been young and in love and full of hope for the future.

'Do you know where Barbara goes during the day?' she says. 'Does she go to a drop-in centre?'

'Yes, she goes to the place by the church. St Matthew's. The one that's full of God botherers.'

'Was Babs religious?'

Bilbo laughs, a big toothless grin. 'Babs? No. Not Babs. She used to say that she was a pagan. Like one of those druids. You know the sort of thing.'

'I certainly do,' says Judy.

CHAPTER 6

Nelson and Ruth are in the UNN cafe. It is not a place that Nelson has seen before, though he once memorably visited Ruth's office, the time when he first came to the university looking for a forensic archaeologist to help him date a child's bones. He looks round at the crowded tables. 'Everyone working hard, I see.'

'Don't the police have tea breaks?' counters Ruth. She has chosen a cappuccino but looks rather enviously at Nelson's large slice of cake.

'Life's one big tea break for Clough,' he says. 'But She Who Must Be Obeyed would probably like to ban tea and replace it with some herbal crap.'

Ruth has no difficulty identifying She Who Must Be Obeyed as Superintendent Archer. Over the last few months she has listened to quite a few of Nelson's monologues on the subject. She'd been sceptical at first. How awful could one woman be? And, despite his protestations, she thought it wouldn't be easy for Nelson to take orders from a woman. But then she'd met Jo.

'How's life at the station?' she asks now.

'Bloody awful,' says Nelson, stirring sugar into his coffee. 'We're short-staffed with Tim gone but there's no chance we can replace him. She'd like to get rid of me altogether.'

'She can't do that, can she?' Ruth can't imagine King's Lynn CID without Nelson. For all his faults, he has always seemed to epitomise the police force: lacking in charm sometimes but matchless in an emergency.

'No. Not if I keep my head. But there are DCIs my age retiring every day. Crazy really. On the scrapheap at fifty with all that experience.'

'What do the others think?'

'Judy keeps her head down but she doesn't like Archer any more than I do. Tanya's happy to play along if it gets her promotion. She's probably after my job. Clough is slagging Jo off one minute and behaving like her puppy dog the next.'

Ruth laughs. 'I heard from Cassandra yesterday.'

'Did you? What did she want?'

'She wanted to offer Kate a part in a play.' She tells Nelson about *Alice's Adventures Under Ground*.

'Acting?' Nelson could not sound more shocked if she was suggesting that Kate start pole-dancing lessons. 'In a play?'

'Yes, Nelson.' Ruth assumes her patient voice. 'She likes drama, as you know.'

'But that's at school. This is a real play, put on for the public. You get all sorts at those festival events.'

'Yes,' says Ruth. 'You get people like me. And it's only one short scene.' That morning, she had still been undecided about letting Kate be in the play but, as usual, Nelson's opposition has the effect of hardening her resolve.

'I don't know,' says Nelson. 'Cassandra's lot put on all sorts of funny plays. You should hear Cloughie talk about them.'

It's nothing to do with you, Ruth wants to say. Nelson is Kate's father but, as Ruth elected to bring her up on her own, she doesn't feel that he has any right to interfere. When Kate was born, Ruth was determined to go it alone: Nelson's name isn't on Kate's birth certificate and Ruth has never taken a penny from him. But Nelson wanted to be involved and, thanks to Michelle's magnanimity, he is now officially part of his daughter's life. That doesn't mean that he can decide on her extra-curricular activities though. To change the subject, Ruth says, 'You were asking about the bones found under the Guildhall.'

This is the official reason for Nelson's visit. They both know that it's an excuse though. The bones are probably at least several hundred years old and it's hardly the job of the DCI to seek out the forensic archaeologist and ask about the excavation. But they are both happy to keep up the pretence. Nelson cuts his cake in two and offers half to Ruth. She put it on her saucer.

'Judy said you thought they were old.'

'Well, they were found in one of the oldest tunnels. I checked with the county archaeologist and he said that the tunnel goes all the way to St John's Cathedral, on the Earlham Road. He'd assumed that it was blocked off though.'

'The Earlham Road? That's where that bus disappeared in the 1980s. Everyone keeps yakking on about it.'

'Yes. It's been on the news a lot with that other hole appearing. Anyway, it's likely that the bones are medieval or even older. There's no flesh on them and they look very clean. It's just . . .'

'What is it, Ruth? I know there's something you're not telling me.'

'It might be nothing. But one of the long bones was broken in the middle and there were cut marks on it. And the bones were so clean, almost shiny, it reminded me of something that I've read about. Pot polish.'

'Pot polish? Sounds like something my granny would do.'

'I doubt it. It's when bones are boiled soon after death. The polish comes from the contact with a roughly made cooking vessel.'

'Jesus wept.' Nelson chokes on his last crumb of cake. 'Are you saying these bones were in a cooking pot?'

'I'm not saying anything yet. But the shattering of the long bone to get to the marrow, that could suggest cannibalism. The cut marks too, those little nicks might come from butchery, cutting tendons, filleting, that sort of thing. It's just an idea. But it's interesting, isn't it? Maybe there was once a whole troglodyte community down there.'

'Yes. A community of cannibals. Pretty bloody interesting.'

'They may not have been cannibals. Sometimes bones are defleshed for religious reasons.'

'When will you know for certain?'

'We might never know,' says Ruth. She is always telling Nelson that, in archaeology, the questions are more important than the answers, but he never seems to take this news well. 'Actually,' she says, 'DNA often survives really well in cannibalised remains. When you take out the organs after death, you take out the gut bacteria that usually initiate decomposition.'

Nelson pushes his plate away. 'Well, you've put me right off my lunch, that's all I can say.'

'Are you allowed lunch breaks too?' says Ruth. 'I'd better get going. I've got a lecture in ten minutes. Are you still picking Kate up on Monday?'

'Of course,' says Nelson.

'Are you sure?' Ruth knows that seeing Kate is more difficult now that Laura is home. Laura doesn't know about Kate and might well ask herself why her parents are constantly entertaining their friend's young daughter. So, this term, Nelson's time with Kate has been limited to meeting her from school once a week and taking her for a McDonald's. Ruth wonders if she should protest on dietary grounds but she doesn't because Kate likes the toys that come with a Happy Meal.

'Of course I'm sure,' says Nelson, in slightly too hearty a tone. He starts piling their cups onto the tray. 'What's your lecture about?'

'Pathological conditions in human skeletal remains. You're welcome to come, if you like.'

'No, you're all right,' says Nelson.

Judy leaves Bilbo in the cafe where, much to the disapproval of the owner, he has obviously decided to stay for the day. She walks back through the shopping centre to the quay, hoping to see Charlie outside the Customs House. It's a beautiful morning, the river calm and still, the boats gently clanking. There are a few tourists taking pictures of the Customs House, neat and symmetrical with its wooden spire. The statue of Captain George Vancouver stands in front of it, holding a scroll with an air of importance. Vancouver, King's Lynn's most famous son, sailed to the north-west coast of America in 1793 with the result that many places in Canada now share names with Norfolk towns. There are a few people taking selfies with the intrepid seafarer but there's no sign of Charlie or of anyone sleeping rough. Judy looks out across the river towards the Wash. Hard to believe that this was once England's most important port. That's what they were taught at school, anyway. Now it seems small and quaint, like an illustration in a picture book. Here are the boats, here are the houses. She looks at her phone. Twelve o'clock. She should probably get back to the station. As she stares at the screen a photo pings up. It's from Cathbad and shows Miranda, their two-year-old daughter, on the harbour wall at Wells, eating a chip. It's not a day to be inside. She decides to walk to the drop-in centre at St Matthew's and ask about Barbara.

She strolls through the Tuesday Market, past the place where the heart of a witch who was burnt at the stake is said to be embedded in the wall, past the almshouses and the converted warehouses. St Matthew's is on the outskirts of the town, near the city wall (another remnant of more important times). It's a sooty Victorian edifice that looks too large for a parish church. Judy doesn't know how many people still go to church on a Sunday but surely they would never fill the cavernous space inside. But next to the church is a modern hall, and this seems full of life. Women are parking their buggies by the steps and carrying their offspring through the double doors. A large sign announces that today it's Mothers and Babies and Weightwatchers. What about Fathers and Babies? thinks Judy, irritated on Cathbad's behalf. At the bottom of the sign is a handwritten notice: 'Drop-in centre. First floor.' Judy makes her way past the mothers and the weightwatchers, looking for the stairs.

Nelson says goodbye to Ruth and watches her walk away along the corridor, her lecture notes under her arm. It's as if she is being swallowed up by the university, that alien organism that intimidates Nelson with its mixture of shabbiness and superiority. The slouching students, the noticeboards advertising string quartets and garage bands, the peeling paintwork, the girls outside playing what looks like rugby: it's all outside his experience, although both his daughters went to university and would presumably feel quite at home here.

He's pleased he saw Ruth in her own environment though. Over the last year their relationship, always delicate, has sometimes been quite difficult to maintain, both of them buffeted this way and that by emotional undercurrents that they can't – or won't – acknowledge. They are bound together for ever as Kate's parents but beyond that . . . Beyond that they can't go. Seeing Ruth at the university reminded Nelson of the first time that he had sought her help and how impressed he'd been by her, this clever woman who seemed so confident that she didn't care what others thought of her. Now that he knows her better he realises that this isn't quite true, but she's still the brightest person he knows. He would never say so but he feels quite proud watching her stride away to lecture on . . . What was it again? Pathology in skeletons? Something like that.

'DCI Nelson?'

Nelson turns. A young woman is looking at him quizzically, as if she too finds him out of place. She has blonde hair in a ponytail and, for some unknown reason, is carrying a broomstick.

'It's Grace. Grace Miller.'

'Oh, hallo, Grace.'

'Were you looking for me?'

'No, no.' He hurries to reassure her. 'I had a meeting with Dr Galloway in the archaeology department. How are you? Hope you haven't seen anyone else disappearing.'

'Did you find my man? The Jesus man?'

'No. But I checked the site and the hole in the road. If he fell into it, he definitely got out again.'

'That's good.' She's still looking slightly worried.

'Everything else all right?'

'Yes, fine. I'm just off to play Quidditch.'

It's as if the young speak a different language, thinks Nelson, as Grace exits through the main doors and joins a group of students on the lawn, all of them carrying broomsticks and baseball bats.

The drop-in centre consists of several rooms on the first floor. There are signs for showers and a laundry room but most people seem to be congregating in a place called the Lounge. It's a big, comfortable room filled with mismatched sofas and chairs. People are sitting drinking tea and talking in low voices. Two men are playing pool at a table in the corner. There's a TV, a computer, a dartboard and a hatch where a large man in a Norwich City football shirt is handing out cups.

Judy makes her way over to the hatch. She's a keen Canaries fan.

'Can I help you?' The man gives her a friendly smile.

'I'm DS Judy Johnson of the King's Lynn police. I'd like to talk to whoever's in charge.'

'I suppose that would be me,' says the man, 'though I don't see it like that. I'm Paul Pritchard.'

'I've heard of you,' says Judy. 'I'm Cathbad's partner.'

'Oh, you're that Judy.' Now the man gives her a proper grin. 'Why didn't you say so?'

'I'm making enquiries about a woman called Barbara Murray,' says Judy. 'I believe she used to come here.'

'Babs?' says Pritchard. 'Yes, she was a regular but I haven't seen her for a bit. Is anything wrong?'

'I hope not,' says Judy.

'Have a cup of tea and a biscuit and we can chat,' says Pritchard. 'There are sandwiches too.'

Judy accepts a cup of tea but thinks she should probably leave the sandwiches for people who need them (a shame as she's suddenly starving). She and Paul Pritchard sit at a table by the window. No one looks across at them. It's as if the visitors to the drop-in centre are used to respecting each other's privacy. It all feels a lot more civilised than the police canteen, closed during the recent round of cuts.

'Cathbad said you were in the police,' says Pritchard. 'I thought he was joking at first.'

'It seems unlikely, I know,' says Judy. 'We actually met through a mutual friend who advises the police.'

'I should tell you that I'm known to the police too,' says Pritchard. 'Ten years for armed robbery.'

'That must have been some time ago,' says Judy, thinking that if Pritchard got ten years the robbery and the violence must have been pretty serious.

'I served eight years,' says Pritchard. 'Got out on licence seven years ago. I'm a different person now. I was born again while in prison.'

He says this in the same matter-of-fact, friendly tone but Judy is taken aback by the mention of religious conversion. She's used to people talking about spirituality (she lives with Cathbad, after all) but, as a cradle Catholic, she is slightly suspicious of evangelicals. She hopes that Pritchard isn't going to start speaking in tongues.

He seems to guess what she's thinking. 'Don't worry, I'm not going to start praying over you. I keep the religious stuff here to a minimum. We offer practical help. I'll pray with people if that's what they want but mostly they just want a meal, a shower, somewhere to pass a bit of time in warmth and safety.'

'Do people sleep here?'

'Sadly no. We have to shut at five-thirty. A lot of people snatch a few hours during the day though. If you're on the streets you may well stay awake all night. I have been known to let the odd person sleep a night on the sofa but I shouldn't do it. It could get us thrown out. The vicar's very supportive but some people don't like the idea of a bunch of down-and-outs in the parish hall.'

'The mother and baby group?'

Pritchard laughs. 'No, they're fine. Partly because it's run by my wife, Meg. She's a midwife and health visitor.'

Pritchard certainly has got his life together, thinks Judy. Marriage to a highly respectable-sounding woman, a job in the centre of the community. No wonder he smiles all the time. But there's nothing really sinister about the smiling. He just seems like a man comfortable in his own skin. And there's a lot of skin. Pritchard must be at least six foot three and big with it, massive rather than fat, a bull elephant in a green and yellow football top.

'So Barbara Murray used to come here?' says Judy.

'Yes. She called in most days for a while, for a wash and a hot meal. I tried to get her into various women's hostels but she wouldn't go.'

'Why not?'

'She said she didn't like being locked up. I think she'd been sectioned once and it really affected her. She had a few mental health issues. She was bipolar, for one thing. It's not unusual. It's a hard life, being on the streets. It doesn't make for perfect mental equilibrium.'

'Was Barbara seeing a doctor?'

'I don't know. She had some medication once so I assume so. It can be hard for rough sleepers to get medical help; most aren't registered with a GP.'

'How old is Barbara?'

'Thirty-nine,' says Pritchard promptly. 'I know because I had my fortieth a few months back and she laughed that she was younger than me. She looked older though. I'm not being ungallant. It's just what living on the streets does to you. Do you know what the average life expectancy of a rough sleeper is? Forty-seven.'

Judy is thirty-eight but Cathbad is fifty and, to her, he seems a young man. He once told her, though, that most prehistoric people didn't live past thirty. It seems that to be homeless is to live in prehistoric times.

'I heard that Barbara had children,' she says.

'Yes. She has a son in his twenties, I think. He's living in Scotland. Barbara had him when she was still a teenager. Her parents threw her out. She mentioned it once when we were talking about forgiveness. She had another child a few years later who was also adopted. Then she came down south and got into a relationship which ended up being abusive. She had two children from that relationship who were taken into care because of her poor mental health. I think that's what finally drove her into despair.'

Judy thinks that the word 'despair' has a rather melo-dramatic, biblical ring to it. The Slough of Despond. But it probably accurately reflects the state of mind of a woman who has lost her children and is forced to live in a cardboard box.

'Some witnesses say that they heard a man talking to Barbara about her children. They said she was upset. Could that have been you?'

'Where was this?'

'On the streets. Near the Customs House, I think.'

'Can't have been me, then. I only saw her here. And we tended not to talk about her children. I think it was too painful. We talked about Lynn, about the other clients here, sometimes about politics. She's a very intelligent woman, Babs, for all that she left school at thirteen.'

'When did you last see her?'

Pritchard looks round the room, thinking. Judy follows his gaze. The centre is filling up. A young woman is now dispensing tea from the hatch. Someone is playing the guitar – rather well, she thinks.

'It must have been at least two weeks ago. It's June now and I remember that it was May because we were talking about that old proverb, Ne'er cast a clout till May be out. You know the one.'

'What does it mean? Something about keeping your vest on all year round?'

'Well, as Babs said, most rough sleepers wear all their clothes all the time. Otherwise things get stolen.'

Judy feels rebuked for her levity.

'Another rough sleeper, Bilbo, he said something about Barbara going underground. Do you know what that means?'

Pritchard shakes his head. 'It sounds almost like prison slang. Prisoners talk about "going up top" if they have a visit or get out on bail.'

'Do you know if Barbara was ever in prison?'

'I don't think so. I'm open about my past and a lot of clients talk to me about their time inside. Not Barbara.'

'Have you any idea where she could be?' asks Judy.

'No, I haven't. Unless she's gone back to Scotland. That's a possibility, I suppose. I pray that's the answer.'

He looks so troubled that Judy decides to forgive him for his use of the p word.

CHAPTER 7

Ruth finds herself rather distracted during her lecture. She keeps reliving her conversation with Nelson, not that it was particularly significant in itself – it was more the fact of Nelson actually coming to see her, sitting down with her in the cafeteria. Apart from that first time, eight years ago, when Nelson came to ask for her help about bones found on the Saltmarsh, she doesn't think that he has ever been inside the university. So much has happened since then. She had an affair with Nelson. Put like that, it sounds at once too trivial and too serious. They slept together and now she has a child. Michelle eventually found out about Kate but, to her eternal credit, did not stop Nelson seeing his daughter. Nelson remains married but last year something happened that seemed to put that rock-solid marriage in jeopardy. For Ruth, the thought that Nelson might be free aroused hope and fear in equal measure. But Nelson is still married and he and Ruth are still meeting in public places, discussing bones, murder and the darker side of human nature. It's quite comforting really.

There aren't many questions at the end. Most of Ruth's MA students are from overseas and few feel confident enough about their English to risk speaking in public. So after a quick discussion about childhood trauma and its effect on bones, Ruth gathers up her papers and heads back to her office. She has a tutorial in an hour. Time to grab some lunch. She's been trying to slim so has brought a salad from home. It occurs to her now, though, that the missing ingredient is probably a cream cheese and smoked salmon bagel. She'll drop off her book bag and make a quick dash to the canteen.

But as she gets nearer to her office she notes, with a sinking heart, that her boss, Phil, is hovering by the staff noticeboard. She knows what he wants, of course. A visit from a detective chief inspector can only mean one thing in Phil's mind. Publicity. Maybe even the chance to appear on TV.

He doesn't even have the decency to pretend to talk about work first.

'I hear you had a visitor today, Ruth.'

'Did you?' Ruth scrabbles for her key card.

'You were spotted in the cafe with DCI Nelson.'

'We were just having a chat.' Ruth finds the card and opens her office door. She tries to slide in without Phil following but he foils her by holding the door open.

'Was it about the bones underneath the Guildhall?' he asks.

'Partly,' says Ruth, putting her bag on the desk. According the clock on the wall, above her Indiana Jones poster, it's already one-fifteen. Her bagel time is running out.

'Is it a murder?' breathes Phil.

'I doubt it,' says Ruth. 'The bones will probably turn out to be medieval.'

'DCI Nelson came all the way here to talk about old bones?' One way or another, there's been quite a lot of gossip about Ruth and Nelson around the university but Phil would never believe that Nelson made the journey across town for the pleasure of Ruth's company.

'It's medieval crime week,' says Ruth. 'A new government initiative. Now, if you'd just excuse me . . .'

Judy arrives back at the office – starving – to find Clough tucking into a giant Subway sandwich. The smell of salami makes her feel slightly nauseous. Whenever she feels sick she worries that she's pregnant again. She starts counting backwards in her head.

'Any luck with the missing dosser?'

Judy loses count and affects not to understand the question. 'Who?'

'You know. The lady tramp.'

'You mean Barbara Murray?'

'That's what I said.'

Judy sighs and gives in. 'No one's seen her in a few weeks. I went to that drop-in centre. Apparently she used to be a regular but she hasn't been seen there either.'

'She's just moved on. These people do.'

'I'm going to trace her son in Scotland,' says Judy. 'See if she's contacted him. I'm going to put in an Intel request.'

'She Who Must Be Obeyed won't like that.'

'Talking about me?'

One of Jo Archer's most sinister attributes is the ability to materialise at will. This is probably because she wears trainers around the office (high heels for public events though). Now she stands smiling in the doorway.

'No, I was talking about Cassie,' Clough lies smoothly. 'Henpecked husband, that's me.'

'You're not a husband yet,' Jo reminds him.

'No, there's still time to escape. You should start a campaign. Free the Lynn One.'

Jo looks at him with narrowed eyes, probably wondering whether to remind him of real prisoners of conscience or women in abusive relationships. Clough continues to eat, unabashed, so Jo says, 'Where's DCI Nelson? He's not in his office.'

Both Judy and Clough know that Nelson's at the university; they also know that Jo would take a dim view of this gallivanting around interviewing expert witnesses. Judy weighs up saying that she's no idea where her boss is (which doesn't say much for their internal communication), or inventing a meeting.

'Think he's at a strategy meeting in Norwich,' says Clough.

'Are you sure?'

'He mentioned it in the morning briefing, didn't he, Judy?'

'Yes,' says Judy. 'I remember now.'

'Hmm.' Jo looks at them for a moment but then turns to leave, pausing only to remind Clough of the number of calories in a Subway sandwich.

*

Ruth manages to make it to the canteen but they are out of bagels. She has to be content with an inferior ham roll, which she eats on her way back to her office. She thinks guiltily of her salad, still in its neat Tupperware box. She doesn't want to meet any of her colleagues so she takes a rather circuitous route through the Earth Sciences department. There should be a staircase around here somewhere that leads back to the Archaeology corridor. As she hurries along the passage she notices a name on one of the scuffed plywood doors: 'Dr Martin Kellerman'. He was the man she heard on the radio. Should she knock and say hallo? It would be a friendly thing to do but Ruth is not always good at being friendly, except to her friends, that is.

As she pauses, undecided, the door opens. A tall, sandy-haired man steps out, then does a double take at the sight of Ruth.

'I'm sorry. Were you waiting for me?'

'I'm sorry,' Ruth apologises back. 'I was just wondering whether to knock. I heard you on the radio yesterday.' She extends her hand. 'I'm Ruth Galloway from Archaeology.'

'Ah! I've seen *you* on the television.'

Ruth is both embarrassed and slightly pleased to hear this. She knows that her two television appearances have made her mildly famous at UNN. This is all very pleasant (especially as it annoys Phil) but it's a pity that one of the programmes was an unashamedly populist number called *Women Who Kill*. Also, she knows that the camera is meant to add ten pounds but in her case it felt more like fifty. When she appeared on screen in her white coat it looked like there had been an avalanche.

'You were very good,' she says to Martin Kellerman. 'Very clear.'

'Thank you,' says Kellerman. He's tall and thin with a large nose and looks rather like a bird of prey. 'I think they wanted me to be more exciting though. To say that the ground is going to open up beneath our feet, just like it did in 1988.'

'The bus in the hole?' says Ruth. 'That's still a hot topic here.'

'Well, there is a network of chalk mining tunnels,' says Kellerman. 'It could happen again.'

'I know. I was in a tunnel underneath the Guildhall the other day,' says Ruth.

'Were you excavating?'

Ruth hesitates, not sure how much she should say. But the discovery of the bones isn't a secret, she's sure that Quentin Swan will have told all his architect friends.

'Some bones have been found,' she says. 'They're probably medieval.'

'Fascinating,' says Kellerman. 'We should have lunch one day, chat about old bones.'

'I'd like that,' says Ruth.

They exchange phone numbers and Ruth continues on her way with, if not quite a spring in her step, a definite bounce.

By the end of the day Judy is feeling frustrated. She hasn't managed to trace Barbara's son. It doesn't help, the Intel officer tells her, that she doesn't know which town in Scotland or even the son's name. Tanya hasn't been able to find a record for Barbara in any of the local hostels. 'And you need ID to get in now,' she says. 'I think Barbara's probably just staying on a friend's sofa.'

But Judy is convinced that there's something odd about Barbara's disappearance and the often-repeated opinions of her colleagues – Clough: 'they're drifters, these people'; Tanya: 'it's a nomadic lifestyle' – only serve to harden her resolve. She keeps thinking of Bilbo's words: *I heard she'd gone underground.*

When she gets home she asks Cathbad if this phrase means anything to him. Cathbad, who is making a curry, stops to think.

'Who said that?'

'Bilbo. Chap who wears a jester's hat. Do you know him?'

'Yes, I think so. Nice guy. Welsh.'

'That's right.'

'He comes to the soup run sometimes.'

Judy is sitting at the kitchen table with Miranda on her lap. The child feels heavy and sleepy; with any luck she'll go down early tonight. Opposite, Michael, still in his school sweatshirt, is finishing his supper. Michael is five but, to Judy, he still seems too young for school. She'd like to keep him at home until he's ready to leave. Thirty seems a reasonable age.

'Do you remember seeing Barbara at the soup run?' she asks.

'Yes,' says Cathbad. 'There's only one woman who comes so I think it must be her. She's always very pleasant and polite. Well, they all are. Much more civilised than my old colleagues at the university.'

'That's what I thought when I went to the drop-in centre. A much nicer atmosphere than the police canteen. Before the canteen got axed, that is.'

Cathbad grates ginger and looks around for something else to add. He's an inspired cook, one of the many unexpectedly domesticated things about him. It's one of Judy's favourite times, sitting with a glass of wine watching Cathbad prepare their supper. In a few minutes she'll give the kids their baths and put them to bed. Michael eats slowly but thoroughly, using his knife and fork carefully although the home-made pizza could easily be eaten by hand.

'What did you have for lunch?' Judy asks him.

'I can't remember.'

Judy's heart contracts. She must ask his teacher if Michael is eating lunch. Maybe she should give him sandwiches instead.

'What did you think of Paul Pritchard?' asks Cathbad.

'He seemed OK. A bit intense but not too holier-than-thou. Do you like him?'

Cathbad pauses, which intrigues Judy. Unlike her, his default position is usually to like people. 'I don't know. He does a lot of good with the drop-in centre and the soup run. But there's something guarded about him. I don't feel like I really know him.'

'You know he's an ex-convict?'

'Yes, but it's not that. He's quite open about his past, almost proud of it. It's more that ... he talks a lot about being born again, but there doesn't seem to be anything particularly spiritual about him. He's a bit like a businessman. Or a politician.'

'Businessmen aren't necessarily bad people. I liked the way that Pritchard was open about having form. When I asked him about the underground comment he said it sounded a bit like prison slang.'

'There are a lot of legends about the underground,' says Cathbad. 'Some people think that in the Bronze Age they believed that heaven was below. That's why there was an upside-down tree buried within the circle at Seahenge.'

'I thought underground was always where hell was.'

'Well, there's the Greek and Roman underworld, of course. And in Hindu mythology there are people called the Nargas, serpents with human faces who live in underground caverns. But in Mayan tradition there's Xibalba, an underground kingdom of gods and superheroes. It means something like "where the sun disappears".'

'Superheroes?' says Michael. 'Like Spiderman?'

'Yes,' says Cathbad dreamily, 'giant spiders too, and –'

'Have you finished your supper, Michael?' says Judy. 'It's time for your bath in a minute. You can watch television for half an hour, if you want.' She doesn't want Michael to have nightmares about giant spiders. She doesn't want them herself, for that matter.

*

The spiders don't make an appearance but Judy does have a strange, confused dream that features Cathbad, Nelson and Ruth in a boat, sailing through an underground tunnel. It's like that terrifying scene in the first Willy Wonka film, the one starring Gene Wilder. She's still remembering bits of it as she gets ready for work. Cathbad and the children are at the kitchen table, eating a leisurely breakfast. It doesn't look as if Michael, still in his Spiderman pyjamas, will ever be ready for school but Cathbad's never been late yet. He'll drop Michael and then he's planning to take Miranda to see the seals at Blakeney. Judy often feels guilty that Miranda has these happy pre-school days with her father when Michael was packed off to a childminder. 'But he loved Debbie,' says Cathbad, which is true. Doesn't stop her feeling guilty though. She leaves at eight, reminding Cathbad to have a word with Michael's teacher about the lunches. 'Lunches,' repeats Cathbad. She's pretty sure he'll forget.

She's at the station by eight-thirty. She parks in the car park and walks round to the front entrance. As she approaches she sees a figure in a sleeping bag propped up against the wall of the porch. Aftershave Eddie, back in his usual spot. She really must do something about getting him into a shelter, or better still into a bedsit.

'Morning, Eddie,' she says briskly.

Eddie doesn't reply. His head is slumped forward and he appears to be asleep. It's only when Judy touches his shoulder that she sees the knife in his chest.

CHAPTER 8

Judy feels for a pulse but she knows in her heart that it's useless. She knows by the caked blood around the knife and on Eddie's filthy army surplus jumper. She knows by the angle of Eddie's head, his grey beard on his chest. She knows by the smell. She is just straightening up when she hears a voice from the street below.

'What's happening, Johnson? Is Eddie all right?'

'Not really, boss.'

Nelson takes the steps two at a time. 'Jesus. Did you just find him like this?'

'Yes. A minute ago. Looks like he's been dead for some hours though.'

'Poor bastard. Let's get this area screened off and call the coroner.'

They go inside. Clough and Tom Henty are chatting at the front desk. Judy hears the word 'penalties'.

'Jesus Christ!' Nelson explodes. 'There's a bloke dead on the front steps and none of you have noticed.'

Clough turns, his mouth open. 'Aftershave Eddie? But he's asleep.'

'Call yourself a bloody detective? There's a knife in his chest.'

There's a general movement towards the doors. Clough looks as if he wants to say more but Nelson is talking on his phone, presumably to the coroner. Clough goes out and a few minutes later Tanya comes flying down the stairs and out through the double doors. By the time Judy goes back outside, there's a screen shielding Eddie's body and police tape across the stairs. Clough is telling anyone who will listen that Eddie looked exactly as if he was asleep.

'I thought it was odd that he was asleep at this hour,' says Tanya.

'Well, you didn't say anything, did you?' growls Clough. 'You walked straight past him, same as the rest of us. It was only St Judy who stopped.'

Judy doesn't rise to this. She knows that Clough is furious at being bawled out by Nelson.

'Who would kill the poor old man?' says Tanya.

'Some nutters do attack tramps,' says Tom Henty. 'There was that case, a few years back, of a rough sleeper being set on fire.'

Set on fire, yes, thinks Judy. Kicked by a gang of mindless thugs, yes. But not stabbed, coldly and efficiently, in the heart. Eddie was murdered a few days after he reported a woman missing. She's pretty sure that they aren't looking for a nutter.

By mid-morning, the SOCO team have been and gone and Eddie's body has been taken away by private ambulance. Normally it would be Judy with her family liaison training who would be contacting the next of kin, in person if possible, and trying to help them through the worst day of their lives. But no one has any idea if Eddie had any relatives. They don't even know his real name.

'He was Irish, wasn't he?' says Clough.

'I thought he sounded Scottish,' says Tanya helpfully.

You never spoke to him, thinks Judy. She'd spoken to Eddie several times and she remembers that he'd mentioned having family 'back in the old country'. She'd once asked him if he ever thought of returning to Ireland and he'd said, 'I can't go back, that's the pity of it.' Why couldn't Eddie go back home? And where was home, for that matter?

Judy rings Paul Pritchard and asks him if he knows Eddie.

'I'm not sure,' says Pritchard. 'What does he look like?'

Judy suddenly has a startlingly clear image of Eddie. She feels oddly reassured that she can recall his face so well, even if she never thought to ask his surname.

'He was about six foot with grey shoulder-length hair and a long grey beard. He had pale blue eyes and weather-beaten skin. Usually wears an army surplus jumper and a long overcoat. Irish accent, smokes roll-ups when he can get them.'

'"Was"?' says Pritchard sharply. 'You said "was".'

Judy curses inwardly. But she can't see any harm in telling Pritchard. The papers might even cover it. They wouldn't normally bother to report the death of a homeless man, of course, but this particular homeless man was stabbed on the steps of the local police station.

'Yes. He's been found dead. I'm trying to trace his relatives.'

'Poor man,' says Pritchard. 'I'll pray for him. But I can't recall seeing someone of that description. We don't ask our clients' names. It's one reason why people prefer to come here than to a hostel.'

'Well, if anyone mentions Eddie, will you let me know? It would be terrible if he was buried with no one being any the wiser. Just the undertakers and a couple of police officers at his funeral.' She'll go to Eddie's funeral, whatever happens, and she's pretty sure the boss will too. She might make Clough come as well. He's usually susceptible to emotional blackmail.

'Judy!' Clough shouts across the room. 'Did the boss take a witness statement when Aftershave . . . when Eddie came in?'

Judy looks at Clough. They both know that Nelson should have taken a statement but Nelson – who is now with the coroner – is not the best at following protocol.

But it's there in the log book.

Witness Statement. 3/6/15. 11.15 a.m. Investigating officer: DCI Nelson. Witness name: Eddie O'Toole.

'O'Toole,' says Clough. 'Like that actor. The one who was always drunk.'

'Peter O'Toole,' says Judy. 'And he wasn't always drunk.'

'He always acted drunk people,' says Clough.

Was O'Toole even Eddie's real name? Or did he just pick

it because of the link with the actor who, as Clough so sensitively put it, was famous for having a drink problem? Anyway, at least she can now try social security. Eddie may well have been claiming benefits. She can ring the hospitals too. Of course, the most likely place to find Eddie is in the police records. A lot of rough sleepers have convictions, if only for begging or being drunk in a public place.

'What's this about a down-and-out dying on our doorstep?'

Jo Archer has made another of her silent entrances. She has obviously been at a meeting because she's wearing a black suit and high-heeled boots. She does have good legs, thinks Judy, even if the skirt is borderline too short for her age.

'A man called Eddie O'Toole was found outside the station with stab wounds to his chest,' she says, emphasising the name, even though she only learnt it a few minutes ago.

'Who found him?'

'I did.'

'Did you administer CPR?'

'No point. I could tell that he'd been dead for some time.'

'So he was lying dead on our steps with my officers walking past and no one noticed? How's that going to look to the press?'

Judy doesn't answer. Clough pulls a terrible face behind Jo's back and Tanya offers her a cup of herbal tea.

'Where's DCI Nelson?' Jo does not answer the question about the tea.

'With the coroner,' says Judy.

'He should have delegated that to a DS,' says Jo. 'Have we got a murder weapon?'

'Yes,' says Judy. 'It was still in his chest. It's at the lab now.'

'What line is the investigation taking?' Jo taps a suede foot.

'Eddie came in on Wednesday to report a fellow rough sleeper missing. We're following up on that.'

'If he was killed on the front steps we should have CCTV footage.'

'That camera's broken.'

Jo looks at Judy as if this is her fault. She is obviously wondering whether to question her further or to wait to interrogate Nelson. 'Tell DCI Nelson to come to see me as soon as he gets back,' she says at last.

'I will,' says Judy.

'Missing you already,' mutters Clough as the door shuts behind Jo.

Ruth is giving a tutorial when her phone pings. She's annoyed with herself; she usually puts her phone on silent when she's with her students. She used to turn it off altogether but since having Kate there's always the chance that she'll get *that* call, the one from the school or Sandra, telling her to rush to the hospital, there's been an accident . . .

This is not the nightmare call. 'Lab calling,' says the message.

Ruth switches it off but it's harder than usual to concentrate on her students' dissertations. Does the world really need another long essay on environmental archaeology and freshwater molluscs? Well, it's going to get one, whether it likes it or not.

As soon as the last of her students has left (and they always take so *long*, dropping papers, wanting to talk about grade boundaries), she switches on her phone and calls the lab. She thinks it must be something interesting because they rang, rather than just sending the results by email.

'Hi, Ros. You called?'

'Hallo, Ruth. It's about the bones you sent us. The underground bones.'

'Yes?'

'Well, we've done carbon-14 and it's interesting. They're a lot newer than they look.'

'Are they? How new?'

'As you know, it's hard to be exact, but I think less than fifty years old. Maybe less than ten. And they look as if they've been boiled.'

'I thought that too.' Ruth thinks about the pot polish that she described to Nelson. That was an interesting historical curiosity when it looked as if the bones were seven hundred years old. But ten years old? That's a modern body. That's a murder investigation.

'Can we get DNA samples?' she asks.

'Sure,' says Ros. 'Just email me the form. Will the university pay?'

'Yes,' says Ruth, though Phil is very mean about any expenditure that doesn't involve him going on a fact-finding trip. 'Or perhaps the police will.'

'We may not be able to get DNA if the bones have been boiled.'

'I know. Let's do isotope testing too,' she says recklessly. 'At least then we'll be able to tell where the victim was living.'

The victim. Suddenly the skeletal matter is a victim. As soon as Ros rings off, Ruth clicks on the name Nelson.

Nelson gets the call as he's driving back to the station. He answers immediately, despite Bev Flinders having told him that even talking on a hands-free device reduces a driver's concentration by twenty per cent.

'What is it, Ruth? Is it Katie?'

A sigh, reverberating round the car. 'No, it's not *Kate*. It's work, Nelson. You remember the bones I found under the Guildhall? I thought they must be medieval but the carbon-14 tests show they're modern.'

'Modern? How modern?'

'They could be fifty years old. They could be ten or less.'

'Can't you be any more specific?'

'No.' They've had this conversation many times before. 'We're going to get isotope testing done. That analyses the minerals present in bones and it'll show us where the person was living when they died.' She's told him that before too.

'We'll need to excavate, won't we? See if we can find the rest of the body.'

'I'd like to do an excavation but the way the bones were found, it was almost as if they were thrown away, not like they were part of a formal burial.'

'Didn't you say that the bones looked like they'd been cooked in a pot?'

'I did say that, yes.'

'Jesus, so we've got a bloody cannibal on the loose. That's all I need. A man was stabbed to death on the police station steps last night.'

'God, how awful. Do you know who did it?'

'Someone with a knife,' says Nelson. 'I'll call you later.'

Nelson gets to the incident room to find that Judy has managed to find some records for Eddie. He was arrested five years ago in Norwich for begging. The warrant gives his name as Edward Fintan O'Toole of no fixed address. His DNA, fingerprints and photograph are all on file. The second, more unwelcome news, is that Superintendent Archer wants to see him.

'She'll have to wait,' he says. 'Any luck with finding next of kin?'

'No,' says Judy. 'I'll go and talk to some of the rough sleepers later. We could put an appeal in the papers too.'

'CSI released his personal effects,' says Nelson. He takes out a paper bag and shakes the contents onto the table in front of him. A thin roll-up cigarette, a holy picture, soft and blurred at the edges, a bus ticket, twenty-four pence in change.

'Is that it?' says Clough. 'Poor sod.'

Nelson looks at the holy picture. It shows the Virgin Mary, eyes uplifted. There's a figure kneeling next to her, probably St Bernadette.

'He was a Catholic then,' he says. 'Might be worth asking at some of the Catholic churches.'

'I rang the St Matthew's drop-in centre,' says Judy, 'and they didn't recognise the description.'

'Ah, but St Matthew's is Protestant,' says Nelson. 'Old habits die hard with some people, especially Irish Catholics. I should know, my mum's one.'

Judy is examining the bus ticket. 'Plusbus ticket,' she says. 'He must have been travelling by bus quite a lot. I wonder why?'

'No Simple Payment card,' says Clough. 'He can't have been claiming benefits.'

'Unless the card is somewhere else,' says Nelson. 'Or was stolen from him.'

'He wasn't on the council's records,' says Judy.

'A man of mystery,' says Nelson. 'Speaking of which, we've got another possible murder case on our hands.' He tells the team about the test results on the Guildhall bones.

'Ruth and Ted thought the bones were old,' says Judy.

'Well, they're not,' says Nelson. 'What's more, it looks as if the bones were boiled in a pot.'

'Boiled?' says Clough. 'To eat, you mean?'

'Who knows?' says Nelson. 'Ruth's getting some more tests done. Right, let's sort our strategy out. Judy, you talk to the rough sleepers. You obviously made some contacts yesterday. Tanya, keep digging in the files. See if there's anything in Eddie's past that may explain this attack. Any fights, altercations, anything like that. Clough, organise some door-to-door. See if anyone saw anything. Coroner thought death occurred at about three a.m. but there might have been people about. Pity about the CCTV camera out front.'

'Superintendent Archer asked about CCTV,' says Judy.

'There might be something from the shops opposite,' says Nelson. 'Look into it, Cloughie.'

'Yes, boss.'

'We'll have to see if CSI picked up anything from the scene,' says Nelson. 'Are they finished?'

'Yes,' says Tanya. 'Shall I liaise with them?' Tanya loves liaising, it sounds so much more important than keeping in touch.

'If you like,' says Nelson, who is looking through the pictures of Eddie's body, hunched on the steps.

'Anything on the weapon?' asks Judy.

'It's with the lab. Ordinary kitchen blade, sharpened to a point.'

'Sharpened?' says Judy. 'So this could have been premeditated?'

'I don't think it was a random attack,' says Nelson. 'Someone knew Eddie slept here and came to find him.'

'Do you think it was linked to the disappearance of the woman?' says Clough. 'Barbara Murray?'

'Well, it's a coincidence,' says Nelson, 'and you know what I think about coincidences.'

They all do.

'Let's step up the search for Barbara. Judy, have you got Intel looking for her family?'

'Yes,' says Judy. 'It's difficult though. We don't even know if her children had the same name as her.'

'Eddie said two were adopted,' says Nelson. 'They might have changed their names. But two are in care. There will

have to be records. I'm going to get us some reinforcements.'

He disappears into his office. No one dares to remind him
about Superintendent Archer.

CHAPTER 9

Judy starts at the quay, hoping to find the elusive Charlie. It's the only clue they have, that Barbara spoke to a man about her children and became distressed. But Charlie – the man who saw Barbara with the mystery man – is nowhere to be seen. It's a dull, rainy afternoon and the grey river – the Great Ouse – merges into the grey sky. A flock of geese flies overhead, honking miserably. Judy makes her way back through the Vancouver Centre to the station. There's an Eastern European woman selling *The Big Issue* but she either doesn't understand Judy's question or doesn't want to be drawn into discussing police business. There's no sign of her earlier informants, the small man and the Viking. She walks to the station, expecting to see Bilbo's jester hat amongst the small knot of travellers heading for London or Cambridge. But there's no multicoloured headgear and no sound of jingling bells. She asks at the Country Line station cafe.

'Bilbo? I haven't seen him today, dear. I normally give him a cup of tea in the afternoon if we're not busy.'

Judy buys herself tea in a polystyrene cup and drinks it

walking to the drop-in centre. There's not necessarily any-thing suspicious about the non-appearance of Charlie and Bilbo, but after the murder of Eddie Judy is not in the mood to take anything for granted. Bilbo had described the drop-in centre as being full of 'God botherers' but that didn't mean that he never used it.

The centre is busy. Paul Pritchard is ladling soup at the counter but he waves at Judy and gestures for her to take a seat. She sits on a sofa next to a man drinking soup. He has a can of Coke on the table and when he opens it, offers it to Judy.

'Want some?'

The thought that this man who, presumably, has nothing, offers her a drink before having one himself, strikes Judy as profoundly moving.

'No. I'm fine. Thank you,' she says.

'It's not good for you,' agrees the man, 'but I need the caffeine.'

He's about fifty, thinks Judy, black with grey dreadlocks. But, remembering what Pritchard said about the life expec-tancy of rough sleepers, maybe he's only about her age. The coroner estimated Eddie's age as early fifties. It seems very sad that no one knows for sure.

The man introduces himself as Scratch, which Judy tends to think is not his baptismal name.

'Have you been coming here long?' she asks.

'Just a few months,' he says. 'I came from London. It's nicer here, more peaceful.'

Judy doesn't imagine that a life on the streets could ever

be called peaceful but she agrees that Norfolk is lovely. 'I've lived here all my life.'

'You're a lucky lady then. You married? Children?'

'I live with my partner. We've got two children. What about you?'

'I've got a child. A daughter. I haven't seen her for ten years.'

'I'm sorry.'

'Probably for the best. A dad out of his head on Spice is no dad, really.'

'Are you still on it?' Spice is synthetic cannabis, a legal high. Pritchard told Judy that it was rife in the homeless community.

Scratch nods sadly. Judy asks him if he knew Barbara Murray.

'Babs? Yeah. She used to come in here. Nice lady. You a street warden?'

'No, I'm with the police.' Seeing the look on Scratch's face, she says hastily, 'I'm only asking about Babs because we're a bit worried about her, that's all. She's not in any trouble.'

'Hi, Judy.' It's Paul Pritchard, resplendent in a check shirt so bright it makes her eyes ache. 'Is Scratch looking after you?'

Scratch smiles politely but after a few moments he gets up and moves away.

'I think I scared him away,' says Judy.

'Most rough sleepers don't have very good experiences of the police,' says Pritchard. Again, Judy feels rebuked.

'I don't suppose that you've heard anything from Barbara?' she says.

'No. I would have told you if I had.'

'I was wondering if you'd seen someone else. A man called Bilbo. He's usually to be found by the station. Wears a jester's hat.'

'Yes, I know Bilbo. He comes to the soup run. I saw him a few days ago. Is he OK?'

'As far as I know,' says Judy. 'I just wanted to ask him some more questions, that's all.'

'Maybe that's why he's lying low,' says Pritchard, but he smiles when he says it.

'Maybe.'

'I'll let you know if I see him. He usually comes in at least once a week for a shower and a hot meal. He plays a mean game of chess too.'

Judy thinks of the shambling figure in the jester's hat. She can't imagine him playing chess but then she realises that she knows nothing about the man. Not even his real name.

'I don't know either,' says Pritchard when she asks him. 'A lot of our clients go by assumed names. *Noms de guerre*, as it were.'

It feels like a war sometimes, thinks Judy, looking around the room where the clients are sleeping, eating or just staring into space. The homeless are like the remnants of a long-forgotten army, still dressed in their ragged uniforms, reminding their more fortunate neighbours that there is a battlefield out there, a place of violence and fear and dread.

This knowledge is hard to take sometimes; you can see it in the faces of people who cross the street to avoid someone begging. But is being made to feel uncomfortable enough reason to kill?

Ruth is in her office, reading about cannibals. Some experts say that archaeologists have never found any evidence for cannibalism, that the only definite proof would be to find a human skeleton with human remains inside its stomach. But there are some disturbing cases. In 1845 a British naval expedition to map the Northwest Passage through the Canadian Arctic ended in unmitigated disaster when everyone on board perished. From the start there were rumours of cannibalism – strongly denied at the time – but recently archaeologists have examined the bones and found definite signs that they were broken for their marrow and cooked. The account in *Archaeology Today* mentions butchery marks on the bones, signs that they were defleshed soon after death. Ruth thinks of the cut marks that she saw on the bones in the tunnel, that eerie sheen which, the article confirms, could have come from contact with a cooking vessel with rough edges. The bones hadn't been burnt, because that would cause discolouration as well as warping and fragmentation. But if they had simply been boiled . . .

A knock on her door makes her jump. Is it Phil? But he normally opens the door before she has time to say 'Come in'. Her students, on the other hand, shuffle outside for ages. She looks at the frosted glass. The shadow looks too tall to be Phil but somehow too substantial to be one of her students.

'Come in.'

'I hope I'm not disturbing you.'

It's Martin Kellerman, the geologist of local radio fame. Ruth arranges her face into a smile and wishes she'd checked that her hair was brushed. It's so windy on her part of the coast that she often doesn't bother in the mornings.

'Not at all.' She pushes the article about cannibalism under a pile of exam scripts.

'It's just . . . We said about having lunch. I know it's a bit late but I wondered if you'd eaten today. We could go to the pub if you've got time. That is, if you haven't eaten yet.'

Ruth looks at her watch. It's nearly two o'clock. She has actually had lunch – another salad – but that was at least two hours ago.

'I haven't had time to eat,' she says. 'I've had a busy morning.'

'Then do say you'll come. It is Friday, after all.' Kellerman peers at her anxiously over his little gold glasses. He looks more like a dishevelled eagle than ever.

'All right,' says Ruth. 'That would be lovely.'

'Lovely for me,' says Kellerman, unexpectedly chivalrous. Ruth is irritated to feel herself blushing.

Judy descends the stairs to find the hallway full of baby buggies again. A woman in a nurse's uniform is standing at the door of the downstairs room welcoming people in. This must be Pritchard's wife, Meg. She's smallish and blonde and even from a distance gives an impression of neatness and order. Despite this, Judy doesn't find herself disliking her on sight.

There's a temporary lull in the convoy of buggies so Judy makes her way over to the door.

'Hi,' she says. 'Are you Meg Pritchard? I'm Judy Johnson. I've been talking to Paul.'

'Oh yes.' The woman smiles. She has blue eyes, tanned skin and a slight South African accent. 'Paul mentioned you. Have you found the woman you're looking for?'

'I'm afraid not. I don't suppose you've seen her?'

'Not recently. But I know the woman you mean. There aren't many women visitors to the centre. And this woman, she stopped me once to talk about the baby clinic.'

'She did?'

'Yes. It was quite sad really. I was helping a mum carry a double buggy down the steps and this woman – Babs, isn't it? – came to help. The mum – I don't think she really meant anything by it – she gave Babs a rather funny look. Babs was obviously a bit upset and when the mum with the buggy left she said, "These people don't realise that I'm a mother too."'

Barbara was a mother four times over but Pritchard had said that she didn't like to talk about her children. Maybe she had opened up a bit to Meg.

'Did she say anything else?' asks Judy.

'She said that she'd had four children. She said that she'd been a good mother – the children were her life, she said – but that they'd been taken away from her. She seemed very sad.'

'I'm trying to trace Barbara's children. Did she say anything else about them?'

'No. I said I'd pray for her. I didn't know what else to say. And she smiled very sweetly and said that she was a pagan.'

Meg doesn't seem shocked by this and Judy likes her for her open-mindedness, even if she did offer unsolicited prayers.

'Well, if you see her again . . .' Judy gives Meg her card.

'I'll ring you. Of course I will. I'd better go. There's hell to pay if I don't open the Jaffa cakes.'

Cathbad says that the cakes are the best thing about mother and baby groups. He's attended a few in his time, never minding about being the only man. Judy dislikes most communal activities. She even tried to avoid antenatal classes. Can she honestly say that she's a good mother? She thanks Meg Pritchard and makes her way out of the church hall. As she closes the door, she can hear the mothers starting to sing 'The Wheels on the Bus'.

Ruth and Martin Kellerman don't go to the pub usually frequented by UNN staff (a noisy chain establishment with mock twenties interior) but to a strange little place in the middle of a roundabout called The Tin Drum.

'I like this pub,' says Martin. 'It has real ale and you rarely see anyone from the university.'

The latter is more important to Ruth. She hopes that Martin isn't going to start talking about beer.

'It has good food too,' says Martin. Ruth orders a sandwich and Martin fish pie. They sit in the almost empty bar talking about the university. Ruth is drinking a small glass of red wine and Martin a pint of beer with an embarrassingly baroque name. They have a few friends in common. Martin knows Phil ('he's very pleased with himself, isn't he?') and Shona. He's also more sociable than Ruth, playing in the university's five-a-side team and going to the chess club.

'I moved from London because I thought that the new universities had more money for the sciences,' says Martin. 'I didn't realise that the money would run out quite so quickly.'

'I was the same,' says Ruth. 'I was promised that I could head up the Forensic Archaeology department. I didn't realise that I'd still be the only one in the department eighteen years later.'

'Have you really been at UNN for eighteen years?'

'I'm afraid so. It was my first real job after I finished my PhD. How long have you been here?'

'Five years. I've been told that it takes twenty years for people in Norfolk to stop thinking of you as an outsider.'

'Oh, longer than that, I should think. Where do you live?'

'Old Hunstanton. What about you?'

'New Road. On the edge of the Saltmarsh.'

'It's stunning out there but isn't it a bit lonely?'

'I like it,' says Ruth, not wanting to get drawn into discussing her relationship with the beautiful, haunted north Norfolk coast. She takes a sip of her wine, wondering if the lunch is going to become awkward. She wonders why she agreed to come.

She thinks this even more when Martin says, abruptly, 'You're quite famous at UNN, you know, Ruth.'

'Am I?'

'Yes. You've been on TV. You've written a book. You've been involved with murder investigations.'

Ruth doesn't answer. She's used to people wanting to pump her about her involvement with the police. They usually want to talk about the first case she ever worked on, the body that was found on the Saltmarsh. But Ruth doesn't want to talk about that. Not now. Not ever.

To her relief, Martin seems to sense this because he says, 'I found TV and radio rather a terrifying experience the other day.'

'You didn't sound terrified,' says Ruth. 'You sounded very cool.'

'I don't really know why everyone got so excited about the hole appearing.'

'Well, it's fascinating,' says Ruth. 'And scary too, in a way. The idea that there's all this going on beneath our feet. I thought that when I was in the Guildhall tunnel the other day. Ted, one of the field archaeologists, he was saying that you could walk the length of the city underground. As if there's another world below, perhaps a mirror image of the one above ground.'

'Have you met Kevin O'Casey in Sociology?' asks Martin. 'He's writing a book about underground societies. It's fascinating. Apparently there are all these communities that live underground, in old subway tunnels and catacombs. There's a group in Paris called The Empire of the Dead. They've got electricity, a movie theatre, restaurants, everything.'

'It seems very French to have an underground restaurant,' says Ruth, thinking of Quentin Swan.

'Well, you get a better class of troglodyte there,' says Martin. 'Kevin was telling me about all these underground cities that were built in case of nuclear war. Mao Zedong built one in Beijing. It had shops, restaurants, schools, even a skating rink. There was even one in England.'

'In England? Where?'

'In Wiltshire somewhere. It was built in an old stone quarry. It had a BBC studio where the prime minister was meant to broadcast to the people.'

'The ones that hadn't been fried by the radiation, that is.'

Kellerman laughs. 'What's worse, dying of radiation poisoning or being trapped thirty metres underground with a bunch of politicians?'

'Someone was telling me about billionaire bunkers the other day. Where the super-rich burrow down to escape nuclear war. Imagine crawling to the surface to find that the only other people to have survived are millionaire arms dealers. Them and the cockroaches.'

'I've heard about those basements,' says Martin. 'They play havoc with the water table and sometimes you get flooding. Seriously though, it's enough to make you pray for a quick death. Remember in the eighties when we were all so terrified about nuclear war? Going on CND marches? Protect and survive? Now no one mentions it but the fact that the super-rich are still worried about it makes you think. They might know something we don't.'

Ruth laughs but she rather resents the fact that Martin assumes that they are the same age and that she is old enough to have been politically active in the eighties. But he's right, she was. She went to university in 1986 and the first society she joined was CND. Their food arrives and the subject of nuclear winter is dropped. Martin dives into his pie with the enthusiasm that only very thin people are allowed to show. Ruth tries to eat her sandwich slowly and to ignore the crisps that come with it.

'What are you doing this weekend?' asks Martin. Ruth is slightly startled by the question. Martin says it casually, still concentrating on his pie but, even so, Ruth stiffens.

'Spending time with my daughter,' says Ruth. 'She's six.'

'I've got a three-year-old daughter,' says Martin. He doesn't say this with the enthusiasm people usually reserve for talking about their children.

Ruth feels that she should say something upbeat and child-friendly. 'They're fun at that age, aren't they?'

'I don't really know,' says Martin. There's a short pause. Ruth eats a crisp and the sound seems to reverberate round the pub.

'I don't live with Olivia and her mother,' says Martin at last. 'Vicky, my ex-wife, she was the reason we came to Norfolk really. She works here, as a matter of fact, in the Sociology department. That's how I know Kevin. Vicky's from Norfolk and she wanted to move back to be close to her parents if she had children. She's still close to her parents, they look after Olivia during the day, it's just me that she's not close to any more.'

He eats some pie crust in a discontented manner.

'But you still see Olivia,' says Ruth, wanting to cheer him up. 'I don't live with Kate's father but she still sees him. He's an important person in her life.'

'It's hard to know what to do with a three-year-old,' says Martin, 'especially in the winter. You can't exactly go to the cinema or out for a meal.'

Ruth thinks that he sounds too defeatist. Nelson, to his credit, has always seemed to enjoy every moment that he spends with Kate. But, then, he has had Michelle to help.

'Well, it won't be long before she can enjoy the cinema,' says Ruth. 'And it's lovely here in the summer. Lots of beaches, the donkeys at Yarmouth, the train at Wells.'

'Yes,' says Martin, but he sounds unconvinced. They talk in a desultory manner about UNN and Norfolk but the ease has disappeared. They decide against coffee and head back across the dual carriageway to the university.

Back in her office, preparing for the afternoon's tutorial, Ruth wonders if she'll ever have lunch with Martin Kellerman again. It's not that she wants him to be interested in her exactly. She decided a few years ago that if she can't have the man she really wants, she is happy on her own, or on her own with Kate and Flint. It's just that it would be rather nice to have a friend at work. She has Shona but she's in the English department and – more distancing still – is in a relationship with Phil. It would be good to have someone with whom she could discuss university politics as well as tunnels and old chalk mines. Her phone beeps. She looks down. Martin has texted her a picture of an underground restaurant. *I enjoyed our lunch*, she reads. *Let's do it again soon. Above ground if possible.*

Ruth finds herself smiling as she sorts out her notes on diseases in bones.

CHAPTER 10

Ruth likes Saturdays. Sunday, with its associations of church and the family, Sunday can be difficult. But Saturday is a day when she can relax and actually enjoy some time with her daughter. She still wakes up early because Kate does but Kate is happy to watch TV downstairs while Ruth drinks coffee and listens to the radio and generally potters about. Then they'll go to the park or the beach in the summer, to the cinema or the swimming pool in the winter. Sometimes they'll meet up with Judy and Cathbad and their children. Kate loves Michael, who is in the year below her at school, even if her love does manifest itself in the form of a series of barked instructions. Even the evenings are fun. They'll watch a Disney film on the sofa, eating pizza and singing along to the soundtrack. Then Kate will go to bed and Ruth will have another couple of hours drinking wine and watching some Scandinavian crime series where everything is grey, even the flowers (not that there are many flowers, unless they are in the form of a funeral wreath). And even if Ruth sometimes wishes she had an adult to talk to, someone who would share the wine and joke about the grey flowers and wouldn't ask her to sing Anna's part in *Frozen*, it's a very small longing really, perfectly manageable. And a man would bring too many complications, not least what would happen when the Scandi crime was over and the prospect of bed loomed. No, she is quite happy with her Saturdays as they are.

But today is different. Today, Kate has a rehearsal.

'Do children usually wear dresses to rehearsals?' she asks, making patterns in her Rice Krispies.

'No,' says Ruth. 'They wear jeans and T-shirts.'

'But sometimes dresses?'

'Cassie's wearing jeans,' counters Ruth. She knows that Kate admires Cassandra, spotting in her a glamour and stylishness sadly lacking in her mother.

Eventually Kate consents to wear jeans and a pink, sparkly T-shirt. Then there's the hassle of finding car keys and digging out the directions to the place where rehearsals are to be held. Flint watches them balefully from the sofa.

'Bye, Flint. Back at one,' says Ruth. She always tells him what time she'll be back.

'Bye, Flint.' Kate blows him a kiss. Flint closes his eyes at her.

The rehearsal is in Norwich, in a room above an old printworks. After a long and irritating drive, Ruth negotiates the one-way systems and eventually finds herself in a small car park, exactly the sort of place that might house a buried king. The printworks is a tall, slightly forbidding building, with outside fire escapes and high industrial windows.

Inside, though, it has been transformed into a modern 'Arts and Culture Centre' with a cafe and a children's play area on the ground floor. The only sign of the building's former life is a rusty-looking printing press which sits rather forlornly in the middle of the room surrounded by squashy chairs and overexcited children. Kate looks at them solemnly; she has no time for play, she has a job to do. Cassandra told them to go up to the third floor and they climb the metal staircase hand in hand. It all feels a bit grown-up suddenly.

On the third floor is a big white-painted room with black and white photos on the walls showing more printing presses and men in overalls holding rolls of paper. As Ruth and Kate stand in the doorway, Cassandra swoops down on them and everything seems much friendlier.

'Katie! Ruth! Leo, this is the brilliant little girl I was telling you about.'

Ruth watches Kate absorb and enjoy this description. She is pleased to see that Cassandra is wearing jeans and what passes for a T-shirt, even though the jeans are skintight and the top is cropped, bearing the legend, 'Venus in Furs'. You wouldn't think that Cassandra had a baby only six months ago.

Leo turns out to be the playwright and director, Leo Chard. He's a small, worried-looking man with a goatee beard and oversized red spectacles. He's trendily dressed in black jeans and black T-shirt, but all the same looks as if he'd be happier in comfy chinos and a golfing sweater.

'Hallo, Ruth. Have we met before?'

'I think I saw a play you did, years ago,' says Ruth, suddenly realising this. 'About the Roman God Janus.'

'Oh yes. At the South Quay Arts Centre. The two-faced God. My work has evolved a lot since then.'

Thank God for that, thinks Ruth. 'This is Kate,' she says.

'Katie!' Leo squats down to her level. 'I'm very glad to meet you. Have you done much acting?'

Kate shakes her head, uncharacteristically shy.

'Don't worry. I'll look after her.' He turns to Ruth. 'I do a lot of acting classes with the little ones.' Kate looks at him dubiously.

'So Katie, do you know the story of Alice in Wonderland?'

'Yes,' says Kate. 'Mum read it to me.'

'Well, this is the same except that it's about Alice as a grown-up lady. Played by your auntie Cassandra.' Leo gestures at Cassandra who smiles encouragingly. Kate looks confused. She has never called Cassandra – or any of Ruth's friends – 'auntie'. 'Do you remember the scene in the book when she gets very small?' Kate nods. 'Well, in my play, the small Alice is Alice as a child. And that's you.' He turns back to Ruth. 'It's very Freudian, you see. The Red Queen is Alice's mother and the caterpillar is her father, a laudanum addict.'

'Interesting,' says Ruth, feeling that she should say something. She wonders who the Mad Hatter will turn out to be.

'So Alice – Cassandra – takes a pill. Acid,' he hisses to Ruth. 'And when she wakes up she sees you in the room, Katie. She says, "Who are you?" and you say, "I'm you."' He smiles encouragingly.

'I'm you,' repeats Kate.

'That's right. Then Cassandra takes you by the hand and you go through a door into an enchanted garden. Her schoolfriends are there – played by grown-up actors – and they're playing a game but they won't let her join in. Then Cassandra drops some more ... takes another pill ... and becomes really, really big.'

'Then she gets stuck in a house,' says Kate, 'and Bill comes down the chimney.'

'Yes, well, we're not doing that bit. The Giant Alice is going to be shown in shadow play. The next scene is her going to a rave with the Cheshire Cat.'

'Gosh,' says Ruth.

'You see,' Leo Chard leans forward, 'my theory is that Alice has multiple personality disorder. You remember that bit in *Wonderland* where she says she's fond of pretending to be two people? Well, in my play, Alice meets her young self as well as her male self and her dark self. The ego, the id and the super-ego, if you like. I'm using underground as a metaphor for delving beneath the surface of the psyche.'

'Where are you performing the play?' says Ruth. She wonders if Cassandra has discussed Leo Chard's script with Clough. She can just imagine his comments on the ego, the id and the super-ego; to say nothing of the Cheshire Cat on acid.

'At Dragon Hall,' says Cassandra. 'It's a super venue. It used to be a medieval merchant's hall.'

'Let's get going then,' says Leo. 'I just want to walk through the scene. See how Katie reacts to Cassie.'

'We'll have fun, won't we?' Cassandra takes Kate's hand.

'Yes,' says Kate, rather doubtfully.

*

After an hour's rehearsal, Ruth has a new respect for Cassandra. It's quite something to make a dusty room full of pictures of machinery into, variously, a rabbit hole, a bedroom and an enchanted garden, but Cassandra manages it. Again and again she falls into the rabbit hole, wakes, looks around her, takes a pill with an all-too-believable mixture of caution and bravado, and opens her eyes again to find Kate looking down at her. Kate, wide-eyed with wonder, manages to say 'I'm you' with just the right combination of solemnity and surprise. Leo is clearly very pleased and tells Ruth that her daughter is 'a natural'. Ruth thinks that he's probably right. The thought frightens her.

Cassandra and Kate then mime watching the children play. As they watch the phantom children, Kate has to move away slowly, pausing only to wave as she disappears into the wings (or, in this case, moves behind a display case of letter tiles). Ruth finds it rather moving, watching her daughter waving from the other side of the room. It's as if she's rehearsing for leaving home, an event already dreaded by Ruth.

'That's brilliant, Katie,' says Leo. 'Tell me, what game do you imagine the children playing when they won't let Cassie – Alice – join in?'

'Kiss chase,' says Kate promptly, and rather worryingly.

'We thought we might have them skipping,' says Cassie. 'Do you know any skipping games, Katie?'

'I know Teddy Bear, Teddy Bear,' says Kate and, without prompting, she chants:

'Teddy Bear, Teddy Bear, turn around

Teddy Bear, Teddy Bear, touch the ground
Teddy Bear, Teddy Bear, show your shoe
Teddy Bear, Teddy Bear, that will do
Teddy Bear, Teddy Bear, go upstairs
Teddy Bear, Teddy Bear, say your prayers
Teddy Bear, Teddy Bear, turn out the lights
Teddy Bear, Teddy Bear, say goodnight.'

Leo and Cassandra look at each other. 'That's perfect,' says Leo. 'I think I could make that sound *very* sinister with a little help.'

'Are you finished with Kate for today?' says Ruth. It's been an interesting experience but she thinks she's had enough of Leo and his Freudian parallels for one morning.

'Yes,' says Leo. 'Thank you very much for bringing her. Could you bring her back in about a week's time so she can meet the rest of the cast?'

'I suppose so,' says Ruth. She's hoping that the play won't take up too much time. She slightly disapproves of after-school activities. The official *Guardian* reader's reason is that children should enjoy being children and not be bothered with dance/gymnastics/football clubs. But the truth is that Ruth finds such places intimidating. They didn't have all these clubs when she was at school. It was the Brownies or nothing. There was Sunday School at the church but that (in Ruth's opinion) was less of an activity and more of an exercise in brainwashing. After school and at weekends Ruth had been free to lie on her bed and read for hours. The perfect hobby and no leotards required.

'She'll only need a couple of rehearsals,' says Cassandra,

perhaps guessing what's in Ruth's mind. No doubt Clough has told her what an unsociable killjoy Ruth is.

'When's the play going on?' asks Ruth.

'First night is tenth of July. I'll send you front row tickets.'

'Thanks very much,' says Ruth. 'Come on, Kate. Let's go and have lunch in the castle cafe.'

Nelson is also in Norwich. He has accompanied his wife and daughter shopping, a circumstance so rare that Laura takes a photograph of him in the shopping centre car park to send to Rebecca. 'She'll never believe it.' But when he heard Michelle and Laura planning the trip, it occurred to Nelson that it was a long time since he'd been out with his wife and elder daughter.

'But you won't want to go into shops,' said Michelle, putting on mascara in the bedroom. She always makes the same face when she puts on make-up, mouth slightly open, eyes intent.

'I can take Bruno for a walk.'

'He's had a walk.' Bruno, sitting on the hall landing, wagged his tail at the mention of his name. In theory he is not allowed upstairs, but in practice the whole house is now one huge dog basket.

'He can have another one. I'll walk him by the castle and meet you afterwards. We can have lunch in a pub somewhere.'

'Let's take Bruno baby shopping.' Laura appeared on the landing and squatted down next to the dog, using the soppy baby voice that she saves exclusively for him. 'Does he want to go shopping? Does he?'

Michelle stared at herself in the mirror and Nelson watched her narrowly. Didn't she *want* him to come? But then she turned and gave him one of her most enchanting smiles, eyes as well as teeth.

'That would be lovely,' she said.

So now Nelson is walking his dog through the castle grounds, waiting for his wife and daughter to finish their female bonding. They have already walked by the river for an hour so Bruno has burnt up some energy and is now walking more or less to heel. He's better behaved with Nelson than he is with Michelle and Laura. This, according to the woman who runs the dog training class, is because German Shepherds are 'one-man dogs'. Nelson had scoffed at the time but he secretly thinks it is true. They are one-person dogs anyway. He remembers Jan Adams and her police dog Barney, two creatures working together in perfect harmony. He can't say that this is true of him and Bruno exactly (pulling the dog away from a particularly fascinating litter bin) but they certainly do seem to have a rapport, perhaps because they are the only two males in the house.

He bought the dog partly for Michelle, to give her an interest now that the girls have left home. After last year's almost-affair with Tim, Nelson and Michelle have been very careful around each other. Nelson tries not to blame Michelle – she has forgiven him for Ruth, after all – but sometimes he is seized with feelings of rage towards Tim, his once trusted sergeant, feelings so strong that he has to punch something or drive fast or take Bruno for a long walk, swearing at the trees. Michelle doesn't mention Tim but she looks sad sometimes and Nelson doesn't know how to cheer her up. Having Laura back at home has helped in some ways – Michelle loves spending time with her daughters – but it has also meant that they haven't had much time together as a couple. Even Bruno gets in the way, trying to sleep on the bed between them and dominating their conversations in the evenings ('Does he want a walk?' 'How's he doing at training class?' 'Is he going to get any bigger/stronger/cleverer?'). It's like having another child, albeit one covered in fur and prone to chasing cats.

Nelson stops and looks up at the castle, a square fortress silhouetted against the sky. Ruth excavated a body here a few years ago, a woman who had been hanged when the castle was a prison. His relationship with Ruth has certainly brought new dimensions to his life. Once he only thought about the surface of things but now he considers all those layers of history under his feet. Now he . . . He stops because, as if summoned by his thoughts, he sees Ruth and Kate crossing the drawbridge that leads to the castle entrance. Kate is wearing a sparkly top and skipping as she walks. Ruth is looking down at her as if she is listening. She's good at listening, Ruth, she always treats Kate's remarks as if they are worth hearing. Should he call out to them? But they seem so contented, so self-contained, another mother and daughter having a morning out together. Nelson and Bruno are outside both happy female circles. Bruno whines slightly as if he realises this.

As Nelson stands there watching, his phone buzzes. He

looks at the screen. The station. A call that needs to be answered.

'DCI Nelson?' It's one of the controllers, a voice he doesn't recognise. 'Can you come to the Red Mount Chapel? A man's body has been found there. Looks like he's been stabbed.'

CHAPTER 11

Nelson leaves Bruno with Michelle and walks to Norwich police station where a squad car is waiting to take him back to Lynn. Bruno whines and tugs on the lead as Nelson walks away and Michelle doesn't look any too pleased either. So much for their cosy pub lunch. Now Michelle has to drive Nelson's car home complete with an overexcited German Shepherd and a daughter weighed down with designer carrier bags. No wonder she doesn't respond when Nelson tells her that he'll see her at home. Laura gives him a kiss though and whispers, 'Is it a murder?' in his ear. She has a morbid mind, his daughter. She should have joined the police.

The police car drives Nelson to a park near the centre of King's Lynn called The Walks. It's a pleasant landscaped promenade that includes a curious building called the Red Mount Chapel, a red-brick, hexagonal structure that stands on its own on a raised mound. Nelson heard somewhere that Red Mount was once a wayside chapel on the way to the shrine at Walsingham. This knowledge doesn't predispose him in its favour exactly.

The chapel has a short flight of steps leading up to a bolted wooden door. Two uniformed officers stand at the foot of the steps and Nelson sees a figure in a blue sleeping bag lying huddled by the door. The positioning of the body reminds him poignantly of Eddie, killed as he slept in the police station porch. The squad car drives over the grass to deposit Nelson by the steps. As he gets out of the car he sees Mike Halloran, one of the crime-scene investigators, approaching from the other direction.

'Glad you got here so quickly,' says Nelson. Crime-scene investigators used to be police employees and Nelson liked it that way better because he had more control. But he respects Mike, who is good at his job and doesn't ask stupid questions.

'I was taking my kids swimming,' says Mike and Nelson sees that his hair is wet and that he's carrying a sports bag.

'We need to secure the scene as quickly as possible,' says Nelson. He climbs the stone steps. 'Who found the deceased?'

'Member of the public,' says one of the uniforms, from below. 'She thought he was just sleeping at first but then she saw the knife. She's over there with a woman officer.' He gestures towards a park bench.

Nelson looks down at the dead man. He doesn't recognise the face but lying next to the body is an incongruously cheerful object, yellow and red adorned with bells. A jester's hat.

The hilt of a knife protrudes through the sleeping bag, which is now more red than blue. Nelson thinks that it looks similar – stainless steel, utilitarian – to the weapon that killed Eddie. He leans forward.

'Don't get any closer, DCI Nelson,' warns Mike. He is looking at the grass at the bottom of the slope. 'There's a track here so we need to secure the entire area around the chapel. It's probable that the attacker came this way. Do you know if the member of the public touched the body?'

'I think she did,' says one of the policemen. 'She said he was cold.'

'I need to talk to her,' says Nelson. 'I think the deceased is a rough sleeper who goes by the name of Bilbo. Or Frodo. Something like that. He's usually to be found near the station. I'm going to ask DS Johnson to meet me here. She interviewed the bloke recently.'

He rings Judy but there's no reply. He leaves a terse message and walks over the grass to the bench where a woman is sitting hunched over a Starbucks cup.

'I was going to give the coffee to him,' says the woman who identifies herself as Rhona McGuire. 'I bought it in the shopping centre but I saw a man sleeping on the chapel steps and I thought he could probably do with a hot drink. I climbed the steps and then I saw . . .' She stops, breathing deeply.

'Take your time,' says Nelson, tapping his foot impatiently.

'I saw the knife,' says Rhona McGuire in a stronger voice. 'I saw the blood on his sleeping bag. I touched his face and he was cold so I called the police. These officers appeared very quickly.'

The woman police officer, who Nelson thinks is called

Campion, says, 'I was on the beat in the Vancouver Centre. I was called in for back-up.'

'Did you take a witness statement?'

'Yes.'

'Thank you very much,' Nelson addresses Rhona. 'I'm sorry you've had such a horrible experience. If you give your telephone number and address to PC Campion here, you're free to go. We may have to call you in and take your finger-prints to eliminate them from the scene.'

Back at the chapel the scene-of-crime team have arrived and have cordoned off the area around the building. A screen has been placed around the steps and figures in white cov-eralls are erecting a passageway so that everyone enters and exits the site the same way. A small knot of interested observers stands watching under the trees.

'Get those people to move on,' Nelson tells the uniformed officers. 'The SOCO team will be some time. In the mean-time, try to keep this area clear. I'll send someone from my team down to supervise.' His phone buzzes. Judy. *I'm on my way.*

Nelson sits on the bench recently vacated by Rhona and PC Campion and waits for Judy. She arrives ten minutes later, panting. 'Sorry I took so long. I was at the swimming pool with Michael. I had to wait for Cathbad to pick him up.'

'Half the world seems to be swimming today. What is it, National Amphibian Week?'

'It's Saturday,' says Judy. 'It's what you do. Michael has swimming lessons at the fitness centre. I want him to learn to swim as soon as possible. It's dangerous for kids not to be able to swim.'

Nelson has vague memories of watching his daughters plough up and down the lanes at the same swimming pool. But it suits him now to act as if everyone else is skiving and he alone is fighting the forces of evil. He has forgotten that he was in the shopping centre an hour ago.

'A man's been found stabbed,' he says. 'I think it might be that bloke from the station. The one with the jester's hat.'

'Bilbo? Oh no. Where is he?'

'He was found by a passer-by on the steps of the chapel.' He gestures to the building which is now half-hidden by a tarpaulin.

'I'd better go and see if it's him.'

Judy approaches Mike Halloran who gives her a paper suit to wear. Nelson watches her climbing into the suit, covering her hair with a cap and putting on a mask. Then she puts on a pair of gloves and follows Mike into the tarpaulin tunnel. Nelson remembers the days when policemen used to flat-foot all over crime scenes in their everyday clothes. He often used to come home to find his cuffs spattered with blood. These days, blood is a precious commodity to be saved and tested and analysed. Then it just meant a hot wash or a new shirt.

Judy is back in a few minutes. She's still wearing the white suit although she has taken off the mask and shaken her hair loose. 'It's him all right. Poor Bilbo.'

'Stabbed. Just like Eddie.'

'Do you think he was killed by the same person?'

'Well, it certainly looks like the same MO,' says Nelson. 'Do you know any more about this Bilbo?'

'Not really. He was from Wales originally. He used to go to the soup run and to the drop-in centre occasionally. He knew Barbara Murray slightly. That's all.'

'When was the last time you saw him?'

'Wednesday. I bought him a coffee and a roll in the cafe opposite the station.'

'Did he say anything significant about Barbara?'

'He was the one who made that remark about her going underground. I wish I'd asked him more about that.'

'Well, someone obviously wanted Bilbo to keep quiet,' says Nelson. 'You go back to the station, see if you can find out anything else about him. We've got another dead man with no name and no next-of-kin. I'll get Cloughie to join me here. Though he's probably at the bloody swimming pool.'

'I think he plays football on Saturdays,' says Judy.

CHAPTER 12

Clough hasn't been swimming. It's worse. He's been babysitting and arrives with Spencer in his buggy.

'What's this?' says Nelson. 'The mothers' union?'

'Cassie's at a rehearsal,' says Clough with dignity. 'She's meeting me here.'

Nelson, who likes babies, can't resist looking at Spencer, who is fast asleep. He's a lovely child, with Cassie's dark hair and, when awake, something of Clough's truculent expression.

'He's growing fast.'

'He's in the highest percentile for his age.'

Nelson is just marvelling at Clough not only knowing about growth percentiles but boasting about them when Cassie appears, loping across the grass in tight jeans and a borderline illegal T-shirt.

'Hi, babe.' She kisses Clough's cheek. 'Sorry I'm late. Traffic was terrible.'

'You're not late really.' Clough kisses her back looking, in Nelson's opinion, extremely foolish. *Babe.* Nelson has never in his life been addressed as 'babe'; he supposes it's a generational thing.

'I was at a rehearsal.' Cassie turns to Nelson. 'In Norwich.'

'Is this the play Katie's in?' says Nelson.

'Yes. Ruth brought her in this morning. She was terrific. A real little star.' So that was why Ruth was in Norwich. Despite his misgivings about acting, he's rather pleased to hear that Katie made such an impression. Rebecca had liked drama as a child too, he remembers.

'We'd better get to work,' he says to Clough. 'Nice to see you,' he says to Cassie, hoping to convey the message that she should leave as soon as possible. And refrain from calling anyone else 'babe'.

Cassie seems to get the hint. 'Lovely to see you too, DCI Nelson,' she says, in a tone which might or might not be ironical.

Clough watches Cassie pushing the buggy along the path until Nelson's voice recalls him to the job in hand.

'Right. We've got a man who's been stabbed. Body's cold so it must have happened a few hours ago. He's a rough sleeper and he knew Barbara Murray. Johnson interviewed him about her disappearance.'

'Blimey, boss. Do you think someone's killing off all the tramps?'

'It looks like it might be the same person who killed Eddie,' says Nelson. 'But we shouldn't assume anything. I need you to take charge here. Organise some door-to-door. I'll send you some uniforms.'

'There aren't many doors,' says Clough, looking around

the sunlit park, full of walkers and cyclists and children on roller skates. One child is blowing bubbles and the wobbly spheres, glinting with rainbow colours, drift past them and up into the sky.

'You know what I mean,' says Nelson. 'Interview the park keeper or warden or whoever looks after this place. There might even be CCTV. We can put some posters up asking for witnesses.'

'OK, boss,' says Clough. 'What was his name? The dead bloke?'

Nelson supposes that it's an advance on 'the tramp' but it's frustrating that he doesn't even have an answer to this simple question. 'Goes by the name of Bilbo,' he says, 'but I don't suppose it's his real name.'

'You'd be surprised,' says Clough. 'Cassie says there's a baby at her NCT group called Gandalf.'

Nelson walks back to the police station. It's quiet on a Saturday with only a skeleton staff working downstairs. Upstairs, in the CID rooms, he finds Judy on the phone.

'Thank you,' she's saying. 'He probably gave his name as Bilbo. B.I.L.B.O. Yes, as in *The Hobbit*. Just let me know if you have anything in the files. Thanks very much.'

She puts down the phone with a sigh. 'Just been ringing round the other local forces,' she says to Nelson. 'It's sad, but our best hope is that Bilbo was arrested somewhere and they've got his records on file.'

'The guy at the drop-in centre. Pritchard? Did he know Bilbo?'

'Slightly. Bilbo came to the centre and to the soup run. Pritchard didn't know his real name though. All we know is that Bilbo was from Wales originally. I'm going to contact the Welsh police but I don't even have a photo to show them.'

'There might be some CCTV from the railway station.'

'That's true. If we can get a photo, we can put an appeal in the paper like we did for Eddie. I've just checked the helpline.'

'Any luck?'

'Not really. One caller saying that he was their long-lost uncle Alan, someone else saying that he's the Devil incarnate.'

'He's unlikely to be both, I suppose,' says Nelson. 'We'd better follow up on the Uncle Alan one though.'

'We've traced his birth records. Born in Dublin in 1955.'

That made Eddie sixty. Nelson was right that they weren't far from being the same age (Nelson is forty-nine) but the ancient figure with the long grey beard that used to sleep in the police station porch could have been a hundred.

'Marriage certificate?'

'No, looks as if he never married. We know his full name and his parents' names though. We can put an appeal in the Dublin papers.'

'Eddie once implied that his family had had trouble with the police. It's possible that they won't want to be involved.'

'Someone must know him,' says Judy. 'It's terrible to think that there are these people living alongside us but we don't know the first thing about them. Cathbad says that it's a powerful thing to know someone's real name.'

'Sounds like the sort of thing Cathbad would say.'

'Well, it's true.' Judy colours slightly and shuffles her papers. 'Boss, have you got any idea who could be behind this?'

'I've got lots of ideas,' says Nelson. He is looking at a map of King's Lynn which is pinned up on the noticeboard. 'Each more ludicrous than the last. But it looks as if the same person killed Eddie and Bilbo. Same MO, even looked like a similar murder weapon. And to stab someone – well, that's a crime that needs real passion.'

'Distantiation,' says Judy.

'If you say so.'

'It's the theory that says it's easier to shoot someone than stab them because it's less intimate. Whoever killed Eddie and Bilbo must have had to come really close to them, must have had to lean over them and thrust the knife in.'

'They knew where to stab too. Eddie was stabbed right in the heart; looked to me like Bilbo was too.'

'Could mean we're looking for someone with medical knowledge?'

'Let's not get carried away. Most people know where the heart is. I'm just looking at the map. The Walks isn't far from here or from the railway station. Could be someone very local. Could be another rough sleeper.'

'Do you think the chapel was significant? Cathbad says that it's very old. People have seen visions of the Virgin Mary there.'

Nelson refrains from saying anything. He hopes that Judy isn't becoming too influenced by her partner. Cathbad's instincts are often right (Nelson knows this from personal experience) but there are only so many visions a person can stand.

'Eddie was killed on our steps,' he says. 'Nothing particularly mystical about a police station.'

'DCI Nelson!'

Nelson mouths 'bollocks' to Judy. He turns to face his boss. 'Yes?'

'What's this about another rough sleeper being found dead?'

'I'm dealing with it,' says Nelson. 'The CSI team are there now. DS Clough is coordinating. I'm just about to send some reinforcements. DS Johnson is trying to trace the family.'

'It doesn't look good for our targets,' says Jo, 'all these deaths.' She's wearing a tracksuit and looks as if she too has just come from Saturday morning exercise. Nelson wonders who told her about Bilbo. It certainly wasn't him.

'That was my immediate concern too,' he says. Judy laughs and hastily turns it into a cough.

'Nasty cough, DS Johnson,' says Jo. 'Keep me informed, DCI Nelson. I want the killer found in twenty-four hours.'

Nelson doesn't answer and Jo turns on her trainered heel and storms out of the room. 'I want doesn't get,' is the phrase that comes to Nelson's mind. It's always a bad sign when he starts quoting his mother, even silently.

CHAPTER 13

Ruth finds the isotope results waiting for her on Monday. The chemicals and minerals in the Guildhall bones are consistent with those found in residents of North Norfolk. But that doesn't make the deceased Norfolk born and bred. What had Martin said – that it takes twenty years in Norfolk to stop being considered a newcomer? Bones renew themselves every seven to ten years and so all the results mean is that the dead person had lived in Norfolk for about ten years. ('Poor bugger,' Ruth imagines Nelson saying.) If they'd found some teeth, then that would have been different. Teeth don't renew themselves so they carry an indelible record of the place where a person grew up. But there was no skull and no teeth found below the Guildhall. Ruth thinks of the small pile of bones, glinting in the darkness. Why were they left there? Where was the rest of the body? If the police commission an excavation then maybe they can find out.

Ros also says that they have been able to extract some DNA from the bones and should have the results very soon, maybe later that day. This should answer a few questions, should tell them the sex of the deceased at the very least.

Is this enough to justify ringing Nelson? The news that the dead person lived in Norfolk is not, strictly speaking, that exciting. But if the body is recently dead, then this is still a murder inquiry. Ruth rings Nelson.

'Nelson. It's Ruth. I've had the results on the bones found below the Guildhall.'

'Anything interesting? It's just that I'm a bit busy.'

She can hear voices in the background. Has she interrupted Nelson in a meeting? Is the dreaded Jo Archer actually in the room? Ruth begins to regret phoning.

'Isotope tests show that the deceased had lived in Norfolk for at least ten years before their death. That's all.'

'Poor bugger.' At least Nelson is consistent. 'Sorry, Ruth,' he says, sounding quite conciliatory for him. 'It's just that we've had another murder. Another rough sleeper. His body was found by the Red Mount Chapel on Saturday.'

'Oh, I'm sorry,' says Ruth. 'I didn't know. There was nothing in the papers . . .'

Nelson laughs harshly. 'Well, those sorts of deaths don't make the papers, do they? Rough sleepers disappear all the time . . .' He stops, then says, in a different voice, 'How old did you say those bones of yours were? The Guildhall ones?'

'Hard to be sure exactly but possibly less than ten years old.'

'I've checked and there are no unsolved missing person cases. What sort of person goes missing for ten years but no one notices?'

Ruth begins to see where this is going. 'A rough sleeper?'

'It's a possibility.' More noises off. 'Look, I'd better go. I'm still OK to meet Katie after school.'

'Are you sure?'

'Of course. I want to see her.'

Ruth thinks of Martin Kellerman saying that there's nowhere for a divorced father to take his daughter. 'I could collect her and we could meet you somewhere, if that's easier,' she says. 'What about The Walks?' She regrets saying this immediately. If a body's been found in the middle of The Walks, Nelson's hardly likely to want to go there for a jolly afternoon with his daughter.

But Nelson isn't one to be squeamish. 'That would be great, Ruth. Thanks. I'll meet you both in The Walks at about four.'

'Goodbye,' says Ruth, but she is speaking to the dialling tone.

Judy hears Nelson agreeing to meet Ruth at four. Bully for him, she thinks. She and Cathbad are going to her parents' in Heacham later to celebrate her mother's sixty-fifth birthday and the arrangements, involving collecting Michael from school and stopping off in King's Lynn for Judy, seem unnecessarily complicated and stressful. Easy enough for the boss to pop out and meet his illegitimate child for fun in the park. It's not openly discussed at the station but everyone knows that Kate is Nelson's daughter. Cathbad, of course, knew from the first but he and Judy don't discuss it much, even between themselves. Clough knows but he's not one to gossip about the boss. Tanya probably doesn't know – she's blind to everything apart from her job prospects. What about Tim, who left last year? Judy had liked Tim – they all did – but there was something closed and secretive about him too. He would never discuss personal matters; Judy doesn't even know if he's gay or straight. They miss him at the station though. His calm good humour was a useful foil for Judy's seriousness and Clough's bluster. The boss was obviously shaken by Tim's defection too. He never mentions him now.

The post-mortem results on Eddie came through that morning. Death by a single stab wound to the heart. That takes planning, whatever Nelson says. Planning and a cool head. The examination also found traces of material and chemicals on Eddie's face and beard. So the killer had drugged him first, probably putting a cloth over Eddie's mouth. The chemical is a version of soda lime which, Judy reads, is commonly used in anaesthetics. Did the killer have medical or scientific knowledge? Where would you find a drug like that?

Judy wonders if the same drug will be found on Bilbo's body. So far she hasn't even been able to find Bilbo's real name or trace his relatives. Like Eddie, no ID was found on him, only a packet of Polos and a flyer for a concert of baroque music. Did Bilbo enjoy Bach as well as chess? No one seems to know. For the tenth time that morning, Judy runs through her conversation with Bilbo in the cafe. He said that he was Welsh and so had a kind of Celtic bond with Babs, a Scot. He knew Charlie, an ex-teacher and another

Scot, but Charlie also seems to have vanished off the face of the earth.

Judy rings Paul Pritchard. She doesn't expect him to have any information about Bilbo (after all, he didn't even know his full name) but she feels she wants to speak to someone who actually knew him and cared for him, in a way.

'Bilbo's dead? That's awful. Is it linked to the other death, the man on the police station steps?'

'It's a possibility.' Judy doesn't think there's much point in denying this. Bilbo's death hasn't been in the papers yet but sooner or later someone will make the link, and even if the two homeless men aren't exactly the most photogenic of victims, surely someone will be interested in their deaths?

'That's terrible,' says Pritchard. 'It means other people could be in danger.'

'Yes,' says Judy. 'It might be an idea to warn your clients.' But what can they do to keep safe? she thinks. If you sleep in the open, you are completely vulnerable. No wonder Pritchard said that some rough sleepers stay awake all night.

'What about Babs?' says Pritchard. 'Have you found her yet?'

'No, we haven't.' They are going to put another advertisement in the local paper, asking if anyone knows Barbara's whereabouts, but Judy isn't hopeful. They haven't had any success with tracing her adult children either. It's likely that social services can trace the younger ones but that won't necessarily get them any nearer to Barbara.

After she puts the phone down, on impulse Judy starts a search for Paul Pritchard. It shouldn't be too difficult if he has a conviction for armed robbery. At first she can't find anything but then it comes up: Dean Pritchard convicted at Norwich Crown Court, April 2000. She's pretty sure that Dean and Paul Pritchard must be the same person. Why did he change his name? It's only when she's walking to the station to ask about Bilbo that she thinks of St Paul on the road to Damascus. Roman soldier Saul changed his name to Paul after his conversion to Christianity. Is that why Dean Pritchard, armed robber, became Paul Pritchard, charity worker? It's a small thing really but it makes her wonder how much she really knows about St Paul of the drop-in centre.

The station is quiet. The London train isn't due for twenty minutes and the only people on the platform are a couple of students with backpacks who look lost. The cafe too is empty which suits Judy fine. She shows her warrant card to the woman behind the counter and asks if she can have a word.

'You were in here the other day, weren't you? Is it about Bilbo?'

'Yes,' says Judy. 'I'm sorry to give you bad news but I'm afraid that he has been found dead.'

'Oh no.' The woman puts a hand over her heart. 'Oh my goodness. Poor Bilbo. Ernie!' she shouts to an unseen figure. 'Ernie, something terrible has happened to Bilbo.'

Ernie appears, wiping his hands on his apron. Judy likes the couple for the obvious distress they show at the news of Bilbo's death.

'He was a gentle soul,' says the woman, whose name is

Pat. 'We always used to give him a cup of tea and a bacon sandwich. He'd play us a little tune on his pipe to say thank you.'

'He loved music,' says Ernie. 'He used to say that he'd sung in a big competition once. In Cardiff, when he was still at school.'

Judy makes a note of this. Perhaps Bilbo was from Cardiff? But Pat and Ernie are unable to help with the most pressing question of all.

'I've no idea what his real name was,' says Pat. 'We always called him Bilbo, didn't we?'

Her husband agrees. 'I asked him once, why Bilbo? He said that Bilbo Baggins hadn't wanted to leave home and nor had he. But he was on the journey and he was going to make the best of it. That was typical Bilbo. He always left you with more questions, if you know what I mean.'

Judy knows exactly what he means. 'Did he ever mention his home?' she asks. 'His family?'

'No,' says Pat. 'I got the idea that he was alone in the world. Ernie and I were talking about our grandchildren – we've got eight – and he said that he didn't have children or grandchildren. It was sad really.'

'Bilbo said something odd to me,' says Judy. 'I was asking about a woman, another rough sleeper, who seems to have disappeared. Bilbo said that she had gone underground. Do you have any idea what he might have meant?'

'No,' says Pat. 'It's like that song, isn't it? By The Jam. "Going Underground". You remember that song, Ernie? Ernie was a bit of a mod once,' she explains in a stage whisper.

'Did you ever see Bilbo talking to anyone strange?' says Judy. 'Anyone unexpected?'

'He talked to everyone,' says Ernie. 'He used to play songs for people and even do little dances. He was a court jester, he used to say. Some people complained about him but I'll miss him. I'll miss hearing those bells jangle and his face appearing in the doorway.'

His wife pats his hand. 'Yes, we'll miss him. Lots of people will. He used to play chess with people in the cafe sometimes. And he knew all sorts. People who lived on the streets, people from the university – he was everyone's friend.'

'Who did he know from the university?' asks Judy.

But Pat is vague again. 'I don't know their names but he once said that he'd been to see his friends "up at the university". I joked that he'd be wearing a cap and gown next.'

'Do you know which university?' asks Judy. 'UEA or UNN?'

'I didn't know there were two,' says Pat. Judy smiles inwardly to think how horrified Ruth would be by this statement.

'Can you let me know if you think of anything else about Bilbo?' she says. 'Anything at all that might help. Here's my card.'

'How did he die?' asks Pat. 'Was it the drink that got him?'

'No,' says Judy. She sees no point in hiding the news, it will be public knowledge soon. 'I'm afraid he was murdered.'

'Murdered!' Pat takes Ernie's hand. 'Who would want to kill Bilbo? He was such an innocent. He wouldn't hurt a fly.'

Bilbo was certainly an innocent in all senses of the word, thinks Judy as she walks back to the police station. The trouble is that innocence is often very dangerous. To guilty people, that is.

Kate is not delighted to see her mother at the school gate.

'Where's Daddy?' is her first question.

'We're meeting him in the park,' says Ruth, trying to maintain a jolly mother expression. Not that anyone is watching her. As usual all the other mothers are in a huddle across the playground, discussing play-dates and handing out after-school treats.

'I don't want to go to the park,' says Kate but she follows Ruth quite cheerfully, waving at her friends as she goes. Unlike Ruth, Kate is very popular at school.

They reach The Walks early and Kate runs around the play area while Ruth surreptitiously checks her texts. She's expecting a message from Ros about the DNA results or maybe a cheerful *I'm on my way* from Nelson. Instead there is a text from an unknown number. She clicks onto it, rather warily. *Hallo Ruth. Have you had any more news on the Guildhall bones? Text me when convenient Yours Quentin.* Quentin Swan. The architect. The David Tennant look-alike. Swan obviously wants reassurance that the bones are medieval and won't present an obstacle to the creation of his underground restaurant. He's got a shock coming, thinks Ruth grimly.

'Hallo, Ruth. Keeping an eye on Katie?'

Ruth jumps. 'Of course I am!' Unfortunately, Kate chooses that moment to fall off the climbing frame. Nelson makes an exclamation and starts forward, but at the sound of his voice, Kate turns round. She grins, all thoughts of her fall forgotten, picks herself up and rushes towards her father.

'Daddy!'

It's so simple, thinks Ruth, a child's delight at seeing her father. It's a pity that it's also so complicated.

They walk through the park, Kate holding Nelson's hand and telling him about her day at school. 'My picture had orange paint not red. Jack said it should be red but I said orange is better because my cat's orange. Isn't orange better than red?'

'Definitely,' says Nelson. 'Orange is the colour of your football team.'

Much against Ruth's better judgement, Nelson has brought Kate up to be an ardent Blackpool fan.

'The Tangerines,' says Kate. 'I like tangerines better than oranges. Why do we only have them at Christmas?'

'Nothing rhymes with orange,' says Ruth, who is feeling rather spare.

'What about borange?' says Kate. 'And zorange and gorange?'

'They aren't real words . . .' begins Ruth but Kate has spotted an ice cream van and is towing Nelson towards it. She is chanting, 'Orange, borange, gorange' as she goes.

In the end Nelson buys ice creams for all of them and they eat them on a bench overlooking the river. Ruth finds herself relaxing and allowing herself to imagine that it could always be like this, just the three of them, sitting in the sunshine, watching the ducks. Hard to believe that there was a vicious murder in this park only two days ago. A steady stream of humanity flows past them. Mothers with children in school uniform, clutching book bags and sandwich boxes. Couples pushing prams. A couple of harassed fathers, checking their phones as their children tug on their arms. Teenagers prowling in packs or walking in pairs, heads together, laughing at something on a screen.

'Can I have a phone?' says Kate.

'Not until you're eleven,' says Ruth. She has arrived at this milestone because that is the unimaginable age when Kate will be going to secondary school (cue another fight with Nelson about state versus private schools).

'I shouldn't really be here,' says Nelson. 'Not with a murder investigation on the go.'

'Have you got any further with it?'

'No. We don't even know the man's real name. We're putting an appeal in the papers and Johnson's going to ask at the soup run on Wednesday. Cathbad helps run it, apparently.'

'He's good, isn't he? I always think I should be doing something like that.'

'Who would look after Katie?'

'That's one reason why I can't do it,' says Ruth. She's irritated when Nelson reminds her about Kate. What does he think she's going to do? Leave her alone with a bottle of gin?

'And then there are the bones under the Guildhall,' says Nelson, unaware that he's said anything wrong. 'Whichever way we look at it, that's another dead body. Another person with no name. Have you heard anything more on the DNA results?'

'No,' says Ruth, but just at that moment her phone buzzes. 'That could be Ros now.'

But it isn't Ros, it's Ruth's father. Her dad never phones her. Ruth stands up, suddenly afraid. Kate, who has been throwing bits of ice-cream cone to the ducks, turns to look at her.

'Ruth. It's Dad. Your mother . . .' There's a long pause.

'What is it?'

'Mum's been taken ill. A stroke, that's what they say. It looks bad, Ruth.'

Another pause. Can her dad actually be *crying*?

'Where is she?'

'In hospital. King's. I think you should come, Ruth. I think you should come quickly.'

'I will,' says Ruth. 'I'll come straight away. Are you at the hospital? Is Simon with you?' Ruth's brother usually manages to get out of anything unpleasant but surely he's doing his bit now. He only lives round the corner.

'Yes, he's here. Cathy too. But I think you should come, Ruth. She'll want you.'

Ruth is touched. She always thinks of Simon as her mother's favourite but her father thinks that she should be there.

'I'll come right away,' she says. 'I can be with you by seven-thirty.'

She clicks off the phone and sees Nelson and Kate staring at her, their faces disconcertingly alike.

'She'll be fine with me.'

'I don't know.'

Ruth and Nelson are standing by her car. Kate is holding Nelson's hand and looking gravely from one parent to the other. Ruth knows that she should be on her way. She should drive straight to Eltham. Her father said that she should come quickly. Her brother, who had rung five minutes later, said the same thing. 'She's in intensive care. It doesn't look good, Ruth. You'd better come at once.'

But what should she do about Kate? At first she thought that she would take Kate with her but what if Ruth ends up having an all-night vigil at the hospital, a vigil that might end in tragedy? Kate would be tired and distressed but she would have to stay with Ruth because there would be nowhere else for her to go. She doesn't know her aunt and uncle that well, and besides, they'll be at the hospital too. Then Ruth had thought of Judy and Cathbad. Kate loves them and has often stayed the night at their house. Ruth phoned Judy but she was on her way to a family party in Heacham. Judy said that she would be happy to collect Kate later and take her home with her but Ruth really needs to leave immediately. So Nelson has suggested that he take Kate back to his house and deliver her to Judy when she gets back. It's a sensible suggestion but it still feels like abandoning Kate. But how can this be if Kate's with her father?

She kneels down beside her daughter. 'Kate, will you be OK with Daddy for a bit? I've got to drive down to see Granny. She's not very well. Daddy will take you over to Judy's later. You can have a sleepover with Michael.'

'You can come back to my house, Katie,' says Nelson. 'See Bruno. Would you like that?'

Kate's face lights up. 'Yes!' She loves Bruno and often paints pictures of him, captioned 'My Dogy'.

'You go, Ruth,' says Nelson. 'You go to your mum.' He sounds uncharacteristically gentle. Ruth has met Nelson's mother and found her rather formidable but she's certain that Nelson would race to her side if she were sick.

'All right then.' Ruth bends down and kisses Kate. 'I'll see you tomorrow, sweetheart. I love you.'

Kate kisses her back but it's clear that her mind is on Bruno.

It's only when Nelson is driving Kate to his house that he remembers its other occupant. What will Laura make of her first meeting with her half-sister?

CHAPTER 14

In a daze, Ruth negotiates the endless daisy chain of round-abouts that surrounds King's Lynn. She is pleased that she is driving her new car and not her old Renault, which had a tendency to stall whenever she stopped. It is not until she is on the M11 that she allows herself to think about what lies ahead. Will she be in time to see her mum? Will her mother be wired up to all sorts of machines, unable to see or hear? Barring the nightmare occasion when Nelson was seriously ill, Ruth has had very little experience of hospitals. She gave birth in one but that's hardly the same as being a patient. Besides, all she remembers about Kate's birth is yelling at Cathbad – her reluctant birth partner – and being embarrassed because he was wearing his robes. The amazing, dizzying joy of seeing her newborn baby seems have wiped out all that went before. Just as well really or no one would ever have a second child.

Ruth can't remember her mother ever being ill. Jean Galloway has always seemed immune to human frailties like colds or toothache or everyday aches and pains. Ruth supposes that her mother has been through the menopause (a life event that she is dreading) but she never remembers Jean mentioning a hot flush, or forgetfulness or depression or any of the delights which, according to the articles Ruth reads in the *Guardian* health pages, are in store for her. Jean had just powered on, omnipotent as ever, dispensing wisdom about both earthly and spiritual matters with the same calm certainty. Best way to get a baby to sleep through the night? Best way to get into heaven? Jean had the answers to both.

By the time that she reaches the South Circular and the Catford Gyratory, Ruth has convinced herself that her mother is dead. She has turned her phone off so that she won't be tempted to look at it while she's driving, but on Sydenham Hill she can't take it any more and pulls over to check her messages. There's nothing from her father or brother which must mean that the worst hasn't happened. There's a text from Nelson. *At park with Bruno. K fine. Drive safely. Thinking of yr mum.* This, from Nelson, is quite expansive. Ruth texts back *Thanks*, and continues on her way. The south London streets look both familiar and strange. It's nearly half past seven and still light and there are tables outside most of the pubs and restaurants. Surely there wasn't this much al fresco dining when she was growing up? Maybe a few tables outside the Windmill on Clapham Common but that was it. So many coffee shops and nail bars and Tesco Metros. So few butchers or greengrocers or off-licences. Even the phone stores that sprang up in recent years have melted into the earth again. Now there are Dickensian-looking pawnbrokers or extravagantly punning hairdressers. Ruth starts to note them as she drives. A Cut Above. Heads Up. Ahead of the Game. Curl up and Dye.

Eventually she reaches Denmark Hill and the looming shape of King's is on her left. She spends a futile ten minutes trying to get into the car park before finding a space in a side road. Then she runs towards the sign saying Emergency because this is an emergency, isn't it? She almost collides with an ambulance driving in the other way. There's a sense that all human life is here. Birth and death and everything in between. A shape on a stretcher is being carried out of the ambulance, the walking wounded are having cigarettes in the porch, and a couple are walking out through the main doors, tenderly holding their newborn baby in a carry-cot between them.

Ruth is directed to a ward, which she takes to be a good sign, until she realises that it's a high dependency unit. When she gets to the doors, though, they are locked and you need a passcode to enter. Ruth almost cries with frustration. To have got through the roundabouts and the motorway and the streets full of hairdressers to be thwarted by this smug little keypad. She wants to give up. She wants to Curl Up and Dye.

She is punching in numbers at random when the door opens.

'Ruth!' It's her brother, Simon.

'Simon.' Ruth grabs at him. 'How's Mum?'

'She's still unconscious.' Simon looks older, thinks Ruth, or maybe that's just the effect of the last few hours. Has his hair always been receding? He looks pale and thin and in need of a shave. 'She's stable,' he says, 'but the longer she's unconscious the less chance of a full recovery.' Simon sounds like he is quoting – he already seems to have been absorbed into the hospital and its alien ways. Ruth, who had looked forward to Simon's support, finds herself backing away slightly.

'Can you take me to her?'

'This way. Make sure you disinfect your hands.'

Ruth does so and Simon leads her into a small ward with four beds. Her mother lies on her back with her mouth slightly open. She's breathing loudly but she's mercifully free from tubes.

'Mum?' Ruth comes closer. Her mother's skin looks oddly waxy. Ruth touches her cheek. It's cold.

'Talk to her,' says Simon. 'That's what the nurses keep telling us to do.'

'Hallo, Mum. It's Ruth.' Her mother's eyes move slightly under the closed lids.

'Where's Dad?' says Ruth, not taking her eyes off Jean.

'Cathy's taken him off for a cup of tea. He's in a terrible state.'

'What happened?'

'Dad just got home from his men's church group and found her on the floor. He didn't know how long she'd been lying there. He called an ambulance but he didn't call me until they'd got to the hospital.'

'Have they operated on her?' Ruth realises that she has been expecting some grand medical intervention of the sort beloved by the TV programme *Casualty*: masks, scalpels, perspiring doctors, bleeping machines. It seems wrong that her mum is just lying here.

'She had a CT scan,' says Simon. 'Apparently there are some drugs that they can give but they only work if they give them within three hours of the stroke and no one knows how long ago it was.'

'What did the scan show?'

'It showed that it wasn't a brain haemorrhage. Apparently this is a different kind of stroke. An ischaemic stroke. And there's nothing much they can do except wait. She's in a coma now.'

'I need to talk to someone. A doctor. Someone has to do something. It's because she's old. They're just not operating because they think she's too old.'

'Ruth . . .'

Simon puts out a hand but before he can say anything, a nurse appears at the bedside.

'You must be the daughter,' he says. 'Your dad will be pleased you're here.'

'What's happening with Mum?' Ruth hears her voice sounding aggressive. 'Why haven't you operated?'

The nurse is checking a device attached to the tip of Jean's finger. 'I know it's hard,' he says, 'but with strokes like this we just have to wait. Her pulse is good, she's stable, we just have to wait for her to wake up.'

'I want to talk to a doctor,' says Ruth.

'The doctor will be doing her evening rounds soon,' says the nurse. 'Can I get you a cup of tea? I know you've come a long way. My name's Denzil, by the way.'

Ruth wants to say no, that she'll sit dry-mouthed by her mother until the doctor arrives. Part of her resents the way that Denzil has expertly defused her anger. But another part of her wants a cup of tea more than anything in the world.

'I'd love a cup of tea,' she says. 'Thank you.'

She sits at Jean's bedside, holding the hand without the device on it. Simon sits on the other side.

'Isn't it strange to see Mum so quiet?' he says. 'I can't remember her ever being so long without speaking.'

'No,' says Ruth. 'She even found quiet times in church difficult.'

'I once suggested that she go on a sponsored silence for Christian Aid.'

Ruth laughs and looks round guiltily. The other occupants of the beds lie quietly, attached to tubes and machines. There's only one other visitor, a man who sits, apparently slumped in despair, at an elderly woman's bedside. Denzil brings tea in NHS mugs for her and for Simon. Ruth hears him offering tea to the other man but can't catch the reply. Outside, someone is cleaning the floors with a loud mechanical device.

'How's Dad doing?' she asks.

'Not too good,' says Simon. 'You know how he relies on Mum for everything. He seems completely lost without her. Cathy's being very good with him.' He says this rather defiantly. Ruth has never particularly got on with her sister-in-law but she can imagine that she would be good in a situation like this. Her dad would be only too happy to swap one capable woman for another.

'It's really kind of her to be here,' she says. 'Who's looking after the boys?'

Simon and Cathy have two sons, George and Jack. Ruth's a bit hazy about their ages but maybe George is old enough not to need a babysitter. He must be about fourteen. She loves her nephews though – nothing complicated about her feelings there.

'They're with friends,' says Simon. 'What about Katie?'

'She's with . . . with friends. They'll look after her tonight so I can stay here.'

'We can take it in turns,' says Simon. 'I really think Dad ought to go home though. He's been here since three.'

'It's awful not knowing what's going on,' says Ruth.

'The doctor said earlier that she could stay like this for days,' says Simon.

Ruth turns to her mother. 'Mum,' she says, 'wake up.'

She's not expecting any response so it's a complete shock when her mother's lips part and she says, 'Hallo, Ruth. Where's Katie?'

Bruno is delighted to see Nelson and Kate. Nelson had been worried that the dog would jump up on Kate and scare her but Bruno seems to understand that this small human needs special handling. He approaches Kate, tail wagging ingratiatingly, and she responds by hugging him. 'Gently, Katie,' says Nelson. He doesn't think that Bruno would harm Kate but he can't help being over-anxious. Both of them are young, after all.

'I love him,' says Kate. 'Can we take him for a walk?'

Nelson hesitates but Bruno does need a walk and it's as good a way as any of passing the time. He has left a voicemail message for Michelle explaining why Kate will be there when she gets home but she hasn't responded. Now he texts Laura, asking cautiously what her plans are for the afternoon. Laura answers that she is going to the gym. Nelson hopes that she will take her time about it.

Nelson and Kate take Bruno to the park where he runs around excitedly and brings them sticks and stones and a single football boot.

'What happened to the other shoe?' asks Kate.

Nelson has no idea. He can't see any irate footballers about the place. 'Drop,' he tells Bruno, who lets the boot fall immediately. Bruno also stands still and lets him put the lead on. Those training classes are clearly paying off. Nelson even lets Kate hold the lead while he texts Ruth. He hopes that her mother will pull through. From the little she has said, he gets the impression that Ruth doesn't get on too well with her parents, but a mother is a mother. He dreads anything happening to his.

They head back through the suburban streets. Kate is interested in everything. Why does that garden have a pond? Why is that man washing his car? Nelson supposes that this is all new to her. Ruth doesn't have neighbours, as such. The two houses on either side are empty most of the time. As far as Nelson can tell one is owned by London yuppies who come down once a year and the other belongs to a strange Aborigine bloke who is always off wandering the world reading his incomprehensible poetry to people.

Nelson doesn't imagine that much car washing goes on. But he's finding it hard to concentrate on Kate's chatter. Who will be waiting for them when they get back to the house? Will it be Michelle offering tea and the brisk kindness that she always shows to Kate? Or will it be Laura asking awkward questions?

As he turns the corner into their cul-de-sac he breathes a sigh of relief. Michelle's car is in the drive. She will understand about Ruth's mother and why Kate had to come to their house. She will be motherly and competent. She'll cook for them (Kate has already said that she's hungry).

'Come on, Katie,' he says. 'Nearly home. We'll have some tea and cake.'

But, before he can put his key in the lock, the door is opened and Laura stands in front of him, dressed in her gym clothes.

'Hi, Dad,' she says. 'Hi, Bruno. Who's this?'

CHAPTER 15

By the time Ruth's dad reappears, clinging on to Cathy's arm, Jean has opened her eyes and said 'Hallo, son,' to Simon. She has mumbled a few unintelligible words too and has shut her eyes again but it's definite progress. Denzil, alerted by Ruth and Simon, appears at Jean's bedside with another nurse.

'This is a good sign,' he tells Ruth. 'The quicker we get her back the better the chance of a full recovery.'

'Jean.' The other nurse, an older woman in a subtly different uniform, leans down to speak into Jean's ear. 'Jean. Can you hear me?'

Another mumble, then, 'Don't shout,' crossly, from Jean. Ruth and Simon burst out laughing.

'What's going on?' asks Cathy from the doorway, shocked at this unseemly mirth. Arthur lets go of his daughter-in-law and comes forward to embrace his daughter. 'Ruth. I'm so glad you're here.' Ruth puts her arm round her father. He seems thin and frail, she can feel his bones under his cardigan. How has he aged so quickly?

'Mum's come round,' says Ruth. 'Isn't that great?'

'Seems like you had the magic touch,' the older nurse says to Ruth.

'I was just there,' says Ruth, but she is rather pleased nonetheless. She approaches the bed to demonstrate her magic touch again.

'Mum,' she says, 'how are you feeling?'

This time Jean opens her eyes and focuses on Ruth. 'Ruth,' she says. 'Where am I?'

'Jean,' Arthur appears on her other side, 'you're in hospital. You fell. Do you remember?'

Jean is still looking at Ruth. 'When did I fall?'

'You fell at home,' says Ruth. 'I don't know exactly when.'

'My head hurts,' says Jean. 'Why's everyone here?'

'You hit your head when you fell, Jean,' says Denzil. 'But you're in hospital. We're looking after you.'

'Well, you can get me some tea then,' says Jean. 'I'm parched.'

'Hallo,' says Laura, disengaging herself from Bruno's welcome. 'Who are you?'

'I'm Kate,' says Kate unanswerably.

'Where's Mum?' says Nelson. 'Her car's outside.'

'She's still at work,' says Laura. 'Remember, I drove her in this morning? She said I could have the car because I want to go to the gym. Debbie's giving her a lift home.'

'Are you off to the gym now then?' says Nelson hopefully.

'In a bit.' She crouches down to Kate's height. 'Hi. Do you want an ice lolly? There are some in the freezer.'

'Yes, please,' says Kate and she puts her hand in Laura's as they walk into the kitchen.

Nelson follows them. 'Kate's Ruth's daughter,' he says. 'You remember Ruth, the archaeologist? Ruth had to rush away because her mum's been taken ill so I'm looking after Kate until Judy gets here.' He had already texted Judy who has said that she will call for Kate on her way home but that won't be until eight at the earliest It's six now. Somehow Nelson has to get through the next two hours.

'My grandma's sick,' Kate tells Laura as they both unwrap popsicles. 'My mum's gone to London to see her.'

'Don't worry,' says Laura. 'The doctors and nurses will make her better. Have you had your tea?'

'No,' says Kate.

'Shall I make us something to eat?' says Laura. 'We shouldn't really have had those popsicles first.'

'But you want to get to the gym,' says Nelson.

'That's OK. You won't want to cook. Tell you what, Kate, we'll have fish finger sandwiches. Have you ever had fish finger sandwiches? They're my dad's favourites.'

Damn Laura with her kindness and domesticity. Shouldn't she be out at a rave with an unsuitable boyfriend? Where did they go wrong as parents?

'My dad likes fish fingers,' says Kate.

'Why don't we all watch a film?' says Nelson, too loudly.

At the hospital things move quickly. By nine o'clock Jean has seen the consultant and has been moved to another ward. Ruth is rather sad to leave Denzil behind but there's no doubt that the new ward is a much jollier place. Some of the patients are out of bed and others are watching TV. A woman is going round with a trolley offering tea and biscuits. 'Turned up like a bad penny again,' says someone, to general laughter.

The new ward sister, who is called Dawn, encourages them to leave Jean to sleep. 'She's had quite a day of it, by all accounts.' Jean seems to have recovered her powers of speech but her face still has an uneven look to it, and when she was finally handed her precious cup of tea she clearly found it hard to grip the handle. The consultant, a scarily young-looking woman called Shamilla, says that there is still a way to go. 'We'll know more tomorrow but it's very good news that Mrs Galloway has recovered consciousness and that she's talking and making sense.' Ruth, who has often accused her mother of not making sense (when she is talking about God, for example), just feels relieved that Jean seems to be out of danger.

'Shall we go home, Dad?' she says. Simon and Cathy have already left.

'Are you going back to Norfolk?' asks Arthur.

'Not tonight. I can stay the night with you and go back tomorrow.'

'That's nice,' says Arthur. 'You can have your old room. It's Jean's sewing room now but the bed's still there.'

'Great,' says Ruth.

She drives her father home wondering when they were last alone together. Jean has always been there with her loudly voiced opinions and general lack of tact. 'You'll never get a boyfriend looking like that, Ruth.' Ruth has always assumed that Arthur shares Jean's views but she can't remember him ever putting this into words. Now he seems pathetically grateful to her, constantly complimenting her on her driving. 'Nicely steered. Oh, that was a bit tight. Well done.'

'I have been driving for nearly thirty years, Dad,' she says, as they take the roundabout onto Eltham Hill.

'Is it as long as that?' Arthur sounds surprised.

'I'm forty-seven in July,' says Ruth though, to be honest, she hardly believes it herself. Especially now as she feels herself getting younger the nearer they get to her childhood home. It's a bit like Alice in Wonderland getting smaller and smaller. Leo Chard would relish the Freudian connotations of Ruth making this journey into her past. Who was the father in his version? Oh yes, the hookah-smoking caterpillar.

The house looks smaller too. It's a pebble-dashed semi sandwiched between Eltham Common and the South Circular. As a child Ruth remembers feeling a sense of claustrophobia, amounting almost to panic, at the view from her bedroom window: the rows of similar houses, the back gardens, the criss-crossing roads. Maybe that's why she now lives in a house which looks out onto miles of marshland, sand, sea and sky. But now, parking in the paved-over front garden, the house seems friendlier than she remembers. Perhaps it's just the relief of being away from the hospital. Inside, everything is the same: the front room with its net curtains and rigidly arranged ornaments, the small kitchen with a hatch looking into the dining room. 'Why don't you knock through?' Ruth used to say, when she still cared about such things. 'Make one long room. It would be much lighter and nicer.' 'No thank you,' was Jean's answer, 'we don't like open plan.' She always managed to make the words 'open plan' sound extremely wicked.

'Shall I make us something to eat?' says Ruth. She and Arthur have somehow gravitated into the kitchen. 'You must be starving.'

'I suppose I must be,' says Arthur. 'It's been such a day. I don't know if I'm hungry or not.'

'I know what you mean,' says Ruth. 'But you should eat something. Shall I make us some tea and toast?'

'That would be nice,' says Arthur. He sits at the fold-out table by the hatch. Ruth guesses that he and her mother usually eat in this room. She can't imagine them sitting at the polished hardwood table in the dining room, where framed pictures of their children and grandchildren stare down at them from the display cabinet: Ruth, pink-faced in her graduation robes, Simon and Cathy on their wedding day, Kate on the beach in Norfolk, windswept and gorgeous.

As she boils the kettle, Ruth reads a text from Judy. She has collected Kate and put her to bed on a blow-up mattress in Michael's room. Ruth texts to say thank you. *How's ur mum?* Judy texts back. Ruth hesitates, not sure how to convey the news about Jean. She's out of danger, it seems, but who knows about the long road to recovery that lies ahead? Will Jean even be able to manage living in this house? The stairs are very steep. Maybe she could sleep downstairs. 'Just as well we didn't knock that wall down,' Ruth imagines her mother saying, never one to miss a chance to be in the right. *Mum on mend*, she texts and hopes that this is the truth.

'Shall we take our toast into the front room?' says Ruth. 'Watch some rubbishy telly before we go to bed?'

Arthur looks worried at the thought of rubbishy telly. 'Can we say a prayer,' he says, 'to say thank you to God and ask for healing?'

'All right,' says Ruth.

It's going to be a long evening.

Nelson watches Kate climbing into the back of Judy's car. He's pleased to see that Cathbad makes sure that she's safely strapped into the booster seat. Michael is on the other side with baby Miranda in the middle. Kate waves happily as they drive off. Nelson, Michelle and Laura wave back from the doorstep.

'Isn't she a cutie?' says Laura. 'I do admire Ruth bringing her up on her own.' Then Laura wanders off to her room, leaving Nelson and Michelle together in a silence that seems to grow bigger and more obtrusive by the second.

Eventually Michelle says, 'You'll have to tell her.'

Nelson knows that she is right. All evening, as he watched his daughters snuggled on the sofa watching *Frozen*, he knew that he had to tell Laura and Rebecca about Kate. Seeing them together like that . . . Kate is dark and Laura is blonde like Michelle but there was something in the shape of their faces, in the set of their eyes, that seemed to shout out the truth, even as, on screen, Elsa was bellowing her defiance to the mountain tops. When Michelle had got in she had taken one look at the two girls and walked from the room. Nelson found her in the kitchen methodically clearing away the debris from the fish finger sandwiches.

'Ruth's mum was taken ill . . .' He started telling the story, aware that, in the face of Michelle's eloquent silence, it had begun to sound like an excuse.

'What if Kate calls you Daddy?' said Michelle. 'What's Laura going to think?'

'They seem to be getting on well,' said Nelson, aware how pathetic this sounded.

'Well, they would, wouldn't they?' said Michelle.

Now, standing with his wife in their suddenly silent house, Nelson knows that he has to act. So far, he has managed to keep Kate separate from his other daughters. Laura and Rebecca have left home, Kate belongs to Norfolk and his other life. In fact, Kate probably slots into the gap left by the departure of his older daughters and makes their absence more bearable. But now Laura has come back and has blown the whole edifice apart. He feels as if his perfect home is going to collapse like a house of cards.

As he hesitates, his phone rings.

'DCI Nelson? You're wanted in Pott Row. A woman has disappeared.'

CHAPTER 16

Nelson collects Clough and they drive to the address given to them by Control. Nelson drives (treating the speed limit with a contempt that would have reduced Bev Flinders to tears) and Clough reads aloud from the email. 'Sam Foster-Jones, aged thirty-five. Mother of four. Missing since five-thirty this evening.'

'It's nearly nine now,' says Nelson. 'When was it called in?'

'Seven,' says Clough, scrolling down through the email. 'Husband came home from work and found the four children alone.'

'Then she could have been missing for longer,' says Nelson. 'What's the husband called?'

'Benedict Foster-Jones. They're one of those couples who hyphenate their names. Very Pott Row.'

Nelson is pretty sure that Clough's son Spencer rejoices in the surname Blackstock-Clough but he decides not to mention this.

'Must be more than a missing person inquiry,' he says, 'otherwise they wouldn't have called us in.'

'My money's on the husband,' says Clough.

Pott Row is a picturesque village on the outskirts of King's Lynn. As Clough implied, it is popular with young, moneyed families. The renovated cottages bristle with burglar alarms and the streets are full of Range Rovers. The Foster-Joneses live in a long, low house – it looks like a bungalow converted to have rooms in the roof – surrounded by a large garden. Standing by the porch are two uniformed officers: Norris and Campion. Jane Campion is the female officer who assisted with the witness outside the Red Chapel. Nelson is pleased. He has formed a good opinion of PC Campion.

They confer by the cars. 'It could be nothing,' says Campion. 'Sam could be with a friend or even a boyfriend. Or she could just be fed up with looking after all the children.'

'There are hundreds of them,' says Norris.

'There are four of them, Chris,' says Campion. 'And that's another thing. The baby is really little. Sam's still breastfeeding. I don't think she would have just walked out on them.'

'What happened?' says Nelson.

'The oldest child, Caleb, said that someone called at the house at approximately five-thirty. He didn't see who it was. Sam went to answer the door and didn't come back. Husband came back at six. He searched the house then he called the police at seven. We answered the call.'

'You've been here a long time.' Nelson looks at his watch. It's just past nine.

Campion colours slightly, although this isn't meant as a criticism. 'We wanted to get all the facts. At first it seemed like she might come back at any time. But now, I'm not so sure. The husband's in quite a state.'

He must know that he's the prime suspect, thinks Nelson. Aloud he says, 'Thank you. You did the right thing in calling us out. It could be nothing but it never hurts to make sure.'

Benedict Foster-Jones greets them at the door, holding a toddler by the hand. He's probably in his mid-thirties, with thinning sandy hair and rimless spectacles. Benedict certainly does seem genuinely anxious but, Nelson tells himself, that doesn't mean he's not guilty of anything. As a young policeman in Blackpool he worked on a case where a mother reported her daughter missing – tears, emotional press conferences, the lot – only to have her body turn up under the floorboards.

Benedict ushers them into a sitting room that seems to stretch the length of the house, with French windows onto the garden. The room doesn't conform to Nelson's preconceived ideas about Pott Row homes. It's very untidy, for one thing; children's toys cover the floor and there are clothes and books piled up on every surface. And, as PC Norris had said, there seem to be children everywhere. As well as the toddler there's a baby asleep in a Moses basket and two older children are watching television, apparently oblivious to the visitors.

Nelson asks the ages of the children.

'Alfie here is three,' says Benedict Foster-Jones, picking up the toddler. 'Caleb's eight and Evie is seven. Freddie, the baby, is thirty-six weeks. It's way past their bedtimes but everything's in such a state.'

'Do you have anyone who can come and help?' asks

Nelson, stepping over a railway track which snakes its way in and out of a half-eaten sandwich and a banana skin.

'My mum lives in London,' says Benedict. 'She's on her way now. Sam's parents live abroad.'

Typical yuppies, Clough would say. Londoners with no close local ties. But Nelson feels sorry for the man. He's not sure how well he would have coped if he'd come home from work when the girls were little and found them alone in the house with no sign of Michelle. He has a sudden vision of his house this evening, Laura and Michelle sitting on the sofa. 'Why exactly was Dad looking after Ruth's little girl?' But he can't think about that now.

'Can you tell me everything that's happened since you came home from work?' says Nelson. 'I know you'll already have told PC Norris and PC Campion.'

'I got in at six,' says Benedict, running a hand through his hair. He's an anxious-looking man, pleasant enough but somehow colourless. It doesn't surprise Nelson to learn that he's an IT consultant. 'I commute to London. My train gets into Lynn at five twenty-four.'

'Do you drive here?' asks Nelson, thinking that if it took Foster-Jones over half an hour it's unlikely that he's ever attended a speed awareness course.

'No, I cycle.' Nelson doesn't look at Clough who would consider this the final black mark against the man, possibly amounting to proof of guilt. 'I got back at six. I came in and found the children watching television and the baby asleep in his basket. I asked Caleb where Sam was and he said he didn't know.'

'Was he worried?'

'No. He thought she must be in the garden. Sam grows vegetables and she often picks something for supper. Well, I looked in the garden and in the shed, then I went to the neighbours. No one had seen her. I knew she wouldn't go out and leave the kids on their own. She's still breastfeeding Freddie. So I called the police.'

'Have you tried ringing her friends? I know it's very worrying for you, but in cases like this, there's usually a rational solution.'

'That's what the other police officers said. Jane and Chris. But Sam doesn't have that many local friends. I rang a couple of the mothers from her NCT group, a friend from the village. No one knows anything.'

'Is anything missing?' asks Nelson, thinking that it might be impossible to tell in this house. 'Could she have packed a bag? I'm sorry to ask but these things do happen, especially . . .' He stops. He was about to say 'especially to mothers with young children' but he doesn't really have the expertise to offer this opinion. He'll be better off leaving the touchy-feely stuff to the family liaison officers.

'No. Nothing's out of place.' Nelson sees Clough looking around the room in disbelief. A pair of children's pants are hanging from the light fitting.

'Do you know Sam's social media passwords?' asks Nelson. 'It's possible she might have been chatting to someone on Facebook.'

'Sam doesn't go on Facebook much,' says Benedict. 'Her passwords are probably the children's names or something.'

Nelson sighs. This means that they will have to go to the service provider with a production order, requesting that Sam's emails be unlocked.

'What about her phone?' he says. 'Is it still ringing out?'

Benedict stares at him. 'Her phone's here. It was on the table in the kitchen.'

Nelson and Clough exchange glances. If one thing is certain these days it's that when people leave their houses they always, always take their phones with them.

'Is it password protected?' asks Nelson. Michelle's is but she always uses the same password for everything (her maiden name plus the year) so Nelson would have no problem hacking her phone. Not that he ever would, of course.

'No, it's not,' says Benedict.

'Have you had a look at her last messages?'

'Yes. Jane asked me to look,' he adds rather defensively. 'Her last message was to me, asking me to remember to pick up some guitar music for Caleb.'

'Well, keep an eye on her phone,' says Nelson. 'See if anyone tries to contact her. So, when you came into the house, did you notice anything unusual? Anything that struck you as strange?'

'No, not really,' says Benedict. 'Except that it's all strange, if you know what I mean. It feels like a nightmare. Sam would never go out and leave the kids. She won't even let Caleb cycle to school on his own, though he wants to. She's the perfect mother. She's always here for the kids.'

Except that she's not here now, thinks Nelson. He starts to ask more about Sam's state of mind but stops when the room becomes full of unearthly wailing.

The older boy, Caleb, looks round from the television.

'Freddie's crying, Dad.'

'Excuse me,' says Benedict, 'I'll have to feed him.' He scoops up the howling baby and leaves the room.

'He's not going to breastfeed, is he?' says Clough.

'Shh.' Nelson nods towards Caleb, who is staring at them solemnly. He's a handsome boy with blue eyes and blond hair that is (in Nelson's view) just slightly too long.

'Hi,' says Nelson. 'Are you Caleb?'

'Caleb Gabriel Foster-Jones,' says the boy. 'What's your name?'

'Harry Nelson,' says Nelson. 'And this is David Clough.'

'Hi, Caleb,' says Clough. 'Did you make the train track? It's a good one.'

'Evie made it,' says Caleb. 'She likes trains.'

'What do you like?' asks Clough. 'Football?'

'No, I like drama and dance,' says Caleb. He turns back to the television. Nelson decides to leave the conversation there. Tomorrow he'll get Judy to do a proper interview with Caleb Gabriel Foster-Jones.

Benedict comes back into the room with the baby on his shoulder and a bottle of milk in his hand. 'Sam expresses,' he explains to the two policemen who, despite being fathers themselves, both look momentarily blank. 'I don't know what I'd do otherwise.' He inserts the bottle skilfully into the open mouth.

'How was Sam's mood when you left her this morning?' asks Nelson, as Freddie's sobs become snuffles.

'Fine,' says Benedict. 'I mean, mornings are always a bit chaotic because Sam has to get the two eldest to school. I catch an early train so I can't be much help.'

'How was she?' Nelson persists. 'Happy? Sad? Stressed?'

'She seemed happy,' says Benedict. 'We talked about Freddie's naming day which is coming up. Alfie had learnt the alphabet song. We all listened to him singing it.'

In a flash of memory that seems to involve a purple dinosaur, Nelson remembers his daughters singing that song. From the sofa, the older children suddenly start up with the chant. 'A, B, C, D, E, F, G . . .'

Benedict's face crumbles and he sobs into the baby's hair.

On the way back to the station Nelson makes his decision. 'I'm treating Sam Foster-Jones' disappearance as high risk,' he says to Clough. 'I'm going to get reinforcements out.'

'Even though she's only been missing a few hours?'

'Yes. If she has been abducted, the next few hours will be vital.' Mentally, Nelson practises making this argument to Jo Archer.

Reading his mind, Clough says, 'What will Super Jo say?'

'That's my problem,' says Nelson. He thinks that Jo will relish the idea of a high-profile hunt for a missing woman. But, if it goes wrong, or Sam is found safely with a friend or a lover, there's no doubt whose fault it will be.

'What about Johnson?' asks Clough, who has found a chocolate bar somewhere about his person and is eating it. 'Shall I call her in? She's done all the family liaison training.'

'She's looking after Katie tonight,' says Nelson. 'We'll tell her tomorrow. She can interview the little boy too. With an appropriate adult, of course.'

'What did you think of Benedict Foster-Jones?' he asks.

'Bit of a new man,' says Clough. 'Sandals, bicycle, organic food.'

As far as Nelson can remember, Foster-Jones had been wearing trainers. He doesn't know where Clough got the organic food from. Perhaps from the fact that Sam had a vegetable patch.

'He escapes up to London every day and leaves Sam to look after the children though,' he says. 'Must have been a lot to cope with. Four children under eight, no family or close friends nearby.' He thinks back to his daughters' early years when they were still in Blackpool. Michelle's mother had been a constant presence in the house. He doesn't know how they would have coped without her.

'Do you think she's done a runner because she's stressed?' asks Clough. 'Post-natal depression and all that.'

'It's a possibility,' says Nelson. 'But I don't think she would have left the children like that, especially the baby. From the little boy's account, someone knocks on the door, Sam goes to answer it and she's gone. Something funny's going on. I'll get some officers going door-to-door and do a fingertip search of the open ground nearby.'

'Shall we get Tanya in?' says Clough, as they draw up outside the police station. 'She'll be longing to be involved.'

'All right. Give her a call. She can organise the door-to-door. I'll need you to talk to the local officers and arrange the search parties.'

'Don't you want to talk to them?'

'I've got to ring Jo,' says Nelson. As he walks up the steps he wishes, not for the first time, that it was Gerald Whitcliffe at the end of the phone.

Ruth lies in her childhood bed in South London. The shrouded shape of her mother's sewing machine looms in the darkness but, otherwise it is still recognisably her teenage hideaway. The room has been painted a tasteful magnolia and the posters of Bruce Springsteen ('Born in the USA' era) and Che Guevara have been taken down but Ruth's books still fill the white-painted bookcase and she can just make out the silhouettes of her stickers on the wardrobe. She has already searched for something to read and has come up with Georgette Heyer's *The Grand Sophy*. There is a whole shelf of Heyers plus sundry Jilly Coopers and a scattering of hardback classics, probably given as prizes in school. There's also *Tess of the D'Urbervilles*, which she studied for A Level, and several books about the Tudors, who had dominated her history syllabus. Henry VIII grew up near here, at Eltham Palace. As a child she had found it hard to equate Tudor magnificence with seventies suburbia. But now she knows better. Now she knows that history is everywhere.

She thinks of her father across the landing. She hopes he'll be sleeping but she knows that before he got into the high old-fashioned double bed, he will have knelt on the floor and prayed for his wife. Sometimes Ruth wishes that she could pray but the best she can manage is a mantra taught to her by Cathbad: 'Goddess bless, goddess keep.' She says it now, thinking of Kate. Please keep Kate safe, whoever is out there. At least she'll see her tomorrow.

Ruth twists round in the single bed, trying to get a good position for reading. Her bedside light (BHS Anglepoise) is the one she had as a child but maybe her eyes have got weaker. She brought no clothes with her so has had to borrow one of her mother's voluminous nightdresses which keeps tying itself in a knot. Ruth untangles her legs and stares at the ceiling which still has a damp spot shaped like Australia. She imagines Nelson walking in the park with Kate and Bruno. What will Michelle say about the unexpected visitor? She'll be kind, knowing Michelle, but Ruth can't help the occasional fantasy that airbrushes Michelle from the picture completely, that has Ruth and Nelson walking across the summer grass with the child and the dog. She sighs and turns back to *The Grand Sophy*.

CHAPTER 17

Judy is furious not to have been told the night before.

'Why didn't you tell me? I could have come over.'

'I thought you had enough on your plate,' says Nelson, aware that he is on shaky ground. 'With Katie and –'

'The children were in bed,' says Judy, 'and besides, Cathbad was there. Are you saying that because I'm a woman I have to stay at home with my children? Dave's a father. Why didn't you think he had to stay behind and look after Spencer?'

'I said we should have called you,' says Clough smugly.

'There was nothing you could do last night,' says Nelson. 'Today you can take over with the family. We need a proper interview with the boy, Caleb. He's the one who saw his mother last. Also, he might be able to remember something about whoever knocked on the door yesterday evening.'

'And there's been no sign of Sam Foster-Jones since?' says Judy, looking at the witness statements from yesterday.

'No. We've searched their house and garden pretty thoroughly. We're draining the septic tank now.'

'Do you think the husband could have killed her then?'

'The husband's always the first suspect, you know that. But from his demeanour last night, I don't think he did it. He seemed genuinely upset and rattled. If we can find witnesses who saw him on the train last night, that should put him in the clear. His train got in at five twenty-four, he got home at six.'

He waits for Clough to say something about the bicycle.

'He could still have killed her and hidden the body somewhere,' says Judy.

'That's true. I've got teams searching open ground nearby and we've got officers going door-to-door.'

When he had rung Jo Archer last night, she had reluctantly agreed to the deployment of manpower. Nelson guessed that she had been torn between not wanting to waste public money and the fear of being found wanting if Sam Foster-Jones's disappearance did turn out to be suspicious. Either way, he is sure it will end up being his fault.

'Did any of the neighbours see anything?' asks Judy.

'No,' says Nelson. 'The houses are quite spread out on that road. There are hedges and trees between them. It would have been possible for Sam to have got into a car and driven away without anyone being any the wiser. It's not like a suburban street where everyone knows what's going on.'

'What about the back way?' says Judy, looking at a map of Pott Row that has been hastily pinned to the incident room wall. 'If she did go into the garden, it looks like there's a path running along the backs of the houses.'

'We've looked along that path,' says Nelson. 'Nothing. It

leads back to the main road. We're searching the neighbouring gardens now.'

'The neighbours were not amused.' Clough attempts a posh accent. 'Worried that we might tread on their precious asparagus beds.' Clough has obviously decided that the area is exclusively populated by organic gardeners.

'Cathbad grows asparagus,' says Judy. 'Samphire too. I've been thinking, is there anything to link this to Barbara Murray's disappearance?'

'I've thought of that too,' says Nelson, 'but it's hard to see what the two women could have had in common. One is a rough sleeper, the other's a middle-class woman with a home and family.'

'I can think of one thing,' says Judy.

'What?'

'They're both mothers of four.'

Nelson and Clough look at each other. Nelson has genuinely not made this connection. He knew that Barbara Murray had two children in care and had had others adopted but he had never thought of her as a 'mother of four' with all the wholesome connotations that phrase carries.

'How could that be relevant?' he says.

'I don't know,' says Judy, 'but you asked if they had anything in common.'

'Could the oldest two be Barbara's kids?' says Clough in a moment of inspiration. 'They were adopted, weren't they?'

'No,' says Judy, looking through her notes. 'Barbara's older children were adopted but the youngest two are in long-term foster care. We've had their files from the local authority. Tommy and Lexy Murray, aged fourteen and twelve.'

'Why weren't they adopted like the older kids?' asks Clough.

'I think social workers hoped that Barbara might be well enough to take care of them again. She was a loving mother by all accounts, it was just that her mental health was poor.'

'Well, we'll have to dig more,' says Nelson, 'see if we can find another link. Will you get over to see them this morning, Johnson? I'm pretty sure that the kids won't be at school.'

'OK, boss,' says Judy, who seems to have recovered her good humour. In fact, there is a sense that they are all relieved to be working on a tangible case, one with real clues and possible lines of enquiry. This feeling of purpose is ruined when Tanya bounces into the room to say that Jo has asked her to lead a press conference later that morning.

Nelson was right. The children are not at school. Judy, coming into the house in Pott Row, finds Marianne Foster, Benedict's mother, trying to interest the three older children in a game of snakes and ladders while Benedict juggles the fretful baby in the kitchen.

'He won't settle,' Benedict told Judy, 'and I've almost run out of expressed milk.'

Judy, at least, understands the importance of this. 'Have you tried him with formula yet?'

'No, but I'm going to have to.'

'Try wearing one of Sam's tops when you give him the

bottle,' suggests Judy. 'I did that when I was trying to wean my daughter. If my partner wore my jumper, she'd take the bottle from him.' Cathbad, she remembers, had rather enjoyed taking over the maternal role. But then he always did like dressing up.

Benedict's face twitches at the mention of his wife. 'I suppose there's no news,' he says.

'I'm afraid not,' says Judy, 'but we're working flat out. I'm sure we'll have some news soon.' She doesn't say what sort.

'I rang her parents in America last night,' says Benedict. 'They said Sam hadn't been in contact since she Skyped last week. I tried her brother too. He lives in the south of France. He hasn't heard from her in weeks.'

Sam's family sound rather jet-set and glamorous, thinks Judy. She wonders what they make of Sam's decision to settle in a Norfolk village and surround herself with children.

'I'd like to interview Caleb if possible,' she says. 'You can be present too.'

'Why do you want to talk to him? He's told you everything he knows. It's just . . . he's a sensitive boy.'

'I'll take it very gently,' says Judy. 'It's just that witnesses often remember more than they thought they did at the time. I'd like to know more about the person who knocked on the door at five-thirty last night.'

'Caleb didn't see them.'

'But he might have recognised the voice. I know he said he didn't, but in a structured interview I might get him to remember more.'

'Does he have to go to the police station?'

'Oh no. We can do an initial interview here. It's better if it's somewhere where he's comfortable. Can you get him to come in? I'll hold the baby,' she says, as Benedict dithers.

Benedict goes out of the room, leaving Judy to look round the kitchen. 'A tip,' Clough had said but Judy can see that some order exists beneath the chaos. The units are expensive for one thing, solid wood with brass handles, and there's a large Smeg fridge even though it is almost invisible under stickers and photos and lower case letters spelling out phonetic sounds like 'pshhtz'. Going closer, jiggling the baby against her shoulder, Judy sees three star charts for the three older children, attached to the fridge by magnetic Disney characters. 'Helping in garden'. 'Tidying room'. There are clearly rules here too, even though it isn't immediately apparent. And the kitchen might be heroically untidy, clothes and toys and muddy vegetables fighting for space on all the surfaces, but Judy thinks that it is probably pretty clean underneath. Has she got time to look in the fridge?

No, she hasn't. Benedict comes into the room with the oldest son.

'This is Caleb,' he says. 'Oh good, you've almost got Freddie to sleep.'

Judy hands over the baby. 'Hallo, Caleb,' she says, 'I'm Judy. I'd just like to ask you a few questions about yesterday. Is that OK?'

'Yes,' says Caleb. He seems quite composed. He doesn't look like his father, thinks Judy. Nor does he resemble his mother, whose photo now adorns the incident room wall. Sam Foster-Jones is attractive, with short, blonde hair and a ready smile but Caleb, with his clear blue eyes and wavy locks, looks like a Renaissance angel.

'Is it all right if I tape it?' says Judy to Benedict. 'I'll let you have a copy. It's just easier than taking notes.'

'That's fine,' says Benedict. He seems preoccupied by the baby, who is almost asleep, eyelids fluttering.

'Witness statement from Caleb Foster-Jones aged eight,' says Judy into her phone. 'Investigating Officer DS Judy Johnson. Also present is Mr Benedict Foster-Jones acting as appropriate adult for Caleb Foster-Jones.'

She smiles at Caleb who stares solemnly back.

'Caleb, can you tell me what happened yesterday after you got back from school? Did Mum collect you from school?'

'Yes,' says Caleb. 'She collected me and Evie. I'm in juniors so I come out of a different door. We had to go back because Evie forgot her recorder.'

'What about Alfie and Freddie?'

'They came too. Freddie was in his buggy. Mum bought us ice lollies at the corner shop for a treat. Alfie dropped his and he cried. Then we walked home. Evie and me went to feed our rabbits. Mine's called Bilbo Baggins.'

This gives Judy a slight shock. Of course, it's quite normal for a bright eight-year-old to like *The Hobbit*. Caleb is not to know that Bilbo was the name of a man who was recently brutally murdered.

'That's a great name,' she says. 'What's Evie's called?'

'Bunny,' says Caleb with withering scorn.

'What did you do next?' asks Judy. 'Did you have tea?'

'Yes. We had pasta and tuna. Alfie didn't like his but Mum wouldn't let him have a yoghurt until he'd eaten some. Mum fed Freddie then he went to sleep. Then Evie and Alfie went to play and I worked on my project.' This was said with tremendous importance.

'What's your project on?'

'Insects,' says Caleb. 'I'm fascinated by insects.'

'Me too,' lies Judy. 'Where were you working?'

'Here,' says Caleb and he points at a book half-hidden by a pile of newspapers on the table. Judy can just make out a meticulous drawing of an ant.

'Were you in here when someone knocked on the door?' says Judy. The kitchen is at the back of the house but the front door is visible if you're sitting in the right place. 'Where was Mum?'

'She was here, cooking supper for her and Dad. Freddie was here too, asleep in his basket. Mum and me were talking. Having a conversation,' he explains, clearly proud of the fact. 'Then someone knocked at the door. Mum said it was probably someone with horse poo.'

'Someone with what?'

'Manure,' Benedict cuts in. 'For the garden. Sam was waiting for a delivery.' He has been listening silently to Caleb, Freddie asleep in his arms, an expression of pure misery on his face.

'So Mum went out. Did you hear voices?'

'Yes.'

'Mum's voice or someone else's?'

'Mum and I think someone else.'

'Was the other person a man or a woman?'

'I don't know.' For the first time, Caleb falters. 'I'm not sure.'

'Did you recognise the voice?'

'I don't know.'

'You're doing really well, Caleb. What happened next?'

'I heard the door shut and I thought Mum had gone round to the garden with the poo man. I went on with my project. I was drawing a really difficult cross-section.'

'Do you remember what the time was?'

'It was after five because Mum was listening to the news on the radio. You know,' he puts on a deep radio announcer voice, 'five o'clock, p.m.'

So Sam was another Radio 4 listener, like Ruth. Judy can't see the attraction herself.

'Do you remember what was on the news when Mum went to the door?'

'Something about the Queen.'

That's useful. They can check the PM podcast and see when the item about the Queen was aired.

'That's great, Caleb,' says Judy. 'Do you remember what happened next?'

'Evie came in saying that Alfie had broken her train track. I told her to find Mum but I don't think she did. Evie went to watch television so I went too. We're allowed to watch for an hour a day,' he adds, rather defensively.

'What did you watch?'

'*Peppa Pig*. For Alfie. Then Dad came home. He asked

where Mum was and I said in the garden. He went out but then he came back and he was all . . .'

'All what?'

'All upset,' says Caleb with a glance at his father. He looks upset too, tears shimmering in the big blue eyes. Recalling yesterday's events has probably reminded him all over again that his mother isn't there.

'One last thing,' says Judy. 'It's a kind of game. I'm going to say two things and you choose one really quickly, without thinking. Ready?'

'Yes.'

'Blue or red?'

'Blue.'

'Cat or dog?'

'Dog.'

'Jelly or ice cream?'

'Ice cream.'

'Man or woman at the door?'

'Man.'

Benedict makes a slight exclamation. 'Is that right, Caleb? Was it a man?'

Caleb looks troubled. 'I think so.'

'I think we'll end the interview there,' says Judy. 'Thank you very much, Caleb. You've been a star.'

'Why did you ask him those questions?' asks Benedict. 'Was it a way of getting him to remember?'

'Yes,' says Judy. 'It's a questioning technique that's meant to raise buried memories but we shouldn't treat it as gospel. There's a danger of response bias, for one thing, always choosing the first option. But Caleb didn't do that. Also Caleb did say that he thought Sam had gone into the garden with the poo *man*.'

Caleb hasn't left the room. He stands quite still looking at Judy.

'Caleb, go and play with Grandma,' says Benedict. 'You've done really well and I'm proud of you.'

But Caleb doesn't move. He looks Judy straight in the eye and says, 'Will you find Mummy?'

The 'Mummy' is particularly heartbreaking. It reminds Judy of Michael.

'We will,' she says, though she knows you should only tell the truth to children. 'We will.'

The ward seems even more cheerful in the morning. Several of the patients are out of bed, physiotherapists are working with two women who are walking the length of the ward with the help of Zimmer frames. When the women pass each other they offer terse words of encouragement: 'Looking good, Mary.' 'Keep at it, Nora.'

'They've been going up and down all morning,' says Jean, half in admiration, half in irritation.

'Have you been out of bed, Mum?' asks Ruth.

'I've been to the loo,' says Jean. 'They were pleased with that.'

'Well done,' says Ruth, knowing that this is an important step. She remembers having to praise Kate for similar feats. It's awful the way your parents become like your children. That morning she had had to restrain herself from cutting her father's toast into soldiers. Her mother does look much better, though. Her voice is still occasionally slurred and her face slightly out of alignment but she clearly does not feel confused or disorientated, as the doctor had warned she might be. Ruth, who has never known her mother confused about anything, is pleased that Jean's omnipotence is still in working order. She has already made Ruth take her tea back because it isn't strong enough.

'Are you going back to Norfolk now?' Jean asks.

'In a little while,' says Ruth. 'I want to be in time to collect Kate from school.' She has persuaded her father to come in later with Simon. In a strange way, she is quite enjoying this time alone with her mother. She can't remember the last time she had her undivided attention, even if the conversation has mostly involved tea and bowel movements.

'Kate's in a play,' she says now. 'It's a proper professional drama club – well, semi-professional anyway. She's playing Alice in *Alice's Adventures Under Ground*, based on *Alice in Wonderland*. She loves acting. I don't know where she gets it from.'

'From me, of course,' says Jean, taking a sip of the new, improved tea.

'Really?'

'Oh yes,' says Jean. 'I loved acting when I was a girl. In fact, I wanted to be an actress for a while but my father wouldn't hear of it. He wanted me to have a proper job in an office.'

Ruth stares at her mother. She had no idea that Jean had ever had theatrical ambitions or that her grandfather, whom she remembers as a mild old man with shaky hands, had thwarted them. She has often wondered whether Kate is more like her or Nelson but it suddenly occurs to her that in character, Kate is actually very like her mother.

'You'll have to come and watch Kate in her play,' she says. She has no idea if her mother will be well enough but she hopes it will give her something to aim for.

'I'd like that,' says her mother. 'Can you ask the canteen for some biscuits? Proper ones. Digestives.'

Judy has a brief chat with Marianne Foster before she leaves. Benedict Foster-Jones's mother is an elegant woman in white jeans and a pale pink shirt. Judy doesn't imagine that her days usually involve squatting on a food-encrusted floor playing giant snakes and ladders. But she seems fond of her grandchildren: Alfie is sitting on her lap twirling a strand of her expensively streaked hair and Evie is leaning against her, obviously in the middle of a long story. Only Caleb, staring at the board, seems intent on strategy. Judy squats down next to Marianne; the children, with one accord, move away.

'How long are you staying?' Judy asks Marianne.

'As long as Ben needs me,' says Marianne. 'I just hope . . .' She glances at her grandchildren, who are now arguing over whose turn it is to roll the dice.

'We're doing all we can,' says Judy. 'I'm sure we'll have news soon.'

'I saw the press conference on television earlier,' says Marianne. 'The policewoman said that it was a major missing person inquiry.'

Typical Tanya, thinks Judy. She always has to exaggerate everything. She can imagine Tanya and Jo making the announcement with identical expressions of slightly gleeful concern.

'That just means that we're putting a lot of manpower into the search,' says Judy. 'It's a positive thing.'

'They were searching the garden this morning,' says Marianne. 'You don't think she's . . .'

'We have to search the surroundings,' says Judy, 'but it's more than likely that Sam has just gone to stay with a friend. Maybe she wanted some space.'

'It is a lot for her,' says Marianne, looking at the squabbling children. 'Ben works hard but he's out most of the day. The two eldest are at school but Sam's on her own with Alfie and the baby. Alfie's only at nursery a couple of days a week.'

'Does she go to any mothers' groups?' asks Judy. 'Ben mentioned a friend from NCT, I think.'

'She goes to a group at a church in King's Lynn,' says Marianne. 'Sam isn't religious but she says that the woman who runs it is nice.'

'Which church is that?' asks Judy.

'St Matthew's,' says Marianne. 'They do a lot of good, Sam says. They even have a drop-in centre for the homeless.'

CHAPTER 18

Ruth is back in Norfolk in good time to collect Kate. In fact, she's the first at the school gates. Usually there's a clique of mothers who arrive early and set up a kind of picnic area on the grass with pushchairs arranged in a circle like wagons on the prairie. But today Ruth is on her own. She sits on the bench at the end of the playground (the friendship bench, Kate tells her it's called) and checks her messages. There's one from Simon saying that he's with Jean and that the doctors say she's making good progress. *Mum v cranky*, says Simon. *Gd sign i think*. Ruth smiles, thinking that cranky is a word that her parents might use. Argumentative would be a better description but maybe Simon couldn't be bothered to type it. There are two other messages, one from Ros at the lab saying that they have the DNA results on the bones and one from Quentin Swan asking if they can meet to talk about the bones. Quentin Swan is obviously still fretting about his underground restaurant. Starting to type a response, Ruth thinks of Martin Kellerman and the Parisian underground dwellers. She hasn't heard from him since their lunch last week. She texts Quentin saying that she has some news and can see him at the university tomorrow. She's not trekking all the way out to Norwich. Then she rings Ros.

'Hi, Ruth. We managed to get some DNA from your bones. I'll be sending you the results but I thought you'd like to know the headlines.'

'Yes please.'

'It's a man, probably red-headed.'

'Really?' Ruth knows that red hair is a mutated gene which can show up in DNA sampling. She thinks of her glamorous red-haired friend Shona. It's not significant as such but red hair probably rules out some ethnicities and might make others, Celtic for instance, more likely.

'Thanks, Ros.' They chat for a few minutes before saying goodbye. The mother cavalcade appears and sets up camp at the opposite side of the playground to Ruth. Other parents and carers are gathering outside the doors. A couple of people wave to Ruth but no one comes to join her. She doesn't really care. It's very pleasant sitting on the friendship bench in the sun, knowing that she's about to see Kate in a few minutes. Her phone pings. It's Quentin Swan. *Can u come to my office? I'd like to show u the restaurant plans.* Bloody cheek. Does Swan think that she's got nothing better to do than look at his plans for underground dining experiences? Her finger hovers over 'delete'.

'Hi, Ruthie.' Ruth looks up. It's Cathbad with Miranda in her pushchair. She's so pleased to see him that she even forgives him for calling her Ruthie.

'Cathbad! Thanks so much for looking after Kate last night.'

'It was a pleasure. They were up at six this morning playing. Having a great time.'

'Oh . . . I'm sorry.'

'It was fine. I always get up early, as you know.' He hands Ruth a carrier bag. 'Here's her school sweatshirt from yesterday. Judy found her one of Michael's to wear today. How's your mum?'

'Incredible. Yesterday she was in a coma. Today she was sending back the tea because it wasn't strong enough.'

'I prayed to the healing spirits,' says Cathbad, as if this settles matters. 'It wasn't her time.'

'No.'

'Hecate really enjoyed her afternoon with Nelson too. His daughter was there, Laura, and she seems to have made a big impression.'

Ruth looks at Cathbad. He has his blandest expression on but she knows that he is getting at something. And it irritates her when he calls Kate Hecate. Why can't anyone get her name right? Also, it is rather galling to see how many of the other parents come over to Cathbad to say hallo and comment on Miranda's growth. Unlike her, Cathbad has clearly conquered the school gate. Mind you, they've never seen him wearing his cloak.

'I think Kate was more interested in Bruno,' she says. 'Where's Thing?'

'At home. You can't bring dogs into the playground. Health and safety.'

Ruth is about to speak (when has *Cathbad* cared about health and safety?) but at that moment the doors open and she can see the Year One teacher, Mrs Shaw, with Kate standing at the front of the queue behind her.

'It's a link,' says Judy. 'It's a definite link between the drop-in centre and Sam's disappearance.'

'And a link to Eddie and Bilbo,' says Nelson.

'And Barbara,' says Judy. 'Remember I thought that the link between Sam and Barbara was the children?'

'You didn't exactly say that,' says Clough. 'You just said that they both had four children.'

Judy shoots him a look. 'The point is that we were looking for something to link the two cases and now we've got it. Meg Pritchard knew Barbara too. She spoke to her at the centre one day.'

'It's a lead,' says Nelson. 'Good work, Judy. You go to the centre tomorrow and interview Pritchard and his wife. She runs the mother and baby group, doesn't she? Take Cloughie with you. It won't hurt to put the frighteners on them a bit.'

'I'm not frightening,' says Clough.

'He means me,' says Judy.

'What about me?' asks Tanya. She looks a little put out. She was on a high after her press conference and now Judy looks as if she is stealing the limelight.

'We'll need you with the family,' says Nelson. 'Especially if there's no news. What did you think of the husband, Johnson?'

'He was pleasant enough,' says Judy. 'Nice with the kids, I thought. I can't see him killing his wife.'

'And we've got witnesses who saw him on the train,' says Tanya.

'He could have come home and killed her,' says Clough. 'All we know is that the children didn't see her after half five. She could have gone into the garden, like the little boy said. Husband comes home, they argue, he kills her. She's probably buried under the compost heap.'

Clough seems determined to blame the garden, thinks Nelson. But nevertheless, he has a point. 'We've searched the garden,' he says, 'including the compost heap. But Cloughie's right. We shouldn't rule the husband out but we'd better go softly on him at first. Fuller, you see what you can get out of him tomorrow. What about the mysterious man at the door?'

'Could have been Benedict Foster-Jones,' says Clough.

'Caleb would have recognised his father's voice,' says Judy.

'Maybe not,' says Clough, more for form's sake than anything.

'We'd better check out this manure delivery man,' says Nelson. 'Sam could have been overpowered and bundled into his van.'

'Why?' says Judy. 'It sounds as if the poo man was a regular caller.'

'Bloody hell,' says Clough. 'How the other half lives.'

'Let's check him out all the same,' says Nelson. 'We'll do another TV appeal tomorrow too. If a stranger did knock at the door, someone must have seen something. Is there any CCTV around? Some of those big houses might have it.'

'I'll check the door-to-door reports,' says Tanya. 'But I don't remember seeing any CCTV.'

'You're going on the soup run tomorrow night, aren't you, Johnson?' says Nelson. 'Keep your ears open for any mention of Barbara or Sam.'

'Yes,' says Judy, 'and it's Eddie's funeral on Thursday. I think we should all try to be there. It doesn't look like there'll be anyone else.' She stares at her colleagues.

'I'll be there,' says Nelson. 'Poor old Eddie. It seems wrong that no one's come forward for him.'

'We still don't even know Bilbo's real name,' says Judy. 'And that's another thing: Caleb Foster-Jones has a rabbit called Bilbo Baggins.'

'That probably just means he's seen the film,' says Nelson. '*The Lord of the Rings.*'

'It's a book,' says Judy. 'Three books. And the first book, *The Hobbit*, is the one about Bilbo Baggins. The Foster-Joneses do seem like a family who read books but it *could* mean that they knew Bilbo – our Bilbo. We should show them a picture at least.'

'Yes,' says Nelson, 'you ask them tomorrow, Fuller. Right, that's probably enough for today. We've got an early . . .' He stops because Tom Henty is standing in the door.

'Sorry to interrupt, DCI Nelson, but there's a girl . . . a young woman . . . downstairs asking for you.'

For one moment Nelson thinks it's Laura, come to confront him about Kate. He croaks, 'A girl?'

'I think it's the same girl who came to see you last week,' says Tom. 'Her name's Grace.'

Grace Miller greets him apologetically. 'Sorry to interrupt you again. It's just . . .'

'Don't apologise,' says Nelson. 'Just tell me what's on your mind.'

Grace looks just as cheerleader fresh as she did last week. She's wearing a summer dress and her long blonde hair is loose. She seems to bring light and colour into the bland interview suite, a promise that life isn't all dead men and missing women, that somewhere people are sitting on the grass enjoying the sunshine. But her face is troubled and she starts apologising all over again.

'I'm sorry . . . It might be nothing. It's just . . . it seemed so odd . . .'

Nelson waits.

'You know last week, when we were in the car and we saw the man, the Jesus man?'

'I remember.'

'Well, I was in my tutor's office at uni waiting for a tutorial to start. He had some papers on his desk. I wasn't snooping. I just glanced at them. And I saw a photograph of him. The Jesus man.'

'A photo?'

'Yes. It was with a pile of other photos but it was the top one.'

'And you're sure it was the same man that you saw that night? I mean, it was dark and you were . . .'

'We were a bit high,' says Grace. 'But I'm pretty sure it was him. I've been thinking about him a lot and he has this really distinctive face.'

'Can you describe him to me?' Nelson is thinking that he would have a hard job describing this 'really distinctive face' in an interview.

'Oh, I took a photo on my phone,' says Grace brightly.

The ability of the public to take instant photographs is both a help and a hindrance to the police. Nelson has had plenty of suspects shoving phones into his face and often wishes that he could do some shoving of his own. In this case, though, it's distinctly useful. He takes the phone from Grace. The screen shows a bearded man, arms outstretched, wearing a long black coat that looks like a cloak. Again, Nelson is reminded of Cathbad.

'Can you send it to my phone?' he says, giving her the number of his police-issue BlackBerry.

'Sure.' Grace's thumbs twinkle over the screen. Nelson has to use his forefinger and, increasingly these days, hold the gadget at arm's length.

'What's your tutor's name?' he asks as his phone pings to say 'message received'.

'Kevin O'Casey. He's the senior lecturer in Sociology. He's really clever, he's written lots of books.'

'I'll pay him a visit,' says Nelson.

'I'm not getting him into trouble, am I?' says Grace. 'It's just, it seemed so weird, so much of a coincidence.'

'Don't worry,' says Nelson. 'I'll just pay him a friendly

visit. One of my forensics experts works at the university so it won't seem odd that I'm there.'

'Oh, Dr Ruth Galloway,' says Grace. 'Everyone knows about her. She's cool. She's been on TV.'

Judy gets home in time to make tea for Michael and Miranda. It's a warm evening and they play out in the garden before bedtime. Cathbad is watering his vegetable patch and before long this turns into a water fight with both adults and children drenched to the skin. Thing runs around excitedly, trying to catch water droplets in crocodile jaws. Cathbad gives the kids their bath but, rather to Judy's surprise, Michael requests her for the bedtime story. She doesn't have Cathbad's gift for invention so she searches Michael's bookshelf and comes up with a handsome illustrated edition of *The Hobbit*. On the flyleaf is written, 'To Michael on his baptism with love from Ruth.' She had almost forgotten that she and Darren had a formal baptism for Michael, with a font and godparents and all the rest of it. There had been tea and sandwiches in the church hall afterwards. The boss had been there with Michelle. They had given Michael a silver goblet. She remembers Ruth confessing that she felt intimidated by traditional baptism presents ('Napkin rings? What is it with napkin rings?') so had opted for a book instead. Miranda didn't have a christening, she had a naming ceremony instead. She remembers Ruth's naming ceremony for Kate, five years earlier. It was the first time that she had really noticed Cathbad.

Glancing at Michael, so sweet and cosy-looking in his

Spiderman pyjamas, Judy spares a thought for the Foster-Jones family. Who will be putting them to bed and reading them a story? She's sure that Benedict and his mother will do their best but the children will know something is wrong. She imagines Caleb refusing a story and reading to himself, a book about insects perhaps, furiously private, unable to admit how much he misses his mother.

She opens the book. 'In a hole in the ground,' she reads, 'there lived a hobbit.'

CHAPTER 19

Judy and Clough are at the drop-in centre just as Paul Pritchard is opening the doors at nine. There is already a small queue outside. Men (all men, Judy notes) carrying bin-liners and sleeping bags and rucksacks. They wait in a diffident way, almost as if they are trying to be invisible, standing in doorways or merging into the shadows of the church porch. When Paul opens the doors though, they surge forward, shouldering their belongings as they go. Paul greets them almost all by name. 'Hi, Bob. Good to see you, Mac. How's it going, Barry?' Are they real names, Judy thinks, or *noms de guerre*? Paul steps back when he sees Judy. 'Hallo, Judy. Have you got some news about Babs?'

'I'm afraid not,' says Judy. 'This is DS Clough. Could we ask you a couple of questions?'

'Of course.' Paul gives them a curious look but leads them upstairs. 'Take a seat,' he says. 'I'll just get breakfast going.'

At the hatch Anya, the young woman who was there the first time Judy visited, is taking the covers off trays of scrambled egg and bacon. The tea urn is hissing and Judy can hear the water running in the showers. A man comes and sits at a table nearby with a plate full of breakfast. Judy looks at Clough. 'No, you can't,' she says. 'It's for the clients.'

'Shame,' says Clough. 'I like a proper breakfast. They've even got fried bread.'

When Paul comes to join them he immediately offers food and drink.

'We're fine,' says Judy firmly.

'So to what do we owe the honour?' Paul sits on the sofa opposite. He has a half-eaten bacon roll in one hand. Clough stares at it hungrily.

'Have you ever seen this woman?' Judy produces a photograph of Sam Foster-Jones, obviously taken in her beloved garden. Sam is smiling in jeans and mud-covered wellingtons. The shed is behind her.

Paul takes the photograph to have a better look. 'No . . . I don't think so . . . Hang on, she's the missing woman, isn't she? I saw her on the news.'

'That's right,' says Judy. 'We believe that she used to come to the mother and baby group downstairs. Is it running today?'

'Yes,' says Paul, 'but it doesn't start until midday.'

'We'd like to have a quick word with your wife,' says Judy. 'Can you give us your address?'

Paul blinks at them. 'Why do you want to talk to Meg?'

'We have information that links the disappearance of Sam Foster-Jones with that of Barbara Murray,' says Clough.

'What information?'

'We're not at liberty to say.'

'But you can't think that Meg has anything to do with it?'

'We just want to ask her a couple of questions,' says Judy soothingly. She thinks it is interesting how quickly Paul's bluff façade has begun to crack. He seems nervous and unsettled. He puts the uneaten roll on the table and looks distractedly around the room. Judy supposes that with his past it's natural to be wary of the police, but even so this seems an extreme reaction to a request for an interview.

'If we could have the address?' she says.

'Yes.' Paul hunts in his pockets, presumably for something to write on. Judy hands him a pen and tears out a page from her notebook.

'It's just round the corner,' says Paul as he writes. 'One of the converted almshouses. It's funny, isn't it,' he adds, with sudden bitterness. 'There's been so much press coverage over this woman's disappearance and nothing at all about Babs.'

'We're still investigating both,' says Judy, though she can't really compare the two inquiries. Police from three forces have been called in to look for Sam Foster-Jones while the search for Barbara Murray has been limited to Judy wandering around asking people questions.

'Have you found out any more about Bilbo?' he asks as they leave.

'No,' says Judy. 'We put an appeal in the paper but nobody came forward. I'm going to ask at the soup run tonight.'

'I'll see you there then,' says Paul, with a flash of his old evangelical smile. 'It's a joyous occasion. Will you be joining us, DS Clough?'

'No,' says Clough. 'I can't face too much excitement on a week night.'

Ruth has arranged to meet Quentin Swan at nine-thirty. She normally drops Kate at school at eight forty-five and is at the university just after nine. It's a good time to work because most of her colleagues don't turn up until ten at the earliest. There are no queues for the coffee machine and she even has the photocopier to herself. To his credit, Swan doesn't protest at driving from Norwich through the morning traffic and he doesn't repeat his request that they should meet at his office.

At exactly half past nine she gets a call to say that she has a visitor in reception. She walks over to the main building to meet him. It's another warm, sunny day, making Ruth look forward to the holidays. Maybe they'll have a hot summer this year. As usual she hasn't got round to booking anything, but if the weather's good there's nothing better than the beaches in Norfolk. She skirts the ornamental lake – looking quite ornamental today – and takes a shortcut across the car park. How can university staff afford all these big cars? BMWs, Range Rovers, Mercedes . . . She stops. That's not just any beat-up white Mercedes – it belongs to Nelson (she's ashamed to say that she recognises the number plate). What's he doing at the university? She feels shaken and oddly hurt. Why would Nelson visit UNN if not to see her?

Quentin Swan is looking at his phone but he puts it away as soon as Ruth comes towards him. She's struck again that he's quite attractive, in a dark, intense kind of way. He gives her a wide, white-toothed smile.

'Dr Galloway. Good of you to make time to see me.'

'Thank you for coming all this way,' says Ruth. She approves of him using her title. She doesn't like it when people she doesn't know assume that they are on first-name terms.

'It's quite a walk to my office, I'm afraid,' she continues, leading the way out of the main doors.

'That's no hardship on a day like this,' says Quentin. 'We don't usually get this weather in June.'

'Norfolk's one of the sunniest places in the country,' says Ruth. 'That's what they tell you, anyway. It doesn't feel like that sometimes.'

They talk about Norfolk and the weather as they walk to the Natural Sciences building. Swan has only lived in Norfolk for a few years but he says that he loves it 'like a convert'. Ruth feels that way too and she warms towards the architect.

In her office, Quentin Swan gets down to business right away. 'I was just wondering if you could tell me any more about the bones you discovered last week,' he says. 'It's just that I'm very anxious to get on with this development.'

Ruth takes out her file. Inside are the photographs she took in the tunnel, plus the carbon-14 results and the DNA graphs (which arrived this morning).

Quentin looks at the photographs. Illuminated by the camera's flash the bones have a ghostly white sheen. 'These must have been in the tunnel for hundreds of years,' he says.

'I'm afraid the carbon-14 tests suggest that the bones are quite modern,' says Ruth.

Quentin stares at her. 'But I thought that they must be medieval. That tunnel is below the undercroft – no one can have been down there for years. I've got some old maps which show all the tunnels.'

'It is a bit of a mystery,' says Ruth. 'I'm hoping to do an excavation to see if there are any other bones down there. This wasn't a whole skeleton, as you know.'

'That tunnel leads to St John's,' says Quentin. 'Maybe the bones were from an old tomb or something?'

'No one's been buried inside the church for over a hundred years,' says Ruth. 'I checked the parish records. The graveyard's full too. These days you can only be cremated and your remains put in the Garden of Ashes.'

She thinks that this garden has a distinctly sinister sound but Quentin doesn't seem to notice. 'You said you had some news,' he says. 'Did you find out anything else?'

Ruth hesitates. She doesn't want to share her ideas about the cuts marks and the pot polish but she can't see any harm in giving a few details.

'We managed to extract some DNA,' she says, 'which shows that the bones were from a male skeleton. Isotope tests show that he lived in this area, at least for about the last ten years of his life.'

'It's amazing the things you can discover,' says Quentin, still looking at the photographs. 'Do you think that this will delay my building work? Do the police want to investigate?'

'Well, the fact that the bones are relatively modern means

that the police have to be involved,' says Ruth. 'I've asked if I can do an excavation. I'm waiting to hear about that now. But if we don't find anything I suppose there's nothing to stop the work going ahead.'

'Can you tell me when the excavation is happening?' says Quentin. 'I'd like to come if possible.'

'All right,' says Ruth. 'I warn you these things aren't very exciting though.'

After a few minutes more of desultory chat Quentin gets up to go. Ruth feels rather guilty that she has dragged him all the way to UNN just to hear rather inconclusive news.

'Oh, that's OK,' he replies when she says something of the sort. 'I know the way. In fact, my wife works here.'

'Really?' That answers the question about Quentin's sexuality anyway.

'Yes. Vicky Swan in Sociology.'

Hadn't someone mentioned a Vicky in the Sociology department to her recently? She racks her brains.

'Her ex works here too,' says Quentin with a slight grimace. 'Martin Kellerman in Geology. Do you know him?'

'Slightly,' says Ruth.

'Take my advice,' says Quentin, 'and steer well clear. He's a very strange bloke.'

Nelson was rather surprised, turning up at nine, to find that Kevin O'Casey wasn't at his desk. 'I'll wait,' he announced grimly to the receptionist. At nine-twenty a figure appears, obviously summoned by an urgent message.

'I'm Kevin O'Casey. Did you want to see me?'

O'Casey is a plump, bespectacled figure, smiling rather nervously. He conforms exactly to Nelson's idea of a university professor (the male version, that is – Ruth has succeeded in making him change his mind about the women) so he is surprised at the strength of the handshake and the shrewdness of the eyes behind the glasses.

'Nothing official,' says Nelson. 'I just wanted to ask you a few questions.'

'You'd better come to my office,' says O'Casey. They walk across the car park, past a rather dirty-looking lake, through some fire doors propped open by an extinguisher, up several staircases and along endless corridors. Nelson is beginning to wonder if he'll ever find his way back when O'Casey stops at a door labelled, 'Professor Kevin O'Casey, Sociology'.

'Here we are.' He is out of breath and even Nelson is panting slightly. If O'Casey does this trek every day it's surprising that he's so overweight.

O'Casey sits behind his desk and leaves Nelson to take one of the inferior chairs scattered around the room. Looking out of the window he can see the lake and another building. He wonders how near he is to Ruth's office. Her view was similar, he thinks.

'Sorry to come unannounced,' he says now to O'Casey. 'I just wondered if you recognised this man.' He hands his BlackBerry across the desk.

O'Casey picks up the phone and peers at it. Then he pushes his glasses on top of his head and peers some more.

'Yes,' he says at last, 'I think . . .' He opens a drawer and pulls out a file. 'Yes, here it is. Is this the same man?'

It clearly is. This is obviously the photograph that Grace Miller saw. The distinctive face is much more noticeable on a larger scale: dark eyebrows, prominent nose, eyes that seem compelling even at this remove. Grace had called him the Jesus man, but to Nelson the figure looks more like an Old Testament prophet about to deliver some particularly nasty news.

'He's a man called Charlie,' says O'Casey, 'a rough sleeper. I interviewed him for a project I'm doing. He's an interesting man, highly intelligent, used to be a teacher.'

'What was the project?' asks Nelson. The name Charlie is troubling him. Where has he heard this name recently?

'I'm writing a book about underground societies,' says O'Casey. 'I interviewed Charlie as part of my research.'

'What do you mean, underground societies?' says Nelson. 'Do you mean people who live in caves and the like?'

'I'm talking about people who live in some of our most affluent cities,' says O'Casey, 'but they're driven to live below the earth. People who – for whatever reason – aren't welcome on the surface: homeless people, addicts, the HIV positive. There are subterranean communities all over the world, in catacombs, sewers and abandoned metros. The Tunnel People in Las Vegas, the Empire of the Dead in Paris, the Rat Tribe in Beijing. A lot of them are proper societies, with electricity and phone lines, even churches and restaurants sometimes. The Rat Tribe in Beijing are mostly migrant workers, some of them brought in to build for the Olympics. The only place they can afford to live is underground, in tunnels and old air-raid shelters. They're actually renting these places from unscrupulous landlords and the conditions are atrocious. I've heard some heartbreaking stories. The Ant People they're called too, because they're working away beneath the surface of the city. There's a lot of secrecy about these places. When the police eventually found the headquarters of the Empire of the Dead in Paris it was abandoned. There was just a note: "Don't try to find us."'

Nelson's head is swimming. 'And you think there's one of these underground groups in Norfolk?'

'There have always been rumours about a community living in the tunnels below Norwich,' says O'Casey. 'I've been trying to find someone on the inside and Charlie's name came up.'

'And was he involved?' says Nelson.

'He didn't confirm it or deny it,' says O'Casey. 'It takes a long time to gain these people's trust. Vicky, my colleague, and I have been interviewing rough sleepers for over a year. This story comes up again and again. That there's a secret society living under the city.'

Nelson thinks of Bilbo saying that Barbara has gone underground. Is this what he meant? Is she even now living below the city? He thinks of Charlie appearing in Denning Road in the early hours of the morning. Did he disappear into the underground world through the newly opened portal? But though the hole in the road had shown an entrance to a tunnel, it had been filled with rubble. No one could have got through. He wishes he could ask Eddie. But Eddie is dead. Did someone kill him to keep the secret?

'How can these places exist without anyone knowing

about them?' he says. 'How do people get in?'

'There are secret entrances all over the place. In Paris there are doorways in the Metro tunnels. In Bucharest you get in through the sewers. Trusted community members know the hidden entrances and the passwords. The gate-keepers, they are called. The rumour in Norwich is that Charlie is one of the gatekeepers.'

'But he denied it?'

'Like I say, he didn't confirm or deny it. He's a clever man, Charlie. He knows how to string people along.'

'I'm anxious to speak to this Charlie,' says Nelson. 'I don't suppose you know where he could be found?'

'That's the thing, isn't it?' says O'Casey. 'There's no way of finding these people if they don't want to be found.'

Tanya is finding it difficult to concentrate on interviewing Benedict Foster-Jones because Caleb insists on playing his guitar throughout. Benedict, jiggling the fretful baby, seems impervious to the noise and to Tanya's suggestions that Caleb might like to 'go out and play with Granny in the garden.'

'She's not Granny,' says Caleb, striking a particularly painful chord. 'She's Marianne.'

Tanya cannot believe that people actually live in this squalor. Maybe Sam isn't missing at all, maybe she's just buried under the pile of coats and footballs and gardening equipment in the hall. But she composes her face into sym-pathetic lines and asks Benedict if there have been any calls on his wife's phone.

'Just a couple. Her parents keep ringing it. I don't know why. I told them she hadn't taken her phone with her. And there was a call from Meg at the mother and baby group.'

'Meg Pritchard?' says Tanya, glancing at her notes.

'Yes. I think she runs the group. Other than that it's just people making moves in online Scrabble. They're driving me mad. I slept with her phone next to me last night and it kept bleeping but it was only people playing that bloody game.'

'You shouldn't swear,' says Caleb.

'Who does she play with?'

'Her brother, I think. Otherwise just strangers.'

Could an online stranger have kidnapped Sam? Is it possible for Scrabble to turn into something more sinister? Tanya resolves to check up on Sam's gaming contacts. She takes a photo from her case. It's a rather grisly exhibit because it shows Bilbo in the morgue. The face is stony and the eyes are closed but it's the only likeness they have.

'I'm going to show you something that you may find distressing,' says Tanya. This, at least, has the effect of making Caleb stop playing his guitar. 'Do you know this man?'

'Is he dead?' whispers Benedict, holding the photo between finger and thumb.

'I'm afraid so,' says Tanya.

'I don't recognise him,' says Benedict. 'Who is he?'

'He's a rough sleeper,' says Tanya, 'who goes by the name Bilbo.'

'Bilbo?' says Caleb. 'Like in *The Hobbit*?'

'Yes,' says Tanya. 'Have you ever met this man, Benedict?'

'I don't think so,' says Benedict. 'Do you recognise him, Cal?'

Caleb looks calmly at the ghastly white face. 'He looks like a statue,' he says.

'Have you ever seen this man before?' asks Tanya.

'No,' says Caleb and goes back to playing his guitar.

When Ruth sees Quentin back to reception, Nelson's car has gone. Perhaps she just imagined it? She's walking back past the lake, deep in thought, when someone says, 'Ruth!' It's Martin Kellerman, as large and untidy as ever, his grey suit flapping on his tall frame.

'Hi, Martin.' She wonders whether Martin saw her with Quentin, his ex-wife's husband, but if he did, he doesn't mention it. He seems delighted to see her.

'I've thought a lot about our lunch last week.'

Was it only last week? So much seems to have happened since then: her mum getting ill, the nightmare drive to London, the worry and then the relief. But of course Martin doesn't know any of this.

'Do you fancy lunch again tomorrow?'

Ruth hesitates. She thinks of Quentin Swan saying, 'He's a very strange bloke.' But Martin had been good company last week (most of the time, anyway), and when it comes down to it, aren't we all strange?

'I'd like that,' she says. 'Thank you.'

Before she goes, Tanya takes a look at Sam Foster-Jones' famous garden. It's mostly vegetables, as far as she can see, but there's an apple tree at the bottom and one of those omnipresent trampolines. Why do all children have trampolines these days? Tanya would have loved one when she was growing up but she'd had to make do with the gymnastics club at the village hall. Another thing to hold against her parents.

'What's in the shed?' she asks.

'Sam keeps her gardening equipment in there,' says Benedict. 'Your officers searched it pretty thoroughly yesterday. I hope they put everything back where they found it. Sam's very particular about her tools.'

That's more than she is about her house, thinks Tanya.

'My animal museum is in the shed too,' says Caleb who has followed them (uninvited as far as Tanya is concerned). 'I've got some dead butterflies, an ant farm and a frog skeleton.'

'Sounds lovely,' says Tanya.

'And the rabbits sleep in there at night,' says Caleb, 'because of the foxes.'

The rabbits are currently frolicking in a run on the lawn. There's a grey one and a white one with a black eye patch. They look extremely glossy and healthy.

'Which one's Bilbo?' asks Tanya.

'The white one,' says Caleb. 'He's a Rhinelander.'

'Is he?' This means nothing to Tanya. She turns to Benedict. 'I hear that Sam used to go to the toddler group at St Matthew's. Did you ever go there?'

Benedict is staring miserably at the rabbits. 'No,' he says. 'I was always at work. I'm afraid Sam always had to go to things on her own.'

'She doesn't mind,' says Caleb. 'She has lots of friends.'

Does she? This isn't what the police have been told.

'Do you know the names of any of her friends?' Tanya asks Caleb.

'No,' says Caleb, bending down to offer grass to the rabbits. 'Grown-ups don't interest me much.'

Ruth is heading back to the Natural Sciences block when another voice hails her.

'Hallo, stranger!' It's Shona, Ruth's closest friend at the university, although they have seen less of each other over the past few years. Shona has a child a year younger than Kate, but when they were toddlers Louis made a habit of hitting Kate so Ruth began to avoid Shona's invitations to play-dates. Besides, Shona lives with Phil, which makes visits rather embarrassing. Shona, who teaches in the English Department, threw herself into motherhood in a big way, cutting down on her working hours. But now Louis is in the reception class of a local private school so Shona is back working almost full-time. Ruth is pleased to see her. She has made a secret vow never to mention the private school. People are free to make their own choices, she accepts that, it's just that the sight of a four-year-old in a blazer gives her an almost allergic reaction. Nelson's older daughters went to private schools too.

'Hi, Shona. How are you?'

'Fine. Getting back on the treadmill. I've just been giving a lecture on the Romantic poets.'

'Sounds fun.'

Shona grimaces, tossing her hair so that it shines in the sun. 'I saw you talking to Martin from Geology,' she says. 'How do you know him?'

'I don't really. We just got talking about bones one day.'

'He's quite attractive, I think,' says Shona. 'Do you know Vicky, his ex-wife?'

'No. Do you?'

'A little. She works in the Sociology department. She's a bit of a hippie. You know the sort: tie-dyed clothes, dyed hair, lots of beads and necklaces.'

Ruth is interested. She can't imagine Martin with someone of this description.

'I'm having lunch with Martin tomorrow,' she says.

'Are you?' Shona gives her a searching look which is replaced by the suggestion of a pout. 'You never have lunch with *me* any more.'

'I'd love to,' says Ruth, meaning it. 'We should meet up in Lynn one day.'

'Or we could get the kids together,' says Shona. 'Louis would love to see Kate.'

'Kate would like that too,' says Ruth, feeling disloyal. Maybe Louis will have changed, she tells herself.

The almshouses in King's Lynn have been converted into neat terraced accommodation. The buildings are in a semi-circle, opening out onto a courtyard with flowers growing in tubs. There's a circle of freshly mown grass in the middle and birds are singing in an apple tree. On a bench below the tree an elderly man is dozing in the shade.

'Not bad,' says Clough. 'Did these use to be poorhouses or what?'

'I think they were for retired workers,' says Judy. 'Or for their widows.'

'Bet they're worth a bomb now,' says Clough. 'More than most working people can afford.'

Knowing that Clough and Cassandra live in a smart apartment in Spalding and will one day inherit Cassandra's family mansion, Judy doesn't comment. She thinks that Cathbad would detect something sad about the houses, the sunny courtyard notwithstanding. She even thinks that she can sense it herself.

Meg Pritchard opens the door dressed in her nurse's uniform. Does she ever take it off? wonders Judy. After all, Meg doesn't have to be at work for another couple of hours. She explains that they would like to ask a few questions.

'Come in.' Unlike her husband Meg doesn't seem at all unsettled by their arrival. She shows them into the sitting room. The room is tastefully decorated in shades of sand but the small leaded windows make it seem rather dark and oppressive. Judy also notes the crucifix on the mantelpiece, slightly too large to be an ornament.

'We're investigating the disappearance of Sam Foster-Jones,' says Judy, taking a seat on the beige sofa. 'We understand that she might have attended your mother and baby group.'

'It's possible,' says Meg, sitting opposite on a darker beige chair. 'We have a few Sams.'

Judy hands her the photograph of Sam in her garden. Meg

nods as soon as she sees it, 'Yes. She comes to my mother and baby group. She brings her older one to my playgroup too. The baby's called Freddie. The little boy is Archie . . . Ollie . . . one of those ie-ending names.'

'Alfie,' says Judy. 'When did you last see Sam?'

'It must have been on Monday,' says Meg. 'The mother and baby group is Monday, Wednesday and Friday. I'm pretty sure Sam was here on Monday.'

'Can you check?' says Clough. 'Do you take a register?'

Meg laughs. 'No, it's quite free and easy, Inspector.' Judy notes Clough doesn't correct her about his rank. 'The mums just come for a coffee and a chat. We have a little light lunch, sing a few songs and play a few games. Nothing too structured.'

'The group starts about midday, doesn't it?' says Judy. 'When does it end?'

'Two o'clock,' says Meg. 'Two hours is enough for most people. The little ones need a nap in the afternoon.'

Meg talks easily about mums and little ones, thinks Judy. Does she have any children of her own? The neat beige house seems a very adult home. There's a picture of Paul and Meg on the mantelpiece, next to the crucifix. Paul is in a suit and Meg in a blue dress with flowers in her hair. There are no photographs of children.

'And you're pretty sure that Sam was there on Monday?' says Judy.

'I think so,' says Meg, crinkling her smooth, tanned brow in thought. 'I remember that one of the babies had some spots. I think it was Freddie. Yes, it was. Sam asked me about it but I didn't think it was anything serious, just a teething rash.'

'Are you a qualified nurse?' asks Judy, hoping that doesn't sound too rude.

'Yes.' Meg waves towards some framed certificates nestling between tasteful seascapes. 'I'm a nurse and a midwife.'

'How long have you been running the groups?'

'Three years,' says Meg. 'Paul and I moved to Lynn four years ago and we wanted to give something back to the community.'

'How long have you been married?' asks Clough.

'Seven years,' says Meg. 'We met while Paul was still in prison. I was a prison visitor.'

'Except that he was called Dean then, wasn't he?' says Judy.

'That's right,' says Meg, unruffled. 'He changed his name when he was born again. "Last of all, to one untimely born, he appeared also to me."'

Judy isn't sure if this refers to Paul's conversion or to Meg herself. She decides to move on. 'When we last spoke, you mentioned seeing Barbara Murray. Babs.'

'Yes?' Meg sounds suddenly on the alert. Her South African accent is also very much in evidence. *Yis?*

'Would Sam ever have come across Babs?'

'I don't think so. I only spoke to Barbara that once, on the steps outside.'

'You mentioned Babs helping a mother with her buggy. That wasn't Sam?'

Meg shakes her head. 'No, that was a mum with twins.

Why, do you think that Babs has something to do with Sam's disappearance?'

Interesting way of putting it, thinks Judy. 'We're following a lead,' she says. 'Did you ever meet any other members of the Foster-Jones family?'

'Sam brought one of the older children with her to nursery once. I think they were off school for some reason.'

'Was that Caleb?'

'No, it was a little girl. Eve or Evie.'

'Did you ever meet Sam's husband, Benedict Foster-Jones?'

'No. Fathers tend to steer clear of mother and baby groups.'

'Not all of them,' says Judy. 'My partner used to go to a group regularly.'

Clough starts to laugh and turns it into a cough. 'You're right,' says Meg. 'It's just that there are no dads in this group. Some of them do come to the Christmas and summer shows though. They always want to video it all.'

'That's natural,' says Clough. 'I'm always videoing Spencer. I want to have it all recorded. His first word, his first step, the first time he says Daddy.'

'Spencer?' Meg turns to look at him. 'Does your partner come to my mother and baby group? An actress, very striking with long dark hair?'

'That's Cassie,' says Clough. 'I didn't know she came to your group. She goes to lots of mother and baby things.'

This seems to prove Meg's point about fathers and their

lack of interest. Judy says, 'Did Benedict Foster-Jones ever come to one of the shows?'

'It's possible, but if he was there he wasn't introduced to me. I always thought of Sam as very independent, bringing up four children, growing her own food, making cakes. The others mums use to call her Superwoman.'

This is interesting. Especially given that at the start of the interview Meg claimed not to remember anything about Sam Foster-Jones.

'You mentioned Sam gardening,' says Judy. 'Did you ever visit her at home?'

'No.' Meg sounds quite shocked. 'I try to keep a certain professional distance. I'm friends with the mums but only up to a certain point.'

This sounds like rather an extreme reaction to the question. Judy looks at Clough, who shrugs. She stands up. 'Thank you very much, Mrs Pritchard. If you think of anything else that might help us, here's my card.'

Meg puts the card on the mantelpiece next to the crucifix. 'I'll pray for Sam,' she says, 'and for Babs.'

'Do you go to St Matthew's Church?' asks Judy as they head towards the door.

'No, it's a bit old-school for us,' says Meg. 'Although the vicar is very kind. Lots of vicars won't have rough sleepers in their church halls but Father Martin is very supportive. Paul and I worship at the Clarendon.'

'Isn't that a bingo hall?' says Clough.

'It is in the week but at the weekends our church holds

services there. We've got a big congregation – too big for most premises.'

'Full house, eh?'

Meg laughs. She opens the door for them and the sunlight floods in. 'God bless you, Inspector.'

'Thanks very much,' says Clough.

CHAPTER 20

'When we were little,' says the Mock Turtle, 'we went to school in the sea. The Master was a turtle but we called him Tortoise.'

'Why did you call him Tortoise if he wasn't one?' says Alice.

'Because he taught us, of course. Really, you are very dull.'

'We learnt Reeling and Writhing,' says the Gryphon, 'and the three branches of Arithmetic.'

He starts to chant and the Mock Turtle joins in. 'Ambition, Distraction, Uglification and Derision.'

'Goodness,' says Alice. 'We have to do French and elocution.'

Leo claps his hands. 'People,' he says, 'I have an idea.' Ruth and Kate, sitting at the back of the room, look at each other. They have only been at the rehearsal for an hour but already Leo has had several ideas, most of which involve starting the scene again with the cast in different positions. Ruth has heard the reeling and writhing line so often that she feels as if her own mind is flailing about at the bottom of a deep, dark sea. Even the actors are starting to look fed up.

The idea was that Ruth should bring Kate to the rehearsal so that she could meet the adult cast members. Ruth had to leave the university early to pick her up from school and then drive to a community centre on the outskirts of Lynn. At least this rehearsal isn't in Norwich. As it is, it is already six o'clock and Ruth likes Kate to be in bed by seven-thirty. Not that Kate looks tired. She has watched every version of the scene with rapt absorption. And the actors were very nice to her. Adrian Linley, who plays the Mock Turtle, the White Rabbit and the Caterpillar, is a spry middle-aged man with an actor's voice and humorous eyebrows. He's a retired actor and Ruth thinks that she recognises him from an old episode of *Midsomer Murders*. Darrell Shaw (the Gryphon, the Mad Hatter and the Cheshire Cat) is younger and quite good-looking, with one of those Victorian beards that all Ruth's students seem to be sporting this year. He told Ruth that he's working as a barman while trying to break into acting. From the look on his face during rehearsals, it's not clear whether he thinks playing various animals in an amateur production of *Alice's Adventures Under Ground* is going to get him very far.

Ruth and Kate also met Flora Frampton, who is playing the Duchess and the Queen of Hearts. She's another familiar face from daytime TV but she seems quite happy to be sitting in a draughty community centre on a Wednesday night. She occupies her time knitting and has endeared herself to Kate by offering her assorted sweets from a large paper bag. Ruth would have liked a sweet too (they only had time for a quick sandwich in the car) but she thinks that this would look greedy. She watches enviously as Kate unwraps a sherbet lemon.

'People,' says Leo. 'An idea. Why doesn't Katie play Alice in this scene? After all, this is about her being at school.'

Kate sits up straighter, obviously keen to be involved. Ruth thinks of her mother and her thwarted theatrical ambitions. Is that really where all this comes from? Her mother is continuing to make a good recovery. According to the nurse, she walked the length of the ward today with the aid of a Zimmer. Ruth must ring Simon for an update when she gets home.

'But Alice is big again in the next scene,' says Cassandra, reluctant perhaps to lose any more lines. 'In the trial.'

'Maybe she could just join in the Lobster Quadrille,' says Adrian Linley. 'Would you like to do a dance, Katie darling?'

Kate is already on her feet. Ruth feels rather embarrassed by such enthusiasm. She thinks that she must seem like one of those stage-school mothers, too large and ungainly to act herself, pushing her daughter to perform for the assembled company. 'Eyes and teeth, Kate. Eyes and teeth.'

'At the end of the scene,' Leo tells Kate, 'Adrian sings a song that starts "Will you walk a little faster?" and Alice dances with the Gryphon. Do you think you could dance with Darrell, Katie?'

Ruth notices that Darrell looks a little disappointed to be losing the chance to dance with Cassandra. She thinks she has noticed the Gryphon watching the adult Alice rather closely during the rehearsal. But Darrell accepts the change with good humour and walks Kate through the steps of the dance.

'Wonderful,' says Leo. 'Beautiful. Now, from the top again.'

'When I was little,' says Adrian as the Mock Turtle, 'we went to school in the sea . . .'

Judy is surprised to find herself enjoying the soup run. It's a long time since she and Cathbad have done anything without the kids, and even if serving soup to rough sleepers isn't everyone's idea of fun, there's a pleasing sense of purpose about it. It seems to her that over the past week and a half they have all been saying, 'Isn't it awful, those poor people sleeping on the streets?' and no one has done anything about it. Giving people a bowl of soup isn't going to solve the problem of homelessness but it's better than nothing.

She doesn't have to worry about the children because Clara, the babysitter she shares with Ruth, is with them. Michael loves Clara and even Miranda (who regards everyone but her parents with suspicion – everyone but her father, to be honest) consents to be left with her. Judy feels young and carefree again, a bit like an urban commando, dressed in dark clothes, helping Cathbad to load the soup onto the trolley. They had collected the soup from Toppolino's earlier (the car will smell of minestrone for days) and Judy had been touched at how the chef had been at pains to emphasise that this was his best soup, the stuff that sells as a starter for a fiver, nothing second-rate about it. Now they are in the car park of St Matthew's, loading up the trolley which they will wheel to the Vancouver centre. Paul Pritchard is there too with a hi-vis vest over his Norwich City shirt.

'That's very bright,' says Judy, shielding her eyes from the yellow on yellow glare.

Paul laughs. 'It'll be dark before we leave. I've got a tabard for you too.'

Judy reluctantly pulls the vest over her black T-shirt. Cathbad, who is wearing his cloak ('people expect it') doesn't have any truck with hi-vis garments, but then he is kind of hard to miss.

Paul doesn't seem at all abashed by the fact that Judy and Clough had been questioning him earlier in the day. He chats quite easily as they push the trolley through the streets.

'You do normally get the same people coming to the soup run,' he says. 'It's quite a community.'

Judy thinks of Bilbo saying, 'There's a group of us who meet regular, like.' Surely she will find someone who'll give her a clue about Bilbo's identity. Otherwise, he'll go to his grave without anyone even knowing his name. Thinking of this, she tells Paul that Eddie's funeral is tomorrow.

'I'm trying to get a few people to go,' she says. 'I'll be there and so will the boss, DCI Nelson.'

'I'll come if I can,' says Cathbad. 'Maybe Clara can look after Miranda for a couple of hours.'

'Where's the funeral?' asks Paul.

'At St Bernadette's,' says Judy. 'The Catholic church.' She has chosen the church because of the holy picture found on Eddie's body and the priest, Father Declan, has been very accommodating. He doesn't think he knew Eddie but he occasionally helps on the soup run and sometimes lets the homeless sleep in his church hall ('It's against the rules, of course, but Our Lord didn't bother much about the law, the way I see it').

Paul nods. 'I know St Bernadette's. Father Declan is a good man. I'll try to come along. Anya can look after things for an hour. What time is the service?'

'Eleven o'clock.'

They have reached the shopping centre. A small group of rough sleepers are standing in a shop doorway and Judy is reminded of the way they had waited outside the centre that morning. They stand patiently, diffidently, reluctant to be the first to move. It's all very different from Costa Coffee.

'Who's for soup?' says Cathbad, getting the ladle out.

A man in a camouflage jacket moves forward slowly.

It's past seven by the time Ruth leaves the community centre. In all that time the group has only rehearsed the Mock Turtle scene and the beginning of the trial scene. Kate has danced the Lobster Quadrille a few times and is in high spirits, pirouetting and curtseying as they walk to the car. But Ruth is keen to get home, feed Flint, ring her brother and watch an hour of mindless television.

'Come on, Kate,' she says. 'It's late and we need to get home.'

Kate dances towards her, singing, '"Will you walk a little faster' said a whiting to a snail." What's a whiting, Mum?'

'I think it's a fish,' says Ruth, doing up Kate's seatbelt.

'How can a fish walk?' says Kate. 'It doesn't have any legs.'

'That's just the writer using his imagination,' says Ruth. It sometimes seems to her that Lewis Carroll's imagination is a very strange place.

They drive through King's Lynn with Kate singing 'Will you, won't you, won't you join the dance?' all the way. Ruth decides to go back along the quayside, which is beautiful in the evening as well as being a shortcut. As she stops at the lights near the Vancouver Centre she sees an odd sight: a metal trolley being pushed by a large man in a yellow shirt, a slight woman with her hair in a ponytail and a druid in a purple cloak. That must be Cathbad and Judy. Who are they with and what are they doing? But the car behind her hoots impatiently and she moves on.

A few people say that they know Babs. 'She's a nice lady,' says the man in the camouflage jacket. 'Haven't seen her around for a while.' The man called Scratch, who Judy remembers from the drop-in centre, comes up to ask if she's still looking for Babs.

'Yes,' says Judy. 'I don't suppose you've seen her?'

'No,' says Scratch. 'But I did hear something about her.'

'What?' says Judy. She looks round. Two of the men are chatting with Cathbad as he dishes up the last of the soup. She hears the words 'positive energies' and 'not your true path', sure signs that Cathbad is offering spiritual counselling. Another man is helping Paul clear up, putting used cups into plastic bags and sweeping the pavement. Judy draws Scratch to one side. 'What did you hear?'

Scratch doesn't make eye contact. He looks up at the sky, still light but with a bluish tinge to it. Scratch has a rather wild look to him and Judy remembers what he said about the drugs.

'I heard she was taken,' he says at last.

'Taken? Who took her?'

'People go missing,' says Scratch. 'Everyone knows that. One minute they're here, next minute they're gone. There was a man, a big red-headed Glaswegian called Archie. He used to sleep outside the library. Then one day, he disappeared. He was taken.'

The night is warm but Judy feels suddenly cold. Michael was taken. She got him back but she will never forget the moment when suddenly he wasn't there, when it seemed that he had fallen off the edge of the world. 'Where do they go?' she says, almost whispering.

'I don't know but people are saying that Bilbo was killed because he knew.'

The deaths of Eddie and Bilbo have been the number one topic that evening. But given that someone is obviously killing rough sleepers, Judy is surprised at how phlegmatic the men are. They are used to death; their friends die in doorways all the time. There is none of the panic you would get if someone was picking off, say, police officers or librarians.

'Who is saying this, Scratch?' she asks. Cathbad must have heard the urgent note in her voice because he looks over questioningly.

'Charlie. I heard Charlie saying it.'

'Charlie? When did you see him?'

But Scratch has gone vague again and wanders away, picking up bits of litter and examining them as if they might contain some profound truth. Judy feels frustrated. Charlie was the person who overheard someone talking to Babs about her children. After that Charlie seems to have vanished and Judy had begun to fear that he had shared Eddie and Bilbo's fate. But Scratch claims to have seen Charlie recently . . .

'All right, Judy?' Paul approaches, carrying a black bin liner.

'Yes, fine.'

'I saw you speaking to Scratch. He's a decent chap but he's prone to fantasy, probably because of the drugs. I wouldn't take him too seriously.'

Judy looks at Paul as he moves away, picking up litter carefully. Of the three of them he is the only one who has bothered with gloves, which gives his hands a smooth, faintly sinister look. Did Paul know what Scratch was saying to her? They had been speaking quietly but sound carries well on the still air. If so, there is some reason why Paul does not want Judy to believe Scratch. And of course this makes her believe him all the more.

Nelson is pretending to watch television. Bruno sits at his feet looking up at him hopefully, though Nelson has already shared more of his supper than was strictly prudent. When Nelson had got home from work he had expected to see Michelle in the kitchen preparing food for the returning worker. Ruth would say that this was sexist, but Nelson tells himself he only expects this because this is what has happened for most of his married life. But Michelle wasn't there and the kitchen was as bare and antiseptic as an operating theatre. Nelson texted Michelle. *R u working late?* was the most tactful he could manage but it was an hour before she replied and that was only to say, *On way back x.* By this time Nelson had eaten an M&S steak and kidney pie for two, although Bruno had come in for quite a lot of pastry. Now he is sitting with a can of beer watching some rubbish about people who have bought a tumbledown house and seem surprised that this means they have to renovate it.

Bruno hears Michelle before Nelson does. He sits up, head on one side, tail wagging. Michelle goes into the kitchen first and Nelson hears her putting his plate into the dishwasher. Then she checks for answerphone messages (he hears the click of the receiver) and hangs up her suit jacket. Then she comes into the sitting room, barefoot in her pink skirt and white silk top. Her hair is loose and, momentarily, she looks like a different person.

'Why are you watching this?' she says. 'You hate property programmes.'

'Maybe I'm thinking of moving,' says Nelson.

Michelle sits down and pushes Bruno away from her lap. 'You'll never move,' she says.

'I might do,' counters Nelson. 'Now that the girls have left home.'

'They haven't left home,' says Michelle. 'Laura is back, in case you haven't noticed.'

'But she'll leave again. She's talking about getting a flat when she qualifies as a teacher. Rebecca looks settled in Brighton.'

'Where do you want to move to?' says Michelle.

'I don't know.' The conversation seems to be moving very fast in a direction that Nelson hadn't intended. 'Into the centre of Lynn, maybe. Or we could move somewhere else altogether. London. Back to Blackpool.'

Michelle stares at him. 'Would you really move away from here?'

Bruno, who had collapsed in front of the television, hears something in her voice that makes him sit up and whine.

'It's just an idea.' Nelson finds himself backtracking.

'Would you really move away from your job? Away from Katie?'

Nelson has no answer for this. He doesn't want to talk about Katie because then Michelle will go on about him telling the girls about her. Instead he says, 'Why are you so late? Is it stocktaking or something?'

'I went out for a drink with Debbie and the girls. I thought I told you.'

'You didn't.'

'I see you got yourself some supper.'

'I had one of those M&S things. Have you had anything?'

Michelle turns away to examine some imaginary mark on the sofa. 'I'm not hungry.'

Nelson looks at her, feeling baffled. Michelle seems cool and remote but she also seems to be waiting for him to say something. But what? It's a relief when his phone rings.

'Boss. I'm sorry to disturb you but I've just come back from the soup run and I heard something rather interesting.'

'What was it?' Michelle gets up and leaves the room. Bruno follows her, his claws clattering on the wood-effect floor.

'One of the men said that he'd heard that Barbara Murray had been taken.'

'Taken? What does that mean?'

'He said that rough sleepers vanish all the time. He said that Barbara had been taken and that Bilbo was killed because he knew about it. And this is the interesting thing. I asked who told him this and he said Charlie. Charlie was the man by the Customs House, the man who heard someone talking to Barbara about her children.'

'Charlie.' The wheels are turning in Nelson's mind. 'Charlie! He's the chap in the photograph.' He explains about Kevin O'Casey and his project.

'So Charlie was the man the students saw that night? The Jesus Man.'

'It seems so. He seems to make a habit of popping up in odd places. A bit like Cathbad really.'

Judy ignores this. 'There's definitely something going on. Paul Pritchard tried to make out that Scratch – the man I was speaking to – couldn't be trusted but I think he was telling the truth.'

'Why did Pritchard say he couldn't be trusted?'

'He said he was a drug addict.'

'Is he?'

'Well, yes, but that doesn't mean that we shouldn't believe him.'

'No,' says Nelson, thinking that all the same courts have a way of disbelieving witnesses if the defence can prove that they are addicts. 'Did anyone say anything about Sam Foster-Jones?'

'No. I told you though that Meg Pritchard turns out to know her quite well.'

'Yes, Paul and Meg Pritchard seem to be in the centre of everything. I don't like that.'

'Any word on the search for Sam?'

'No. There was CCTV on a couple of houses. I've got digital media investigators looking at it now but I'm not hopeful. Fingertip search has found nothing. She's been missing for forty-eight hours now.'

He doesn't need to tell Judy what this means.

Ruth is snoozing in front of another property improvement programme when she hears screaming. She's awake immediately but it takes her a few seconds to realise that the sound is coming from Kate's room. She bounds upstairs faster than she's ever moved at the gym, or anywhere else for that matter.

Kate is sitting upright under her green spotted duvet. Her eyes are open but she doesn't seem to be looking at anything. She is still screaming, a high undulating sound that seems to be pouring out of her without any effort on her part. It's the spookiest thing Ruth has ever seen.

'Kate.' She touches her lightly on the shoulder. 'Kate. It's OK. Mummy's here.'

Kate stops screaming, but when she looks at Ruth her eyes are still glassy.

'He said he'd take me underground. I don't want to go underground.'

'Shh, Kate. No one's going to take you anywhere.' Gradually Kate's breathing slows down and her eyes close. Ruth lowers her gently onto the bed but she stays there, sitting on the floor, for a long time, holding Kate's hand until she is sure she is asleep. And when she finally goes downstairs she checks all the windows and puts the security chain on the door.

CHAPTER 21

In the end there are four people in the church waiting for the undertakers to carry in Eddie's coffin. Judy and Nelson sit awkwardly in the front pew, in the seats usually reserved for the deceased's nearest and dearest. For a long time it seemed as if they would be the only people there apart from Father Declan, a slight grey-haired man, who is sitting by the altar rails with his head bowed in prayer. Then, five minutes before the service is due to start, Cathbad appears, closely followed by Paul Pritchard. Cathbad joins them in the pew and Paul sits on the opposite side of the aisle. Judy is rather touched to see that he is wearing a shirt and tie rather than his usual football shirt. Nelson, too, is formally dressed in a dark suit which Judy thinks looks rather good on him. You wouldn't call the boss handsome (well, she wouldn't anyway) but there's no denying that he has a certain presence and the sombre clothes seem to emphasise this. Cathbad, of course, is wearing his cloak.

At eleven o'clock precisely the undertaker's men enter the church carrying the coffin, the cheapest kind available.

The Serious Crimes Unit have clubbed together and bought a wreath so at least there are some flowers on it. After much discussion Judy settled on red and white roses and a small card with the message 'RIP Eddie'.

Judy is relieved that there aren't any hymns. It would have sounded too pathetic, just the four of them singing in the huge church, though maybe the undertaker's men are trained to join in on such occasions. They are sitting in the pew behind them, which at least swells the congregation a bit, and the main undertaker is making all the responses in a sonorous bass voice. He's a singer, Judy is sure of it.

Father Declan leads the prayers in a soft Irish accent. He talks about Eddie as a free spirit who, even if he wasn't known that well by those gathered in the church, was 'known to God and loved by him'. It's a nice thought, thinks Judy, that someone was watching over Eddie. All the same, it would have been even nicer if that someone had managed to prevent him being knifed to death as he slept. 'Man that is born of woman,' intones Father Declan, 'has but a short time to live.'

The only awkward moment comes with the scripture readings. Father Declan looks up and asks if anyone in the congregation would like to read. Nelson stares at his feet. Judy has heard him read in church once, at the funeral of a murdered child, and he had looked and sounded as if every second was pure torture. She herself can think of nothing worse than reading aloud. She hated it at school and she hates it now. She looks imploringly at Cathbad who nods, but before he can stand up, Paul Pritchard has made his way to the pulpit.

It's that reading from St John: 'Do not let your hearts be troubled . . . in my father's house there are many rooms.' Has Father Declan chosen it because there was no room on earth where Eddie could lay his head? Paul reads confidently and well. Judy supposes that he takes a leading role in the services conducted in the bingo hall. 'I am the way, the truth and the life.' Paul looks towards the back of the church and gives a slight theatrical start, as if the Truth is being revealed to him there and then. 'No one comes to the Father except through me.'

Then it is nearly over. A few more words, a quick blessing and a sprinkling of holy water and Eddie's coffin is on its way back out of the church. As Judy turns to follow it she sees that there were, in fact, five mourners in the church. A man was sitting at the back and he stands up now as the coffin passes, his head bowed respectfully. He's a tall man with long dark hair and a beard. She thinks he might be a rough sleeper because he's wearing a heavy coat on a warm day but there's nothing else to suggest that the man is down on his luck. He has a rather proud bearing, looking Judy in the eye as she passes, a look that is composed of challenge and a certain wry humour. Does the man know her? She's sure she's never seen him before which is why she is amazed to hear Nelson, beside her, saying, 'Charlie?'

'Some people call me Charlie,' says the man. 'My name's actually Richard. Richard Latham.'

'I'd like a word with you,' says Nelson, 'if you don't mind.'

They walk out of the church, which opens directly onto the street. The hearse is moving off, followed by Father Declan in a battered-looking Mini.

'Where are they taking Eddie now?' says Charlie/Richard.

'To the crematorium,' says Judy. 'His ashes are going to be scattered in the garden of remembrance.' This is the usual thing, the undertakers told her, when there are no funeral instructions. Judy has seen the garden and it's a pleasant walled space with rose bushes and brick paths between the flowers. Not a bad place to end up.

'It was good of you to give him a proper funeral,' says Richard.

'That was Detective Sergeant Johnson's doing,' says Nelson.

Richard gives her a slight bow. 'I'm glad. Eddie was a good man, a deep thinker. I'm sure he would have been grateful. A Catholic church too. That was a nice touch.'

'I thought Eddie was a Catholic,' says Judy. 'We found a holy picture on him when he died.'

'He was brought up a Catholic,' says Richard, 'though he stopped going to church after he left Ireland. I'm sure he would have wanted a Catholic funeral though.'

'You seem to know Eddie quite well,' says Nelson.

'We often talked,' says Richard. 'He was an interesting man.'

'Well, would you mind having a chat with Sergeant Johnson and me now?' says Nelson. 'We're anxious to know a bit more about Eddie. It might help us find his killer.'

'I'd be happy to help.' They walk to the car park where they find Paul and Cathbad, deep in conversation.

'Hallo, Paul,' says Richard.

'Hallo, Richard. Good to see you again.'

Despite this, Judy doesn't think that the two men are remotely pleased to see each other.

They drive back to the police station in Nelson's car. Nelson had been worried that Richard would refuse to come with them but the man looks quite relaxed, arms stretched along the back seat, for all the world as if he's a passenger in a minicab and Nelson's the driver. He doesn't smell either, Nelson can't help noticing, remembering poor old Eddie. They chat about the funeral, about St Bernadette's, even about Norwich's chances of promotion (slim). When they get to the station, Nelson asks Judy to take Richard to the interview suite. He makes a quick dash upstairs to get his notes.

Not quick enough.

'Hallo, Harry. You're looking very smart today.'

'Thank you. I've just come from a funeral.' Nelson wonders if Jo was hoping that he'd been to a job interview.

'Ah, the homeless man,' says Jo. 'Well done. Good PR for the force, you being there. Was there anyone from the press?'

'No,' says Nelson. 'There were only a handful of us in the church.'

'Pity. Still, I might draft a statement. Judy Johnson set all this up, didn't she?'

'Yes. She's worked very hard.'

'I'll make sure she gets a mention. Oh, DCI Nelson . . .' As

Nelson tries to sidle past. 'I've just had Ruth Galloway on the phone.'

Nelson stops. 'Ruth? Why?'

'She's had the DNA results on the bones found below the Guildhall. She wants to excavate the area. She said that she'd raised this with you.'

'She did,' says Nelson. 'And I raised it with you.' Why is Ruth talking directly to Jo Archer? And why didn't she tell him about the DNA results?

'Well, I've managed to pull a few strings,' says Jo. 'The excavation is set for tomorrow. I assume one of your team will want to be there.'

'I'll go myself,' says Nelson.

'Is that an effective use of your time?' Jo puts her head on one side and smiles sweetly but Nelson gets the message.

'It could be an important lead,' he says.

'Then send DS Johnson. She liaised with the archaeologists before, didn't she?'

'I'll think about it,' says Nelson. 'Excuse me. I'm in the middle of an interview.' He waits for Jo to say that he shouldn't be interviewing either but she just gives him an irritatingly knowing look and allows him to carry on up the stairs.

Nelson gathers up his notes. He wonders again why Ruth didn't speak to him. He had almost called in to see her at the university yesterday but had thought that she might be teaching or holding a tutorial (he's never quite clear what that entails). He knew that Ruth wanted to do a proper excavation and had put in an official request. What can have prompted her to ring Jo directly? Or maybe she rang the office number and Jo answered the phone. He wouldn't put it past her.

He walks back downstairs to the interview suite. Judy and Richard are drinking tea and chatting like old pals. Richard and Judy, ho ho. Maybe they should start a TV show.

Nelson explains that this is a witness statement and asks permission to record the interview. Richard inclines his head graciously.

'Your name is Richard Latham and you're how old?'

'Forty-five.'

He looks older, thinks Nelson, though not as old as Eddie with his bleary eyes and long wizard's beard. But Eddie had only been sixty, fifteen years older than Richard.

'Have you got an address at the moment?'

Richard laughs. 'Put "care of the park bench".' Nelson watches Judy write 'no fixed abode' on the witness statement pad.

'Out of interest,' he says, 'why are you called Charlie?'

Richard laughs. 'When I was first on the streets I used to do crazy things, just to show that I wasn't completely down and out, I suppose. Once I got a bit of money handing out flyers and spent it all on champagne. Just sat there in front of the Customs House swigging champagne from the bottle. People started to call me Champagne Charlie and the name stuck. Lots of rough sleepers have nicknames. You lot used to call Eddie Aftershave Eddie, didn't you?'

This is said rather nastily and Nelson feels embarrassed.

He had no idea that Eddie knew about his nickname. He says hastily, 'How did you know Eddie?'

'You get to know everyone who sleeps on the streets,' says Richard, 'but I always got on well with Eddie. He was a gentle man, he looked out for some of the younger ones. He used to drink a bit but when he was sober we had some interesting talks.'

'Did you know Bilbo too?' asks Judy. 'The man with the jester's hat outside the station.'

'Bilbo? I never called him that. I loathe Tolkien. His name was Stuart. Stuart Hughes, I think.' Nelson sees Judy making a note. He knows how pleased she'll be to have this name.

'I knew Stu,' says Richard. 'We used to play chess together sometimes. I don't think he had much schooling – he was an innocent really – but he played a good game of chess.'

Nelson thinks that Richard sounds rather patronising. 'I take it you have had some schooling.'

'I've got a degree in maths,' says Richard. 'All mathematicians are mad, as you know. You're at your best at twenty then you burn out slowly. I was teaching maths at a secondary school. I drank too much so I lost my job. My marriage broke up. I started to take drugs. I ended up on the streets. I burnt out.'

His eyes do have rather a mad, burning look, thinks Nelson, like a martyr about to go to the stake.

'And Barbara, Barbara Murray,' he says. 'Did you know her too?'

'Yes. There aren't many women who sleep rough. I knew Babs by sight. I'm Scottish originally and she was from

Scotland so there was a connection there. Eddie was the one who knew Babs. She was vulnerable, he tried to look after her.'

Eddie had tried to look after Barbara, thinks Nelson. He had even braved the dreaded police because he was worried about her. And the result was that this gentle, kind, troubled man ended up dead.

'Eddie mentioned that you had heard someone talking to Barbara,' says Nelson, 'saying something about her children. He thought that Barbara was upset. Do you remember this?'

Richard is silent for a moment, looking into his empty polystyrene cup. 'Yes,' he says at last. 'I was outside the Customs House minding my own business. Babs was just across the bridge, asking passers-by for money. I kept an eye on her because some people get nasty with women begging. I saw a man talking to her so I went over the bridge, just to check that she was all right. I heard the man saying something like, "The children are important" or "Your children are important". It seemed to make Babs upset, she was wiping her eyes. I called out and asked her if she was OK and she said yes. The man went away. I didn't ask Babs about it but I suppose the incident stayed in my mind, which is why I mentioned it to Eddie.'

'Could you describe the man?'

'Forties, quite smartly dressed, glasses. I didn't get a long look at him but at the time I took him for a charity worker of some kind. He had that look about him.'

'It wasn't Paul Pritchard then,' says Judy.

Richard laughs, rather harshly. 'No, it wasn't Paul. I would have recognised Paul.'

'Do you go to the drop-in centre at St Matthew's?' asks Judy.

'No. It's too happy-clappy for me but everyone on the streets knows Paul. He's all right, I suppose. A bit holier-than-thou for my taste.'

'I understand that you know a man called Kevin O'Casey,' says Nelson. 'Could you tell us a bit about your connection with him?'

Richard laughs, this time more naturally. 'Kevin's an academic. He works at the university. The new one outside Lynn. Kevin's got this thing about underground societies. He thinks that there's this community of rough sleepers living underneath Norwich. He thought that I might know something about it.'

'And do you?' asks Nelson.

'It doesn't exist,' says Richard. 'Ever since I've been on the streets I've heard people talking about The Underground but it's a fairy story.'

'Bilbo told me that he'd heard that Barbara had gone underground,' says Judy. 'Do you know what he meant by that?'

'It's this same fantasy,' says Richard. 'Someone disappears, and instead of admitting that they've moved on or that they're dead, people say that they've gone underground. It's just an urban myth.'

'You were seen in Denning Road in Norwich just over a week ago,' says Nelson. 'It would have been about three in the morning. Some students in a car saw you. Could you tell us what you were doing there?'

'There's no law against being in Norwich, is there?' says Richard. 'Homeless people are allowed on buses, you know.'

Nelson thinks of the bus ticket in Eddie's pocket. Eddie obviously liked to travel too.

No buses will have been running at three in the morning but Nelson senses that this is all the answer he is going to get. He decides to try another tack.

'Have you ever met a woman called Sam Foster-Jones?'

Now Richard does look surprised. 'No, I don't think so. Why?' Sam's disappearance has been all over the news but Nelson doesn't suppose that Richard ever gets to watch TV. According to Judy, there's a set at the drop-in centre but Richard claims never to go there. He must go somewhere though, if only to wash. Richard's hair and clothes look clean and, long coat aside, he could be any bearded, hippyish man in his forties. He could be Cathbad in the old days.

'We're investigating her disappearance,' says Nelson, 'and we think there might be a link to Barbara.'

'Why? Has she gone underground too?'

'It's a possibility,' says Nelson.

'We wanted an extension,' says Martin. 'We had Olivia and we thought we'd want more children. We decided to extend the kitchen and build a study off it. Vicky wanted to work at home more. We got an architect in and . . . well, the rest is history. Checkmate to Quentin Swan.'

He laughs rather unhappily and takes a bite of his

sandwich. They are sitting outside the pub – a different one this time, by the quay – and the ducks wander around their feet looking for crumbs. Ruth isn't sure how they got onto the subject of Quentin Swan, but once on it it seems they can't get off.

'He's got quite famous since then,' says Martin. 'I'm sure he doesn't do extensions any more. He did that arts centre on the South Quay and he's designing some swanky new apartments in Norwich.'

'He wants to build a restaurant under the Guildhall,' says Ruth. 'Where I found the bones I was telling you about.'

'So you've met him then?'

'A couple of times.'

'Women find him attractive, I believe.'

There's no good answer to that. 'I didn't,' says Ruth, although this isn't entirely truthful.

'He might be good-looking,' says Martin, 'but that's not everything.'

This seems unanswerable so Ruth doesn't answer it. She takes a sip of wine and looks out over the river. The water is as still as glass and the Customs House is reflected perfectly in the looking-glass world.

'Men like that,' Martin is saying, 'they're dangerous. They're dangerous to women. Women fall for them and before they know it they're drawn into their web.'

Ruth always suspects people (particularly men) who claim to be experts on 'women' but Martin sounds as if he is talking specifics rather than generalities.

'These things happen,' she says. 'I know it's awful at the

time but life goes on. And sometimes things work out even if they weren't in the original plan. I've learnt that myself.'

She waits for Martin to ask her what didn't work out in her life but he's not listening to her. He's gazing out over the water, his eyes hard behind the scholarly glasses.

'Vicky was taken in by him,' he says. 'She was always so sensible, so level-headed. We met when we were both teaching in London and she was the one with the career plan, even then. She's a really good sociologist. She was going to write books, even make television programmes. But then Quentin Swan swans in' – mirthless laugh – 'and she jumps into bed with him without a second thought.'

Ruth doubts that it was without a second thought but talking about adultery always makes her nervous. After all, didn't she jump into bed with someone else's husband without many thoughts at all?

'And now he's Olivia's stepfather. I'm sure people think he's her father too. He picks her up from playgroup, takes her to the zoo. He's even promised to buy her a cat.'

Ruth is becoming a little fed up. It's not as if Quentin Swan's crimes sound too awful. People have affairs all the time and the fault is rarely just on one side. And surely every home is better with a cat? Martin is spoiling what started out to be a good day. Earlier that morning Ruth had a call from Superintendent Jo Archer telling her that she has secured permission for the excavation below the Guildhall. It can take place tomorrow. Ruth has already booked Ted to help. 'Nelson seemed to be stalling so I pulled a few strings,' said Jo. 'Thank you,' said Ruth although she can't believe that Nelson has ever stalled in his life. Ruth decides to tell Martin about the excavation. It might distract him from his marital woes.

It seems to work. 'I'd love to have a look in those tunnels,' says Martin. 'The geology must be extremely interesting.'

'Yes, it's fascinating,' says Ruth. 'This tunnel seems to lead to St John's, the Catholic cathedral, but there's apparently a tunnel from the Guildhall to the Castle too. I think this one is quite old because it looks as if it was hand dug. The later Victorian tunnels were wider. You could get a horse and cart down some of them.'

'There were chalk pits on Rosary Road and Barrack Street,' says Martin. 'The area used to be known as Chalk Hill. The easiest way to dig is from an open pit in the valley side. But it's fair to assume that there are tunnels there too. There might even be an underground railway system for bringing the chalk back to the surface.'

'I don't think this is a mining tunnel,' says Ruth. 'It's too narrow and twisty. But it's quite well constructed – the walls are even plastered in places.'

'Probably lime plaster,' says Martin. 'A mixture of sand, water and lime. It stays hard for ever. Versions of it are still used in construction today.'

'I think I've read about it being used in the pyramids,' says Ruth.

'Yes. It's quite remarkable really. I wish I could see those tunnels of yours. Will Swan be there tomorrow?'

'I don't know,' says Ruth, though she's pretty sure he will be. She has left him a message about the excavation.

'Do you see your daughter's father?' asks Martin, obviously brooding again.

'Yes,' says Ruth. 'We're quite . . . friendly.' She wonders how long it will be before Martin hears the gossip about her and Nelson. 'He's married,' she says. 'He has another family. Grown-up children.'

'That must be difficult.'

'I'm used to it,' says Ruth. This is true though she's always surprised that the situation still has the power to hurt her. When Kate talks about Laura, for example. When Nelson lets slip that he and Michelle have been out 'for our anniversary'.

'Vicky and I are civilised now,' says Martin, 'but it's tough. I try to be a good father. I go to things like Olivia's Christmas play but Swan is always there too. I keep thinking, it was Vicky's fault that I came to bloody Norfolk in the first place and now I've got to live here on my own.'

Ruth prickles. She doesn't like to hear her adopted county criticised, although Nelson does it all the time.

'You won't be on your own for ever,' she says.

'I suppose not,' says Martin, taking a meditative sip of beer. He is smiling in a way that Ruth doesn't understand and doesn't quite like.

CHAPTER 22

Ruth remembers this conversation when she arrives at the Guildhall the next day to find the tall, rangy figure of Martin Kellerman waiting for her outside the main doors.

'I hope you don't mind,' he says. 'I just couldn't resist seeing the tunnels.'

Ruth does mind. The excavation is meant to be a sober, professional affair. 'You owe it to the dead to treat their remains with respect,' she tells her students, 'even if you don't know their names or how they died.' Besides, she had been hoping to spend some time with Nelson. Pretty desperate, she tells herself, to be looking forward to spending quality time buried in a fetid tunnel looking at old bones. But hey, each to their own.

'There might not be room for more than three people in the tunnel,' she tells Martin. 'There'll be me, Ted from the Field Archaeology team, and DCI Nelson from the King's Lynn police.'

'A policeman?' says Martin. 'Why is there a policeman here?'

'Because human bones are involved,' says Ruth. 'Excuse me. I need to get down to the undercroft.'

She doesn't invite Martin to follow her but he does anyway. And below the ground, worse is to come. Standing in the stone-vaulted cellar she finds not only Ted and Nelson, but Quentin Swan accompanied by a plump, bespectacled man and an attractive woman with hair dyed traffic-light red.

Martin speaks first.

'Vicky,' he says. 'What are you doing here?'

So this is Vicky, Martin Kellerman's ex-wife and mother of his child. It's hard to imagine the two people together. Vicky, with her red hair and artfully ripped jeans, looks far more suited to Quentin Swan in his designer casuals than to Martin Kellerman with his rumpled suit and little glasses.

Vicky blushes, which clashes rather nastily with her hair. 'Kevin and I wanted to see the tunnels. You know about our research on underground societies.'

So the other man must be Kevin whatsit, the sociologist who knows about the Empire of the Dead. To Ruth's surprise, he seems to be deep in conversation with Nelson.

'Why are you here?' Vicky asks Martin. Whatever Martin's claims of a civilised relationship with his ex-wife, there is definite animosity here. It fizzes and crackles in the dimly lit room. Ted looks from one to the other as if he's at a tennis match.

'Dr Galloway told me about the excavation,' says Martin. 'I'm interested from a geological perspective.'

Vicky turns a curious gaze on Ruth. With her powerful sense of her own attractiveness, Vicky reminds Ruth of

Shona. No wonder Shona had been rather dismissive in her assessment. Vicky flashes a smile at Ruth now, very Shona-like both in its impact and its brevity. On, off.

Ruth decides to assert herself. 'I'm afraid you won't all be able to come down. There's not enough room in the tunnel.'

'I need to come,' says Nelson immediately. Ruth is irritated (this is her dig, after all) but also slightly relieved. However annoying Nelson can be there's no doubt that she also feels safer when he's around.

'OK,' she says. 'DCI Nelson and one other.'

'I should go,' says Quentin. 'After all, it's my project.' He looks quite agitated, thinks Ruth, fiddling with his phone and not making eye contact with anyone. Maybe it's the presence of his wife's first husband or maybe it's just worry about the fate of his restaurant. Even so, Ruth resents him trying to take ownership. At the moment the tunnels are *her* project.

Martin looks as if he's about to protest but just lets his arms fall to his side in a rather deflated way. Silently Ruth hands Quentin a vest and hard hat. She wonders what Martin, Vicky and Kevin will find to talk about while she and the others are below ground.

Ted has removed the planks from the tunnel entrance. This time Ruth knows that she has to go first. She takes the torch and steps into the darkness. Ted follows, carrying the excavating equipment, pick over his shoulder. Ruth doesn't like the thought that Ted, Quentin and Nelson are behind her, blocking her exit route. They descend into the darkness, Ruth's torch picking out the ground below them, brick giving way to smooth chalk and then rubble.

'Bloody hell,' says Nelson from the back. 'How far does this thing go?'

'It goes all the way to St John's, we think,' says Ruth. 'But it's blocked a little bit beyond where the bones were found.'

'Who has access to this place?'

'It's closed off most of the time,' says Ruth, 'but the surveyor got special permission to come down here.'

'Mark Copeland,' says Quentin. 'He's very thorough.'

They have reached the passage where the bones were found. The pile of earth – the spoil heap, archaeologists call it – is still there. Ruth can even see the marks of her trowel. Normally a site will change every day. Wind, rain and sun will all affect the trench and the surrounding land. But here, underground, nothing has changed; it's as if it has been sealed, awaiting their return.

Ruth and Ted decide to dig in two locations: where the bones were originally found and another site a few metres further on. They have brought a crude lighting rig and Ted sets that up now. It's just two battery-operated lights on a stand but it casts an eerie glow in the tunnel, picking out the rough chalk walls and ceiling, the dusty rubble underfoot. The light has the effect of making the space feel even smaller and more claustrophobic. Ruth can feel herself breathing faster and wills herself to take slow, calming breaths. This is just an excavation like any other, she tells herself. Ted is marking out the trenches, humming to himself, for all the world as if they are in a field under the sun.

Ruth photographs the trenches and plots them on a graph.

'I'll do the new one,' says Ted. He takes a swing at the earth with his pick. Quentin gives an exclamation. 'I thought archaeology was meant to be delicate stuff? Brushing earth from priceless artefacts. That sort of thing.'

'Some of it is like that,' says Ruth, 'but digging is hard work, especially when the ground's packed hard like this. Sometimes we even use mechanical diggers.'

They could do with one today, she thinks. She bends to dig in the disturbed soil where the earlier bones were found. After shifting impatiently behind her for a few minutes, Nelson says, 'Can I help?' Ruth hands him a trowel and he kneels down opposite her. It's the first time that they have ever worked together and Ruth finds it oddly soothing. They dig in silence for a few minutes while, a few metres away, Ted unearths huge clods of earth. Quentin Swan doesn't offer to help. He watches carefully though, shining his iPhone torch on the widening hole.

After about ten minutes, Ruth says, 'I think I've found something.'

'What is it?' Ted comes over.

'A bone.'

Ruth pulls the white object out of the chalky soil. It's a piece of a long bone, completely defleshed but without the eerie glossy sheen of the previous bones.

'Do you think it's from the same body?' asks Nelson.

'I don't think so,' says Ruth. 'It looks like a tibial shaft and we found both of those last time. This looks a little shorter too. Could be a woman.'

'Or a child?' asks Nelson.

'Children's bones have growing ends on them called epiphyses,' says Ruth. 'This looks fully grown to me.'

'Does it have the same pot-whatsit as the other bones?' asks Nelson.

'No,' says Ruth. 'But it is broken off in the middle. Like I said, that could mean someone was after the marrow.'

'What do you mean?' Ruth had forgotten that Quentin Swan was there.

'Nothing,' she says. 'We won't know anything until we do some tests.' She marks the bone with a number and places it in a paper bag.

'Are there any more?' calls Ted from the neighbouring trench.

Ruth works the earth gently with her trowel. 'Yes,' she says. She pulls out another bone, flatter and more discoloured.

'What is it?' Nelson looks up.

'Looks like part of a pelvic bone. This could be useful. Will help us find out whether the bones are male or female.'

Gradually Ruth unearths several more bones: a femur, a patella and several ribs. There are some small bones which she thinks are from a foot. She marks them all on her skeleton sheet.

'No skull,' she says. 'We could really do with a skull or some teeth.'

'Do you think these are old bones?' asks Quentin Swan.

'Given that the other bones were modern,' she says, 'there's a good chance that these are too. They were found in the same context.'

Nelson leans over for a closer look but doesn't say anything. Ruth is glad that he doesn't say any more about her earlier suspicions. She's not ready to share these thoughts yet. She doesn't think that Quentin or Ted would go to the press but if they did, she could just imagine the headlines: 'Cannibal's lair beneath city.'

They dig for about half an hour longer. Quentin goes over to help Ted although Ruth can't imagine that the architect is a great one for physical labour. It's very hot in the tunnel and Ruth's back is starting to ache. She takes a swig from her water bottle.

'Should we stop for the day?' she says to Ted. They haven't found any more bones, but given what they have uncovered so far, it might be worth coming back another day and digging in a different part of the tunnel.

Ted doesn't answer at first. He has already created a shallow trench and is now on his knees sifting through the soil. So far, this section hasn't yielded any bones.

'Ted?'

He straightens up. 'Yes. Sure. It's getting bloody hot down here. Hang on a minute . . .'

'What is it?' Ruth hears the note of excitement in Ted's voice and comes to look.

'It was here . . . in the soil . . . yes, here.'

Ted straightens up and extends his hand. On his chalky palm is a small object that glints in the darkness.

A necklace, tarnished gold, spelling the name 'Babs'.

*

Judy is excited. She has her first real breakthrough. A message from Intel is in her inbox saying that they have traced Barbara's oldest children. They were adopted by the same family and their names are Rory and Siobhan McTavish. Both are still living in Scotland and Siobhan is at Herriot Watt University. 'Three guesses what Rory does for a living??' writes Poppy from Intel in her characteristically breathless style. Poppy has obviously not thought it worth giving Judy time to guess because underneath she has written, 'He's a copper!!!!'

Judy calls Clough over.

'Barbara Murray's son is a policeman.'

'Bloody hell.' Clough finishes his Mars bar and comes to look at the screen. 'What was that thing you were telling me the other week? Looked-after children have higher rates of mental and emotional problems. Here's your proof.'

'He's done well,' says Judy. 'But he wasn't in care, he was adopted. There's a big difference. He's working in Portobello. Shouldn't be too hard to find the number of the station.'

'Are you going to call him?'

'Why not?'

'Well, he might not want to know about his mum. Maybe he doesn't even know he's adopted.'

'He could have applied to the Adoption Contact Register at eighteen to see if he wanted to trace his birth mother,' says Judy. 'He's twenty-three now. I just want to know if Barbara has been in touch.'

Judy has found a number and is dialling.

'Well, be careful.'

'I'm always careful,' says Judy.

After all that, she fully expects PC McTavish to be away or out on the beat, but after a short break a pleasant Scottish voice comes on the line. 'Hallo?'

'Constable Rory McTavish? It's Detective Sergeant Judy Johnson here from King's Lynn CID. I hope it's all right but I just wanted to ask some questions about your birth mother.'

'My birth mother?' He sounds confused. Oh God, please don't let Clough be right.

'Your birth mother. Barbara Murray.'

'What about her?' The boyish voice sounds hard now. 'Is she dead? The drugs, was it?'

'No,' says Judy. 'But we're a bit worried about her. She hasn't been seen for a couple of weeks. I just wondered if there was any chance that she'd been in contact with you.'

'She hasn't been in contact,' says Rory. 'I haven't seen her since I was a bairn. I heard she was living on the streets. A down-and-out. In a real bad way.'

'How did you hear that?'

A short silence. 'I looked in the police records,' says Rory. 'She's got convictions for drug offences, begging, all sorts. No wonder she couldn't bring up her children.'

'You looked her up but you didn't get in contact?'

'Why would I get in contact? I've had the perfect parents. They've given me and Siobhan everything. Why would I get in contact with a drug addict who abandoned me?'

'Look,' says Judy, 'it's none of my business but I understand that Barbara was a child when she had you. She probably wasn't ready to be a mother, especially when she didn't get any support from her own parents. But I've been finding out a lot about her in the last week or so, talking to people who know her. Barbara's had her problems but everyone says she's a very nice lady, very kind, very intelligent. She talks a lot about being a mother. It's very important to her. I'm sure you're very important to her.'

There's another silence and Judy wonders if she's totally overstepped the mark. Then Rory says, 'Thanks for ringing anyway.'

'Thanks for talking to me.' Judy rings off.

Clough is watching her across the desk. 'St Judy strikes again,' he says.

'Oh, give it a break, Dave.'

Clough is about to say more when Tanya prances into the incident room.

'The digital media bods have found some CCTV,' she says. 'I think Sam's on it. They're sending it through now.'

Barbara momentarily forgotten, Judy and Clough gather round the computer.

'What did you find?' Martin, Kevin and Vicky crowd round as they emerge from the tunnel.

'We're not at liberty to say,' says Nelson at his most repressive.

Ruth takes off her hat and shakes out her sweaty hair. More than anything she just wants to sit down with a cold drink. But Vicky is at her elbow, doing that Belisha beacon smile again.

'Did you find any more bones?'

'I can't say, I'm afraid,' says Ruth. 'This is a police inquiry.'

'Are the bones modern then?' Vicky turns to Quentin who doesn't reply. Ruth has no doubt at all that he'll tell his wife all the details later, but at the moment Quentin seems more concerned with brushing chalk dust from his black jeans.

'It was filthy down there,' he says. 'Boiling hot too.'

'All right for you,' says Ted, upending his flask and letting the water drip down his face. 'You didn't do any digging.'

'I did a bit.' Quentin looks rather hurt.

'Did you find any signs of human occupation in the tunnel?' says Kevin. 'That tunnel leads to St John's and there are rumours that the crypt at St John's is one of the portals to the underworld.'

Portals to the underworld. Ruth can't believe what she's hearing. It's as if she's wandered into one of Kate's beloved C.S. Lewis books. What was that line in *The Silver Chair*? 'Many come down and few return to the sunlit lands.'

'There were no portals as far as we could see,' says Nelson. 'I need to get back to the police station now.'

'Why don't we all go to the cafe for a cup of tea?' says Quentin.

'I ought to get back too,' says Martin, obviously not fancying a tête-à-tête with Quentin and Vicky. Ruth wonders if he regrets coming. It's a long drive just to wait in a cellar with your ex-wife and her colleague.

'I'm off too,' says Ted, swinging his tool bag onto his shoulder. 'People to see, bones to excavate.'

'I'll take this for you, Ruth.' Nelson reaches for the pathology box. 'Can I have a word before you go?'

Ruth follows Nelson out of the undercroft, trying not to

show how pleased she is. Outside, in the sunshine, Nelson says, 'I couldn't face going to a cafe with that lot. Shall we talk in the car? I'll get us something cold to drink and we can have the air conditioning on.'

This sounds a perfect plan to Ruth. She waits in Nelson's car which he has parked in the market place beside the Guildhall, oblivious to signs telling him not to. The air conditioning is whirring away but it still feels like a sauna. It's blissful to be sitting down though. Ruth opens the door to let in some air and sees Vicky, Quentin and Kevin heading off down the cobbled street, in search of a pub or cafe. Martin has obviously gone in the other direction. Quentin and Vicky are arm in arm, Kevin struggling to keep up with them.

Nelson appears carrying two sweating cans of Coke.

'You're a life saver,' says Ruth.

'I do my best.'

They sit in the car drinking in silence for a few minutes and then Nelson says, 'Did you ring Jo about the excavation today?'

Ruth is surprised. 'No. *She* rang *me*. She said that she'd pulled strings to get it authorised.'

'Typical,' says Nelson, but he seems rather cheered by this news. 'So,' he says, 'do you think those were Barbara's bones in the tunnel?'

'I don't think so,' says Ruth, holding the can against her forehead. 'These bones were buried below the previous ones. That suggests that they've been there for some time and Barbara's only been missing for a couple of weeks.'

'But the necklace though,' says Nelson. 'That could mean that Barbara was in the tunnel recently.'

'Or that someone who had the necklace was in the tunnel.'

'Yes. You do think like a policeman, Ruth.'

'Don't say that,' says Ruth, but she knows that it is meant as a compliment.

Nelson is silent for a few minutes, drinking his Coke and frowning into the distance. 'The thing is, Ruth, when we were asking about Barbara, this man, another rough sleeper, said that he'd heard that she'd gone underground. Then we find her necklace in a tunnel below the Guildhall.'

'Did you ask the man what he meant?'

'I'd love to ask him a few questions,' says Nelson, 'but unfortunately he was murdered on Saturday. He was the man found dead by the Red Mount Chapel. You might have read about it in the local paper.'

'I must have missed it. The papers have all been full of the missing woman from Pott Row.'

'We haven't got any leads on her either,' says Nelson. 'It's hard to see any link to Barbara, but two women disappearing into thin air – we've got to look at the possibility. Maybe they've both gone underground.'

'Martin Kellerman, one of the men who was here today. He was telling me about underground societies recently. He knows about them because Vicky, his ex-wife, works with that Kevin bloke.'

'It's all very complicated,' says Nelson. 'Vicky was the red-headed woman, right?'

'Yes. It was a bit of a surprise to see them all here today.'

'I went to see Kevin O'Casey at the university on Wednesday,' says Nelson. So that's what he was doing there, thinks Ruth, rather pleased to add this piece to the jigsaw. 'He's writing a book about underground societies. The weirdest stuff you ever heard.'

'Why did you go to see him?'

'I had some information that he knew a man we wanted to speak to. Another rough sleeper.'

'And did he?'

'Yes. He'd interviewed him for his book. He thought that this man was one of the organisers of a secret society living in the tunnels below Norwich.'

'Is there really a society like that?' The thought gives Ruth an unpleasant, dizzy feeling. She thinks of *Alice's Adventures Under Ground*. Is it possible to fall down a rabbit hole and find yourself dancing the Lobster Quadrille with a Gryphon and a Mock Turtle? It sounds impossible, but doesn't Lewis Carroll have a character who believes six impossible things before breakfast?

'Richard, the man I was talking about, he's says it's all a fantasy, an urban myth. But I don't know. Richard's a clever man – he could be hiding something. Bilbo, the chap who said that Barbara had gone underground, was murdered. Maybe that was to stop him saying any more. Judy and Cathbad did the soup run last night and one of the homeless men there was talking about people disappearing – "being taken", that's how he described it. Barbara Murray and Sam Foster-Jones have disappeared off the face of the earth. But now I'm thinking, what if they're not off the face of the earth? What if they're below it?'

Ruth looks out at the busy Norwich scene: the open market, the council offices, the chequerboard Guildhall building. As a child Ruth had been fascinated by the London Underground, especially by the thought of the abandoned stations: Aldwych, Down Street, Brompton Road. She sometimes used to think of the deserted platforms, the 1930s advertisements still on the walls, the rats running along the silent lines. She had read somewhere that during the war Down Street had been used as a shelter by Churchill and his cabinet. Is there really an underground beneath Norwich too? Yesterday Martin Kellerman had talked about an underground railway system for bringing chalk to the surface. Ruth imagines a network of subterranean tunnels, carts moving in silence along the dark rails. Are they still there, part of a secret metropolis? Are people being taken from the surface so that they can work in these hidden mines? And she hears Kate screaming, *'He said he'd take me underground.'*

Nelson offers to drive Ruth back to the university but she says that her car is parked a few streets away. 'Anyway, I want to go home and have a shower. I don't have to go back to work this afternoon. I'll go home now and then I'll be in good time to pick up Kate.'

'How is she?' says Nelson.

'She's fine,' says Ruth. 'She really enjoyed going to your house that time. She keeps talking about Laura.'

Ruth's face is unreadable. Nelson says, carefully, 'She liked Laura.'

'Does Laura know about Kate?'

'No,' says Nelson. They are standing by his car, now hemmed in by market stalls. Ruth has turned away from him, almost as if she doesn't want to know the answer to her question. He says, 'I know I should tell the girls. Michelle keeps telling me I should. It's just . . .' He stops, not knowing how to finish the sentence. Just impossible? Just too difficult? Just terrifying to think that, with one conversation, he could lose the love and respect of his daughters?

Ruth takes pity on him. 'It must be hard,' she says. 'Kate hasn't really asked who Laura is. She just seemed to think she's a nice lady who lives at your house.'

'They were drawn to each other,' says Nelson. 'I suppose it's natural, really.'

'I suppose it is. Not that I'm that close to my brother. I mean, I love him but if we weren't in the same family I don't think we'd ever be friends.'

'It's the same with my sisters,' says Nelson. 'I haven't got that much in common with them. Laura and Rebecca though, they've always been close. Like Michelle and her sister.'

There is a rather awkward pause then Ruth says, 'I suppose I'd better be getting on.'

'Don't forget the bones,' says Nelson.

'No.' Ruth lifts the box from the back seat. 'I'll let you know when we have the test results,' she says. 'Bye, Nelson.'

'Yes,' says Nelson. 'Thanks, Ruth.' And he drives back to

the station deep in thought, hardly noticing how often he breaks the speed limit. He always enjoys seeing Ruth at work. He admires her calm professionalism, the way that she takes charge of the situation. She hadn't had any truck with any of the academics observing the excavation, for example. He had thought that she hadn't enjoyed the dig today – the dark journey underground, the cramped conditions in the tunnel – but it hadn't showed, not really. Afterwards it had been good to sit in the car with her, with their cold drinks, discussing the case. There are things that he can say to Ruth that he can't say to anyone else, not even to his team. That he's got no idea what has happened to Barbara or Sam, for example. That he's beginning to believe in this underground world. The Empire of the Damned, or whatever it's called.

But then Ruth had to spoil it all by mentioning Laura. He knows that he has to tell the girls. It's just . . . It's just he would do almost anything in the world to avoid this conversation. He can imagine Laura's tears, Rebecca's disgust. 'You mean you've had a child with another woman and she's six years old? Why didn't you tell us before? Why didn't Mum leave you as soon as she found out?'

Back at the station he finds Tanya, Judy and Clough looking through some new CCTV from Pott Row. The local primary school has cameras fitted which show the road outside. 'We have a lot of problems with parents parking on the zigzags,' the headteacher had explained. The footage from Monday night shows a lot of cars going to and fro (and some stopping on the zigzags), but at a quarter to six it shows a black car waiting at the pedestrian crossing. In the passenger seat is a woman who could possibly be Sam Foster-Jones. Judy and Clough are peering at the screen.

'She's got short blonde hair,' Judy is saying. 'It could be her.'

'She's wearing a dark top,' says Clough. 'What was she wearing when she disappeared?'

'I'll have to check,' says Judy. 'T-shirt and hoodie, I think.'

'Can you see the driver?' asks Nelson, coming forward.

'Not very well. The camera's on the passenger side. Looks like a man, dark hair or a hat, wearing glasses.'

'Glasses? Charlie said that the man who spoke to Barbara was wearing glasses.'

'Doesn't get us very far though,' says Judy. 'Half the population wears glasses and they're the easiest thing to take off and put on if you want to change your appearance.'

Nelson often thinks that he should probably wear glasses. His phone screen seems strangely blurred and he finds himself holding the newspaper at arm's length, just like his mum used to.

'She seems to be going with him of her own accord,' says Clough. 'After all, the car's stationary. She could have jumped out.'

'We don't know that,' says Nelson. 'She could be drugged, for all we know. Her head looks a bit as if it's lolling to the side.'

'Eddie was drugged,' Judy says. 'Bilbo too.' The autopsy on Bilbo had also shown traces of soda lime around his mouth.

'Have you got a number plate for the car?' says Nelson.

'Yes.'

'Let's get it out there. Intel should find us a match in seconds.'

'I was just going to,' says Judy, sounding irritated. 'Did Ruth find anything in the tunnel?'

'Another set of bones,' says Nelson, 'possibly female. And this.' He places the bag containing the necklace on the desk.

'Bloody hell,' says Clough. 'Do you think she's dead then?'

'Ruth didn't think the bones were hers,' says Nelson. 'She thought that they'd been down there too long. But the necklace – it's almost too big a clue. As if someone left it there for us to find.'

'And would Barbara wear a necklace anyway?' says Clough. 'You don't see many rough sleepers with jewellery.'

'It looks quite cheap though,' says Judy. 'The metal's tarnished. It's not real gold. Maybe she wore it for sentimental reasons. Maybe one of her children gave it to her.'

'We could show it to her younger children,' says Nelson. 'She had some contact with them, didn't she? We'd have to be sensitive about it, mind.'

'Intel managed to trace her older two children,' says Judy, 'the ones that were adopted. I spoke to the son about an hour ago. He's called Rory McTavish and he's a police officer.'

'A policeman? Where?'

'Portobello in Scotland. But he hadn't been in contact with his mother. He sounded very bitter about her, actually. He'd looked up her records, the drug convictions, all the rest of it.'

'Judy gave him some worldly-wise advice though,' says Clough. Judy flashes him a look.

'What about the daughter?' says Nelson.

'She's at university.'

'Give her a ring,' says Nelson. 'Just check whether she's been in touch with Barbara. She may have made contact but not wanted to tell her brother. It's a long shot but we can't leave any stone unturned. Cloughie, you get onto the number plate.'

It's an odd phrase, thinks Nelson, as he runs the CCTV footage one more time. He thinks of the tunnel that morning, the journey below the stones of the city. Nothing good ever comes of turning over a stone.

Once again Ruth is in good time. She sits on the friendship bench in glorious isolation until Cathbad arrives and takes pity on her. Miranda is out of her buggy for once and is trotting around the playground, picking daisies and being admired.

'She's growing up so fast,' says Ruth.

'She's an old soul,' says Cathbad. 'Like my mother.'

Cathbad often says that Miranda is like his mother, who died when he was a teenager, and there is something stereotypically Irish about the little girl's dark hair, pale skin and blue eyes. Ruth actually thinks that Miranda is the image of Judy but then Judy, too, is Irish on her father's side.

'How's your mother?' says Cathbad.

'Doing well,' says Ruth. 'She's in a rehabilitation place now but she's hoping to get home soon. I'm driving down to see her on Sunday.'

'We can have Hecate if you like.'

'I'm taking her with me. I thought Mum would like to see her. She adores Kate.'

'I bet she does. I imagine they're quite alike.'

'Why do you say that? You've never met my mother.' Ruth looks at Cathbad sitting serenely in the sun with Miranda's pink cardigan on his lap. Just when you dismiss Cathbad's second sight he comes out with stuff like this.

'Just an idea. I imagine that your mum was like Kate when she was young – bold and outgoing and clever.'

'I think you might be right,' says Ruth. 'She certainly doesn't get bold and outgoing from me.' She doesn't add 'clever' because she secretly does think that Kate gets her intelligence from her.

'Oh, you have your moments, Ruthie,' says Cathbad.

There's a definite Friday feeling as the cavalcade of mothers and buggies heads out of the school gates. Ruth and Cathbad take the children for ice creams in Wells. It's very pleasant sitting on the harbour wall, watching the fishing boats bobbing in the shallow water. Ruth doesn't really want to leave but she has work to do that evening and even Kate says that she has some spellings to learn. Ruth doesn't approve of homework for primary school children, but just as she is planning a stiff letter to the headteacher Kate tells her that this task is self-imposed. 'I asked if I could learn ten new words beginning with D.'

'Try druid,' says Cathbad, putting Miranda into her buggy. 'And dendrochronology.'

*

'What does that dendo word mean?' asks Kate as they drive back along the coast road.

'Telling a tree's age by the rings on it,' says Ruth. 'I'll show you next time we see a tree stump.' She loves teaching Kate things and luckily archaeology, involving as it does a lot of digging in the mud, is endlessly fascinating to her daughter.

The Saltmarsh is beautiful in the afternoon sun, pale pink with sea lavender, criss-crossed by countless sparkling streams. The tide is coming in, inlets turning to lagoons, the bright blue water reflecting the sky above. They eat their supper in the front garden, watching the birds flying over the mud flats. Then Kate writes out her words in large wobbly letters and Ruth reads exam scripts. They watch a DVD (*The Voyage of the Dawn Treader*) and Kate has her bath and goes to bed without undue struggle. Ruth prays that Kate won't wake with a nightmare, but when she checks on her at nine she is sleeping peacefully with her favourite toy (a cuddly chimpanzee from Nelson) at her side. It's still light outside and Ruth is just wondering whether to sit in the garden with her laptop when her phone rings. 'Dave Clough' says the display. Surprised, Ruth presses 'accept'.

'Ruth,' says Clough's voice, sounding slightly odd. 'Is Cassie with you?'

'Cassie? No.'

'I thought you had a rehearsal tonight.'

'Kate wasn't needed.'

'It's just . . .' Ruth can hear Clough breathing and another sound, possibly Spencer, in the background. 'She was meant to be home at eight and it's past nine now.'

'Maybe she went out for a drink with the cast.'

'Maybe, but she usually rings and there's no answer from her phone.'

'It's probably just run out of battery. That happens to me all the time.'

'Probably. Just let me know if you hear anything, will you?'

'Of course.'

The house is silent after Clough has rung off but Ruth doesn't go into the garden. She locks both doors and sits in front of the television watching two delusional Londoners build a house in Tuscany. Though she doesn't quite know why, she is very scared.

CHAPTER 23

Nelson is still at work when he gets the call.

'Boss, I'm worried. Cassie hasn't come back from her rehearsal.'

Nelson looks up at the wall clock. Christ, is it as late as that? He should have been home hours ago. But from Cassie's point of view it's probably still early. He says as much.

'It's nine-thirty,' says Clough. 'The rehearsal ends at eight.'

'Maybe they've all gone out for a drink,' says Nelson. 'It's Friday night after all.'

'That's what Ruth said.'

Nelson is rather disconcerted that Clough has already spoken to Ruth but he supposes that it's because Katie is in this weird play too (against his better judgement). His own feeling is that Cassie has almost certainly gone for a drink with some adoring man. He's not sure why, but he has never quite trusted Cassandra. Maybe it's just because she is so glamorous, as out-of-place in rural Norfolk as a gazelle in a petting zoo. But Nelson's own wife is also extremely beautiful and he trusts her, doesn't he?

'I'm sure she'll be back soon,' he says.

'I keep trying her phone but there's no answer.'

'Give it another ten minutes. She's probably on her way.'

'The thing is, boss, I'm in Lynn. At the rehearsal place. Her car's here.'

'You're in Lynn? What about the baby?'

'He's with me. I thought I'd have a look round the local pubs. See if she's here.'

The thought of Clough trailing round the pubs with Spencer in a baby sling, in search of his missing partner, makes Nelson's heart twist in mingled exasperation and pity. He sighs. 'Stay where you are. I'll come and join you.'

When Nelson arrives Clough is walking around the community centre car park. He's moving in an odd way and when Nelson gets nearer he sees that it's because he's jiggling Spencer up and down to stop him crying. Whatever else he does, Nelson decides, he has to persuade Clough to take the baby home.

Clough has his phone with him and he's texting, with some difficulty because of the baby, as he walks.

'I've just tried her parents,' he says as Nelson approaches. 'They haven't heard from her since yesterday.'

'Where's her car?' says Nelson.

It's a stupid question. There's only one car in the car park besides Nelson's Mercedes and Clough's Saab. It's a Fiat 500, bluish-green (Nelson is hazy about those colours), exactly the car he would have expected Cassandra to drive. Nelson's daughters are crazy about those little Fiats and even Michelle says that she would like one in a colour called latte.

'Her pashmina's on the back seat,' says Clough. 'I'm sure she would have taken it with her if she'd gone out anywhere.'

Nelson can't believe that Clough has even heard of a pashmina, let alone be thinking about when one should be worn. He doesn't think it's that suspicious himself. It's a warm evening – both he and Clough are in shirtsleeves – and he's pretty sure that Cassandra could survive without her posh scarf.

'Let's think about this calmly,' says Nelson. 'When did you last hear from Cassie?'

'I got home at six,' says Clough, 'and Cass went straight out to her rehearsal. She was a bit pissed off with me for being late. She said that she'd be back at eight-thirty. I started to worry at nine.'

Nelson is willing to bet that Clough started to worry at eight thirty-one. It's ten o'clock now. 'Did you call anyone else in the play?' he says. 'They could all be out drinking somewhere. Have you checked in any pubs?'

'Yes. Bar Red and Dr Thirsty's. They looked a bit shocked to see Spencer in there. And I called Leo Chard. He's the wanker who wrote the play. He said that he said goodbye to Cassie here, at the community centre, at eight. He said she was standing in the porch texting when he drove away.'

'Look, Cloughie.' Nelson tries to make his voice reassuring. 'You've got to get Spencer home. Cassie might already be back. Maybe her car wouldn't start. Someone could have given her a lift home. I'll check the local pubs, and if there's no joy I'll put a missing person out. OK?'

'OK,' says Clough. Spencer starts to whimper and Clough jiggles him again. 'I keep thinking,' he says, 'is this how that poor sap Benedict Foster-Jones felt?'

'This is completely different,' says Nelson, though he feels a cold chill to the heart. 'You said yourself that Cassie was a bit pissed off with you. That's probably why she's not answering your calls. I bet she's at home now.'

'You think?'

'Yes, I do. Go on, Cloughie, take Spencer home. He needs his bed.'

Clough still looks unconvinced. 'I'll ask if anyone has seen her,' says Nelson. 'Have you got a picture of Cassie on your phone? Text it to me. What is she wearing?'

'Black jeans and a cropped T-shirt. The T-shirt has "Venus in Furs" written on it.'

'"Venus in Furs". What does that mean?'

'It's a song. From a band called Velvet Underground.'

They look at each other as a sudden wind sweeps through the car park, scattering the rubbish from an overflowing bin in a swirl of newspaper and crumpled paper cups.

Eventually Clough allows himself to be persuaded and drives off with Spencer asleep in the baby seat. Nelson calls Michelle to let her know that he'll be late.

When he tells her about Cassandra Michelle says, 'I just had a text from her earlier.'

'When?' says Nelson.

'Eightish, I think. Let me look. 8.02.'

'What did she say?'

'Nothing much, just how was I. That sort of thing.' Nelson thinks Michelle sounds rather evasive but maybe she is worried because then she says, 'Do you really think something's happened to Cassie?'

'No,' says Nelson bracingly. 'I'm sure she's just with some of the cast.'

'Yes, she says they're all really good friends.'

'Any idea where they might have gone?'

'In Lynn? I don't know. Somewhere nice, knowing Cassie.'

'I'll have a look round the restaurants. See you later, love.'

Nelson sets out to search for 'somewhere nice'. Clough has visited the only places in walking distance so he drives into the centre of town and starts with the places likely to appeal to Cassandra, establishments with real tablecloths and complicated-sounding menus. But no one has seen a stunning dark-haired woman, either alone or accompanied. The picture Clough texted to Nelson shows Cassandra peering over her naked shoulder in a cloud of hair and this causes much unnecessary ribaldry.

After trying the last possible restaurant Nelson walks through the deserted Vancouver Centre. He passes several shapes huddled in doorways. Do these people know where Barbara is? Could one of the shapes even be Barbara? But he doesn't like to wake them and besides, Cassandra is now in the forefront of his mind. He no longer thinks that she's having a jolly, flirtatious evening with an admirer. He is starting to feel very worried indeed.

Clough calls just as he gets back to his car.

'Any luck?'

'No,' says Nelson. 'I'm going to put out a missing person alert. Just as a precaution.'

'Cassie's parents are coming over to look after Spencer,' says Clough. 'Then I'll come and help you look.'

Nelson groans inwardly but doesn't think he can stop Clough. And he understands only too well the need to be doing something at moments like this.

'I thought I'd go and see the director,' says Nelson. 'After all, he was one of the last people to see her. Do you have his address?'

'Somewhere. Hang on. Here it is.'

Leo Chard lives in a new apartment block by the quay. 'I'll meet you there,' says Clough. 'As soon as Sally and George get here.'

Nelson knows Cassandra's parents from an earlier case. Sally, at least, is very sensible. He hopes that she'll talk Clough out of any vigilante justice.

'I'll see you later,' he says.

Ruth wants to ring Clough to find out if Cassandra is home but she imagines him pouncing on the phone only to slump back in despair when he realises that it's only her. No, she'll have to wait until the morning and ask Judy. After all, she tells herself, Cassandra is probably back by now, airily blaming a flat battery and laughing at Clough's fears. She's a grown woman, why shouldn't she be out past nine o'clock? But Sam Foster-Jones was a grown woman who managed to disappear in broad daylight. Ruth looks at the unreliable carriage clock on her mantelpiece that was a leaving present from some of her overseas students last year. It's now past eleven. She goes to the window. She's used to the utter blackness outside, no street or house lights, just miles of darkness with the occasional faint phosphorescent glow out towards the sea. What is happening, out there in the dark world? Has Cassandra been taken, as Barbara was taken, as Sam was taken? She jumps when Flint appears on the table beside her, butting his head against her arm to make her stroke his ears. 'Don't worry, Flint,' she tells the cat. 'It'll all be OK in the end.' Her words sound hollow in her own ears.

She feeds Flint (this is probably what he was after all along) and turns out the lights downstairs. Upstairs, she checks on Kate one more time. Kate is still sleeping peacefully. Ruth thinks of her father, all those miles away in London, alone in the big double bed. She hopes it won't be too long before her mum can come back home. The Eltham house is too big for one person and her father doesn't fill it, as she, Kate and Flint fill this cottage. 'Goddess bless, goddess keep,' says Ruth aloud. Back in her room, she takes one last look out of the window. The marshes whisper with a sudden breeze, an owl hoots and she hears another night bird answer. The liminal zone, that's what Erik used to call it – the bridge between life and death. This underground world described by Nelson seems another in-between place, a waiting area between life on earth and death in the grave. Why do we bury bodies underground? So they will rise again. Ruth pulls the curtains and gets into bed.

*

Even though it's now nearly midnight, Nelson doesn't telephone to say that he's on his way to Leo's flat. Memories of watching an earlier play of Leo's, some god awful nonsense about Janus, have not made him kindly disposed towards the director. However, he has no actual reason to suspect him.

The address given to him by Clough is one of those new developments that looks like it's been made from children's building blocks, all multicoloured bricks and plasticky-looking balconies. Leo answers the entryphone sounding worried, but Nelson's peremptory bark of 'Police' would do that to anyone. By the time he opens the door to his flat he is looking more or less composed. He is wearing a weird black outfit, a cross between martial arts gear and pyjamas, but Nelson decides not to hold this against him.

'What's this about?' Leo shows him into a sitting room which is just what Nelson would have expected: white walls, black furniture, arty posters.

'Cassandra Blackstock has gone missing,' says Nelson, sitting on an unpleasantly squeaky sofa. 'When did you see her last?'

Leo sits opposite him, take off his glasses and rubs his eyes. 'Cassie? Oh my God. How awful. Are you sure?'

'She hasn't been seen since eight o'clock,' says Nelson. He glances at the clock on the wall, too trendy to display any numbers. The hands are almost together at the top. 'So, can you tell me when you last saw her?'

'It was outside the community centre,' says Leo. 'We'd finished the rehearsal and I was going to my car. Cassie was standing in the porch texting. I said goodbye and she said it back but she seemed preoccupied. Then I went to my car and drove off.'

'Was she still there when you drove away?'

'I think so.' Leo looks up. Nelson can never remember if this means that you're lying or not. Tim was the one who knew all that neurolinguistic programming crap. 'I think I saw her under the porch lights as I drove away.'

'Have you any idea where she could be? Was she friendly with any other cast members?'

'All the cast get on well. Cassie seems close to Adrian Linley, who plays the Caterpillar, her father in the play. Flora Frampton, who plays the Queen of Hearts, she mothers everybody, and Darrell Shaw . . .' He pauses.

'Yes? What about Darrell Shaw?'

'He's a young actor. Very talented. Plays the Gryphon, the Mad Hatter and the Cheshire Cat. I just have a feeling that he has rather a crush on Cassie.'

'Does she have a crush back?'

'No.' Leo sounds quite shocked. 'She seems blissfully happy with that oafish policeman partner.' He stops. 'Oh, I'm sorry . . .'

'It's OK,' says Nelson. 'He's not a big fan of yours either.' He wonders whether Leo, too, has a crush on Cassandra and that's why he dislikes Clough. He doubts that Clough, who earlier called Leo a wanker, has gone out of his way to ingratiate himself.

'Do you have this Darrell's address?'

'Yes.' Leo takes out a flashy gold phone. 'But you can't think that he's got anything to do with this.'

'I don't think anything,' says Nelson. 'I just want to find Cassandra.'

Clough is waiting outside, a dark, miserable shape standing beside his car. 'What did Leo say?' he asks as soon as he sees Nelson.

'He says he last saw Cassie at eight o'clock, standing in the porch of the community centre, texting. Michelle got a text from her at 8.02. Did you hear from her later?'

'No,' says Clough. 'I haven't had a text or a call from her all evening. I asked her mum and she hadn't heard from her either.'

'So Michelle might have been the last person she contacted.'

'What did she say to Michelle?' asks Clough.

'Nothing much, apparently.' Nelson remembers that Michelle hadn't told him Cassandra's exact words. 'Just chit-chat,' he says. 'Leo mentioned a young actor, Darrell Shaw, who might have a crush on Cassie. Has she ever mentioned him to you?'

'Darrell.' Even in the dark, Nelson can see the cogs working. 'I think she might have mentioned him. She thought he was a good actor. What are we waiting for? He could be obsessed with Cassie. He could have kidnapped her.'

'Not so fast,' says Nelson. 'I'm not taking you anywhere in this state. You've got to get yourself under control.'

'I am under control,' says Clough through gritted teeth.

'Let me lead the interview,' says Nelson. 'Remember, this Darrell isn't accused of anything. He lives quite near her, in

Gaywood. We'll talk to him and then I'll get a team to search the area around the community centre.'

He thinks that Clough might break down at this evidence that he is taking Cassandra's disappearance seriously but Clough just nods and says, 'Let's go. I'll follow in my car.'

Nelson rings the number given to him by Leo and warns Darrell that they will be calling. When he arrives at the semi-detached house, he's glad that he took this precaution, because it turns out that the dashing, bearded Darrell lives with his mother. Meeting them at the door, Darrell ushers them into the sitting room and asks them to keep their voices down so as not to wake this parent. 'She's a nurse,' says Darrell. 'She has to get up early.' He smiles, slightly ruefully, 'It's not the most glamorous thing for an aspiring actor, is it? Living with your mum.'

'Happens a lot these days,' says Nelson. 'My daughter's just come home to live with us.'

'I keep telling myself it's just until I get my big break . . .' His voice trails off.

'As I said on the phone, we're slightly anxious about Cassandra. She hasn't been seen since rehearsal ended at the community centre. When did you see her last?'

'At the community centre. When I left she was chatting with Leo, the director.'

'Then what did you do? Drive home?'

'Yes, I've got a little moped. I left just before eight, met some friends in the pub for a quick drink, then came home.'

'Which pub?'

'The Lord Nelson.' Darrell tries a quick smile but Nelson looks at him stonily.

'Someone told us that you've got a soft spot for Cassandra,' says Nelson.

Darrell blushes in the parts of his face not covered by hair. 'I . . . no, I haven't . . . it's just . . . well, she's really good-looking. Have you seen her?'

Clough makes an angry movement but Nelson quells him with a look. 'Have you ever made a pass at her?'

'No. She's got a boyfriend and a baby.'

'These friends of yours in the pub,' says Nelson, 'can they vouch for you?'

'Yes,' says Darrell. 'I'm well known in the pub. I do bar work there sometimes. But you can't think that I've got anything to do with Cassie going missing?'

People keep telling him what he can't think, muses Nelson. The trouble is, the unthinkable is often the only solution. But if Darrell's friends give him an alibi, it looks as if he's in the clear. Besides, it's hard to imagine him bringing Cassandra back to the house that he shares with his mum. He thanks Darrell and drives back to Lynn, followed by Clough, grim-faced behind the wheel of his sporty Saab.

Outside the community centre they find the search teams going over the waste ground behind the car park. At the sight of this activity Clough's composure fails him. He turns away, his shoulders shaking. Nelson pats him on the back. 'Come on, Cloughie. This is just a precaution, you know that.'

Clough raises an anguished face. 'She's dead, boss. I know she is.'

'No, she isn't. We'll find her, I promise.' Clough continues to sob, and in the end Nelson puts both arms round him. They stand in the car park as Clough, who never sheds a tear, cries on Nelson's shoulder.

CHAPTER 24

Ruth is woken by Kate asking her if she can give Flint a bath.

'No,' says Ruth, struggling to wake up. 'He hates water. What time is it?' Kate has recently learnt to tell the time.

'I think it's nine,' says Kate. 'Or three.'

Ruth feels a moment of panic and then she remembers that it's Saturday, a blissful day of rest. Tomorrow they'll have to be up early for the drive to Eltham so she should make the most of today. She stretches out a hand and switches on Radio 4.

'. . . missing woman has been named as Cassandra Black-stock, the partner of a local police officer. Police are said to be taking her disappearance very seriously.'

Ruth stares at Kate.

'Did they say Cassandra?' says Kate, who is arranging Ruth's bedside reading into neat stepping stones.

'I think they did,' says Ruth.

Downstairs she rings Judy. Yes, says Judy, it is Cassandra. She went missing last night. They think it's linked to Sam Foster-Jones's disappearance. They've got reinforcements from three forces looking for her. Yes, Clough is here. The boss keeps telling him to go home but he won't. Cassandra's parents are looking after Spencer. Yes, she will give Clough Ruth's love. She has to go now. Goodbye.

Ruth sits on the sofa with her phone in her hand. Sensing her distraction, Kate switches on the television. A chef is preparing something that he calls 'food heaven'. Ruth thinks about Cassandra – beautiful, cool Cassandra. Can she really have disappeared? What did Nelson say? *What if she's not on the face of the earth?* And Clough, who finally seemed to have found contentment with his gorgeous girlfriend and their baby. What is he feeling now? She can just imagine Nelson urging him to go home and Clough refusing. The team always sticks together at moments like this. Not for the first time, Ruth feels rather left out. She's accepted by the Serious Crimes Unit but she's not really one of them. All she can do is sit at home and wait. If only she could pray or summon up a few helpful spirits. Well, she imagines that Cathbad must know about Cassandra and he'll be summoning spirits for all that he's worth.

Kate peers into her face. 'Are you sad?'

'A bit,' says Ruth. 'Let's have some breakfast and go for a walk on the beach.' They'll visit the henge site. If there's natural magic around, that's where it will be.

'I don't like walking,' says Kate but she says it quietly. Maybe she too secretly wants to commune with the nature spirits.

The incident room is in a frenzy. A large map of King's Lynn is on the wall with pins showing where Cassandra and Sam were last seen. Teams are going door-to-door and searching waste ground by the community centre. Tanya, who is coordinating the fingertip search, is in seventh heaven (though she puts on a suitably concerned face whenever Clough is in sight). Even Jo Archer has put in an appearance, urging the team to 'give a hundred and fifty per cent because our reputation is on the line here.' She's planning a press conference for midday.

Nelson, Clough and Judy are holed up in his office. Clough is grey-faced and hollow-eyed. Judy thinks he looks as if he hasn't slept all night. Nelson, who stayed out with the search parties until the early hours, doesn't look much better. Judy reckons that she'll have to carry them both.

'We'll find her,' she says now. 'We search every house in Lynn if we have to.'

'We haven't found Sam yet though, have we?' says Clough. 'Even though we've got a lead on the number plate.'

The car spotted on the school CCTV turned out to be a black Volkswagen Golf, owned by a Norwich woman called Margaret Shaw. The car was reported missing two days ago and has not been seen since.

'What will I tell Spencer when he's older?' says Clough. 'He won't remember her at all.'

Judy and Nelson exchange glances. 'Cloughie,' says Nelson. 'You should go home. Get some rest. You're no good to anyone like this.'

'No,' says Clough. 'Cassie's missing. I can't stay at home. We worked all night when Michael was missing, didn't we?'

'Yes we did,' says Judy. 'And we found him. *You* found him, Dave. We'll find Cassie.'

Clough rubs his eyes. 'Thanks, Judy.'

'I've been thinking about the bus ticket in Eddie's pocket,' says Judy. 'We're concentrating our search on Lynn but people travel around. The car that was seen in Pott Row was registered in Norwich.'

'That's what Richard said,' says Nelson. '"Homeless people are allowed on buses, you know." He was in Norwich that night, when the students saw him.'

'I think we should talk to Richard again,' says Judy. 'I had a feeling he was holding something back last time.'

'There's no link to Cassie or Sam though,' says Nelson.

'There's a link to Barbara and she's the one who started the whole thing.'

Nelson looks as if he is about to protest but Clough says suddenly, 'I agree. I think we should talk to Richard. If this underground place exists, he's the only one who knows about it.'

'We haven't got an address for him,' says Judy, 'but he obviously goes to one of the shelters to wash every day. We should be able to find him.'

'You go, Johnson,' says Nelson. 'Take Cloughie with you.' Judy knows that he just wants Clough out of the station. The trouble is, she thinks Nelson could probably do with going home for a rest too. But she can't say this, of course.

'All right,' she says. 'Come on, Dave. The A-Team rides again.'

*

They go to the drop-in centre at St Matthew's first. Richard might have claimed that he wouldn't be seen dead in the place but there's a chance that Paul Pritchard will know his whereabouts. Also, Judy hasn't forgotten that Cassandra, too, had been to Meg Pritchard's baby group. The mother and baby group won't be running today, because it's Saturday, but she thinks it wouldn't hurt to find out what Paul and Meg were doing last night.

At the drop-in centre it is business as usual. There's a queue for the showers, two young men in bathrobes play cards while they wait for their clothes to wash, Anya is stirring soup in the kitchen and Paul is at a table helping Scratch with some paperwork.

'Hallo again,' he says to Judy. 'Have you come to give us a hand?'

'We're looking for someone,' says Judy. She shows him Nelson's picture of Richard. 'Has he been here recently?'

'I don't think so,' says Paul, looking intently at the photocopy. 'I think I recognise the face though.'

'That's Champagne Charlie.' Scratch leans over. 'He sleeps by the Customs House.'

'Have you any idea where he goes during the day?' asks Judy. 'Does he go to a centre like this one?'

'He goes to a place in Norwich,' says Scratch. 'By the cathedral.'

'In *Norwich*?' says Judy. It seems a long way to go for a shower.

'He likes Norwich,' says Scratch simply.

'Are you investigating that other woman who's gone missing?' says Paul. 'I saw it on the news this morning.'

'Yes we are,' says Clough. 'Do you know anything about it?'

Clough's tone is so aggressive that Paul takes a step back and Scratch melts away altogether. Several other clients look up. Judy puts her hand on Clough's arm.

'We are investigating the disappearance of Cassandra Blackstock,' she says to Paul. 'Did you know her?'

'No.' Paul is still looking rather nervous. 'An actress, isn't she?'

'Do you mind telling us where you were last night between eight o'clock and midnight?'

Paul hunches his massive shoulders and Judy thinks she can detect a weariness in his manner, as if he had hoped to shake off this kind of question with his old name.

'I was at home,' he says, 'with my wife.'

'All evening?'

'Yes.'

'Can anyone verify that? Did you make any calls? Text anyone? Update your Facebook status?'

'I texted a couple of people from church. Look, what's all this about? I don't know anything about this woman.'

'Just eliminating people from the inquiry,' says Judy, willing Clough to stay silent.

'Meg said that you'd been asking her questions too.'

'Just following up on a lead,' says Judy. 'We'll leave you in peace now.'

'I'm all in favour of peace,' says Paul. It's a standard quasi-religious line but the look on Paul's face as he says it is not particularly Christian. Or especially peaceful either.

Nelson has the search results spread out in front of them. Tanya has converted them into a rather useful diagram with dots of various darkness showing possible sightings. There is a rash of spots around the community centre where people remember seeing Cassandra earlier in the evening. Apparently she went to the local Co-op to buy chocolate biscuits, presumably for the cast, at six-thirty. Was this an apology for being late? The assistant remembers Cassie, 'a very beautiful young lady', chatting in a friendly way. He recalled that she was wearing a T-shirt with writing on it. Nelson remembers the ominous-sounding name: 'Venus in Furs' by Velvet Underground.

Different colour spots show the last sightings of Sam Foster-Jones. There are no overlapping points between the two women. Sam walked to the school in Pott Row, took her children for an ice cream, and then walked back home. Cassie was in King's Lynn. She left the rehearsal and then stood on the steps of the community centre texting someone. Was that Michelle or did she contact someone else later?

Nelson's head starts to ache and spots dance in front of his eyes. Last night had been gruelling, searching the streets, trying to keep Clough, going while all the time feeling that cold, sick dread. At three a.m. he had forced Clough to go home to get some sleep but he doubts if this is what happened. Nelson got home at five, had two hours'

sleep in the spare room so as not to wake Michelle, woke at
seven, showered and came straight to work. Now he feels
as if he's been awake for ever. Were Sam and Cassandra
taken by the same person? But why and for what reason?
And what about Barbara, the woman who apparently disappeared underground? Nelson leans back and closes his eyes.

'Having forty winks, Harry?' It's Jo, of course.

Nelson's eyes snap open. 'Just thinking.'

'It doesn't look good, does it?' Jo sits opposite him and
crosses her legs. She's wearing tight jeans which Nelson
does not consider suitable for the workplace, even if it is
Saturday.

'We've got four teams searching,' says Nelson. 'We'll find
her.'

'But you haven't made any headway with the Foster-Jones
case, have you?' Nelson notes the use of 'you'. In her team-
building talks Jo is a great one for 'we'.

'We've got some CCTV and a number plate.' Both of which
got them nowhere, but he doesn't add this.

'We need a result,' says Jo. 'It'll be all over the news
tonight, especially with a photogenic victim like Cassandra
Blackstock.'

'We'll get a bloody result.' Nelson doesn't realise that
he's shouting until he sees Jo's face. He's standing up too,
looming over his superior officer. He knows he's commit-
ting professional suicide but he can't stop himself. 'We'll get
a result because it's a woman who's gone missing – Clough's
partner – not a victim or a statistic. We'll get a result because
we're police officers, not bloody PR people. And I might not

be able to write a strategy report but I know how to work the streets. I know how to find her.'

'Calm down, DCI Nelson.' Jo stands up. 'You need to address these anger issues.'

Someone else once said this to Nelson. Who was it? He takes a deep breath, trying to get back in control.

'We'll find her,' he says again. 'We'll find them all.'

'I hope you're right, DCI Nelson,' says Jo very quietly. 'I hope you're right.'

Clough wants to drive straight to Norwich but Judy persuades him to look for Richard near the Customs House first. The quay is crowded with visitors this sunny Saturday. They are filing in and out of the Customs House, which houses the Information Centre, stopping to take photographs of the house, the giant anchor and the statue of Vancouver. But there is no rough sleeper outside the building, making them feel uncomfortable and spoiling the selfies.

Outside the elegant Bank House Hotel, Judy spots a man selling *The Big Issue*. He looks vaguely familiar and she realises that he's the bearded giant – the Viking – who first pointed her in Bilbo's direction.

The man looks nervous when Judy approaches him but he seems to recognise her and isn't averse to talking. She asks if he's seen Richard, 'Charlie', today. 'No, this is his pitch though. He doesn't mind me selling here.' The Viking looks nervous and fiddles with his beard.

'We've heard he goes to a shelter in Norwich. Do you know where that is?'

'I think it's in a church. In Tombland.'

'Do you know the name of the church?'

'Our Lady of something. Sucker, some funny word like that. Near the cathedral.'

'Thank you.' Judy gives him a fiver but declines the magazine. As she and Clough hurry away, the Viking shouts after her, 'Have you found Babs yet?'

'We will soon,' Judy shouts over her shoulder.

Judy drives to Norwich; she wouldn't trust Clough at the wheel. The traffic is heavy but Judy is skilful; she weaves through the meandering day-trippers, looking out for short-cuts, cutting through car parks and industrial estates. She tells Clough to Google churches in Norwich.

'There are hundreds of bloody churches in Norwich,' he says.

'This one's called Our Lady of something. And it's in Tombland.'

'I went to a wedding at St George's in Tombland once.' Clough's voice falters slightly, perhaps thinking of his own forthcoming nuptials.

'The *Big Issue* seller said by the cathedral,' says Judy. 'That's right in the middle of Tombland.' It's an inauspicious name, she thinks, but she read once that it comes from an old word for an open space and not from a grave at all. At any rate, she mustn't let Clough's mind wander towards tombs.

In the end they find an address: Our Lady of Perpetual Succour, drop-in centre for the homeless. It's just off Tomb-land Alley, beside the cathedral. Judy parks in a spot marked 'Reserved for the Dean' and they set off through the cobbled streets. The houses here are undeniably picturesque, all beams and uneven roofs, but they are also slightly oppressive, leaning over as if to watch the streets below. It's an odd, dizzying feeling to be in a place that doesn't have one single straight line. Judy and Clough push their way through the photographing tourists. The shops are squashed together, all different heights and widths: Tombland Bookshop, Tombland News, Tombland Antiques. The occasional modern building pushes its way through the wattle and daub, looking bland and sinister. The trouble is that the church could be almost anywhere – hidden in an alley, masked by a new building, disguised as a cafe. Judy has the location on her phone and knows that it's tantalisingly near but the streets seem determined to lead them in a circle. Time and again they turn a corner to find the cathedral in front of them again. The clock on the tower of St George's strikes two. Time is running out.

Just when Judy is considering stopping and trying to telephone, Clough shouts, 'It's here!' He's standing by a shop which has second-hand books displayed in old packing cases on the pavement. Next to the shop is a flight of stairs with a tiny signpost, grey on black, pointing downwards: 'Our Lady of Perpetual Succour (decommissioned)'. The steps lead down to a cobbled yard and there is the church, a squat, flint-faced building, its door hospitably open. Clough disappears inside without waiting for Judy. She texts Nelson quickly to say where they are and follows him.

Inside, the church is empty of what Judy thinks of as the 'holy stuff': altar, statues, candles, paintings. All that is left are the pews and these are full of what are obviously rough sleepers, lying stretched out on the benches or just sitting staring into space. There's a table with an urn and paper cups, at the back are signs for showers and washrooms. As Judy and Clough approach the pews, a voice calls, 'Can I help you?'

A grey-haired woman with a kind but formidable face is coming down the aisle towards them.

Judy shows her badge. 'We're looking for a man called Richard Latham.'

'I can't give out the names of clients,' says the woman.

'It's very important,' says Judy.

The woman looks sceptical but behind her a voice says, 'It's all right, Geri.' Richard Latham appears out of the gloom, barefoot in black shirt and trousers, long hair wet.

'You don't have to speak to these people,' says the woman.

Judy is just about to put her right on this when Richard looks past her and says, 'Hallo. No jogging pants today then? Still supporting that clapped-out London team?'

Clough stares. 'It's you.' He turns to Judy. 'This is the man I told you about. The one I talk to about football.'

'We need your help,' Judy says to Richard. 'Clough's girl-friend is missing. We think she might have been taken underground.'

Richard looks at Clough for a moment and then sighs. 'You'd better come into the back room.'

CHAPTER 25

'The entrances are in the churches,' says Richard. 'Lots of the old churches have tunnels linking them. But only a few people know all the doorways.'

Judy stares at him. They are in a small room which may once have been the vestry. It's now mostly full of boxes although there is a desk and a chair. Richard sits in the chair, which gives the impression that he is in charge. He has put on his socks and boots though his hair is still wet and dripping down his back. Judy and Clough perch on boxes which seem to be full of catering supplies. Judy's is marked 'Tea Bags'. Geri has come along too, uninvited, and stands by the door.

'You mean there really is an underground society?' says Judy.

'Yes,' says Richard, with a glance at Geri. This obviously isn't news to her because she smiles thinly. 'We started it about five years ago. We weren't wanted on the surface. Nobody really cares about the homeless. They just want us to go away so they don't have to see us and feel guilty. Well, a group of us decided to go away, to disappear, to dig down. Geri told us about the tunnel beneath this church. It leads to an undercroft, quite a big space, so we started living there. But then we found other tunnels, one leading to St John's and one to St Etheldreda's on Denning Road.'

'Denning Road,' says Judy. 'That's where the students saw you.'

'Yes. Stupid idiots, swerving all over the road. One of the tunnels under Denning Road was blocked off by the hole appearing. There are tunnels everywhere, we haven't penetrated half of them.'

'When Bilbo said that Barbara had gone underground, what did he mean?'

Richard is silent for a moment, looking up at the ceiling where there is still a dusty crucifix hanging from one of the beams.

'There have been rumours,' he says at last. 'When we started it was just a small group of us living here, under Our Lady's, but then it got bigger. Other groups started living in different tunnels. People started to talk, about kidnapping, cannibalism, murder, about women being forced underground. There aren't that many women on the streets, and I suppose if you're starting a new society you need women. Like I say though, it was all talk, no evidence.'

'Do you know what happened to Barbara?'

'No, but what I think is that someone is taking these women and keeping them underground.'

'For Christ's sake,' Clough explodes. 'You must know where they are. You're the leader of this bloody group.'

Richard smiles. 'I'm not the leader. We don't have leaders. That's a mistake that the overgrounders made. We're a brotherhood, everyone is equal.'

'That all sounds very high-minded,' says Judy, 'but we're talking about abduction and murder. You must have some idea who is taking these women.'

'I don't,' says Richard. 'What I think is that they've found an entrance somewhere. Like I say, there are tunnels everywhere.'

'What about the man you saw talking to Barbara?'

'I didn't recognise him. But it's possible he's the man you're looking for.'

'Why didn't you go to the police?' says Clough. 'If you suspected that women were being abducted?'

It's Geri who answers. 'Rough sleepers have no reason to trust the police. You move them on, you arrest them for begging. Why should Richard talk to you?'

'Because people are being murdered,' says Judy. 'What about Eddie? Did he know about this society?'

'No,' says Richard. 'I liked Eddie but you couldn't trust him with a secret like this. He drank too much. You can't have drinkers in the Brotherhood or people out of their heads on legal highs. That cuts down our options, as I'm sure you'll appreciate.'

'I thought you used to have a drink problem?'

'That was years ago. I'm teetotal now.'

'And Bilbo? Stuart Hughes?'

'He knew something, I think. He wasn't one of the Brotherhood but he knew things, Stu. He kept his ear to the ground and maybe he found out what was going on under-neath.'

'I heard that Bilbo had friends at the university. Do you know who they might have been?'

'Kevin O'Casey's always sniffing around. He's the man who's writing a book about underground societies.'

'Kevin O'Casey talked to you,' says Judy. 'What did he want?'

'He'd heard some rumours,' says Richard. 'He's researched other underground societies. He knows what's possible. Someone must have given him my name, linking me to the Brotherhood. But I didn't tell him anything. I don't trust him or any of these so-called academics.'

'So why are you telling us?' says Judy.

'Because I like him.' Richard nods towards Clough. 'He talked to me as if I was one of his mates. I've missed that – those ordinary conversations, talking about football over a pint. And if his girlfriend's missing, I want to help.'

'Can you show us into the tunnels?' says Clough.

Richard looks at Geri and then, without speaking, they start to move boxes.

Nelson can't quite take it in at first. 'You're saying there is a group living in the tunnels? And Richard thinks that the women are there too?'

'He doesn't know where they are,' says Judy. 'But he thinks they might be in the tunnel system somewhere. Clough and I are going down now. We're in Our Lady of Perpetual Suc-cour in Tombland. There's an entrance in the old vestry, hidden behind some boxes. I wanted to ring you before we went down. I'm pretty sure I won't get a signal down there.'

'Are there any other entrances?'

'Yes. Richard says there's an entrance below St Etheldreda's in Denning Road and another below St John's.'

'Which is more likely?'

'Richard thinks St Etheldreda's. Apparently no one's been there since the rock fall, when the hole appeared.'

'Right. I'll go to St Etheldreda's. I'll take a couple of firefighters in case there's rubble to get through. I'll send Fuller to St John's.'

'Richard says the entrance at St Etheldreda's is in the crypt. At St John's it's behind the statue of St Hugh of Lincoln.'

'Right. Don't take any risks, Johnson. Don't let Cloughie do anything silly.'

'I'll try,' says Judy. 'I've got to go now. I can see the doorway.'

She rings off, leaving Nelson feeling slightly uneasy. This unease, though, is overshadowed by a greater feeling of excitement and relief. At last they have something to go on. He reaches for his phone to call the fire station. He has forgotten that he ever felt tired.

As always, Ruth feels a thrill – a mixture of so many emotions – when she sees the site where the henge was found. Now there's just an expanse of sand rippling like frozen water, the gold fading to brown and blue in the distance. Kate runs across the beach, paddling in the shallow streams and inland pools left by the tide. Ruth takes off her shoes and follows her, the razor clams sharp beneath her feet. It's another beautiful day but the sea is still cold and only a few swimmers have ventured in, shivering as they walk out to the deeper water. Ruth knows that Kate will want to swim – she adores the water, a true Scorpio according to Cathbad – and if Kate goes in she will have to as well, as least as far as her knees. She has towels and bathing things in her bag, as well as snacks, a change of clothes for Kate and a flask of coffee. What was it like before having a child, when you didn't have to carry a heavy bag everywhere, when you could go out with just your purse and a mobile phone? Ruth can hardly remember. She dumps the bag by the dunes and walks by the water's edge, trying to find the exact place where the wooden henge once stood.

It's nearly twenty years since they found the posts that formed the Bronze Age timber circle. Twenty years since Erik, Ruth's one-time professor and mentor, knelt in the sand and raised his face to the skies. 'We've found it.' Twenty years since Peter, Ruth's ex-boyfriend, was stranded out on the mud flats with the tide coming in. Twenty years since Cathbad and the other druids stood in the centre of the circle and vowed not to give the sacred wood to the museum. So much has happened since then and all that remains of the henge is a few streaks of discoloured sand. Some lines from a favourite Wilkie Collins book come back to Ruth. 'Nothing in this world is hidden forever . . . Sand turns traitor and betrays the footstep that passed over it.'

'What are you looking at?' Kate comes skipping up, already wet as far as her shorts.

'Nothing,' says Ruth.

'Can we go swimming?'

They do swim in the end. Even Ruth gets her shoulders under and Kate, who has just learnt to swim without armbands, manages a few splashy strokes. Afterwards they sit on the beach wrapped in their towels, Ruth drinking coffee and Kate nibbling a rice cake. Ruth is thinking about Cassandra – how beautiful she is, how kind she has always been to Kate, how happy she has made Clough. Can she really be gone for ever? Is it really true that nothing is ever lost?

It seems that Kate has been thinking along the same lines. 'You know Cassandra?' she says.

'Yes,' says Ruth.

'Maybe she's gone underground,' she says, 'like Alice.'

'Maybe,' says Ruth.

'There's a whole world underground,' says Kate. 'With underground bedrooms and tables made of stone. There's a prince living down there.'

Ruth turns to look at her daughter who is busily sketching in the sand.

'Kate,' she says, 'you know when you woke up screaming that time? You said that someone was going to take you underground. Who were you talking about?'

'Leo,' says Kate, still drawing. 'He said he was going to show me the underground room. With the prince. He said it that day when we danced the Lobster Quadrille.'

Ruth is scrabbling for her phone. Please God let her get

a signal. She has a single dot of reception but there's no answer from Nelson. Where the hell is he? Surely he'll be glued to his phone today. She tries Judy. No answer. Then Clough. The same. Where are they all? Eventually she rings King's Lynn police and asks for the Serious Crimes Unit.

'Hallo. Jo Archer here.'

Ruth almost drops her phone. Why is She Who Must Be Obeyed acting as the receptionist?

'It's Ruth Galloway,' she says. 'I think I know who took Cassandra.'

Jo tells Ruth that she'll pick her up in twenty minutes. 'I've got my daughter with me,' says Ruth.

'Get a babysitter,' says Jo.

That's easier said than done. Ruth rings Clara but she's in London with friends. There's no time to take Kate over to Cathbad's house. Ruth and Kate walk back over the dunes, Kate complaining and dragging behind, Ruth's shoulder aching from the heavy bag. As the cottage comes into view Ruth sees something else, a rare sighting these days: a Range Rover parked by the house next door. The weekenders must be down for the weekend.

Ruth knocks on the door. It is opened by Sammy, slim and elegant as ever in cropped white trousers. Her husband Ed is bobbing in the background.

'Ruth! How nice to see you. Come in.'

Sammy and Ed have always been friendly, thinks Ruth. They even invited her to a party once. She wishes that she'd been a better neighbour in return. It wouldn't have hurt her to ask Sammy and Ed over for a coffee instead of trying to avoid being in the garden whenever they have a barbecue.

'Can I ask you a favour?' says Ruth. 'I need to go out. It's really urgent. Could you possibly look after Kate for an hour or so?'

'Of course,' says Sammy. 'Our son Cameron's here with some of his friends. They'll entertain her.'

Kate, who has been looking sulky, brightens at this. She loves teenagers. Sammy ushers Kate into the house just as a Porsche that can only belong to Jo Archer screeches to a halt outside.

CHAPTER 26

Behind the catering boxes is a small wooden door. It looks old but there is a very modern-looking keypad beside it. Richard punches in some numbers and Geri hands him a torch.

'Are you ready?' he says.

'Let's get on with it,' says Clough. He switches on his torch app. Judy leaves her phone in her pocket; she has a feeling that she will need to conserve the battery.

Judy has to duck to go through the door. Clough and Richard are bent almost double. 'The ceilings get higher soon,' says Richard. They are in a brick tunnel, heading downwards. It's unpleasantly tight; Judy can't stretch out her arms. She concentrates on Clough's back in its white shirt. In a hole in the ground, she thinks, there lived a hobbit.

After a few minutes Judy hears Richard say, 'This is the undercroft.' She can tell by his voice that they're in a much bigger space, and a few seconds later she's standing in a vaulted cellar with archways covered by metal grilles.

'This is the crypt,' says Richard. 'The parish priests used to be buried here.' Judy looks down and sees that the floor is made up of large stones with inscriptions on them. 'Father Philip Hannoth 1432–1467. All flesh is graff.' The stones must date from before the Reformation, when Our Lady's was a Catholic church. Also from the days of fs for s.

'Is this where your group lives?' says Clough.

'No,' says Richard. 'We're going lower down.' He takes another key from his pocket and approaches one of the grilles. Again, it opens easily. This route must be in frequent use.

'Ignore the bones,' says Richard over his shoulder.

A few metres into the new tunnel, Judy sees what he means. There are shelves on both sides and these are full of skulls, row upon row of white orbs with black, hollow eye sockets.

'Jesus,' says Clough. 'What is this place?'

'When they built over the graveyard they put the bones here,' says Richard. 'The bones are all in boxes. Someone must have arranged the skulls like this. Quite creepy, isn't it?'

It's a charnel house, thinks Judy. She crosses herself surreptitiously. The tunnel goes on and on. Eventually the skulls stop and the walls become rougher, chalk-hewn, with uneven sides. It's also very cold. How far are they now? thinks Judy. She thinks that they may have already left Tombland. Maybe they're almost at the Guildhall, where the first bones were found.

Eventually the tunnel divides into two. 'That way is

blocked,' says Richard, pointing to the right fork. 'I tried to go down it once but it's impossible. We're going this way.'

The left-hand tunnel is also blocked by a steel door with a keypad on it. Richard types in some numbers and the door opens, scraping slightly over the chalky floor.

The first thing that strikes them is the light. It's just a bare bulb hanging from a beam but it seems so bright after the tunnels that Judy has to shade her eyes. The swinging bulb illuminates a large round space – another undercroft, Judy thinks – with a brick ceiling and supporting pillars. Around the edge are alcoves and Judy sees that these have beds in them; some even have pictures on the walls and rudimentary bookshelves. One alcove is clearly the kitchen, with what looks like a camping stove and a fridge. In the middle of the space there are sofas and a large table with a laptop on it. It reminds Judy of the drop-in centre at St Matthew's.

A young man is sitting at the computer. He looks up when they come in.

'What the fuck . . .' he says, seeing Judy and Clough.

'Relax, Nathan,' says Richard. 'They're friends.'

'You didn't clear it with the brothers,' says Nathan, sounding like a disgruntled trade unionist. He's in his twenties, Judy thinks, pale with dusty blond dreadlocks. There are three other men in the room, all lying on their beds, but only one looks over in their direction.

'We're looking for a missing woman,' says Clough. 'Cassandra Blackstock. Do you know anything about her?'

'There aren't any women down here,' says Nathan. 'I bloody wish there were.' There's an answering laugh from one of the beds.

'Nathan's got a map of the tunnels,' says Richard. He speaks to Nathan in an undertone, and with some reluctance, Nathan opens a drawer and unfolds a piece of foolscap. It is covered with neat lines, hand-lettered with a fine-nibbed fountain pen. Judy and Clough crowd round to look.

'This is the blocked-off tunnel,' says Richard, pointing. Even his nails are clean, Judy notices. 'There's another tunnel that leads from here to the Denning Road entrance. That was the tunnel I used the night the students saw me. But there was a rock fall soon afterwards when the hole in the road appeared. Nathan says that he went down the other day and that way was completely blocked.'

Clough is poring over the map. 'All these tunnels. Cassie could be in any of them.'

Judy notes that he has completely forgotten that they are looking for Sam and Barbara too. Also, that he is now convinced that Cassandra is somewhere under the city.

'Only a few are navigable though,' says Richard. 'Here's the tunnel from the Guildhall to St John's. That's blocked just before it gets to the church. These are the undercrofts under Jarrolds, the department store. They don't go anywhere now. The tunnel from the castle is sealed off. I think the only ways in are through St John's or the crypt at St Etheldreda's.'

'The boss is going to St Etheldreda's,' says Judy. 'He says he's taking some firefighters with digging equipment. They might be able to get through the rubble.' She turns to Richard. 'Who else knows about the tunnels?'

Richard shrugs. 'I don't know. I found this place by accident. Nathan here studied as an architect and he drew this map. I don't think there's another like it.'

Judy looks at Nathan. He has pale blue eyes and a complexion that looks as if it doesn't see the sun much. She wonders what drove a trainee architect to live this underground life.

'Where should we go?' she says. She feels trapped. This room is a dead-end and time is running out.

'Let's try the blocked-off tunnel,' says Clough. 'We might be able to get through.'

They leave the underground room and make their way to the fork in the tunnel. They take the right-hand path, but about a hundred yards in it is completely blocked by chalk and rubble. Clough starts to clear away the stones but he has to give up after a few minutes. He and Judy stare at each other in the ghostly light from Richard's torch.

'What do we do now?' says Clough.

Nelson drives to Denning Road, taking with him Roy 'Rocky' Taylor, a police constable sometimes seconded to the Serious Crimes Unit. Rocky is not a deep thinker but Nelson hopes that he will be quite good at shifting rubble.

It's just past three o'clock when they reach St Etheldreda's. Denning Road is quiet, the big houses secretive behind their high hedges. An ice-cream van is playing an enticing Pied Piper tune, but apart from a mother with two children trudging slowly up the hill, there's not a customer in sight. The church itself, a grey stone building with a squat square tower, is set back from the road behind chestnut trees in luxuriant leaf. Standing by the porch are two members of the King's Lynn fire brigade, Tom Summers and Bob Lam.

'What's going on, Nelson?' says Tom. 'Is someone trapped inside? We've tried the doors. The church is locked.'

'Let's see if we can track down the vicar,' says Nelson. But this isn't necessary. A tall figure with a clerical collar is marching down the path.

'Can I help you?'

'DCI Harry Nelson.' Nelson shows his warrant card. 'I'm looking for the vicar, Reverend Dominic Howe.'

'I'm Dominic Howe.' Apart from the collar, he doesn't look like a priest. The Reverend Dominic is young, in his thirties probably, lean and rangy like an athlete. He's wearing headphones which he takes off now.

'I need to look in the tunnels below the church,' says Nelson. 'Richard Latham told me about them. He told me to say "Persephone".' He feels stupid saying the password, especially as Tom and Bob seem to find it extremely amusing, but it has its effect. Father Dominic gives him a searching look and says, 'This way.'

He leads them through the church, which is beautifully decorated with yellow and white flowers. The air smells headily of roses and candles. 'We had a wedding this morning,' explains the priest. 'We're popular for weddings and not much else these days.'

They go through a side door into a room filled with robes

and prayer books. The vestry, thinks Nelson, remembering his altar server days when putting on your robes was called 'vesting'. They had to pray while they were doing it, a decade of the rosary. Well, St Etheldreda's is C of E now so there won't be much praying to Our Lady going on. Dominic Howe doesn't look as if he has Anglo-Catholic leanings.

Dominic opens another door and tells them to be careful of the steps. He leads them down a spiral staircase into a large underground space with curved walls. The word 'crypt' had led Nelson to imagine coffins and sepulchral gloom but this is actually a light, pleasant room, with small windows high up. He imagines that the tunnels will be different though.

Another door and a heavy-looking key.

'I think some of the tunnels were blocked by the rock fall the other week,' says Dominic. 'One of the Brotherhood came down a few days ago and he couldn't get through.'

The Brotherhood. Nelson can hardly believe his ears. In his experience it's a bad sign when people start messing about with passwords and silly names. It leads them to ignore reality.

'How well do you know the so-called Brotherhood?' he asks.

'Not that well,' says the vicar. 'Richard came to me a few years ago saying that he'd heard about the tunnels under the church. He asked if some rough sleepers could use them. It's quite organised – only a few people have keys and passwords and they're choosy about who they admit. You can't have anyone with drug or alcohol issues, for obvious reasons. It's enough to drive you crazy, living underground, without the added complication of drug-induced hallucinations.'

'And you didn't think to tell anyone about this?'

'My bishop doesn't know, if that's what you mean, but my conscience is quite clear. These people need somewhere to go, and if they're not welcome above ground, well, it makes sense to go below.'

Someone else said something similar to Nelson but he can't remember who it was.

'Has anyone been down recently?' he says. 'You mentioned someone who couldn't get through.'

'Nathan,' says Dominic. 'One of the gatekeepers. He tried to get through to the base under Our Lady's in Tombland but the tunnel's blocked. A few people have been down in the last week. They're using the arches – you'll see for yourself. But I don't think you'll be able to go much further.'

'We've got digging equipment,' says Nelson.

'You're welcome to try,' says Dominic, 'but I think it's completely impassable.'

The new door leads into a tunnel lined with brick and flint, rather like the one below the Guildhall. Nelson goes first, Rocky and the two firefighters following. After a while the tunnel opens out with arched spaces on either side. These show distinct signs of recent occupation: camp beds, burned-out candles, even a large earthenware pot and some cooking equipment. But when they get past the arches, their way is blocked by a mound of chalky rocks.

'Do you think you can get through this?' Nelson asks Tom.

'We'll try,' says Tom, who is shining his torch on the

tunnel roof. 'You have to be careful in spaces like this. We don't want to bring more stones down on top of us.'

Nelson looks at his watch. Nearly four o'clock. It's unlikely, he thinks, that anyone can have got through this tunnel recently. If Cassandra and the other women are held somewhere below Norwich, it probably isn't here.

'Do what you can,' he says. 'Rocky, let's you and me go and look at the arches again. People are obviously living there. Let's see if we can find anything.'

Rocky follows him silently. He seems completely unfazed by the experience of being underground, which supports Nelson's view that he must have been a troglodyte in a former life.

'Wait here a minute,' Ruth says to Jo, who looks slightly surprised but nonetheless turns off her roaring engine. Ruth dashes into her house, dumps her bag and goes to the cork board where there is a list, given to her by Leo, with the names and addresses of all the *Alice Under Ground* cast.

She's still wearing her swimming costume under linen trousers and top. She wonders if she has time to change – the costume is still slightly damp and the straps are digging into her shoulders. But Jo is starting to rev again and Cassandra is in danger. Ruth snatches up her phone and keys and goes back out to the Porsche.

'Leo Chard,' she says as they set off, bumping over the uneven road. 'He's directing this play called *Alice's Adventures Under Ground*. Kate, my daughter, said that he threatened to put her underground.'

'Is that the play that Cassandra Blackstock is in?' asks Jo. She's intent on the road, frowning slightly. Ruth finds her extremely intimidating at close quarters. Perhaps it's the sports car. Or the tight jeans.

'Yes,' says Ruth. 'And he does drama clubs for young children. Perhaps that's how he knew the other woman, the one from Pott Row.'

'This Leo was the last person to see Cassandra yesterday,' says Jo, checking in the mirror before pulling out into the main road. 'Where does he live?'

'King's Lynn,' says Ruth, looking at her list. 'One of the new apartment blocks by the quay.'

Jo speeds up. They must be doing nearly eighty on the narrow road, thinks Ruth. And this is the woman who sent Nelson on a speed awareness course. Jo's hands are completely relaxed on the wheel. Ruth notes that she's wearing an Apple watch, matt black, and that she doesn't have a wedding ring.

Ruth, of course, messes up the navigation, twice sending Jo the wrong way down one-way streets around the quay. Jo's jaw clenches but she says nothing. She asks Ruth to ring Nelson. 'I can't reach him. He and most of his team are off on a wild goose chase in the tunnels under Norwich.' She doesn't ask whether Ruth has Nelson's number, which Ruth finds rather telling. Ruth rings Nelson and Judy but both are still unavailable.

Eventually they draw up outside the smart new apartment block. Ruth checks the list. 'It's on the first floor,' she says. She looks up at the tiny balconies, barely big enough for a chair. Is Leo inside one of these bijou residences or is he in some underground lair plotting the next abduction? She thinks of Kate's skipping rhyme. *Teddy Bear, Teddy Bear, turn out the lights. Teddy Bear, Teddy Bear, say goodnight.* Leo had liked that, thought he could make it sound very sinister. Oh please God, don't let him have killed them.

Leo doesn't answer when they buzz the entryphone but Jo presses the button marked 'caretaker' and says briskly, 'Police. Open up.' The door opens silently and Jo runs up the stairs, two at a time. Will she shoulder-barge the door, thinks Ruth, following more slowly. Or will she shoot out the lock? The Serious Crimes Unit don't carry guns but she wouldn't put anything past Jo.

But by the time Ruth reaches the landing, the door has been opened and Leo stands there, blinking behind his red glasses.

'Superintendent Jo Archer.' Jo shows her warrant card. 'I believe you know Dr Galloway? Can we come in?'

'Yes, of course.' Leo stands aside to let them into the flat. 'Hallo, Ruth. What's this about?'

'It's about the disappearance of Cassandra Blackstock,' says Jo. 'I believe you were the last person to see her yesterday.'

'I already spoke to that other policeman, DCI Nelson. I said goodbye to Cassie at the community centre. I haven't seen her since.'

'Did you say to Ruth's daughter that you were going to put her underground?'

'No!' Leo looks at Ruth, his eyes pleading. He looks smaller than usual, standing in the white-painted hallway, slightly ridiculous in his trendy clothes. 'I think I said that I'd show her the underground room – at the printing works, you know. There's an undercroft there.'

Ruth remembers Kate saying, 'There's a prince living down there.' Prince, prints. That could be the explanation, she supposes. The printing place probably does have an undercroft and after all, Kate hadn't seemed frightened by the conversation at first.

Leo is still talking, 'The architect, Quentin Swan, he told me about it. He built the arts centre on the South Quay where I put on my first play. The one you came to see, Ruth.'

Quentin Swan. Ruth thinks of the day that the architect came to see her at the university. *I've got some old maps which show all the tunnels.* Quentin, who seems intent on burrowing below the oldest buildings in the city. Is it possible that his underground rooms also hold another secret?

CHAPTER 27

Tanya has some trouble finding the statue of Hugh of Lincoln. Eventually she finds him. He's a monk (who knew?) and his statue is in the darkest corner of the cathedral. PC Bradley Linwood, the uniformed officer assigned to help her, stares at the cowled figure.

'Is there a secret passage or something?' he says.

'There's a doorway,' says Tanya. She doesn't want to admit that she doesn't know. The cathedral is open to the public but she can't see anyone official to ask, just a woman praying at the altar and a group of foreign tourists who look lost.

'What's this?' Linwood is opening the door of what looks like a cupboard.

'I think it's where Catholics go for confession,' says Tanya. The boss would know. He was raised a Catholic. Judy, too, even though she's probably now a pagan like Cathbad. Tanya has never had much time for religion, although meeting a woman priest last year had almost changed her mind. She even thought that when she and Petra get married next year, they might do it in church with a female celebrant.

But Petra hadn't been keen and, on balance, Tanya isn't about to forgive the church for centuries of misogyny and homophobia just because she once met a cool woman in a dog collar.

Linwood is inside the confessional box. 'Hey, Tanya,' he says, 'look at this.'

Tanya wishes he wouldn't use her first name. She's his superior, after all. Secretly, she'd like to be addressed as 'Ma'am'.

'What?' She looks into the dark cubbyhole. It's a tiny space with a crucifix on the wall, a kneeler and a grille that opens into the adjoining box (presumably for the penitent). But there's also something else. A second door with an electronic keypad.

Judy has given her a number and Linwood keys in the digits. Tanya isn't really expecting it to work but there's an immediate click and an exclamation from Linwood. 'Bloody hell. We're in.'

The door opens onto a flight of steps. Tanya takes out her trusty Maglite torch and shines it into the void. The steps lead into a cellar which appears to be full of old statues: a headless angel, a one-armed St Joseph, a garishly coloured Mary. But at the back there are three archways, like one of those computer games where you have to choose the right way. This time, though, the decision is easy. Someone has cleared a path through the statuary to the middle arch and there are clear footprints in the dust.

'Someone's been down here recently,' says Linwood. Unnecessarily, in Tanya's opinion.

'Come on,' she says, starting to descend the steps. 'I'll go first.'

Ruth doesn't know Quentin Swan's address but a quick Google offers up his offices, which are in the centre of Norwich, near the castle. Jo rings and ascertains that the offices are open today. 'Let's go then,' she says. She gets back into the Porsche and takes the Norwich road, other cars hastily moving out of the path when they spot the speeding black shape in their rear-view mirrors. Once more Ruth has the job of contacting Nelson, and to her surprise he answers on the second ring.

'Ruth? What's wrong? Is it Katie?'

'No.' Ruth hopes Jo hasn't heard this. 'I'm with Superintendent Archer. She wants you to meet us at Quentin Swan's office, One Castle Place, near the Mall.'

'You're with Jo? Why?'

'It would take too long to explain but we think Quentin Swan might be involved with the women's disappearance. Can you meet us there? Where are you?'

'I'm not far away. Denning Road. I've just come out of a tunnel. I'll meet you there.' And he rings off. Next Ruth tries Judy, and once again, the phone is answered.

'Ruth. What is it?' Ruth thinks that Judy sounds out of breath.

'I'm with Superintendent Archer. She wants you to meet us in Norwich.' She gives the address. Judy doesn't waste time asking why Ruth is driving around with Jo Archer. She just says that she and Clough will meet them at Castle Place.

Jo keeps driving, eyes on the road. This time she has her satnav on and doesn't ask Ruth for directions. As they approach the castle walls, she says, 'You're very close to DCI Nelson, aren't you?'

'We've worked together quite a lot,' says Ruth.

'He's a good man,' says Jo. 'But I'm not sure he's very happy at the moment.'

'What's he got to be unhappy about?' says Ruth, aware that she is not sounding exactly neutral. 'Perfect wife and family and all that.'

'Things are not always as perfect as they seem,' says Jo.

Ruth doesn't know how to respond to this and luckily Jo doesn't seem to expect an answer. She hums as she threads through the weekend traffic, moving the powerful car as if it's a toy.

The central arch leads to a brick-lined tunnel, well-kept and high enough for even the burly Linwood to walk without difficulty. There are occasional alcoves in the wall, possibly for lanterns, Tanya thinks. She tries to think what direction they are heading. Judy had said that this tunnel leads to the Guildhall but that it was blocked somewhere along the way.

'Do you really think they might be down here?' Linwood's voice echoes in the enclosed space. 'The missing women?'

'I don't know. DS Johnson seemed to think they had a strong lead.'

Tanya had hoped that the tunnel would lead to an underground room where dauntless DS Fuller, with minimal help from PC Linwood, would find and rescue Sam Foster-Jones and Cassandra Blackstock. She can see the headlines now. Would she be Terrific Tanya or Fabulous Fuller? But the tunnel shows no sign of leading to a hidden room. They must have been walking for five minutes now. Occasionally Tanya shines her torch down and picks out a footprint. A man's print, she thinks, walking quickly in heavy shoes. Eventually the path seems to head upwards and the ceiling seems slightly lower. There's a white shape ahead.

'This must be where it's blocked,' she says.

But when they reached the rock fall, they see that someone has cleared a path through the rubble. Stones are piled on either side and there's room for a person to scramble through. Tanya does just that, and after clearing a wider space, Linwood follows. The path continues to lead upwards. The walls are now no longer brick but chalk and it's much tighter. Linwood has to crouch slightly and even Terrific Tanya is starting to feel rather uncomfortable. Then, without warning, they are in a wider space and Tanya almost falls into a trench that has opened up beneath her feet.

She shines her torch and sees that there are two trenches, too neat and symmetrical to have appeared by accident.

'This must be where Ruth found the bones,' she says.

Nelson is waiting for them outside the office block. He looks hot and dusty, his greying hair almost white with chalk. Beside him Rocky Taylor looks like a ghost. Jo has left the Porsche by the castle but Nelson has just parked in the street. As they approach, Judy and Clough appear from the other direction. They too look dusty and dishevelled.

Jo briefs the team quickly. 'We've had a lead that Swan might be involved. I don't want us to go in mob-handed though. Ruth and I will go in and talk to him.'

'Let me,' says Nelson. 'I'm in charge of this investigation.' He sounds extremely belligerent, thinks Ruth, and is surprised when Jo answers him calmly.

'No. You look as if you've been underground. It'll put him on the alert. Ruth knows him. He won't be suspicious of her.'

'Let me go in.' Clough's fists are clenched.

'Not a chance,' says Jo briskly.

Ruth presses the entryphone button and asks for Quentin Swan. She is buzzed in but when she and Jo enter the plate-glass open-plan offices they are told that Mr Swan is not working today. Jo throws her weight around a bit but the receptionist, though perfectly charming, says she has no idea where her boss can be. She does give Jo his home address though. Lurking in the background Ruth looks at the framed architectural plans on the walls. She had liked Quentin Swan, had even found him rather attractive. Can he really be responsible for two deaths and three abductions? The bland chrome and glass office gives nothing away.

Downstairs Jo consults with her team. 'He lives in Newmarket Road. You go there, Nelson. I'll send some back-up. Ruth, thanks for your help but you can go home now. DS Clough can take you.'

Almost everyone finds fault with this plan. Clough flatly refuses to leave. Nelson thinks that they should send a squad car to Newmarket Road immediately. Jo reminds everyone that she's in charge. Rocky wanders off and comes back with bottled water and a packet of Polos which he silently offers around.

'Excuse me,' says Ruth. They all turn to look at her with expressions ranging from interest to irritation.

'I've got an idea,' she says. It came to her when she was looking at the plans in the reception area. She hears Martin Kellerman's voice as he sat by the river enumerating Quentin Swan's iniquities. *He did that arts centre on the South Quay and he's designing some swanky new apartments in Norwich.*

'Quentin Swan's building some flats near here,' she says. 'They're half finished. I saw the plans just now. Is it possible that he's keeping the women there? Maybe there's a basement or something.'

'Where are these flats?' says Jo.

'Castle Meadow,' says Ruth. 'Walking distance.'

They set off, Jo leading, although she knows the area the least well. Ruth turns on her navigation app and sees the little blue dot that is her moving towards the jaunty pin that represents Quentin Swan's new apartments. Clough sprints ahead, disappearing into an alleyway between two shops, Judy at his heels. Nelson turns to Ruth. 'Are you coming?'

'You bet I am,' says Ruth. 'It was my idea.'

Nelson smiles but says nothing. Rocky brings up the rear, sucking noisily on a Polo.

The new apartments are on the north side of the castle, that square fortress that somehow looks foreboding even in bright sunlight. A sign outside reads: 'Castleview Apartments. Deluxe living in the heart of the city.' Ruth notes that the builders are Edward Spens and Co. She and Nelson have had dealings with the Spens family before.

There's no one on site today and the building, a smooth white shell that reminds Ruth of the flats where Leo lives, looks completely finished. A new sign boasts that half the units are already sold. Clough has climbed the fence before Nelson and Rocky have forced the gate open. Nelson tells Rocky to wait there and crosses the gravelled courtyard to the main doors, which Clough is trying to break down single-handedly.

Clough looks quite wild, thinks Ruth, throwing himself against the locked doors, his hair and clothes white with chalk. The single eye of a CCTV camera is observing them balefully. Jo is on the phone calling for back-up but Nelson joins Clough, and in a few minutes the doors start to splinter. Clough, Nelson and Judy enter the building. Ruth hesitates. Should she go in? Part of her really wants to see if her hunch was right, but on the other hand she is a mother with a dependent child. It would be irresponsible to put herself in any danger.

Jo decides her. 'Stay here,' she barks at Ruth. That does it. Ruth isn't going to be bossed about by a woman in tight trousers who thinks she's Helen Mirren playing Jane Tennison. She follows Jo through the broken doors into the lobby.

There's a lift but the controls are still covered in plastic. 'There's a B for basement,' Judy is saying. 'Let's go down.'

The twenties-style uplighters are also plastic-covered but Nelson switches on his torch and lights their way down the stairs. The basement contains a large space which is obviously destined to be a home cinema, as well as a laundry room and a room containing a boiler and fuse boxes. The place is deserted, smelling of paint and new carpets. The wiring obviously hasn't been completed and electric cables hang in colourful garlands from the ceiling.

It's Judy who spots a second door by the lift. 'There's a lower basement,' she says.

Ruth thinks of Quentin Swan telling her about the oligarchs with their countless basements digging down into the rarefied soil of west London. *They can't build horizontally any more so they build vertically. Down and down. Floor after floor with no natural light. Cinemas and gyms. Even swimming pools.* She follows the police officers down a second flight of stairs. This time they are in a dark corridor with no designer features, just a vestibule with doors leading off it. Then, all at the same time, they hear something. A cry that sounds as if it has been muffled. Clough lets out a cry of his own and hurls himself at the nearest door. It's not locked and the shock of the door opening knocks Clough off balance. Standing behind Jo, Ruth only has a confused view of a darkened room, shouts and voices. She hears Nelson say, 'Steady, Cloughie' and another voice, Quentin Swan's, saying, 'Keep back!' Edging closer, Ruth sees Swan holding a knife to Cassandra's neck. There are other people in the room and she hears Jo speaking into her phone, 'They're all here. All three women.'

The next bit happens so quickly that Ruth only manages to put it together later. Clough, ignoring Nelson's warning, throws himself at Quentin Swan. There's a scuffle and several people fall to the floor. Nelson goes to Clough's aid and Ruth hears him telling Cassandra to run. Then Nelson makes a sound somewhere between a grunt and a shout.

'Nelson!' yells Ruth, coming to life. A figure tries to push past her but Jo rugby-tackles it neatly. Then a bright light shines behind them and a new voice says, 'Anyone hurt?'

'I think I am.' Nelson is lying on the floor, holding his shoulder. Blood is gushing out in horrible profusion. Ruth runs over and puts her hands over the wound.

'Don't die, Nelson,' says Ruth.

'I'll try not to,' says Nelson.

Clough holds Cassandra in his arms. Ruth thinks they're both crying. Judy is on her knees untying huddled shapes who must be Barbara and Sam. Free from their bonds, the two women cling to each other. In the doorway, Jo Archer is still sitting on the prone figure of Quentin Swan. 'Cuff him,' she says to the back-up team who have just arrived. 'And get an ambulance for DCI Nelson.'

'I'm fine,' says Nelson, but the blood is still flowing through Ruth's fingers and his face is frighteningly pale.

'Quentin Swan,' says Jo, getting to her feet and dusting down her designer jeans, 'I'm arresting you for the abduction of Barbara Murray, Sam Foster-Jones and Cassandra Blackstock. Do you understand the nature of the charge?'

Swan makes a sound which could be 'yes'. Jo continues, 'You do not have to say anything. However, it may harm your defence if you do not mention when questioned something which you later rely on in court. Anything you do say may be given in evidence.'

Ruth takes off her cotton top and rolls it into a pad which she puts over the wound in Nelson's shoulder.

'Going swimming?' says Nelson with a weak grin. She had forgotten that she is still wearing her swimming costume. Judy comes over. 'Keep up the pressure,' she tells Ruth. 'The paramedics will be here in a minute.'

'Are Barbara and Sam all right?' asks Nelson. His hand is underneath Ruth's, holding the makeshift dressing tightly.

'We're fine,' says Sam. 'I wouldn't have coped without Babs though. She kept us all going.'

'Did he keep you here all the time?' asks Judy.

'Yes. He kept us locked in,' says Barbara Murray, speaking for the first time. She has a soft voice with a faint Scottish accent. 'He talked about this new society he was going to build underground. He kidnapped us because we'd all had children. We're good breeders, apparently.' To Ruth's surprise, both Sam and Barbara laugh.

'Babs and I have four children each,' says Sam. 'That makes us prime breeding stock.'

'I knew that was the link.' Judy can't stop herself sounding smug.

'I only had one child.' Cassandra comes over to stand with the other women. All three hold hands. 'I wasn't in the same class as the others.'

'But he fancied you,' says Sam. 'So he was prepared to overlook that.'

'Did he . . . ?' Clough's voice is thick with rage.

'He didn't rape us, if that's what you mean,' says Sam. 'I think the great breeding plan was all in his head.'

'His wife is a sociologist,' says Ruth. 'She knows all about underground societies.'

'We'll put out a warrant for her arrest,' says Jo. 'Take him away.' She motions towards the handcuffed Swan. 'Let's get you to the ambulance, Harry. Can you walk?'

'I'm fine,' says Nelson, but he leans heavily on Ruth as they walk towards the door.

'You three need to get to the hospital too,' says Jo to the women.

'Can I ring my husband first?' says Sam.

Ruth goes with Nelson in the ambulance. She sits beside him as the paramedic winds a professional-looking bandage round the wound. Nelson's eyes are shut and his face looks very pale. Ruth can see the muscles in his jaw and the faint stubble around his chin. His shirt is open and Ruth can see the hair on his chest. She has an insane desire to touch it.

The paramedic is an old friend of Nelson's called Bishoy. 'What's going on, Harry?' he says. 'I thought you were untouchable. I thought you had super powers.'

'I slipped up,' says Nelson.

'It's lucky someone was looking after you.' Bishoy hands Ruth her bloodstained top. She almost considers putting it back on. Judy has lent her a jacket but it's too small and doesn't meet over her swimming costume.

'I've got some spare scrubs,' says Bishoy, watching her trying to tug the edges together. Ruth pulls on the green top, feeling like an extra in *Casualty*.

'Very fetching,' says Nelson, opening his eyes.

'Thank you,' says Ruth. 'How do you feel?'

'Champion.'

But he's still very pale and Ruth sees his jaw clench as the ambulance bounces over speed bumps.

'He'll be OK,' says Bishoy. 'He's as tough as they come.'

'Do you want me to ring . . . to ring anyone for you?' says Ruth.

'Yes,' says Nelson. 'Can you text Michelle and say I'll be late back? Say I've had to go to the hospital but it's not serious.'

Ruth has to lean over Nelson to get his phone from his pocket. It feels like the closest she has been to him in years. The ambulance seems to shrink around them, like the house in *Alice's Adventures in Wonderland*, getting smaller and smaller until the confinement is almost unbearable. She can smell his aftershave and the antiseptic tang of bandages.

She types the message, trying to sound as reassuring as possible. *Be a bit late. Had to go to hospital. Nothing serious. Don't worry.* She doesn't know whether to add a kiss but doesn't like to ask.

'We're here,' says Bishoy, looking through the window into the driver's compartment. 'And it looks like there are some reporters waiting for us.'

'Can we go round the back?' says Nelson. 'And we should let Judy get Cassandra, Sam and Barbara into the building first.'

When the ambulance doors open, Ruth sees Judy shepherding the three women into the back entrance of the hospital. She and Nelson follow at a slower pace. A stretcher is waiting for Nelson but he refuses to get onto it. Ruth can hear him arguing with the doctors as they lead him away.

Ruth sits in the waiting room with the broken bones, the drunk and the confused. It reminds her of her trip to King's College Hospital. Was it really only five days ago? Time appears to be moving in a very strange way. She looks at her phone and sees that the battery is dead. Normally this would make her feel very stressed (what if Kate needs her?) but in her present dream-like state it barely registers. It seems like weeks since she was on the beach with Kate. She sees the other patients looking curiously at her quasi-medical outfit and bloodstained hands. She gets up to find the loos.

In the Ladies she washes her hands, watching as Nelson's blood drains away, reddish brown in the sink. Hardly knowing what she's doing, she licks a drop that remains on the back of her hand. It tastes like iron.

Back in the waiting room she spots a familiar figure in police uniform wandering about but doesn't like to call out because she doesn't know his real name. Luckily Rocky recognises her.

'I've brought the boss's car,' he says. 'It's in the car park.'

'Thank you,' says Ruth. 'You can give me the keys. He'll be very grateful.' She is amazed when Rocky just hands over the keys and ambles away again. Nelson appears a few minutes later.

'Your car's here,' says Ruth, showing him the keys. 'Rocky brought it back.'

'Great,' he says. 'I'll drive you home.'

'Should you be driving?' says Ruth. His shoulder is band-aged, making a bulky shape under his bloodstained shirt.

'I'm fine,' says Nelson. But Ruth has to change gears for him all the way back to the Saltmarsh. It's nearly seven o'clock when they get to Ruth's house and the tide has come in, the water whispering against the edges of the grassland. Ruth sees Sammy at the window and waves but she does not go next door to collect her daughter. She and Nelson go straight upstairs where they make love on her unmade bed, the whole thing full of joy and tenderness and pain.

When Nelson has gone, Ruth goes to retrieve Kate. 'She's been a joy,' says Sammy. 'Do let me babysit again. I'm longing for grandchildren but neither Cameron nor India seem to be getting on with it.' Cameron, watching television in the background, raises an arm in ironical salute.

It is only when Ruth gets back into her house that she sees the answerphone flashing. It's Simon, telling her that her mother died an hour ago.

CHAPTER 28

Judy and the three women are ushered into a waiting room that has been closed to the public. Judy thinks it's a place for delivering bad news. The pink walls show sad landscapes of empty beaches and sombre light-dappled trees. There is a large box of tissues on the table. But the atmosphere in the room today is febrile and euphoric. Sitting on the stiff-backed sofa the three women hold hands as if they can't bear not to be in contact. They were tied up most of the time, says Barbara, but they managed to get close enough to hold hands. Swan untied their hands to give them food and they had discussed the possibility of overpowering him in those moments but their legs had been tied, and besides, Swan was always armed with a knife.

'It's lucky you didn't,' says Judy. Swan hadn't hesitated to use a knife to kill Eddie and Bilbo. Swan hasn't admitted to the murders but Judy's going to have a good go at getting a confession out of him. Jo has promised that she can be the one to interview him ('Under my supervision, of course').

Barbara doesn't know about Eddie and Bilbo yet. She's

clearly the leader of the three women and seems in good shape, although she was incarcerated the longest. Judy is rather fascinated to meet the woman she has been searching for. Barbara Murray is tall with dark hair pulled back into a ponytail. Her face is handsome and high-coloured with an aquiline nose and a humorous mouth. It's a strong face, thinks Judy, and Barbara is not the fragile creature she expected, the woman with mental issues and countless unspecified 'problems'. 'Babs kept us going,' says Sam, drinking the tea brought to them by an orderly. 'She was amazing – she told us stories, sang us songs, told jokes. I was in pieces but Babs kept telling me that it would be all right in the end.'

Sam Foster-Jones is buoyant, almost manic. Reaction, thinks Judy, watching Sam nibbling a biscuit then putting it down, unable to settle to anything. After she had rung her husband and ascertained that the children were OK, Sam seemed almost to be enjoying the moment of rescue. 'I've never been in an ambulance before,' she kept telling everyone.

'Calm down, Sam,' Barbara had said. 'It's all right now.'

Judy wonders how often Barbara has said those words over the last week.

'Babs is the one who should be an actress,' says Cassandra. 'She acted out all these plays and stories for us, doing all the voices and everything.'

Cassandra seems stunned by the events of the last hour. Maybe she can't quite believe that she saw her partner bursting in through the door and hurling himself on her abductor. She keeps asking about Nelson. 'Is he OK? Dave will never forgive himself if he's badly hurt.'

'He'll be fine,' says Judy. 'He was cracking jokes in the ambulance.' She doesn't mention the expression on the boss's face when he looked at Ruth. She has her own misgivings about that.

Judy is also rather irritated to see that even after all that she has been through, Cassandra still looks effortlessly glamorous.

The doctors will have to examine the women separately but Judy wants to ask them a few questions first.

Barbara says that she first met Quentin Swan at St Matthew's. 'I'd been to the drop-in centre and he was collecting his stepdaughter from the toddler group. He was nice. He talked to me. A lot of the mothers used to look at me like I was dirt but he spoke politely, even introduced me to the little girl. Then I saw him when I was begging by the Customs House. He bought me a coffee and we talked about my children. He said that he knew lawyers who might be able to help me get custody of Tommy and Lexy.'

'Richard . . . Charlie . . . he said that he saw you talking to someone and that they mentioned your children. He said you seemed upset. Was that Quentin?'

'Yes. At first he seemed really helpful and kind. But then he kept talking about the kids, saying that they were important and that I shouldn't forget them. As if I would! I've got their names tattooed on my back but they're in my heart always . . .'

She stops, overcome for the first time. Sam puts her arm

round her. 'It's OK, Babs. I'll help you get back in contact with your kids. I promise.'

'Then one day Quentin told me that he had some important information about Tommy and Lexy. He said he had some papers in his car. I went with him. I know it was stupid but I trusted him. He seemed so respectable. He said he was married too.'

'Did you ever meet his wife?'

'No. He talked about her a lot though. He said that she had a child from a previous marriage but hadn't had a baby with him. He seemed disappointed about that.'

'What happened when he asked you to go to the car with him?'

'He opened the door and I got into the passenger seat. Then he put something over my mouth and I suppose I passed out. When I woke up I was in the basement room.'

'Same thing with me,' says Sam. 'He came to my door and said that he was lost. I recognised him vaguely from the toddler group so I wasn't worried at all. I even offered him a cup of tea. He said that he had a map in the car and asked me if I'd show him the route on it. What an idiot I was! Who has a map these days? Everyone uses satnav. Anyway, he was fumbling with the map and I got into the passenger seat. I vaguely remember him putting a handkerchief over my mouth. Next thing I knew, I woke up in the basement next to Babs.'

'"I've brought you some company." That's what he said to me,' says Babs. 'Nutter.'

'All the same, I was very glad to find you there.' Sam

reaches for Barbara's hand again. 'When I opened my eyes in the dark I thought I was dead. Then I heard your voice saying that everything would be all right.'

'I kept saying that,' says Babs. 'I had no way of knowing if it was true.'

Judy thinks of the chemical traces found on Eddie and Bilbo. Quentin must have used the drugged handkerchief trick on them too. Soda lime. She's willing to bet that lime is used in construction somehow.

'I was the same,' says Cassandra. 'I feel such a fool now. I met Quentin at Meg's Easter play so when I saw him in the car park I wasn't scared at all. He said that his car wouldn't start and would I come and look at it. I was actually flattered that he asked me. People always ask Dave about cars and he knows nothing about them. I went over to have a look. He had the bonnet up and I . . .' She stops because there is the sound of raised voices outside the room. For a second the three women look at each other with identical expressions of fear.

'It's OK,' says Judy, moving towards the door. But, before she can reach it, Clough bursts into the room, making a dramatic entrance for the second time that day.

'Some idiot in a white coat trying to keep me out,' he says, crossing to Cassandra's side. 'Are you OK, babe?' He strokes her hair.

Clough is followed by the rather more reticent figure of Benedict Foster-Jones. 'Is it OK to come in?' He stops, seeing Sam. She gives a cry and rushes into his arms.

Judy glances at Barbara, wondering if she'll see some

bitterness or sadness on her face as she watches her companions being embraced by their partners. But Barbara is smiling with genuine kindness and pleasure. She's a nice woman, thinks Judy.

A disgruntled-looking orderly has followed the two men, accompanied by a nurse and the A and E consultant, a woman Judy has met before.

'Hi, Judy. In the thick of it again?'

'That's right, Harpreet. You know I like to keep busy.'

Harpreet addresses herself to Barbara, as she is the only woman not locked in a passionate clinch. 'Hi, I'm Dr Kaur. I just need to check you over. I've got a forensic nurse practitioner with me and she'll take photographs of your injuries to assist with the police case. Is that OK? How are you feeling?'

'Very well, considering,' says Barbara. 'It's amazing what a couple of weeks off the streets will do for you.'

'Would you come with me? It shouldn't take long.'

'Could you see Cassandra and Sam first? I think they're keen to get home.'

This too is said without bitterness. Harpreet turns to Cassandra and the two of them leave the room, closely followed by Clough. Judy hopes Harpreet will not let him into the examination room.

Sam and Benedict sit on the sofa, holding hands. 'I can't believe you found her,' says Benedict, wiping his eyes.

'I told you we would,' says Judy.

'Caleb always said you would,' says Benedict. '"Judy promised", that's what he kept saying.'

'Have you met Caleb?' Sam turns to Judy, eyes shining. 'Isn't he amazing?'

'Amazing,' agrees Judy. 'Seriously impressive.'

'DS Clough says you've arrested some architect,' says Benedict. 'Why did he do it? DS Clough said he was under arrest for murder too.'

'Murder?' The two women look at Judy. Typical Clough. He could never keep his mouth shut.

'I'm sorry.' Judy addresses herself to Barbara. 'We think Quentin killed two men. One of them was your friend Eddie O'Toole.'

'Eddie?' Barbara puts her hand to her mouth. 'Oh no. He was always so kind to me. He gave me that necklace. Quentin took it.' Sam gets up and goes to her friend's side, putting her arm round her shoulders.

'The other man was Stuart Hughes – Bilbo. I'm sorry. I think he was also a friend of yours.'

'Yes,' says Barbara sadly. 'Poor Bilbo. Why would anyone want to hurt him?'

'We think that Eddie was killed because he raised the alarm about you,' says Judy. 'And I interviewed Bilbo. He said something about you being underground. Quentin must have got to hear about that. I suppose Quentin thought that if we started looking underground, the trail would lead to him.'

'Is the Underground real then?' says Sam. 'Quentin kept talking about it.'

'It's real,' says Judy, remembering the crypt below Our Lady of Perpetual Succour, the rows of skulls in the dark, the underground room with men sleeping in alcoves. She supposes the police will have to close it down now. Then she thinks of Nathan and his map – so many tunnels, so many entrances and exits. She's pretty sure that the Underground will rise to the surface again.

Later, when Cassandra and Clough have gone home and Sam is being examined by the doctor, Judy has a few minutes alone with Barbara.

'I can get you a hotel for tonight,' she says. 'Then maybe I can help you get housing somewhere.'

'That's very kind,' says Barbara, 'but Sam has invited me to stay with her for a bit. It would be nice to be with a family again.'

For the first time Barbara looks really vulnerable, her hands shaking as she readjusts her ponytail. Old woman's hands, thinks Judy, although she knows that Barbara is still only in her thirties.

Judy says, choosing her words with care, 'Barbara, when we were looking for you, I got in touch with your oldest two children.'

Barbara looks up. 'You spoke to Adam and Kirsty?'

'Well, they're Rory and Siobhan now, but yes. They're both still in Scotland and are doing really well. Siobhan's at university and Rory is a policeman.'

'Oh my God.' Barbara lets out a shaky laugh. 'I don't know whether to laugh or cry.'

'I can understand that,' says Judy, 'but the point is that he's doing well.'

Barbara looks at her, her eyes shining with tears. 'Does he . . . do they . . . do they want to see me?'

'Not yet,' says Judy gently, 'but I think there's hope. I'll help if I can.'

'Thank you,' says Barbara. And they sit in silence until Sam comes back into the room.

CHAPTER 29

Jo told Nelson to go home after leaving the hospital but instead he drives back to the station. His shoulder aches but he welcomes the pain. It stops him from thinking.

At the station he finds Tanya in the incident room, looking disgruntled.

'Judy and Superintendent Archer are still interviewing the suspect,' she says.

'Where's Cloughie?'

'He went home with Cassandra. He said to say he was sorry.'

'What for?'

'He says it was his fault you got stabbed. He went charging in without thinking and you went to help him.'

'It wasn't his fault,' says Nelson. 'It was just a bit of a mad moment.' It was Clough's fault, he thinks, but anyone would have done the same. He remembers Clough sobbing in his arms the night before. More than anything, he's glad that he kept his promise to Clough. They have found Cassandra alive and well.

'Did you find anything in your tunnel?' he asks Tanya.

'It had been cleared recently,' says Tanya. 'It led all the way to the Guildhall. Linwood and I came out in the under-croft just as a load of tourists were being shown around.'

Quentin Swan must have cleared it, decides Nelson. He thinks about the gold 'Babs' necklace found during Ruth's excavation. Quentin had been there – he could easily have dropped the necklace into the trench, to draw attention away from the women's true hiding place. Quentin must have explored the tunnels when planning for his underground restaurant. He wonders at what point Swan's empire-building turned into something darker.

'Come on,' he says to Tanya, 'let's listen in to the interview.'

Tanya does not need telling twice.

Through the two-way mirror, Nelson sees Swan accompanied by a man who must be his solicitor. Sitting opposite him are Judy and Jo. Judy is speaking. 'When did you first decide to abduct Barbara Murray?'

The solicitor makes a movement to object but Swan answers quite calmly. Nelson wonders whether the solicitor originally advised a 'no comment' interview. If so, Judy has broken through Swan's defences.

'I met her at the drop-in centre,' says Swan. 'She told me that she had four children. I knew that I would need fertile women for my society so I thought that I should take her. It was the same with Sam. I first met her at the Christmas show. Her son was Joseph. Olivia was an angel.'

Olivia must be the stepdaughter, thinks Nelson. Didn't Ruth say that Swan's wife used to be married to one of the lecturers at UNN?

'Tell us more about this society,' says Jo.

Swan sighs and looks at the ceiling. 'I found out about the Brotherhood through my wife, Vicky. She was researching underground societies and she knew that there was one in Norwich. I started going out at night and talking to the rough sleepers. It was Bilbo who told me about the entrances in the churches. He knew a lot, Bilbo, but he never knew when to keep his mouth shut.'

'Is that why you killed him?' asks Judy in a deliberately casual voice.

'My client declines to answer that question,' says the solicitor. But Swan has already said, in the same dreamy voice, 'Yes. I didn't feel too bad because I was putting him out of his misery. He'd had a very sad life, Bilbo. I killed him as he slept by the Red Chapel. I drugged him first so he wouldn't know anything.'

'Did you kill Eddie too?' asks Jo. From her tone, with its carefully suppressed excitement, Nelson guesses that this is the first time Swan has admitted to the murders. His solicitor once more attempts to stop him speaking.

'Yes,' says Swan, waving his legal advisor away. 'Eddie didn't know about the Brotherhood but he was asking questions about Barbara. He might have found out. It was easy to find him. He always slept on the police station steps. I knew that the CCTV wasn't working. I know quite a lot about CCTV for my job.'

'What about Sam Foster-Jones?' asks Judy. 'Did you drug her too?'

'Yes,' says Swan. 'I went to the door and pretended that I was lost. I asked her to come and look at my map. Poor woman. Far too trusting. When she was in the car I put a handkerchief impregnated with soda lime over her mouth. Always lots of lime about on a construction site. It was quite safe. I didn't used much, just enough to knock her out for a bit. I drove her to the basement. I'd taken the precaution of acquiring a car. Too much CCTV around these days. There's no privacy. Britain has more CCTV per square metre than any country in the world.' He sounds quite indignant.

'Why did you kidnap Sam?' asks Judy.

'I told you,' says Swan. 'I needed women. That was the mistake the Brotherhood made. You can see it in their name. There were no women. You can't have a perfect society without women.'

'Was that what you were doing?' asks Judy. 'Building a perfect society?'

'Yes,' says Swan, as if this is obvious. 'Vicky had done a lot of research on utopian societies. You need a shared ethos. Well, we had that. All the Brothers were united in wanting to live together in peace and harmony. No hierarchies, no leaders, everyone equal. And the world's overpopulated. There's no room on the surface so it makes sense to go underground. I was going to build a beautiful underground city like Setenil de las Bodegas in Spain or the City of the Gods in Giza. But we needed women to populate it. The Brotherhood had forgotten about the women.' He shakes his head.

'What about the wife?' Nelson whispers to Tanya. 'Are we holding her too?'

'No,' says Tanya. 'She was charged with aiding and abetting the abductions but she was released on bail. Her ex-husband paid.'

'And Cassandra Blackstock?' Jo is saying. 'Why did you abduct her?'

'Ah, Cassandra.' Swan's voice thickens. 'A beautiful woman. I knew her from the toddler group too. She was just what we needed in the society. Barbara was all very well but she was a bit old. Sam was younger and fitter but still not a prime specimen. Cassandra was physical perfection. And she'd proved her breeding abilities too.'

Nelson can just imagine what Judy will make of this view of women as brood mares. But, to her credit, Judy's voice is expressionless as she says, 'Tell us what happened with Cassandra.'

'I knew she was rehearsing in the community centre,' says Swan. 'I'd talked to that ridiculous director, Leo. He put on a play in one of my buildings once. I didn't rate him at all – completely lacking in talent and originality – but he was useful. I waited for Cassandra on Friday night. I watched her texting in the porch, then, when she started walking towards her car, I called her over. I pretended my car wouldn't start. As she came over to look, I put the handkerchief over her mouth. Then I put her in the car and drove her to the base-ment. It was quite simple. I'd forgotten her partner was a policeman though. He never came to any of the events at the nursery. Clearly not a fully committed father.'

Is Swan, a self-confessed murderer and abductor, really criticising Clough's parenting skills? It seems so.

'Who else knew about your plans?' says Judy. 'Did Richard Latham know?'

'No,' says Swan. 'I knew Charlie – Richard – by sight, but I'd never spoken to him. I knew he'd been an alcoholic once and I didn't trust him. Some of the Brothers said that he was brilliant but that made me distrust him more. I have a genius level IQ myself so I'm wary of brilliant people. I was careful who I spoke to. My main contact was Nathan, one of my old apprentices. He was deep in the Brotherhood. He knew all about my plans for building the perfect city. He was going to help me.'

'What about your wife?' says Jo. 'I expect you confided in her. I'm sure she was very helpful, with all her sociological knowledge.'

But suddenly Swan seems to come out of his trance. 'I refuse to answer that question,' he says. He turns to his solicitor. 'I can refuse to answer, can't I?'

'Yes,' says the solicitor wearily, 'you can.'

'Interview suspended at twenty-one hundred hours,' says Jo into the microphone. 'That's all for today.'

The team meets for a final briefing in Jo's office. There is a celebratory feeling in the air. The women have all been found safe and well and Quentin Swan has confessed to the murders as well as the abductions. Jo takes a bottle of wine from a drawer in her desk and Tanya gets some mugs from the canteen. Jo claims not to be able to drink from a mug and produces a wine glass from another drawer.

Nelson refuses a mug of wine. His shoulder is hurting quite badly now and he thinks it will be hard enough to drive home without the added complication of being slightly over the limit. Sitting in Jo's office with its flowers and inspirational posters and listening to Jo, Judy and Tanya laugh and talk, it occurs to Nelson that he's now in a predominantly female environment at work, just as he is at home. Even when Clough is there, they are outnumbered. Tim would have made the difference, metrosexual and smooth as he was. With Tim the sexes would have been evenly balanced but now Nelson is definitely in the minority. He doesn't really mind, he likes the company of women, it just takes a bit of getting used to, that's all.

Judy tells him that Barbara, Sam and Cassandra have all been discharged from hospital.

'They're in quite good physical shape, all things considered. Swan brought them food and water, he even brought them weird little treats like chocolates and wine. They were locked up all the time but he didn't mistreat them physically, apart from drugging them, of course. Both Sam and Cassandra say they couldn't have coped without Barbara. Babs kept them all going. It's strange, she was the one who was considered mentally frail – too frail to have custody of her children – but she was as tough as anything in the basement. She was definitely the leader.'

'What's happened to Babs now?' asks Nelson. He can

imagine Sam going home to the bosom of her family, to that messy, friendly house in Pott Row, but where will Barbara go? Who will want to hear of her trauma and release? Eddie, her only friend, is dead. Will Barbara just go back to her life on the streets?

'I offered to put her up in a hotel for the night,' says Judy, 'but she went home with Sam. The two of them seem close. I really think that Sam will help her now.'

'What about Cassie?'

'Cloughie took her home as soon as he could. He didn't want to let her out of his sight.'

Judy sounds quite indulgent towards her old sparring partner but Jo says briskly, 'Let's hope this doesn't make him too overprotective. Cassandra's a strong, independent woman. She doesn't need Dave fussing over her all the time. That's why I've never married.'

She manages to convey the impression that she has been fighting off desperate suitors for years. Tanya hastens to agree that the patriarchy is to blame for everything.

'I think it's just the shock,' says Nelson. 'I would say Cassandra can stand up for herself. Actually, I'm surprised the three women didn't overpower Swan. He's not exactly well-built.'

'They were tied up most of the time and the room was locked,' says Judy. 'They said they did think about overpowering him when he gave them their food but he always had a knife on him. And don't underestimate the psychological power Swan had as their jailer.'

'He's an unlikely nutcase, isn't he?' says Nelson. 'I mean,

a respectable architect, swish offices and all that. I wonder what set him off?'

'Architects can be megalomaniacs,' says Judy. 'Look at Albert Speer. Hitler's architect,' she adds for Tanya's benefit. 'I think Swan was attracted to the idea of building the perfect city. Then his wife tells him all that stuff about underground societies. It became an obsession.'

'Do you think his wife knew?' says Nelson. 'I heard you'd charged her.'

'She claims not to know a thing,' says Judy, 'and the women say they never met her. But it's hard not to think that she influenced him in some way.'

'I think he'll try to protect her,' says Jo. 'You saw how he was just now as soon as we mentioned her name. But I think she must have known something. He knew Sam and Cassandra through Meg Pritchard's baby and toddler groups. If it turns out that Vicky Swan knew them too then we might be able to prove that they worked together.'

'We should bring Nathan in too,' says Judy. 'I met him in the undercroft below Our Lady of Perpetual Succour. Swan says that Nathan knew about his plans. He might have known about the abductions and the murders too.'

'You did well to get Swan to cough to the murders,' says Nelson. 'I didn't think he would.'

'Nor did I,' says Jo. 'His brief was having kittens. That was all due to DS Johnson. She conducted a pitch-perfect cognitive interview.'

Judy looks modest and Tanya rather annoyed. Nelson's phone buzzes and he reaches for it. As he does so, his shoulder gives a sudden twinge, violent enough to make him feel sick.

'You should go home, Harry,' says Jo, who is watching him closely. 'You've been stabbed, don't forget. We're charging Swan with malicious wounding of a police officer. Another one to add to the list.'

'I'd better go,' says Nelson, standing up. He's annoyed to find himself feeling rather light-headed.

'I'll go to the front door with you,' says Jo.

Nelson imagines that Jo wants to rebuke him for shouting at her earlier. In fact, he half expects to be suspended pending disciplinary proceedings. He's certain that Jo feels that he mismanaged the inquiry and that it was only her quick thinking in following up Ruth's phone call that led them to Swan. Ruth's part, he is sure, will soon be forgotten.

But as they go downstairs, Jo says, 'Well done, Harry. We caught the bastard.'

'More by luck than judgement,' says Nelson.

'Isn't that always the way?' says Jo. 'Policing's fifty per cent luck, fifty per cent hard graft. You and your team did the graft and in the end we had the luck. Good police officers, not bloody PR people.'

Nelson is rather embarrassed to hear his words quoted back at him. 'I'm sorry if I spoke out of turn earlier,' he says. 'Lack of sleep, pressure, you know how it is.'

'I do know,' says Jo, 'and I wanted to thank you.'

'Thank me? For what?' They are at the main doors now, a few feet from the place where Eddie breathed his last.

'For the chase,' says Jo with a grin. 'It was the most fun

I've had in years. I bloody hate being stuck behind a desk. Goodnight, Harry.'

Nelson drives home, pleased that Bev Flinders isn't around to witness his complete disregard of speed limits and other driving niceties. He spends the whole journey in fourth because it hurts to change gear and he doesn't think he looks in the rear-view mirror once. 'I'm not interested in what's behind me,' he had said to Ruth once. She had been shocked, of course. She's passionately interested in what lies behind, in the past, in the echoes. Don't think about Ruth, he tells himself.

It's past ten o'clock when he gets home but any thoughts of trying to slip in quietly are ruined by Bruno doing his Hound of the Baskervilles impression as soon as he hears Nelson's key in the lock.

'Down,' he says, trying the stop the dog jumping up against his shoulder.

'Harry.' Michelle appears in the sitting room doorway. 'Are you all right? I've been really worried. Down, Bruno, there's a good dog.'

Nelson remembers Ruth sending a text to Michelle when they were in the ambulance. What had she said? He had never checked.

'Where's Laura?' he says.

'She's out with friends,' says Michelle. 'What happened? You said you were in hospital.'

'I got stabbed,' says Nelson. 'I could murder an aspirin and about a pint of whisky.'

'Stabbed! Oh my God, Harry.' Michelle looks so white that Nelson is afraid that she will faint.

'It's not that bad. It bled a bit at first but it didn't touch any vital organs.' He remembers Ruth stemming the blood with her hands. *Don't die, Nelson.* Is the heart a vital organ?

Michelle makes him sit down while she brings him aspirin as well as tea and toast. 'I don't think you should have a whisky,' she says.

'It's good for shock,' says Nelson, drinking the tea gratefully. 'You should have one too, love. You look dead pale.'

'No,' says Michelle. 'I can't have a drink.' She sits opposite him and plays with Bruno's ears.

'Harry,' she says. 'We have to talk.'

Suddenly the room is as cold as the deepest underground cellar. Nelson knows they have to talk. He's known it for weeks and the matter became urgent at the precise moment when he followed Ruth up the stairs in her cottage, past the accusing eyes of the cut-out Star Trek figure on her landing.

'Michelle,' he says. 'I—'

'No,' says Michelle. 'I want to talk.' She looks at him, her beautiful face somehow illuminated by something that he does not understand and instinctively fears.

'Harry,' she says. 'I'm pregnant.'

'What?' Whatever he expected, it wasn't this. He stares at his wife, who smiles timidly back at him.

'But that's impossible. We're . . . you're . . .' He almost says 'you're too old', but even at this moment he knows this is not a statement he can make.

'You're on the pill,' he says at last.

'It's not infallible,' says Michelle, 'especially as you get older.'

'But . . .'

'I'm forty-six,' says Michelle. 'Dr Patel says it's unusual but not unheard of. Many women conceive naturally in their forties.'

'You're sure then?'

'Yes. I went to the clinic today. But I've suspected for weeks. I've been feeling odd, a bit sick, not liking certain foods. It took me back to when I was expecting the girls.'

You were in your twenties then, thinks Nelson. His mind isn't reacting properly, plodding along the byways and cul-de-sacs because it can't face the traffic on the main highway. But when it comes to it, his life has once more become a straight road leading in one direction. Until death us do part.

'Are you pleased?' says Michelle. 'Please say you're pleased.'

'Of course I'm pleased.' And he gets up, painfully, to embrace her.

EPILOGUE

15 August 2015

For reasons of their own Clough and Cassandra decide to abandon their plans for a register office wedding and get married in St Matthew's Church, King's Lynn, where Paul Pritchard runs the drop-in centre upstairs and Meg Pritchard hosts her mother and baby groups. 'Cassie likes the place,' said Clough when he explained the change of venue to Ruth. And what Cassie wants, Clough hastens to get her these days.

The first person Ruth sees as she is dragged up the steps by a thoroughly overexcited Kate is Judy, standing at the door handing out the order of service. Judy is one of Clough's ushers, a compliment she takes in the spirit with which it was intended. She even attended Clough's stag night, an event she described to Ruth as 'truly awe-inspiring'. Now, looking poised and pretty in pale green, Judy greets Ruth and admires Kate's dress.

'It's got petticoats.' Kate lifts her skirt to show.

'That's so cool,' says Judy. 'I like your shoes too.'

Kate's outfit is by far the fanciest she has ever had. Ruth squashed her inclination to buy Kate something that she could wear again and splashed out on a pink-flowered dress and matching shoes. She did this not just to please Kate but because she knew it was what her mother would have wanted.

The last month has probably been the hardest of Ruth's life. The telephone call from Simon had felt like an axe blow. She had thought that her mother was recovering, back to her omniscient best, establishing herself as undisputed queen of the rehabilitation centre. Then, on the Saturday afternoon when Ruth was at the hospital with Nelson, her mother had suffered another massive stroke from which there was no recovery. Ruth drove to London the next day, dry-eyed and in shock. Her father was moving like a ghost around the house in Eltham, which was full of flowers and cards and worthies from the church but still felt achingly, devastatingly empty without Jean. Ruth and Simon threw themselves into death paperwork and organising the funeral, Kate and her cousins played subdued games of football in the garden, and Cathy cooked what felt like a never-ending series of mince-based dishes. It was only when Ruth drove back to Norfolk that she wondered why she hadn't heard from Nelson. She had felt so sure that something was about to happen. She and Nelson had hardly exchanged a word during the drive from the hospital and the subsequent detour but she knew that the events in her darkened bedroom had changed their relationship for ever. So why hadn't she heard from him?

When Nelson contacted her on the Wednesday, she already knew something was wrong. They met in The Walks and he told her that Michelle was pregnant. It was the second axe blow. Nelson would never leave his wife now, she knew that. He would feel that the family should stay together for the sake of this late, unexpected baby. 'It was a bit of a shock to us both,' he said. 'But a nice shock, I'm sure,' said Ruth, hardly recognising her own voice. 'I'm sorry,' Nelson began and then stopped himself, perhaps realising that this was the wrong thing to say and anyway, what was he apologising for?

'It's OK,' said Ruth. 'I'm happy for you, really. I'm happy for you both.' Nelson had put his head in his hands and Ruth had stood up. 'Congratulations,' she said, and walked carefully away. Later, this seemed very important, that Nelson hadn't known how she felt inside. He hadn't followed her.

Jean's funeral was a week later, a fervent affair in the strange Nissen hut where Ruth's parents had always carried on their love affair with God. Arthur asked Ruth to read a passage from the Bible, which she did to the best of her ability, using her clear lecturing voice. 'For I know that my Redeemer lives, and at the last he will stand upon the earth.' Simon read a short eulogy composed by the two siblings and his sons read a psalm. Arthur played no part in the ceremony; he sat with his arm round Kate as if drawing comfort from her stalwart young presence. Cathy had suggested that Kate was too young to attend but somehow Ruth knew that this too was what her mother would have wanted. She remembered that day in the hospital when Jean said that Kate took after her. *I loved acting when I was a girl. In fact, I wanted to be an actress for a while but my father wouldn't hear of it.* Jean's acting ability isn't mentioned in any of the tributes from the congregation ('a true Christian', 'a humble apostle', 'a woman of God') but this only makes the memory more precious to Ruth. It is a secret she shared with her mother, perhaps the only one in all their life together.

Alice's Adventures Under Ground was performed at the Dragon Hall in July. Ruth still couldn't make head nor tail of the story, which seemed to fuse Lewis Carroll with Freud and come out with *The Muppet Show*. But there was no doubt that Kate performed her part with aplomb. She got a big cheer at the end and Leo presented her with a bouquet of pink roses. Nelson and Michelle attended, Michelle pale but glamorous in a loose blue top. She didn't look pregnant – in fact she appeared thinner than ever – but she smiled when Ruth congratulated her. 'Thanks. I'm feeling exhausted at the moment but I'm sure the blooming bit will come later.' Ruth said that she was sure it would. Kate doesn't know about the expected sibling because Michelle wants to wait until the three-month check-up before making the news public. Rebecca and Laura know though. Nelson says that they are delighted.

Cassandra was wonderful as Alice. Her beauty and talent transcended Leo's production and created something quite remarkable. She received two bouquets at the end – roses from Leo and half a flower shop from Clough, who videoed the entire production. Clough says that Cassandra has been offered an audition for a West End play. 'But she's not sure whether to go for it, not while Spencer is so young.' Ruth wonders whether Cassandra will be seduced by the lure of London and disappear into the sunset, taking her family with her. If so, she will miss her – and Clough too.

Inside, the gloomy church is lit with candles and flowers, white and gold against the sooty Victorian brickwork. Ruth sees Clough sitting at the front next to his brother Mark, his best man. Clough's mother, disconcertingly glamorous in a big hat, is sitting behind them. Cassandra's mother, Sally, who Ruth remembers from another case, is sitting across the aisle from them. Sally is holding Spencer, dressed in white satin. Next to Sally is Cassandra's brother Chaz and a woman who must be his wife or partner. The church seems very full: Cassandra's theatrical friends, Clough's police colleagues (the men in three-piece suits, the women in tight dresses and high heels), friends, family and even an onlooker or two who has wandered in to see what all the fuss is about. On Cassandra's side of the church Ruth spots Sam Foster-Jones and Barbara Murray. According to Judy the three women have become close friends and Barbara is now living with Sam and her family. Looking at Barbara, smartly dressed and surrounded by the Foster-Jones children, it's hard to imagine that she ever lived on the streets. Well, perhaps that part of her life is over. Maybe she will even be able to win back custody of her own children.

As Ruth watches, Sam and Barbara stand up to greet a newcomer. It's Jo Archer, stunning in a red dress and one of those feathery hat things which Ruth understands is called a fascinator. Jo embraces both women and goes to sit behind them. Ruth admires the way that Jo seems quite happy to attend the service on her own, no man at her side, confident that all eyes will be upon her. She has become quite a fan of Jo's since their mad dash through the countryside. For her part, Jo has made a point of keeping in touch with Ruth, telling her that Quentin Swan has entered a mental disorder defence and discussing the possibility of further excavation of the tunnels below the Guildhall. Ruth remembers Martin Kellerman saying that Quentin Swan was dangerous. She had dismissed it as jealousy at the time but it turned out that he was right. Martin had also compared Swan to a spider trapping women in his web and that, too, turned out to be an apt image. Ruth hasn't heard from Martin since term ended but Shona says that he's back with Vicky. She hopes it works out for them.

Ruth thinks of the bones she discovered that day in June. They haven't managed to identify them but Nelson told her about a rough sleeper called Archie, a big red-headed man apparently, who disappeared about five years ago. Could those first bones, which contain the gene for red hair, be the remains of Archie? No one knows but Nelson arranged a burial in the Garden of Ashes all the same. They have had no such luck with the bones found on the second excavation. The DNA results were inconclusive but from the pelvic bone she excavated, Ruth thinks that the skeleton belonged to a woman. Who was the woman who came to be buried under the city, unknown and unmourned? Ruth still thinks that the bones may have been boiled but despite Jo's best efforts, it seems unlikely that they will be able to continue the investigation. 'Let it go, Ruth,' said Nelson. 'That's all you can do. Let it go.'

Ruth is relieved to see Cathbad and the children sitting near the back of the church and she and Kate go to join him. Michael is solemn in a blue waistcoat and Miranda is wearing a stiff white dress that surrounds her like a tent. Kate immediately shows Michael her petticoats. 'Kate,' says Ruth weakly, 'please sit nicely.'

'That reminds me of going to mass as a boy in Ireland,' says Cathbad. 'Sit nicely and don't fidget. It's no wonder children get fed up with church.' For all his protestations, Ruth notes that Cathbad has dressed his children up for the occasion and that he is looking unusually smart in a grey suit, his long hair in a ponytail. At least he isn't wearing a tie. Ruth doesn't think she could cope with Cathbad in a tie.

'I saw Judy at the door,' says Ruth. 'Doing her ushing. Half the Norfolk force seem to be here today.'

'Did you see Tim?' says Cathbad. 'He's near the front with Tanya and her partner.'

Ruth cranes her head to see where Tanya is sitting with Petra. Next to them is Tim, elegant as ever in a dark suit. He looks distant and forbidding but as Ruth watches, Clough turns round and says something that makes Tim laugh. Tim's very good-looking when he smiles, thinks Ruth, but she has always considered him a rather serious person. He must be fond of Clough though, to have come to his wedding, considering everything that has gone before.

Of course, the one person Ruth is looking for isn't here. She's sees that there's a space in the pew next to Clough's mother and wonders if this is reserved for Nelson, his boss and father figure. Then, just as she begins to think that maybe he isn't coming, she hears Cathbad say, 'At last!' and Nelson sweeps into the church accompanied by Michelle in a silvery dress and another one of those little hats. Nelson sits next to Lindsay Clough and Ruth watches as he leans forward and pats Clough on the shoulder. He doesn't turn to speak to Tim or Tanya. Michelle glances round briefly but Ruth can't see her expression. She can see Tim though and his face looks, briefly, stricken.

Judy joins them just as the organ is cranking up. 'The bride's here,' she says. 'She looks beautiful.'

It's what everyone always says but in this case it really is true. Cassandra, gorgeous in jeans and a Venus in Furs T-shirt, looks beyond beautiful in a low-cut white dress, jewels in her cloudy dark hair. As she walks up the aisle on the arm of her father, George, Ruth is annoyed to find her eyes prickling with tears. It's a feminist nightmare, she tells herself. The woman dressed in white to represent virginity, handed over from one man to another. Ruth has never been married and she has never really regretted this. She knows her mother dreamed of a white wedding, even after Kate came along, but Ruth never encouraged those fantasies. Now it's too late for her mother to attend her wedding. She watches as Clough turns to Cassandra, his face a perfect pattern of joy, pride and a sort of incredulous happiness. George goes to sit beside his wife and Clough and Cassandra stand hand in hand in front of the altar. Clearing his throat, Father Martin begins the service.

*

'Doesn't she look beautiful, Harry?' says Michelle.

'Very nice,' says Nelson. He hasn't been looking forward to this day: seeing Clough and Cassandra in wedded bliss, seeing Ruth and Kate and knowing that he can never really be with them. But he knows that it means a lot to Clough to have him there. Clough is a traditionalist at heart; witness the church and the candles and the three-piece suits. Clough wants his family and friends around him on his big day and Nelson is not about to deprive him of this.

The last few weeks have felt dreamlike and unreal. By day, Nelson has been going about his business, tying up the loose ends on the Quentin Swan case, opposing bail, trying to make a case against Vicky Swan as an accomplice. In the evenings, he mimes domestic bliss with Michelle. His daughters, at first amazed and slightly shocked by the pregnancy, have now thrown themselves wholeheartedly into preparing for the baby. 'We'll be like aunts rather than sisters,' said Laura. 'Cool aunts,' said Rebecca. 'This child is going to be so spoilt.' Michelle, who has been feeling very sick (something that did not happen with either of her earlier pregnancies), had smiled in a rather pained way. Maybe a spoilt baby isn't quite what she planned for her middle age. Nelson and Michelle are careful with each other, polite and almost embarrassed by this new development in their lives. Nelson often wonders if Michelle had known or guessed the confession that had been on his lips before she forestalled it with her news.

Luckily work is busy enough to prevent him thinking too much about his domestic situation. Even so, at odd moments during the day he sees Ruth's face when he told her about the baby. 'I'm very happy for you both,' she had said, before walking away, past the Red Chapel and the formal gardens. He thinks about this rather too often as the warm June and July give way to a cold, grey August. Nelson's shoulder aches in the unseasonable weather and this is the reason he gives, both to Michelle and to himself, for his irritability and distractedness and for the nights when he can't sleep and gets up at four a.m. to walk Bruno through the empty streets.

Quentin Swan has been charged with the murders of Eddie O'Toole and Stuart Hughes. He has also been charged with the abduction of Barbara Murray, Sam Foster-Jones and Cassandra Blackstock, as well as the malicious wounding of DCI Harry Nelson. It's no surprise to Nelson when Swan puts in a mental disorder defence. It's fairly easy to claim insanity when you've admitted plans to build an underground city populated by rough sleepers and women you have abducted. All the same, Nelson thinks that Swan was pretty sane when he stole a car and lured Sam away from her family, or when he drugged Cassandra and forced her into his car. To say nothing about killing two defenceless men while they slept. To Nelson's disappointment they have had to drop charges against Vicky Swan. Quentin has refused to implicate his wife and they have no evidence that she was involved. But, whether deliberately or not, Vicky's research into underground societies certainly stirred something in the brain of her second husband. And Quentin's loyalty hasn't done him much good. Nelson has heard that Vicky is now back with her first husband,

Martin Kellerman, who stood bail for her when she was first arrested.

There will be no charges against Richard Latham or any of the Brotherhood either. In theory, the police have closed the underground rooms but Nelson has no doubt that the rough sleepers will find other ways into the labyrinth below the city. He has his own suspicions too. Ruth thought that those first bones had been cooked in a pot. Were they the bones of big red-headed Archie? When Archie died (probably of natural causes), were his remains cooked and eaten? There's no way of proving if this is true but Nelson remembers the cooking pots in the undercroft under St Etheldreda's and thinks that the Brotherhood may have some dark secrets. Nathan, the ex-architecture student, has admitted telling Quentin Swan about the underground tunnels – and even giving him some of the passwords – but no charges have been brought against him either. Swan obviously spoke to other rough sleepers too, including Bilbo. Judy has become obsessed with finding out more about Stuart Hughes, aka Bilbo. She has even written an obituary for him which appeared in several local papers. Whatever happens, Bilbo and Eddie won't be completely forgotten.

In gratitude for his help on the case, Nelson tried to get Richard onto the council housing list but his assistance was politely declined. 'I can't live within four walls any more,' Richard had said. 'It might surprise you to know, DCI Nelson, that some people actually prefer living on the streets.' It did surprise Nelson. He pointed out that Richard hadn't seemed to mind living in a claustrophobic windowless cell several metres underground. 'But that was my choice,' Richard said, 'don't you see?' And Nelson did see, in a way. It probably helps Richard's lifestyle that he is clearly having an affair with Geri Anstruther, the woman who runs the shelter in the old church of Our Lady of Perpetual Succour.

At least Barbara Murray seems to be getting her life together. She is living with the Foster-Jones family, acting as a kind of nanny and home help. 'Though it's more like living with your big sister,' said Sam, when Nelson visited them last week. Sam had been digging in the garden while Barbara helped the children make a tree house. Caleb, Evie and Alfie were sorting out planks from the remains of old packing cases. The baby was sleeping in his pram and the rabbits scampered around their run, disturbed by the noise and the laughter. Nelson spoke briefly to Barbara as she supervised the construction task. 'We need an architect,' she said. 'Joke.' 'Joke,' agreed Nelson, though he can never see crime as a laughing matter. Barbara is now having regular contact visits with her younger children and there's a real hope that she might be able to win back custody if she manages to get a place of her own. Nelson asked Barbara whether she had been in touch with her older children. 'I've written them a letter,' she said. 'It's up to them to respond now. Judy's been very kind, she's helped me a lot.'

Before Nelson left Caleb showed him the corner of the shed where he had what he called his 'insect museum'. This included an ant farm, a Perspex box which showed a cross-section of an ant colony: tunnels and chambers and thoroughfares, all filled with scurrying bodies, some laden with food, some, it seemed, actually carrying other ants. Nelson stared at it for quite some time. He remembered Kevin O'Casey talking about the 'ant people' in Beijing, tunnelling away beneath the city. Is this what Quentin Swan had wanted to create? An underground world complete with fertile females (Caleb tells him that they are called 'queens'), worker ants and soldiers? A place where even the dead ants serve a purpose?

There had been no sign of Benedict Foster-Jones. Presumably he had escaped back to his office in the city.

'Repeat after me. I, David Elvis Clough . . .'

A ripple of laughter runs round the church. Nelson grins. Judy had told him that Clough's middle name was Elvis but he hadn't believed her. 'I was a big fan,' whispers Clough's mother.

'I, David Elvis Clough take you, Cassandra Harriet Blackstock to be my lawful wedded wife, to have and to hold from this day forward; for better, for worse, for richer, for poorer, in sickness and in health, until death us do part.'

Mark Clough steps forward smartly with the rings. Nelson can see Cassandra's face, smiling mistily, as Clough slides the gold band onto her finger.

'With my body I honour you, all that I have I give to you . . .'

Nelson looks at Michelle's profile. Is she remembering their wedding day, all those years ago in Blackpool? He knows that he should probably take her hand but he's too conscious of Tim sitting behind them and of Ruth somewhere in the church.

'I now pronounce you man and wife.'

Clough and Cassandra are kissing, slightly too passionately for the sacred surroundings perhaps. A cheer goes up throughout the church. After all the trauma and heartache, it's an unashamedly happy ending.

Afterwards, as Clough and Cassandra pose on the steps of the church, the air full of confetti (in defiance of Father Martin's express request), Nelson looks for Ruth. Eventually he sees her, standing with Cathbad and Judy. The children, Michael and Katie, are jumping up and down in excitement. Cathbad has Miranda on his shoulders. Ruth looks unusually smart in a navy blue dress, her hair pulled away from her face. Instinctively, Nelson looks for Michelle before making his way over to Ruth. Michelle is talking to Cassandra, catching a rare moment between photographs. Nelson watches as Michelle kisses Cassandra on the cheek. These two women have always got on and Nelson wonders again what was in the text that Cassandra had sent to Michelle just before she was abducted. Michelle moves away and Nelson sees Tim approach. At first it looks as if he's going to walk straight past Michelle, but at the last moment he veers off to say something to her. They exchange a few words and then Nelson gets a clear look at Tim's face as he walks away through the laughing, confetti-throwing crowd. His expression is one of sadness, mingled – Nelson is sure – with a certain cautious paternal pride.

Obituary: Stuart Robert Hughes

Stuart Hughes was born in Newtown, near Cardiff, in 1950. He was the youngest child of Megan and David Hughes. At school Stuart excelled in music. His family couldn't afford formal lessons but he taught himself to play the recorder, clarinet and guitar. Stuart sang in the church choir and even performed at the National Eisteddfod in 1960. Stuart was also a talented chess player who competed for his primary and secondary school. Stuart loved reading, especially the works of C.S. Lewis and J.R.R. Tolkien. While still at primary school he acquired the nickname Bilbo because of his identification with the character in *The Hobbit*.

When Stuart was ten his father died and the family seem to have undergone some financial hardship. The two older children, Davy and Jane, went to live with their grandparents but Stuart stayed at home with his mother. Then, when Stuart was thirteen, his mother married Ivor Williams, a dock worker. At first the marriage seemed happy and Williams appeared kind to his stepson, buying him a bicycle and even paying for guitar lessons. But after the birth of his own two children – Bryony in 1964 and Edward in 1966 – Williams became violent towards Stuart. The police were called after one incident on Christmas

Day in 1966 and Stuart was put in foster care for a while. He appears not to have liked his foster parents and ran away several times, once to join his older siblings with their grandparents in Swansea. Stuart eventually went to live with his grandparents and in Swansea he enrolled as an apprentice printer. This appears to have been a happy time in Stuart's life. He enjoyed working in the printworks, especially as the workers were sometimes given free books. He played in a band, The Shire Men, and became involved with a girl called Iris, the daughter of one of his colleagues. But in 1971 Stuart's grandparents died within a few months of each other. Stuart lived with his brother Davy for a while but the two quarrelled and Stuart moved away. He was also unhappy at the break-up of his relationship with Iris, who eventually married another colleague from the printworks.

Stuart seems to have drifted to London, where he had various casual jobs. He struggled with drink and depression and was hospitalised several times. At some time in the 1980s he moved to Suffolk where he worked at the printers Williams Clowes. Having his occupation back seemed to have a restorative effect on Stuart and he lived happily in Beccles until Clowes relocated in 2003 and he was made redundant. Stuart started drinking again and soon lost his council accommodation. By 2005 he was living on the streets in King's Lynn.

Even while he was living rough, Stuart retained his good nature and his love of music. He played the pipes and the harmonica and earned money from busking.

He also continued to play chess, finding opponents at the local drop-in centre and even at the University of North Norfolk chess club. Pat Butler, who runs the Countryline Cafe at King's Lynn station, said, 'Everyone liked Bilbo. He was a gentle soul. He must have been through a lot in his life but he was never bitter. He always had a smile and a joke for everyone.' Paul Pritchard, who coordinates the St Matthew's Project for the Homeless, said, 'Bilbo was a kind, intelligent man who suffered a lot in his time on earth. But I never heard him say an unkind word about anyone. He did no harm. Let that be his epitaph.'

Stuart was murdered on 7th June 2015. He is survived by his brother and sister.

Judy Johnson, 2015

ACKNOWLEDGEMENTS

As far as I know there is no underground society below the streets of Norwich. However, Norwich is rich in tunnels and undercrofts and many of the places in the book – the Guildhall, St John's Cathedral, Tombland – actually exist. There was a famous incident in 1988 when a bus disappeared into a hole that opened up on Earlham Road in Norwich. However, Denning Road is imaginary, as are St Etheldreda's and the St Matthew's centre. The Countryline Cafe at King's Lynn station is real but Pat and Ernie are fictional characters. Many thanks to Carole Slaughter for showing me the undercroft below the famous Jarrolds department store.

Thanks to Lisa Cutts and Elizabeth Haynes for advice on the ways that the police would trace the families of homeless people. Thanks also to Giulia de Rosa and the Soup Run Team at Our Lady of Lourdes Church, Rottingdean. Many thanks to archaeologist and osteologist Linzi Harvey for the fascinating information on bones, and to Cain Weibel for the insights into the work of a surveyor. However, I have only followed the experts' advice as far as it helps the plot and any subsequent mistakes are mine alone.

Special thanks to Richard Latham, who made the winning bid in an auction organised by CLIC Sargent, the teenage cancer charity, for a chance to appear in these pages. By a stroke of serendipity Richard actually works with rough sleepers but I need hardly say that he bears no resemblance to the character who bears his name.

Thanks, as always, to my editor, Jane Wood, and my agent, Rebecca Carter. I'm the luckiest writer alive to have these two in my corner. Thanks to everyone at Quercus and Janklow and Nesbit for all their hard work on my behalf. Thanks also to my American agent, Kirby Kim, and all at Houghton Mifflin Harcourt, especially Naomi Gibbs, Katrina Kruse and Michelle Bonanno-Triant. Thanks to all the publishers around the world who have taken a chance on Ruth.

I'm also very grateful for the support and friendship I have received from my fellow crime-writers, especially David Harrison (Tom Bale), William Shaw, Lesley Thomson and Susan Wilkins. Love and thanks always to my husband, Andrew, and our children, Alex and Juliet. This book is dedicated to my dear friend Sarah Huber. I would say that she's one of my oldest friends but neither of us have aged *at all*.

Finally, thanks to Sussex Police for sending me on a speed awareness course. Not only am I now a more careful driver but I left the course knowing how to start this book.

Elly Griffiths, 2017

WHO'S WHO
IN THE DR RUTH GALLOWAY MYSTERIES

Dr Ruth Galloway

Profession: forensic archaeologist

Likes: cats, Bruce Springsteen, bones, books

Dislikes: gyms, organized religion, shopping

Ruth Galloway was born in south London and educated at University College and Southampton University, where she met her mentor Professor Erik Andersen. In 1997 she participated in Professor Andersen's dig on the north Norfolk coast which resulted in the excavation of a Bronze Age henge. Ruth subsequently moved to the area and became Head of Forensic Archaeology at the University of North Norfolk. She lives an isolated cottage on the edge of the Saltmarsh. In 2007 she was approached by DCI Harry Nelson who wanted her help in identifying bones found buried on the marshes, and her life suddenly got a whole lot more complicated.

Surprising fact about Ruth: she is fascinated by the London Underground and once attended a fancy dress party as The Angel Islington.

Harry Nelson

Profession: Detective Chief Inspector

Likes: driving fast, solving crimes, his family

Dislikes: Norfolk, the countryside, management speak, his boss

Harry Nelson was born in Blackpool. He came to Norfolk in his thirties to lead the Serious Crimes Unit, bringing with him his wife Michelle and their daughters, Laura and Rebecca. Nelson has a loyal team and enjoys his work. He still hankers after the North though and has not come to love his adopted county. Nelson thinks of himself as an old-fashioned policeman and so often clashes with Super-intendent Whitcliffe, who is trying to drag the force into the twenty-first century. Nelson is impatient and quick-tempered but he is capable of being both imaginative and sensitive. He's also cleverer than he lets on.

Surprising fact about Nelson: he's a huge Frank Sinatra fan.

Michelle Nelson

Profession: hairdresser

Likes: her family, exercising, socializing with friends

Dislikes: dowdiness, confrontation, talking about murder

Michelle married Nelson when she was twenty-one and he was twenty-three. She was happy with her life in Blackpool – two children, part-time work, her mother nearby – but encouraged Nelson to move to Norfolk for the sake of promotion. Now that her daughters are older she works as a manager for a hair salon. Michelle is beautiful, stylish, hard-working and a dedicated wife and mother. When people see her and Nelson together, their first reaction is usually, 'What *does* she see in him?'

Surprising fact about Michelle: she once played hockey for Blackpool Girls.

Michael Malone (aka Cathbad)

Profession: laboratory assistant and druid

Likes: nature, mythology, walking, following his instincts

Dislikes: rules, injustice, conventions

Cathbad was born in Ireland and came to England to study first chemistry then archaeology. He also came under the influence of Erik Andersen though they found themselves on opposite sides during the henge dig. Cathbad was brought up as a Catholic but he now thinks of himself as a druid and shaman.

Surprising fact about Cathbad: he can play the accordion.

Shona Maclean

Profession: lecturer in English Literature

Likes: books, wine, parties

Dislikes: being ignored

Shona is a lecturer at the University of North Norfolk and one of Ruth's closest friends. They met when they both participated in the henge dig in 1997. On the face of it Shona seems an unlikely friend for Ruth – she's outgoing and stunningly beautiful for a start – but the two women share a sense of humour and an interest in books, films and travel. They also have a lot of history together.

Surprising fact about Shona: as a child she won several Irish dancing competitions.

David Clough

Profession: Detective Sergeant

Likes: food, football, beer, his job

Dislikes: political correctness, graduate police officers

David Clough ('Cloughie' to Nelson) was born in Norfolk and joined the force at eighteen. As a youngster he almost followed his elder brother into petty crime but a chance meeting with a sympathetic policeman led him into a surprisingly successful police career. Clough is a tough, dedicated officer but not without imagination. He admires Nelson, his boss, but has a rather competitive relationship with Sergeant Judy Johnson.

Surprising fact about Clough: He can quote the 'you come to me on my daughter's wedding day' scene from The Godfather off by heart.

Judy Johnson

Profession: Detective Sergeant

Likes: horses, driving, her job

Dislikes: girls' nights out, sexism, being patronised

Judy Johnson was born in Norfolk to Irish Catholic parents. She was academic at school but opted to join the police force at eighteen rather than go to university. Judy can seem cautious and steady – she has been going out with the same boyfriend since school, for example – but she is actually fiercely ambitious. She resents any hint of condescension or sexism which can lead to some fiery exchanges with Clough.

Surprising fact about Judy: she's a keen card player and once won an inter-force poker competition.

Phil Trent

Profession: professor of Archaeology

Likes: money, being on television, technology

Dislikes: new age archaeologists, anonymity, being out of the loop

Phil is Ruth's head of department at the University of North Norfolk. He's ambitious and outwardly charming, determined to put the university (and himself) on the map. He thinks of Ruth as plodding and old-fashioned so is slightly put out when she begins to make a name for herself as an advisor to the police. On one hand, it's good for the image of UNN; on the other, it should have been him.

Surprising fact about Phil: at his all boys school, he once played Juliet in *Romeo and Juliet*.